W9-ALU-323

By Carole Nelson Douglas from Tom Doherty Associates

MYSTERY

MIDNIGHT LOUIE MYSTERIES

Catnap
Pussyfoot
Cat on a Blue Monday
Cat in a Crimson Haze
Cat in a Diamond Dazzle
Cat with an Emerald Eye
Cat in a Flamingo Fedora
Cat in a Golden Garland
Cat on a Hyacinth Hunt
Cat in an Indigo Mood

Cat in a Jeweled Jumpsuit
Cat in a Kiwi Con
Cat in a Leopard Spot
Cat in a Midnight Choir
Cat in a Neon Nightmare
Cat in an Orange Twist
Cat in a Hot Pink Pursuit
Cat in a Quicksilver Caper
*Cat in a Red Hot Rage***
Midnight Louie's Pet Detectives
(anthology)

IRENE ADLER ADVENTURES

Good Night, Mr. Holmes
The Adventuress (Good Morning, Irene)*
A Soul of Steel (Irene at Large)*
Another Scandal in Bohemia (Irene's Last Waltz)*
Chapel Noir
Castle Rouge
Femme Fatale
Spider Dance

Marilyn: Shades of Blonde (anthology)

HISTORICAL ROMANCE

Amberleigh†
Lady Rogue†
Fair Wind, Fiery Star

SCIENCE FICTION

Probe†
Counterprobe†

FANTASY

TALISWOMAN

Cup of Clay
Seed upon the Wind

SWORD AND CIRCLET

Six of Swords
Exiles of the Rynth
Keepers of Edanvant
Heir of Rengarth
Seven of Swords

* Reissued editions
** Forthcoming
† Also mystery

Cat in a Quicksilver Caper

A MIDNIGHT LOUIE MYSTERY

Carole Nelson Douglas

A TOM DOHERTY ASSOCIATES BOOK
NEW YORK

This is a work of fiction. All of the characters, organizations, and events portrayed in this novel are either products of the author's imagination or are used fictitiously.

CAT IN A QUICKSILVER CAPER: A MIDNIGHT LOUIE MYSTERY

Copyright © 2006 by Carole Nelson Douglas

All rights reserved, including the right to reproduce this book, or portions thereof, in any form.

A Forge Book
Published by Tom Doherty Associates, LLC
175 Fifth Avenue
New York, NY 10010

www.tor.com

Forge® is a registered trademark of Tom Doherty Associates, LLC.

ISBN-13: 978-0-765-35269-9
ISBN-10: 0-765-35269-9

First Edition: July 2006
First Mass Market Edition: April 2007

Printed in the United States of America

0 9 8 7 6 5 4 3 2 1

For Janice Carlson-Buffie aka Ashland Price,
my longtime great and foresighted friend
through all the thick and thin of writing
and publishing

Contents

viii • Contents

Contents • ix

Cat in a
Quicksilver
Caper

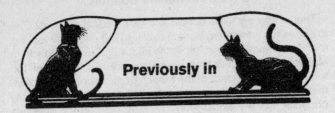

Midnight Louie's Lives and Times . . .

I cannot say why I am always hip-deep in dames.

Not that I object to said state.

It is just that I am a noir kind of guy, inside and out. My singing voice is more scat than lyrics, and my personal theme song would have to be "There Is Nothing Like a Dame."

I admit it. I am a shameless admirer of the female of the species. Any species. Of course, not all females are dames. Some are little dolls, like my petite roommate, Miss Temple Barr.

The difference between dames and little dolls? Dames can take care of themselves, period. Little dolls can take care of themselves also, but they are not averse to letting the male of the species think that they have an occasional role in the Master Plan too.

That is why my Miss Temple and I are perfect roomies. She tolerates my wandering ways. I make myself useful by looking after her without letting her know about it. Call me Muscle in Midnight Black. In our time, we have cracked a few cases too tough for the local fuzz of the human persuasion, law enforcement division. That does not always win either of us popularity contests, but we would rather be right than on the sidelines when something crooked is going down. We share a well-honed sense of justice and long, sharp fingernails.

So when I hear that any major new attraction is coming to Las Vegas, I figure that one way or another my lively little roommate, the petite and toothsome, will be spike heel–high in the planning and execution. She is, after all, a freelance public relations specialist, and Las Vegas is full of public relations of all stripes and legalities. In this case, though, I did not figure just how personally she would be involved in murder most artful.

I should introduce myself: Midnight Louie, PI. I am not your usual gumshoe, in that my feet do not wear shoes of any stripe, but shivs. I have certain attributes, such as being short, dark, and handsome . . . really short. That gets me overlooked and underestimated, which is what the savvy operative wants anyway. I am your perfect undercover guy. I also like to hunker down under the covers with my little doll. My adventures would fill a book and, in fact, I have several out. My life is just one ongoing TV miniseries in which I as hero extract my hapless human friends from fixes of their own making and literally nail crooks.

After the recent dramatic turn of events, most of my human associates are pretty shell-shocked. Not even an ace feline PI may be able to solve their various predicaments in the areas of crime and punishment . . . and PR, as in Personal Relationships.

As a serial killer finder in a multivolume mystery series (not to mention a primo mouthpiece), it behooves me to update my readers old and new on past crimes and present tensions.

None can deny that the Las Vegas crime scene is a pretty busy place, and I have been treading these mean neon streets for eighteen books now. When I call myself an "alphacat," some think I am merely asserting my natural male and feline dominance, but no. I merely reference the fact that since I debuted in *Catnap* and *Pussyfoot*, I commenced with a title sequence that is as sweet and simple as B to Z.

That is when I began my alphabet, with the B in *Cat on a Blue Monday*. From then on, the color word in the title has been in alphabetical order up to the current volume, *Cat in a Quicksilver Caper.*

Since I associate with a multifarious and nefarious crew of human beings, and since Las Vegas is littered with guidebooks as well as bodies, I wish to provide a rundown of the local landmarks on my particular map of the world. A cast of characters, so to speak:

To wit, my lovely roommate and high-heel devotee, Miss Nancy Drew on killer spikes, freelance PR ace MISS TEMPLE BARR, who has reunited with her elusive love . . .

. . . the once missing-in-action magician MR. MAX KINSELLA, who has good reason for invisibility. After his cousin SEAN died in a bomb attack during a post–high school jaunt to Ireland, he went into undercover counterterrorism work with his mentor, GANDOLPH THE GREAT, whose unsolved murder while unmasking phony psychics at a Halloween séance is still on the books. . . .

Meanwhile, Mr. Max is sought by another dame, Las Vegas homicide detective LIEUTENANT C. R. MOLINA, mother of teenage MARIAH . . .

. . . and the good friend of Miss Temple's recent good friend, MR. MATT DEVINE, a radio talk show shrink and former Roman Catholic priest who came to Las Vegas to track down his abusive stepfather, now dead and buried. By whose hand no one is quite sure.

Speaking of unhappy pasts, Miss Lieutenant Carmen Regina Molina is not thrilled that her former flame, MR. RAFI NADIR, the unsuspecting father of Mariah, is in Las Vegas taking on shady muscle jobs after blowing his career at the LAPD . . .

. . . or that Mr. Max Kinsella is aware of Rafi and his past relationship to hers truly. She had hoped to nail one man or the other as the Stripper Killer, but Miss Temple prevented that by attracting the attention of the real perp.

In the meantime, Mr. Matt drew a stalker, the local lass that young Max and his cousin Sean boyishly competed for in that long-ago Ireland . . .

. . . one MISS KATHLEEN O'CONNOR, deservedly christened by Miss Temple as Kitty the Cutter. Finding Mr. Max impossible to trace, she settled for harassing with tooth and claw the nearest innocent bystander, Mr. Matt Devine . . .

. . . who is still trying to recover from the crush he developed on Miss Temple, his neighbor at the Circle Ritz condominiums, while Mr. Max was missing in action. He did that by not very boldly seeking new women, all of whom were in danger from said Kitty the Cutter.

In fact, on the advice of counsel, aka AMBROSIA, Mr. Matt's talk show producer, and none other than the aforesaid Lieutenant Molina, he had attempted to disarm Miss Kitty's pathological interest in his sexual state by supposedly losing his virginity with a call girl least likely to be the object of K the Cutter's retaliation. Did he or didn't he? One thing is certain: hours after their iffy assignation at the Goliath Hotel, said call girl turned up deader than an ice-cold deck of Bicycle playing cards. But there are thirty-some-million potential victims in this old town, if you include the constant come and go of tourists, and everything is up for grabs in Las Vegas 24/7: guilt, innocence, money, power, love, loss, death, and significant others.

All this human sex and violence makes me glad I have a simpler social life, such as just trying to get along with my unacknowledged daughter . . .

. . . MISS MIDNIGHT LOUISE, who insinuated herself into my cases until I was forced to set up shop with her as Midnight Inc. Investigations, and who has also nosed herself into my long-running duel with . . .

. . . the evil Siamese assassin HYACINTH, first met as the on-stage assistant to the mysterious lady magician . . .

. . . SHANGRI-LA, who made off with Miss Temple's semi-engagement ring from Mr. Max during an onstage trick and has not been seen since except in sinister glimpses . . .

. . . just like the SYNTH, an ancient cabal of magicians that may deserve contemporary credit for the ambiguous death of

Mr. Max's mentor in magic, Gandolph the Great, not to mention Gandolph's former onstage assistant and a professor of magic at the University of Nevada at Las Vegas.

Well, there you have it, the usual human stew, all mixed up and at odds with each other and within themselves. Obviously, it is up to me to solve all their mysteries and nail a few crooks along the way. Like Las Vegas, the City That Never Sleeps, Midnight Louie, private eye, also has a sobriquet: the Kitty That Never Sleeps.

With this crew, who could?

Eve of Destruction

Max Kinsella was the Man in the Moon.

Here at the Neon Nightmare club, he was part of the dark, neon-lit dreamscape. A hybrid of magician, acrobat, and superhero, he hung high above everybody else, a nightly phenomenon easily taken for granted. Anonymous. Easily over- or underestimated.

Sometimes he was a star swinging down on a bungee cord into the mosh pit on Neon Nightmare's black Plexiglas floor, sprinkling firework tricks on the well-oiled crowd dancing the night away.

Beyond one perfectly safe confederate, no one knew he was the Phantom Mage, not even the love of his life, Temple Barr. It was a little bit of knowledge that was really too dangerous to have and to hold, especially for anyone he cared about deeply.

But he was playing double solitaire this time. No one knew that hidden rooms honeycombed the pyramid-shaped night-club's inside walls. There, he came and went using his real persona: Max Kinsella, who had performed as the Mystifying Max until forced out of Vegas. Now, for a select audience of conspirators, he played the disgruntled ex-magician. He was consorting with the group of aggrieved old-time magicians who called themselves the Synth, magicians who might be behind high stakes Las Vegas villainy like murder and money laundering and even international terrorism. His real role was infiltration, investigation. His purpose was exposing and bringing the Synth down. That sole act might save innumerable lives. But the Synth did not run on blind trust.

So, to his nightly role at Neon Nightmare, he had added a Synth-demanded assignment: playing high-flying technician in the "heavens" over the New Millennium Hotel's extravagant soon-to-open exhibition of White Russian nineteenth-century treasures. Ripping off the exhibition was Max's entry fee for membership in the Synth. They'd always suspected his motives. If he committed a high-profile crime in their service, they controlled him.

So, here he stood at midnight on a dark pinnacle inside Neon Nightmare, timing the first of many risky plunges to the abyss below. In the morning's wee hours, he'd be moonlighting at the New Millennium, planning a daring art heist.

And sometime in between, he should be making a few personal appearances before an audience of one. Temple. He'd been forced to neglect her, and them. She was feeling it and saying so.

He remembered the overpowering plunge of falling for her more than two years earlier when they'd met in Minneapolis. He'd lured her to follow him to Vegas where they'd settled like newlyweds into a co-owned condo at the Circle Ritz. That was when he'd first started to investigate the possibility of slipping out of the undercover counterterrorist role that had been forced on him as a teenager. He could retire at the ripe age of thirty-four and become a magician, pure and simple.

It hadn't worked out that way. Someone had tumbled to him. Someone hounded him out of Las Vegas and into hiding for a year.

He'd come back to find that Temple, smart and spirited and cute as a kitten, had stood her ground like a tiger when the police came sniffing around about his past and present whereabouts.

He'd known female assassins who were stone killers, but Temple had her own brand of toughness all the more lovable for being so unexpected in such a petite package.

Now he couldn't even manage regular appearances in her bedroom, and his promises of finally breaking free of his past had become as empty as an old-time magician's top hat.

He had so many roles to play, public and hidden, professional and personal, that even an expert juggler like himself couldn't keep them all up in the air.

Max had become the man in the mirror, the middle, the mirage. He was the magician, the mechanic, the pawn, and the power player . . . depending on whose casting card you read.

For the first time, this position seemed untenable. Undoable. Doomed. He had split himself into too many personas. Some would not, could not, survive. That was the curse of the double agent. He had acted that role for many years. Now, all aspects of his various personas dueled each other. He wore the three faces of . . . not Eve, but Eventual destruction.

He had the sinking feeling that he stood on the Eve of Destruction.

He swung off his high, invisible perch into the darkness eighty feet below, into the laser lights and neon, losing his misgivings in the sudden enthralling swoop of risk and danger.

Flying, falling, flying while people below gasped and cheered and some few hoped, in the darkest corner of their too human hearts, that he would fall for real and truly thrill them.

Chapter 1

Swept Off Her Feet

Temple Barr woke up at 10:30 A.M. in her own bed, which was hardly unusual, and supposed that there wasn't a woman in America who didn't ache for one of those Scarlett O'Hara moments.

Maybe it was Scarlett swearing to heaven that she'd never have to choke down another raw turnip (or broccoli or cauliflower floret . . . or diet book) again.

Maybe it was the spunky freshman Scarlett, telling that blind-stupid Ashley Wilkes right out that he ought to be dating her instead of some wimpy prom queen from the next plantation down along the Sewanee.

Maybe it was Scarlett cornered on the stairs of Tara shooting an attacking Yankee soldier dead.

Or Scarlett in any of the dazzling fashion-show gowns in which she schemed, fought, and flounced her way through the Civil War and its aftermath . . . especially the gutsy gown made from green velvet drapes she wore to convince a jailed Rhett Butler that she wasn't down and out when she was.

But the most perfect Scarlett moment of all involved the crimson velvet dressing gown she wore as Rhett carried her upstairs when he'd had it with her fickle, bewitching, bitching Scarlett ways.

Feminists long removed from the 1930s debut of Margaret Mitchell's *Gone with the Wind* choked on their turnips over that scene, which to modern sensibilities plays like date rape—or, in that case, wife rape.

But no matter how a woman might land on the swept-upstairs-scene issue, she couldn't fault the famous morning-after scene.

What a wake-up call! That was when Vivien Leigh's Scarlett awoke in a cat-contented camera close-up. When her eyes recalled the-night-before-the-morning-after with the devilish satisfaction of a distinctly un-downtrodden Southern belle indeed. . . .

Temple awoke this day to one of those classic dawning moments. It made her world take an unexpected lurch toward a totally different axis than it had previously been twirling around like a ballerina in a well-known routine.

Oh. Right. Yes. Oh. My. Oh. Dear. Oh!

Because all morning-afters have their down as well as their up sides, and Temple was starting to see that. It didn't help that Midnight Louie, all fully furred twenty pounds of him, was sitting on her chest like a guilty conscience, staring at her with unblinking feline-green eyes.

His mesmerizing eyes and shiny black hair reminded her that she was betrothed (as much as you could be in a modern world) to raven-haired Max Kinsella, a magician on hiatus. Louie's watchful presence also reminded her that Louie had been on patrol in the apartment early this morning when she'd returned from her supposedly bland dinner date with neighbor Matt Devine, during which certain overly neighborly things had occurred and mention had been made of the M-word: marriage.

Louie knew. Somehow.

And that gloriously green stare said that he understood every miserable nuance of her now hopelessly complicated love life. And that he did not approve.

Neither, she knew, would Max.

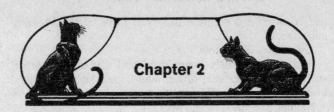

Chapter 2

Louie Agonistes

What is a loyal bodyguard and bedmate to do? (And I am not asking you, Mr. Kevin Costner; I am no fan of anyone who dances with wolves.)

My charming roommate, Miss Temple Barr, is obviously undergoing a major life crisis. Now, were a serial killer breaking into our humble but homey unit at the Circle Ritz, I would not be at a loss for direction.

I would leap upon a pant leg, ratchet my way up to his chest and shoulder area—making three-inch tracks a quarter-inch deep—lash out with my built-in switchblades and take out his eyes, then execute a thorough bit of plastic surgery on his mug for a finishing touch.

All of the above before the average bear could say "Hannibal Lecter."

But nerve and brain, my two greatest assets, will not work here. I am at a loss for once, waylaid by the tangled webs of human emotions when it comes to what are such simple matters to the rest of the animal world, i.e., what people call the Mating Game.

This is not a game, folks! It is the call of the jungle, the survival of the species, and the triumph of the Alpha Male. Of which I am, naturally, one. Although perhaps not so naturally anymore since I was relieved of the possibility of fatherhood by a villainous B-movie actress who had hoped to de-macho me. Whatever. Despite Miss Savannah Ashleigh doing her worst, I am still catnip for the dames and no back-alley offspring will ever come back to haunt me.

I am the 007 of the feline world, four on the floor and one in the backseat, with an unlimited license to thrill. Even the animal protection people cannot fault my condition and habits.

And I face no messy consequences who might want to slash a dude across the whiskers and call him a philandering absentee father. I am thinking here of Miss Midnight Louise, my erstwhile daughter from the old pre-chichi cut days. According to her.

Anyway, this stuff among my own species I have aced.

Humans are a different plate of Meow Mix entirely.

I pace back and forth in front of the French doors that lead to our triangular mini patio. By now my Miss Temple is out for the day, pretending that she is going about business as usual, but I saw her disarray the previous evening and am most . . . unsettled.

True, she lavished more than the usual affection on me, even clutching me to her breast (which is not such a great treat for a dude such as I, if you wish to know; we do not like forced confinement, even in comfy places). Please, let us come to you. It works out much better.

Anyway, I put up with this mushy stuff because we go back a long way and have done some heads-up crime-solving together. A dude owes it to his partner, even when the going threatens to get slushy.

And it is not that I am such a big fan of Mr. Max Kinsella, who previously occupied pride of place here at this Circle Ritz unit, i.e., the bed. I mean, he is probably an okay magician and he does have undercover aims for the betterment of humankind—not that humankind much deserves it, from my observation—but there is only room for one black-haired, agile, and sexy Alpha Male in this unit, and it is I.

You will note that I am schooled in the nuances of human grammar as well as kung fu.

And I have nothing against Mr. Matt Devine, who once devoted himself to the service of humankind (boy, they do get a lot of devotion for such a sorry species) and, during his priesthood days, actually gave up using what I almost lost. Even Miss Midnight Louise has a soft spot for him and she is one hard mama, let me tell you, speaking as her delinquent supposed-daddy. So I do sympathize with a well-meaning dude who is trying to enter the Alpha Male sweepstakes so belatedly in life. Not everyone can have my advantage of being born to be bad.

But my first and foremost loyalty is to my Miss Temple. She is not only Recently Blonde, she is recently tempted by the New Dude on the Block.

Well, I am the grayer head here by a single hair. I will not tell you where it is.

So, I sense that I will have to seek advice outside my usual, normal guy-type venues.

Ick!

However, for the good of my devoted roomie, no sacrifice is too extreme.

Chapter 3

The Deal of the Art

The New Millennium Hotel's vast, soaring, empty exhibition space rivaled the square footage and chambered nautilus design of the Guggenheim Museum West at the Venice Hotel and Casino up the Strip. Temple eyed its scope with a frisson of pride that this might be her next assignment.

The Guggenheim Museum in New York City and its Western branch at the Venice Hotel in Las Vegas made strange bedfellows, but Las Vegas was built on making strange bedfellows. Or making bedfellows of strangers.

Nowadays in the City That Never Sleeps, though, class is a more cherished commodity than wretched excess for its own gaudy sake. To this has Las Vegas ascended: the city now boasts a mini Guggenheim Museum as well as a mini Eiffel Tower. Pretty soon it may boast a mini me.

New York's famous Frank Lloyd Wright–designed museum was created decades ago for its Manhattan setting. It is a top-heavy organic space, with galleries spiraling upward around a soaring central atrium.

The vaulted exhibition space at the New Millennium is less natural and more high-tech, an eight-story Star Trek holodeck now vacant but capable of running any exhibition "program" needed.

"You like, I see," said Randall Wordsworth, the New Millennium's chief PR honcho.

He was an affable, well-fed, graying guy who looked liked he had been born with the low blood pressure needed to navigate a major Las Vegas attraction through endless media hoopla.

"It's a totally blank canvas in three-D," Temple said, trying to get her focus right despite three cups of espresso. It was 12:30 P.M. and she still was not quite there yet. "There's nothing you can't do in this space."

"Exactly. We plan to use it for three-dimensional multimedia, multicultural exhibitions. The opening art exhibition will be spectacular, but so will the elevated magic show occurring above it. A double bill of eye candy and live entertainment. You see our problem."

"Two-dimensional artworks like paintings, no matter how rare and spectacular, are static."

"Exactly."

"But the more you jazz up the exhibition itself," Temple went on, "the less respect you get from the major national media, and the higher risk you run of something invaluable being damaged, or even stolen. What to settle for? Glitz or guilt? Essentially, this new upscale trend has made the Las Vegas we know and love bipolar."

Wordsworth laughed. "That last analogy earns you a free lunch at our Jupiter restaurant. And my dedicated admiration."

* * *

Over a sumptuous lunch of Martian greens and Saturn scampi (the New Millennium boasted a relentless solar system theme), Temple and Randy Wordsworth discovered that they were both pros at public relations.

That wasn't surprising. What was surprising was discovering that they both performed the same tightrope act of being meticulously honest with the press while keeping the interests of their billion-dollar-baby employers foremost.

Lying to one for the other never came out as well as it was supposed to.

"Truth will out," Randy mused over the arugula and other less identifiable but no less trendy greens, "and show up on *Access Hollywood*."

"Or *Sixty Minutes,* even worse."

"So our jobs—" he began.

"—are to prevent anything bad from happening that might make the six P.M. news, et cetera."

"I'm amazed some major hotel hasn't snagged you for PR director," he noted, sipping the white wine spritzer the canny PR person uses to imbibe socially without losing an ounce of keen observation.

Or weight, unfortunately, Temple thought.

"I'm happiest working with a variety of projects," she explained. "And I'm the semiofficial permanent floating PR consultant for the Crystal Phoenix Hotel and Casino."

"Nicky and Van Fontana's place! Class act. 'Choice,' as Spenser Tracy said when he met Katharine Hepburn. Sad that they're both finally gone now."

"You mean Tracy and Hepburn, not Nicky and Van, of course. Sad and a heck of a lot less interesting."

"That's exactly why I'm looking for outside assistance with the White Russian exhibit."

"I can't see why. You're a total pro."

"Thank you. I'd like to keep it that way."

Temple nodded. "When what we do works, nobody notices."

"With this exhibition, the New Millennium competes directly against the Bellagio and the Venice, which started the Art of Vegas trend. A lot is on the line, going upscale like this.

Your reputation for, er, uncovering crime scenes is another reason we'd like you on board. An exhibition like this attracts the criminal elements. We have security, of course, but we'd like someone on staff who can blend a suspicious mind with publicity concerns."

"You need a Nancy Drew with a communications degree."

"Right. And since you've done PR in the past for purely cultural institutions, I could use you to handle special touchy corporate sponsor events and high-gloss artsy-fartsy print media. Glitz I get. With quiet snobby stuff, I gotta admit, I'm out of my element. If *Art in America* deigned to notice us, I'd swoon."

"I can't guarantee that, but I can give it the old art college try. What about the show's basics, like security?"

"Absolutely the latest high-tech world-class museum paraphernalia. I can't be specific—"

"Of course not. The fewer who know how and where, the safer the installation. But with all that archaic bling from days of empire, your prime audience will be women, and we're generally a rule-abiding lot. Sometimes too much so."

"Yes. Women will be dazzled by the paintings, the artifacts, the jewels, the gowns, the tragic death of the Romanovs, and the brutal end to empire."

"And they'll hopefully urge their honeys to dazzle them after a tour of the exhibition with the costly but less arty goodies in the exhibition gift shop and the hotel's Milky Way shopping arcade."

"You got it." He frowned as he sipped the de rigueur watered-down wine. "Apparently, you don't place all your faith in high-tech security."

"I've . . . dated a magician. I think you'd do well to import some human bloodhounds to mingle with the patrons. Just in case the lasers and eyes-in-the-sky don't work."

"You have a security firm in mind?"

"No."

Wordsworth lifted pale, caterpillar eyebrows.

"I have a discreet family business in mind, given that your patrons will be mostly middle-aged women."

"Paying twenty bucks a head to eyeball the exhibition? Yes. And if they can't drag hubby along, they'll view it on their own. Diamonds and rubies and emeralds and sapphires and *plique-à-jour* enamels and Fabergé and all."

"Exactly. The, uh, gentlemen I have in mind for the job are impeccably continental and most amenable to middle-aged ladies. To ladies of all ages, in fact."

"I will get some references—?"

"Certainly. My aunt, the well-known novelist Sulah Savage, for one. And Nicky Fontana at the Crystal Phoenix, for another. They're his brothers."

"The Fontana boys?" Wordsworth sputtered a discreet swallow of wine spritzer into his napkin. "You *do* think outside the box."

He sipped again to recover, then nodded, as if approving the wine's vintage. It was something else he was approving. "They do discreetly straddle the line between legit and illegal."

"To catch a thief . . ."

Randy nodded. "Perfect casting, now that you mention it. You have a theater background also, don't you?"

Temple nodded. "Rather minor and very distant."

"Still, with the *Ocean's Eleven* and *Twelve* caper movies so popular, we wouldn't want a nouveau Rat Pack trying a heist at the New Millennium."

"I and six million women might, if George Clooney came along for the ride. After all, he and Brad Pitt almost put together a new Las Vegas hotel deal."

"You know, that's not a bad idea. Turn it around to focus on the star and not the deplorable use of robbery for entertainment. It's like turning the Fontana Brothers out on security detail. I imagine they'd take extreme issue with anyone challenging their protective services."

"Yes. Picture them as pit bull–Italian greyhound crosses. They've been extremely protective of me in the past. Sometimes I think 'shady' is just another word for sex appeal."

Randy laughed until he needed to quiet his hilarity with another tepid sip of wine spritzer.

Temple went on. "Getting Clooney to attend the exhibition

opening shouldn't be too hard. Tape-cutting. Lots of high-roller comps from the hotel, the five-thousand-square-foot Nebula Suite, and flashy media up the ying-yang."

"I'll let you look into that. I'll do all the traditional stuff: local press, major national general interest media. Anything off the wall is your area."

"Don't use that expression! We *are* talking about an art exhibition, after all. Nothing will be 'off the wall' on our watch."

"Done." Randy gave Temple a rather anemic high-five. They were talking serious culture here, after all.

Temple couldn't believe it. The contract Randy would be sending to her home office at the Circle Ritz could keep her in everything, including Stuart Weitzman shoes, for a year. This was her first truly major PR commission for a major Vegas hotel. It took her breath away and almost took a girl's mind off of all things Scarlett.

When she got home, Louie was waiting on the kitchen countertop, white whiskers twitching on his Jack of Spades black face.

Temple opened three cans of mixed shrimp, scallops, and red snapper supper, and then added dollops of caviar and capers over the Free-to-Be-Feline cat health kibble he'd only eat if it was adulterated.

Or maybe not. After gazing at the lavish stew, he turned tail and thumped down. She followed him anxiously into the living room, thinking he was expressing annoyance at her recent absences. Although he had hardly been confined to quarters lately himself. . . .

By following him, she discovered that her answering machine was blinking red with a message.

"Temple, you formerly red-headed little rascal!"

Her aunt Kit's dramatic contralto boomed into the room like a bolt of energy. "Thanks for the fix-up date. What a morning after! I felt like Judy Garland in the production number of 'Get Happy.' Remember that one? Judy in fedora and legs and black-tie jacket, borne aloft at the end by rows of chorus boys?

"As chorus boys go, the Fontana Brothers are the cat's pajamas, all nine of 'em. Does that have anything to do with lives? Unfortunately, not mine. One can't have everything all at once. Listen, my dear. I'd love to spend some time with you. I'm not needed in New York for ages. Well, a week or two. No bloody book deadline. I'm at the aging Oasis where the damn reality TV show put us poor judges up. Can we get together?"

Temple laughed at the message until she cried a little. (Scarlett O'Hara wake-up moments had a very bad effect on one.) Aunt Kit. Her Midwestern mother's never-married sister, an actress turned novelist. In the old days, she would have officially been designated "spinster," (kinda what Temple did for a living now, media wise). But Aunt Kit was the only woman in Temple's family who'd gone somewhere and done something . . . adventurous.

Yes, they could get together!

Temple dialed the number Kit left and suggested that her aunt might want to do Vegas with a transplanted native and maybe bunk with her for a while.

When Temple hung up, she cringed. *What a coward!* Aunt Kit in residence would keep both Matt and Max at bay while Temple tried to adjust to her brave new role as a woman with two equally appealing beaux: playgirl of the Western world.

Chapter 4

Eat Till You Drop

"Are you ready?" Randy asked the next day at the New Millennium.

He looked almost as quizzical as Danny Dove, Temple's choreographer friend, at his most frantic or antic. She should be ready for anything, on the work front at least.

Aunt Kit had been installed that morning in Temple's humble home-away-from-Manhattan and was left to her own devices. Why did Temple think those started with the initial *F*? *Rule, Fontanas, Fontanas rule the Strip. Their ladies never, ever will be anything but hip.*

Temple regarded the hotel's deserted, gray flannel–upholstered media room, wishing she and Randy could sit here forever, playing tiddlywinks and video games with art and commerce.

"Ready for what, Randy?"

"Lunch with the Bigwigs."

"Why do I think that title is capitalized?"

"Because it is. Today. Russia is no longer a Red State, excuse the expression."

"Politics," Temple said. "Damned if you don't play politics, damned if you do."

"This exhibition is a touchy blend of Russians Red and White. Ready to walk the tightrope?"

Temple thought about walking her own personal tightrope between two guys and a gal: Max. And Matt. And C. R. Molina, the interfering homicide lieutenant. Guess which one was the gal? If you could call it that.

"Tightrope walking? What," she asked Randy, "do you think a self-respecting freelance PR person in Las Vegas has been doing all these years?"

"Excellent. We'll be lunching in the Red Planetarium Room."

"Why am I not surprised?"

Temple seriously wished for her natural red hair back when she sat down to lunch in the Red Planetarium Room fifty stories above the Strip.

The restaurant revolved, of course. In a city dominated by mini-me skyscrapers like the Eiffel Tower and the New York, New York faux skyline, real elevation was a turn-on. The ceiling was a slowly spinning electrified night sky as seen from Mars, with Earth a marbleized blue-and-white beach ball dominating the distant glittering galaxies.

Larger-than-life-size Greek-style nude statues in red marble depicted Mars, the Roman god of war, and his Greek counterpart, Ares. Not to mention several naked unnamed goddesses. The room was awash in red velvet and stainless steel.

Although the rococo decor befit the last Romanov czars of Russia, the dominating red color scheme was a slap in the cool white-marble faces of White Russians, the aristocracy ushered out of the mother country so violently by the "Red" Communist Revolution in the early twentieth century.

At least the tablecloths were whiter than the snow-capped Ural Mountains separating expansive European Mother Russia from equally sprawling Siberia and Asia. At a huge round table curled into the tufted shell of a crimson velvet banquette sat a coven of strangers, eight, from Temple's hasty summation.

Let the introductions begin! Shortly thereafter, she concluded: too bad the table was surrounded by the most dyspeptic mugs on the planet.

The exhibition curator was a tall, snowy-polled stork of a man named Count Ivan Volpe. A French citizen, his family had fled the 1917 Russian revolution for Paris, as had so many aristocratic White Russians, or supporters of the czars. Ever after, French culture had a distinct Russian accent in such artistic circles as dance and graphic design.

Temple couldn't decide whether Volpe would be best typecast as an impossibly snobby Parisian head waiter or an autocratic Slavic prince. Either way, his accent was divine. The women at the table, though few, perked up to hear it.

A decidedly proletariat-looking man—strong nose, strong back, weak chin—who spoke neither English nor French, was introduced as Dimitri Demyenov. This Russian government representative was accompanied by two Russian tractors who stood silo-still behind him throughout lunch.

Not literal tractors, mind you, just the human equivalent of same: bull-necked, rhino-chested men in black-green suits with the no-nonsense tailoring of flak jackets.

Temple was surprised that the Terrible Two didn't overtly taste Dimitri's dishes before he did. Who could forget the dioxin poisoning of presidential candidate Victor Yushchenko in the Ukraine?

Olga Kirkov was the exhibition designer, obviously a former ballerina—such a tiny, fragile creature, as creased and transparent as old lace. Imperial in mein and manner, her eyebrows were so elevated they could have been McDonald's golden arches etched in mourning black. There was something childlike about her immobile, disciplined features, like a doll with seven facelifts.

Her opposite was the thirty-something feature writer for *Artiste* magazine, a glossy national review of multimedia events. This tall, awkward bundle of hyper-intelligent bones with popping doe eyes had a name ideal for her job, though Paris Hilton it was not: Maven Abernathy.

The portly gentlemen were harder to distinguish: expensive but not too-designer suits, ebbing age-paled hair, glittering rimless glasses, soft pink hands that honed their only calluses on board reports, not elite gym weight machines.

Two represented sponsoring corporations, adding luster to their corporate logos for backing a bona fide crosscultural coup. And for flashing their company names in front of the millions who visited Las Vegas and the hundreds who covered its every wink and twinkle and buzz on multimedia outlets day in and day out.

Temple nodded and shook hands where offered and finally sank onto her cushy red velvet place with spinning brain and rejoicing haunches.

Randy would give her a remedial course in Mass Introductions 101 after lunch. For now, she just had to speak softly and make intense mental notes on the personalities and politics surrounding this ballyhooed event.

First, there was the ordering ritual.

A waitress in green body paint—whose costume was designed to show the most of it that was legal—declaimed the innumerable specials and took orders.

Boris and Natasha, Temple's nicknames for the unidentified standing goons, made furtive notes on everybody's orders. Looking for poison or planning on planting it?

Even the pre-luncheon drinks took on a political cast. Some ordered Black Russians, some ordered White Russians. Some ordered raspberry-red white-chocolate martinis, shaken, not stirred, renamed Pink Russians for this occasion. She and

Randy shared a peace-keeping order: pink Zinfandel wine spritzers. The chitchat began over appetizers, a pan-galaxial platter of haute French, Russian, Asian, and Tex-Mex teasers.

Every PR person in the business knows that meals and drinks are a professional hazard, rather like sand traps in golf. You have to play through them, but it isn't pleasant or easy and you may end up looking like an idiot. Or in this case, fat.

This was a crosscultural sand trap: Post-Communist New Russia huckstering its once-despised Old Russian aristocracy meets New Wave Las Vegas and American know-how/hype-now via the intervention of the delicate and decidedly iffy French connection.

Snobbery and savvy were having an arm-wrestling contest in the subtlest of terms. Temple couldn't help thinking that something had to give.

The art people really couldn't stomach the publicity hype and the tacked-on magic show. The hotel people couldn't swallow Culture with a capital *C* when it didn't include generous amounts of media slap, dash, and tickle.

The expanding New Russia's sense of enterprise couldn't unloose the Old Red State need for heavy-handed control. The Old Las Vegas free-roulette-wheeling love of the art of the deal couldn't slick down its cowlicks to kowtow to High Culture on a roll.

Talk about a marriage made in Hell. This was a miscarriage made in Hellespont: Byron versus Hulk Hogan. Erté versus Eminem. Fabergé versus Rasputin.

Something, Temple told herself for the second, third, and fourth time, has got to give. If this exhibition opened without a major media glitch, Temple and Randy would be so lucky they ought to enter the lottery.

She couldn't think of anything else that could be added to this recipe for disaster.

Except . . .

Elvis, we hardly knew ye. And you're way better off left out of this fiasco.

Chapter 5

The Softer Side of Vegas

The empty lot opposite Maylords Fine Furnishings is a scruffy bit of sand and sagebrush not far from the Las Vegas Strip.

Folks who fly into Sin City only see the high-profile skyline, not the flat lots in between. Granted these checkerboard squares of empty real estate are worth the ransom of an Enron executive (pre-downfall). Yet to the tourists who trot by on their way to the next overblown attraction, they look pretty tacky.

And here is where my kind has always set up shop: on the outcast fringes of populated areas, where they can forage, be overlooked . . . and sometimes be tended by the soft-hearted.

So. I got Ma Barker and her north-side gang transferred down-Strip to the softer side of Vegas during one of my recent capers. They are all summa cum laude graduates of the Feral Seize and Suture program, meaning they are the last of their breed.

I admit I am sorry to see the last of us street folk subdued. We are like the lonesome hobos of decades gone by: free and free living. Railriders and kings and queens in disguise.

But it is a rabies tag world these days. My goal is to ease this ragtag community over to the parking lot of the Circle Ritz, where they can live out their days, and nights, as local celebrities, thanks to the attentions of Miss Electra Lark and her tenants, who are also lone strangers in their own human way.

My Miss Temple, of course, would be the first to offer them shelter, did she but realize that they existed. Although I have come to know her circle of loved ones and acquaintants well during our mutual adventures, she has never quite wised up to my extended family.

It is about time that she did.

So, I round up Miss Midnight Louise, who occupies my old post of house detective at the Crystal Phoenix Hotel and Casino. Some say she is the spitting image of myself. Black, ballsy, and cool. Well, delete the ballsy. What is the female version of that? Gallsy? And I am Palsy?

Some say she is just spitting mad.

She says she is my unsanctioned daughter and that I am a deadbeat dad.

I say . . . call me a Clairol blond. Who knows for sure?

Meanwhile, I am stuck with her. Being a practical cat à la T. S. Eliot's streetwise breed, I allow her to delude herself. So, I sidle over to the Phoenix and find my partner in Midnight Inc. Investigations lounging under my old favorite stand of canna lilies next to the koi pond.

"Popster!" she greets me.

I look around to see if anyone feline or human has overheard this humiliating term. Kits, these days. Tattooed and microchipped. Born to be wild but happy to be post-modern media children.

"I need an inside kit and an outside herder."

"Tell me more." She settles onto her haunches, a sign of budding maturity.

Louise is not quite my spitting image, although her temperament sometimes matches mine. Her eyes are 24-karat gold where mine are emerald green. And her coat is longer and softer, as becomes a girl. I hunker down as well, ready for a cat-to-kit talk.

I start. "You know Ma Barker and her gang have moved downtown." Ma Barker is my, well, ma and possibly Louise's grandma. We had a touching reunion during one of my recent cases. That is to say that shivs and whiskers were brushed, but nothing came of it but a mutual resolve to keep out of each other's hair.

"Thanks to you," Louise acknowledges. "But Ma Barker and her crew are still a feral gang. Anybody might be after them to wipe them out."

"Right. But I have plans."

"You always have plans."

"This is a good one. I want to relocate them to the Circle Ritz."

The hair on the back of her neck stands up. "You did not want to relocate me there."

"You have a good position here at the Crystal Phoenix. The house executive chef is in the palm of your paw. These are, well, street people in fur. They need someone to watch over them."

"You?"

"Somewhat. Mostly they need my human associates, which are all a soft touch, once their potential is pointed out to them."

"Hmm." Louise settles deeper into her ruff, which has grown fluffier as she has matured.

I admit I am taken aback by her new Mae West look.

"So, you need my help?" she asks.

"We need a Moses."

"I am a girl cat."

"Well, a"—boy, am I stuck—"a Joan of Arc. To lead them to the light."

"She led the French to battle and darkness."

"This is different. Plus, I could use you later on the scene of what may become a foul crime."

"That sounds more up my alley."

"The New Millennium."

"Oh, that New Age planetary place!"

I explain what is going down there nowadays.

"The Czar's Scepter? I do know a couple of Russian Blues who might give me an in."

"Russian Blues? Those are pretty aristocratic cats."

"I am a modern girl, Daddy-o. I can do country or haute couture."

Manx! I am not sure I can "do" either. But leave us not let Miss Midnight Louise know that! Like the Mystifying Max, misdirection is one of the few weapons I have left in a tricky, hostile world.

"So," I say, "if you could hang around the New Millennium when you are not chatting up the Ma Barker gang for the move, it would help me out a lot."

"And what will you be doing?"

"Fixing my Miss Temple's personal and professional life, as usual," I growl.

"She seems to have an inordinate amount of both, for a ginger-cream."

I have never heard Miss Louise sound so . . . catty before.

"Just do your job. I will handle the delicate diplomatic bits."

"Yes. I have glimpsed your delicate diplomatic bits and they leave a lot to be desired."

That is Miss Midnight Louise these days. Ma Barker all over again.

Chapter 6

Designing Man

"Thanks for coming," Danny Dove greeted Matt at the door.

Matt wished that he was still so naive that he didn't detect the inadvertent pun in that greeting.

The door Danny opened was one of a shining black enameled double set. This neighborhood was high-end and this Big White House (a domestic version of Hollywood's Big White Set) was palatial. Still, Danny Dove, Temple's bereaved friend and Las Vegas's prime big-time show choreographer, stood in its doorway looking like death warmed over and fricasseed for good measure.

Matt felt uneasy, unsure quite how to take openly and obviously gay men like Danny. The church's longtime "don't ask, don't tell" policy had put it crosier-deep in unaddressed issues about gay and pedophile priests. Who could hurl the first stone?

Matt the priest had been heroically virginal, playing by all the ancient rules. He was heterosexual, but he couldn't disown his non-hetero seminary peers. Or non-seminary non-heterosexuals. Dogma was one thing. Real life was a lot more complicated, including his.

"How are you doing?" he asked Danny. Carefully.

"Rotten. Why else would I have asked you over?"

Matt didn't mention his own resemblance to Danny's recently dead significant other, Simon. He understood the need to clutch at a lost past. He still felt uncomfortable acting as a stand-in for a dead man, but his job wasn't his own ease. Only the ease of others.

"Drink?" Danny asked.

Danny Dove was a sophisticated man. The toast of the Las Vegas Strip. A world-class choreographer. The best of his generation. Today, at high noon, he held his cocktail glass like Captain Hook had hoisted his metal claw. Part of him, but hated.

"Yeah," Matt needed to roll with Danny's needs before he could fully understand and address them.

"I always knew you were all right." Danny headed for the cocktail cart.

Well, no. Matt had not always been all right, but he was getting there.

"To our mutual friend Temple," Danny said, lifting his glass. "She tried to help." He bowed his head over a major piece of Baccarat crystal.

Sometimes people needed the Eucharist. Sometimes some people needed St. Glenlivet more.

"I'm not sure why you called me," Matt said.

"Raised Catholic, what else?"

"I'm not a priest anymore."

"No, but . . . you feel like one, only as freaked out as I am."

"Thanks. I think."

"And. You look like Simon. You have his innocence. That's

what got him killed. Innocence. Tell me how to live in a world without innocence."

"I can't. I can't live in it either."

Danny sat, hard, on a white leather sofa. The whole house was a Big White Set from a thirties movie. Matt realized that anyone who didn't fit into Here and Now invariably harked back to There and Then.

"I need a counselor," Danny said. "I'll go crazy with Simon gone like this. I'll hurt someone, probably myself. I was raised Catholic, did you know?"

Danny had repeated himself, but Matt said no.

"If you guys don't accept me, where'll I go now?"

"I accept you."

"But do they accept *you?*"

"Maybe not. I haven't asked yet."

"So, you ask? You leave it up to them?"

"I'm not sure."

"You're supposed to be sure! You're the goddamned religious nut."

Matt held back a glib answer. Pain was a powerful force. Was he a freak, as Danny and Simon had felt in their own small, painful world? And if not, what was he?

Everyone wanted to be part of something.

He wanted to be part of Temple's world. Part of that was Danny. A bigger part of that was what he felt for her, no matter what.

"So . . . Temple," Danny said as if reading his mind. "You like her."

"You could say that."

"I can help you with that."

And then Matt understood that the best thing for Danny right now was helping someone, in his view, worse off than he was. Like Matt himself. "How?"

"Lord! You don't have the slightest idea about dealing with women."

And a gay guy did? Maybe.

"So how far has it gone?" Danny was asking.

"I'm up against the great Max Kinsella."

"Know about him. True love . . . and then love on the run. Temple's a girl who likes to set her spikes into a groove and stay there."

Matt sipped the expensive Scotch from the expensive glass. It tasted sharp and stung him.

"She's loyal beyond belief," he said.

Danny nodded. "You didn't get what I said. She's loyal. She'd go to the wall for me. Did." He looked down so Matt wouldn't see the tears in his eyes. "But she's like a lot of women. Stability, security is Job One. She's not getting that from Max anymore."

"It's not his fault," Matt the ever honest heard himself say.

Danny laughed a little. "You do need a Cyrano de Bergerac to speak for you, pal, if you're going to keep apologizing for your romantic rival."

"I'm only trying to be fair."

"You know the old saying: nothing's fair in love and war."

"Then neither of them should be that way."

Danny rolled his eyes. He was looking decidedly perkier. " 'Shouldn't' is a delusion. 'Is' is. That's what you mean by the word 'is.' "

"What should I do?"

"Depends on what you've done."

Matt sat back. Took a real sip of Scotch, then leaned back on the white leather couch, which was actually quite comfortable, and told him.

"I took her out on a surprise dinner date. The dinner wasn't a surprise, the date part was."

"Sounds good. Someplace expensive?"

"Someplace very cheap."

Even as Danny frowned, Matt went on. He described the drive to the desert. The corsage; the taped dance music from the era of Temple's prom night. The lights of Las Vegas like an aurora borealis in the distance.

Danny kept nodding so often he forgot to drink. "Outstanding. You don't look that inspired."

"Temple did the same thing for me, months ago. I was just a copycat."

"*Hmmm.* Your relationship goes back that far?"

"I wouldn't call it a 'relationship.'"

"The hell it isn't! Where have you been all your life? In a seminary, that's right. So, it went . . . well?"

Matt steeled himself for candor. "Yeah. I guess you could say we . . . made out. I proposed—"

"Oh, my God! Too soon. Disaster."

"I proposed," Matt repeated a bit stiffly, "that we could have a civil marriage."

"Why on earth would an ex-priest do that? That's a mortal sin anyway. Totally unrecognized by the church. Almost as bad as that horrible religious-political-social bugaboo 'gay marriage.'"

"Temple had said that—modern women, and I suppose non-Catholic women, want—she did say this, but it's not as hard-bitten as it sounds . . . 'free samples.'"

It had been hard for Matt to report this, but if he was going to do any good as a counselor he had to reveal his own feet of clay.

Danny practically rolled on the floor laughing.

Matt sat stunned.

"Oh, my God!" The tears welling in Danny's eyes now had been undammed by laughter, not sorrow. "What a magnificently naive counterplay. You made the girl put her money where her mouth was. What'd she say?"

"That she'd have to think about it."

"Blessed are the pure of heart. They will drive you crazy."

"Are you saying I blew it? Or not?"

"Not! Temple is not stupid. She realizes what a risk you're taking to offer her that out. So . . . where are you two star-crossed lovebirds now?"

"I don't know," Matt said. "I haven't seen her since."

"Why not?"

"It's only been a couple of days. Our paths haven't crossed, and I don't feel right about pressuring her."

"Pressure her." Danny set his drink, half-drunk, aside. His blue eyes were clear now, not blurred, and he leaped up, like someone who thought best on his feet. Which a choreographer did.

"You're right," he told Matt. "Max Kinsella is one hell of a rival. He could be frozen in a block of ice in a river, like some Arctic Houdini, and no one would take their eyes off him or take any bets on him not coming out of the coffin and walking on water and eloping with the girl to Monte Carlo."

Matt didn't see how that was supposed to make him feel better, but Danny apparently thought this was a pep talk.

"Okay," Danny said. "You grooved in the desert. What's the next step?"

"She tells me what she thinks about my offer?"

"No! You're right not to approach her. Next. You make her wonder what *you're* up to. Next."

"Talking to you?"

"No. Wait! Right! Yes. That's brilliant." Danny was directing a show now: Romeo and Juliet at the Rialto. "Keep her guessing. You're neighbors at the Circle Ritz, right?"

"Right. Actually, I rent the unit above hers. And Max's."

"Forget Max! If you can't, she can't. That's a highly cool place. She must be aware of you right on top of her, excuse the expression."

Matt blushed. Must have been the alcohol.

"So. What's your place like?" Danny alit on the couch again.

Matt eyed the palatial surroundings. "Plain. I haven't had much time or inclination to buy stuff. Decorating wasn't necessary in the rectory."

"You have anything the slightest bit hip in your place?"

"Only the red suede Vladimir Kagan sofa Temple found at the Goodwill and browbeat me into buying."

"Vladimir Kagan? Fifties suede? Simon would have killed for that."

Neither could find any right words to say for a couple of minutes.

Then Danny lifted his head, assuming the dancer's ramrod posture even though he was only sitting, not standing on a stage.

"And the bedroom? Don't blush, my boy, this is serious business."

"A disaster. Empty. What I was used to."

"Tsk, tsk." Danny was looking Puckish again. "You clearly need *Queer Eye* help. You do know what that is?"

"I do have a television set in there."

"A feeble beginning, but well-intended. I must see this Disaster Zone. I must . . . choreograph a more positive future from your rather bleak past."

"It didn't feel bleak when I was in it."

"It never does. Let me help you. I'm afraid my dear Temple isn't happy anymore, and I desperately want someone to be happy just now." Danny looked down, mumbled. "I was . . . am . . . one of those unsung subjects of newspaper stories these days. The perfect altar boy. So perfect that my parish priest molested me."

"My God, Danny, I am so sorry."

"We are all sorry." Danny invoked his dancer's posture again, as much a ritual as any religious rite.

Matt knew the bitter truth that what he had spent half his life believing in had been twisted to serve carnal self-interest. It made him doubt his vocation, his gender, his past.

"Let me help you," Danny was saying. "It restores my faith a little, to see a nice naive virginal heterosexual ex-priest like you flailing around trying to be both honest and sexual. You don't know what a rare bird you are."

Matt didn't know what to say.

"I just hope that Temple appreciates that, and I mean to see that she does. For both your sakes."

Chapter 7

The Russians Are Coming

The only thing wrong with working for a mega hotel was the meetings. Lots and lots of meetings.

Temple supposed some PR persons enjoyed numbing their rears until they could hear the cellulite piling on underneath them, but she liked to be on her toes in more ways than one. There were always so many chiefs at meetings that the foot soldiers spent all their time deferring to rank instead of getting anything done.

Which was why she was a freelancer.

At least the operations meeting room at the New Millennium was spectacular: a huge, black-marble-topped conference table, brushed stainless-steel chairs upholstered in black leather. A shrimp-colored marble floor. Every chair had a wireless silver flat-screen computer in front of it, the screen as big as a place mat and the sleek keyboard the size of a videotape.

No ashtrays. No cups of coffee or glasses of water or booze. No chitchat.

Around the perimeter were honest-to-God, gray-flannel vertical blinds that could be operated from the computer keyboards, Randy had said, to cast shadows in various shades of gray.

Pete Wayans, the hotel's operations manager, was a beefy middle-aged guy wearing wire-framed half-glasses that looked like a pair of tsetse flies posed on a hippo snout.

He stood in front of the giant plasma TV, narrating the exhibition layout and contents while the same scenario played on their individual computers.

Temple tapped in notes and observations (on the eerily silent toy keyboard), like her fellow attendees. And they were all fellows. This was when she began to seriously lament her blond dye job at the *Teen Idol* reality TV show. She couldn't yet testify that blondes had more fun (although it was beginning to look like it).

Dang! She'd typed in "Matt blond" instead of matte black to describe her idea for an invitation card.

Temple backspaced to erase the error, aka Freudian slip, noticing that the men in her vicinity all noticed her retreat. Blondes attracted much closer examination, she'd discovered, which Temple didn't welcome. At half an inch per month, it would take almost a year for her natural coppery red color to reach its usual below-the-ear-length. She didn't know if she could take the stress that long.

Wayans droned on, but the computer show was so spectacular and self-explanatory that it didn't matter what he said or didn't say.

Essentially the exhibition would funnel guests up a circular ramp of paintings hanging between bullet-proof Lexan-plastic display cases sparkling with court dress, jewels, furniture, and precious artifacts of every conceivable type, ending in a translucent onion dome apex, where Czar Alexander's scepter could be displayed upright on a block of rock crystal, like the Sword in the Stone from Arthurian legends.

A close-up of the scepter revealed a silver and gold rod circled by a lacework of diamonds, emeralds, rubies, and pearls twining its two-foot length. The crowning orb held a yellow diamond of three hundred and sixty-five carats. It was called the Calendar Diamond, for the days of the year.

As Wayans read the laundry list of the pieces: jewels and their weights and history and values, Temple found her mind drawn back to the Sword in the Stone analogy.

Set an object up as a modern-day Sword in the Stone and what do you get? Something a lot of people might compete to unseat. Of course, Temple thought like a crook—she was the significant other of a world-class magician and had undone a few crooks of her own.

Pete Wayans thought like a hotel mogul with the artiest state-of-the-art-security system and the hottest high-class act in town.

Then he got to the good part. On Temple's screen, multiplied by sixteen around the table, the viewpoint swooped above the scepter to show a life-size jewel-enlaced human figure spinning slowly in the gallery's upper blackness.

It was a woman wearing a headdress that duplicated the scepter's daggerlike lines, her arms close to her lithe body, straight legs crossed at the ankles and arched into one sharp point, like a ballerina's toes, her head straining upward on a long swanlike neck.

Temple had seen acrobats at the Cirque du Soleil spinning like this by their teeth, but not invisibly and not—here her blood ran cold, just like in the cliché, and Temple hated clichés—with a white-painted face with exaggerated features drawn in Oriental shades of black and blushing crimson as in a Chinese opera.

Before Temple could fully register who this scepter sylph was, a huge male figure came striding out of the darkness, booted, caped, and wearing a dark tiger-pattern mask that covered his entire head.

At a gesture of his gloved hand, the scepter woman sank lower, like a spider on an invisible web. Lower, lower, turning faster and faster, a blur now. A flick of the magician's wrist, and a glittering web of empty cloth floated down, tenting the onion dome in a lacy cobweb.

Everybody applauded the stunning effect.

Everybody except Temple. She wasn't surprised, of course, to see the Cloaked Conjuror appear. He headlined at the New Millennium, after all.

What had shocked the accumulating cellulite off her behind was seeing the made-up countenance of a magician who'd done her—and Max, and Midnight Louie—wrong, and had never been seen again. Shangri-La, last glimpsed several months ago at the Opium Den, a low-end casino off the Strip.

As part of her disappearing act, this woman had stolen Temple's almost-engagement ring from Max right on stage. The only time Temple had been called out of a Las Vegas audience to do an onstage turn had almost cost her, and Louie, their lives.

Max needed to know about this . . . pronto!

Chapter 8

Friendly Fire

"What is *she* doing here?"

Max's annoyed tone roused Garry Randolph from the humble task of coiling a rubber snake of electrical cord in one corner of the New Millennium's exhibition area scaffolding, fifteen feet above the construction-littered floor.

This place wasn't just a room, that was for sure.

The whir of power drills backgrounded their conversation. A faint miasma of sanded Spackle dusted their workmen's white jumpsuits a whiter shade of pale.

"You look like you've seen a ghost," said Garry, who once had performed as Gandolph the Great.

"Two," Max said grimly, looking up, and then back down

again. "The worst part is that they've both seen me, one more than the other."

Gandolph followed Max's quick flick of eyelashes both up and down.

Up, the problem was obvious. A lithe figure in pale tights and leotard was cavorting like the Sugar Plum Fairy on a distant tightrope invisible against the flat black ceiling of the museum-to-be.

"I don't know where Shangri-La came from," Garry admitted, "but I know you had an unpleasant run-in with her months ago—"

"More than one, and the last one way too recently," Max interrupted, looping his own length of cable into the tight coil of a striking cobra.

Garry eyed his one-time apprentice at both magic and counterterrorism work. The painter's cap hid Max's thick dark hair. Spackle dusted the arched Faustian eyebrows. His eyes were their natural blue. He expertly hunched his four inches over six feet into a droop-shouldered stance that kept him from literally standing out in a crowd, rather like Sherlock Holmes on a stakeout.

"Where did you last see her?" Garry asked.

"At the Cloaked Conjuror's estate. Creepy old place near a cemetery. Keeps the tabloids and the tourists away. Crazy young woman, always wears her stage makeup. We had a little talk, she and I, and it wasn't peace negotiations."

"What happened?"

"A few months ago, she lured Temple up on stage in her act in an audience-participation gig."

"Always a crowd-pleaser."

"Not that time. She did the take-the-item switch, only it was the Tiffany ring I gave Temple in New York. And not only that but she whisked Temple into a transformation box."

"That's risky to do with a civilian. Going down that trapdoor in the floor."

"And then into another cabinet and into a departing semi trailer loaded with magic box illusions and illegal designer drugs. Also napped was Temple's cat, Midnight Louie."

As Gandolph regarded him with gaping jaw, Max said, "Don't ask. I mean it. I got them back again, but it didn't help my low profile with the Las Vegas Metropolitan Police Department."

Gandolph chuckled. "Low profile was always a job for you. So, I get the lethal lady in the sky. What's the problem on the ground?" Max shrugged in a direction that directed Gandolph's attention down over his shoulder to a cluster of people way overdressed for the floor of a resort hotel and casino with summer coming on.

Gandolph frowned at the men in suits. FBI? No. Open-necked shirts. Still, pretty boardroom for the New Millennium main floor. And who else? Max would never worry about executive suits. A blond head at three o'clock caught his eye.

Garry reeled off his diagnosis. "There's the odd one out in that crowd. That little gal. Has to wear high heels for the top of her head to reach the shortest guy's shoulder. Cute."

"Don't say that! She'd kneecap you if she heard it."

"That *your* Temple?" Gandolph straightened in surprise, even though it strained his back. At sixty and two-hundred-sixty pounds, life was not a cabaret when it came to sudden motion. Good thing he had retired from the stage. So to speak.

"Maybe," Max said mysteriously.

"Ah. I saw her at the séance where I 'died' last Halloween. She was a redhead then."

"She *is* a redhead."

"Adorable girl. And she's a blonde now because—?"

"I don't know," Max said, visibly trying not to let the tension in his jaw affect his voice. "Obviously, having her on the scene is a huge kink in our operation."

"Perhaps you should find out why she's here," Gandolph said quietly. "And you last saw her as a redhead when—?"

"Just two weeks before last and way too many nights ago." Max tossed the drills and cords in a long metal workbox the size of a coffin for a midget.

He glanced up to the deceptively frail female figure twirling above. That was Max Kinsella these days. Caught between heaven and hell, only hell happened to be on high in this latest scenario. With Temple on the scene, his assignment for the cadre of magicians he was infiltrating had just become three times more difficult.

He tried not to straighten up fully as he and Gandolph climbed down and shambled out, their blue-collar shift over, right on time.

All right, lady! he challenged Shangri-La from above. *Bring it on!*

But first he had to catch up with Temple, fast.

Chapter 9

Brothers Under the Fur Skin

I go through the usual contortions to slip into the New Millennium Hotel unobserved. The word "observed" is very apropos, as the hotel exterior is ringed by a giant neon solar system. Mars, Venus, Mercury, Jupiter, Saturn, and that goofy little outer quasi-planet, Pluto, shine luminescent red, blue, green, pink, white, and yellow.

This decorative hallmark hangs about six stories above the Strip, the better to be seen. So a lightweight but heavy dude like me is risking life and limb and family jewels to be crawling around on the hotel signage in the blinding and alternating dark of night and glare of blinking neon.

Still, I have found and used the hotel service channels before, and I do so again. Before you know it, I have slid down the interior laundry chute called a service hatch, and immediately head for the hotel's backstage area.

This is not hard. I need only follow my nose. Few of us *felidae* rove and ramble inside a major Las Vegas hotel. Luckily, Vegas hotels are built like anthills or Egyptian pyramids: high and imposing, and slicked up with impressive façades, but basically three-dimensional puzzles riddled with hidden entrance and exit tunnels.

Instead of worker ants constantly plying these routes in service to queens of the insect world, the hotel conduits are so seldom used that I end up with a cobweb mask over my puss by the time I find my quarry.

Calling two acquaintances of the Big Cat family "quarry" is a little nervy on my part, but my part has always been nervy, or I would not be where I am today. Which is in the belly of the beast, in the offstage areas below and above the theater and museum arena, going nose to nose with dudes who outweigh me by twenty times. At least.

If you are going to be intimidated by the canine incisor-advantaged in this detection business, you have no business being in it.

Besides, they are caged and I am free range.

I amble over to the bars that separate them from me.

"Hi, boys. I was in the neighborhood and decided to check in. I hear you will be the centerpiece of another custom-bustin' Las Vegas show."

"Where is the delightful Miss Midnight Louise?" Lucky, the black leopard, asks.

He will never forget that she finessed him a fine shank of beef when he was being kept in chains and underfed for nefarious purposes during one of my previous adventures. It is one of *my* previous adventures, and not his, because *I* am the pioneering feline PI in this town and he is just a main attraction.

"She is having a manicure at the Crystal Phoenix," I say.

Because she is the house detective there since I moved up to bigger and better things, like heading our own firm, Midnight Inc. Investigations, it is fair to say that her nail sheaths are getting a workout, even as we speak.

"That is one feisty little doll," Kahlúa, the other black leopard, puts in with a baritone chuckle.

These Big Boys are way too indiscriminating, in my opinion. They have no idea what I have done for them. But a PI is most effective when he is most unnoticed, so I do not belabor the point. Besides, their "points" are way bigger than mine are. An effective PI is not a dummy.

"You are still working with the Cloaked Conjuror?" I ask.

"So far," Kahlúa says, growling a little.

Lucky adds a bit of a roar in support of his foster brother. I am getting the impression of discontent under the big top.

"What is going on?"

"The Boss has gone soft."

"No!" This I say with a straight puss, for there is hardly a human on the face of the planet—even the neon ones outside the New Millennium—who is not capable of leaving an animal companion down and out . . . flat!

"He is all taken with this new dame in the act," Lucky says with a snarl.

"And her damn housecat—no offense," Kahlúa adds.

"None taken." I am many things, but housecat is definitely not one of them.

"I am," so I inform them, "a street cat who happens to maintain an in-town condo and a live-in girlfriend. That is a whole different kettle of moray eels."

"A live-in girlfriend, really?" Kahlúa is practically panting.

"Yeah. You have seen her around. Cute little thing. She used to be a ginger-top but she has recently gone platinum, like a record."

I cannot tell whether they are purring or growling. That is the trouble with the really Big Boys. You walk a narrow line with them. Irritation and agreement often sound the same.

"We have seen nothing," Lucky notes with a disconsolate purr turned groan. "We have been in rehearsal, but have not been allowed to strut our stuff on the stage here. It will be our first aerial act."

"Aerial act!"

I am impressed, though I do not wish to let them know it. Nobody uses these Big Boys higher than a few piled drum pedestals. This idea is so innovative, I half suspect Mr. Max Kinsella of being behind it. But he has been AWOL of late. Not even my Miss Temple knows that he has been moonlighting as the masked Phantom Mage at the Neon Nightmare nightclub. The Shadow, however, knows. That is me.

"So," I speculate, "the Cloaked Conjuror is going up, up, and away. He always struck me as the earthy sort."

"He is." Kahlúa shows his teeth. The big white vampire fangs in front are maybe two inches long. That is almost as long as my . . . never mind.

"It is that Oriental longhair dame he started associating with all of a sudden," Lucky says. "We were doing fine as an all-guy act. CC is not built for aerial acts. He is all bone and boots and heavy-metal costuming."

"You got that right," I tell the boys.

If Mr. Max onstage and off as the Mystifying Max floats like a butterfly and stings like a bee, the Cloaked Conjuror thumps like an elephant and lands like a sledgehammer. His shtick is outing magical illusions, not creating them. And creation takes brains, guts, and elegance. "Outing" takes greed, anger, and envy. My opinion. So sue me. I will see you in People's Court, where I recently won a case, paws down.

"We think this is a mistake," Lucky tells me.

No kidding. "So what will you guys be doing up there?"

"Jumping from black-painted platform to black-painted platform and vanishing." Lucky boxes a huge black-gloved mitt over his prominent cheekbone. "In the dark. Black light. With mirrors."

I whistle low through my quarter-inch front fangs. "Sounds like a suicide assignment."

"For our faux master."

They are speaking of CC, for whom they actually feel great affection. He is a big galoot but he treats them well. I understand that they think little of this new act; that they are risking their own hides for his sake.

"It is all *her* fault," Kahlúa murmurs bitterly.

I know that "her" well and concur. She has done my Miss Temple and me no good. And so I tell the Big Boys, who are all eyes and ears and fangs.

"Shangri-La," Lucky hisses, showing his awesome fangs. "What can we do? Our faux master is besotted."

"It is more than a business arrangement?"

"He is hated, threatened, masked, though feared and famous," Kahlúa says with some fellow sympathy. "He has no friends but us, and does not understand how loyal we are. He falls prey to a capering female."

Well, I have fallen prey to a capering female or two in my day, so I do not add anything to their summation.

"He is human," I say finally. "The breed requires constant shepherding, more subtle than a mere dog's. We will just have to do our jobs and theirs too. As usual."

"Amen," the Big Cats growl in unison.

You would think I was leading a revival meeting. But then, I am in a way.

"I will be in touch," I say airily. "I have a delinquent human to mind too."

"Awww," they growl in sympathy.

Chapter 10

Kit and Caboodle

"This is the cutest place," Aunt Kit exclaimed as she moved from Temple's small entry area into the living room.

"Your mini Flatiron building in Greenwich Village isn't anything to whistle Dixie at," Temple said.

"Yes, but the whole interior has been renovated. This is the real schlemiel, as they said on *Laverne and Shirley*. Oops! I'm dating myself, aren't I?"

"Aunt Kit, you will never date, only improve with time," Temple said. "The couch unfolds into a bed."

"That big thing? I don't need a bed in your living room. At my height, the sofa will be as comfy as a cradle."

"At *our* height," Temple said ruefully, watching Kit kick off her four-inch heels and bump hips with a lounging Midnight Louie as she claimed the sofa for her own.

It'll be an interesting bedtime around the Circle Ritz tonight, Temple thought. "I've got the Porthault sheets ready," she said, kidding. "You can use the sofa open or closed."

"Mr. Big Boy and I can share just fine," Kit growled in a super-satisfied Mae West voice. "I'm sure he'll come up and see me sometime. In the night."

Every naughty implication in the phrase was punched out perfectly. Kit wasn't an ex-actress for nothing.

"You're sure I'm not intruding?" her aunt added, pushing her large-framed glasses atop her head.

"No," Temple said without thinking.

"No, you're *not* sure I'm not intruding, or no, I'm not intruding?"

"No, you're not intruding," Temple said firmly. "I imposed on your hospitality in New York last Christmas."

"You did not impose, my dear. Midnight Louie did, as I recall. But we are old friends now, eh? And happy to cohabitate. Right, Chief?"

Louie's green eyes had become narrowed slits in his handsome head. He didn't like humans to speak for him. Kit ran her long painted fingernails along his whisker-stubbly chin and down his chest hair.

He rolled over like a kitten.

Temple beamed on this happy domestic scene. Having her aunt here was amazingly comforting. She was bewitched, bothered, and bewildered at the moment, which she might confide to Aunt Kit later, when there weren't feline eavesdroppers around.

They had a microwave dinner and luxuriated their bare toes in the faux goat-hair rug under the coffee table. Louie had taken himself off somewhere through the open bathroom window, fleeing the girly ambiance.

Their wineglasses were on the third refill.

"So." Kit was settling into her confidante mode. "How's your tall, dark, and handsome fella?"

"Fine. I guess."

"Not fine! A wishy-washy answer if I ever heard one."

"Max has . . . a lot of issues."

"Family?"

"In a way."

"Work then?"

"In a way."

"Why can't you say in what way?"

"Because . . . his life is a secret that could get other people killed."

"He's mob?"

"No, he's hero, which is much tougher."

Kit kept silent for a bit. "What's with keeping the blond hair?"

Temple shook herself upright. Blonde was a badge of courage, in this instance, from going undercover and nailing a killer.

"I don't know what to do. If I dye it my natural Little Orphan Annie red, the dye job will fade as the roots grow out and I'll have to redye it all to match. If I don't dye it red, I'll have crimson roots and glitzy platinum hair. Going completely white at the roots might work best, but not all of my brushes with crime and murder have scared me that much so far. No roots are showing yet, so I have a couple weeks to decide. Besides, I may discover I like being a blond bimbo."

"Temple! This is the little scabby-kneed roller-skating niece I knew and loved in Minneapolis?"

"This is my glamorous Aunt Kit, who came to the family reunion picnic at Minnehaha Park with her boyfriend with the sexy convertible and the ear stud?"

"You still remember that?"

"The handsome boyfriend?"

"No, the sexy convertible."

"Nobody in Minnesota drove convertibles. Too cold and too many mosquitoes when it was warm."

"Morgan," Kit recalled.

"The car?"

"No, the boyfriend."

"How come you never married?"

Kit sighed. Set down her wineglass. "My era. Liberation. Independence. A career. The big city. *Sex and the City.* Enough success to become a carousel. Some great guys, always moving on and upward. Getting 'too old' for acting when I was thirty-five. Finding I could write as well as act. That was a woman's world. Any guys I met after that were all unhappily divorced. All needed shoulders and understanding baby-sitters. My time was past. And . . . I did what my stars allowed. I was always more, or less, Me, not Somebody's Wife or Somebody's Mother. But—" Kit smiled at Temple. "I have always been excessively proud to be your aunt."

"Kit. I . . . have a marriage proposal."

Kit's hands clasped at her breastbone, the universal theatrical gesture for joy. "Max has proposed? I knew it in New York! I feel like a mother hen whose chick has landed in her own safe little nest!"

"No. Not Max. Matt."

"Matt?"

"You remember. You saw him when you were out here for the romance writers' convention." Temple had not sounded very sure.

"Matt." Kit was visibly gathering her improvisational skills. "Ah, yes! Blond, dreamy. Ah . . . I thought he was a friend."

"Where do you think proposals come from?"

"I don't think. Temple, I'm sorry. I'm in a fantasy fog most of the time. Acting, writing. Not reality. I do indeed remember Mr. Caramel Smoothie. Frankly, I'd assigned you to Max and felt free to . . . well, appropriate Matt for one of my books. So. He's proposed. Isn't he . . . forbidden fruit, somehow? I remember importing him as the luscious and of course forbidden first cousin in . . . er, *Bayou Bewitched,* a Louisiana-set romance."

"'By you bewitched'? Quite the obvious pun, Auntie."

"You'd be surprised how many don't get it. How old are you anyway?"

"Thirty," Temple announced in tones of doom, not mentioning that thirty-one was just around the corner, suddenly next month, like June.

"A chick fresh out of the egg." Kit frowned. "But it's true. I

followed my acting career just long enough to lose out on the
first round of romantic link-ups."

"Women," Temple quoted a magazine article, "who don't
marry by thirty-five are unlikely to."

Kit winced and drank wine. "I can't deny it. So. You wanna
get married?"

"Actually, no. I mean, I would, but mainly I want a guy who
loves me and vice versa, who I can trust and try to get through
this mess called Life together with. That's awful sentence
construction, isn't it?"

"Horrid. But the sentiments are pretty universal. I did like
Max."

"So did I."

"Did?"

"I thought he was Mr. Right, like there is any such mythical
beast, but . . . it's not that he doesn't want to commit, he can't.
Not with his job history."

"And Matt can."

Temple nodded. "Now. Except that he comes with all these
religious strictures that aren't mine."

"You've always liked him."

Temple rolled her eyes, Mariah style, left over from the
Teen Idol competition. *"Ye-es."*

"Maybe some of those strictures have something to do with
that."

Temple nodded. "He's so honest you sometimes want to
kick him in the shins. He really does care about what I think
and feel. He's willing to sell himself down the river if I'll give
him a shot, though he didn't tell me that part. I figured it out.
And he's really hot for me, but he's aggravatingly able to control it."

"Grrrrowl. Take it from Auntie, that is *not* a problem when
it comes to female satisfaction. Would that they taught that in
high school instead of abstinence and friends with benefits."

"What are friends with benefits?"

"Are you out of the talk show circuit! Girls are preserving
their virginity, all right, but by giving out oral sex to boys as a
substitute. Can we say 'not a fair trade-off'?"

Temple couldn't say a thing. Girls always lost something,

somehow, in the dating game, and she was very glad not to be the mother of one. Yet. Maybe she could become a Red State conservative and marry Matt yet. She and Kit finished their wine and conversation, yawned, and hugged each other good night.

Temple's mind and emotions were in turmoil despite several glasses of wine. A woman's future options were much rockier than she'd suspected. Her own immediate options made her stomach churn with an unhealthy surfeit of emotion and indecision. Max. Matt. Matt. Max. It was coming down to a duel in the sun. Her heart and libido were giving her emotional whiplash. She took a Tylenol PM to help her to sleep, and so to bed.

It was past two in the morning, so Max did the Midnight Louie trick. Push, bounce, click and the left French door from the balcony let him into Temple's living room with barely a sound.

Unlike the White Rabbit, who was too late to say hello/good-bye, Max was the black cat burglar. He knew it would soon be too late to say hello/good-bye/good night, so he wanted to explain himself to Temple before he became entangled in the inexplicable again. Perhaps for a good long time.

The parking lot lights cast shadows over the living room's familiar topography: potted Norfolk pine in corner, pale sofa grazing like a White Buffalo in the middle, and various tricky tables and lamps to tiptoe around.

Max was almost around the sofa when it sat up and took notice.

"Ahhh!" it said, switching on the floor lamp at its right end.

There was Max, in the spotlight again.

He blinked to see a pale imitation of Temple: small, indignant, red hair faded to strawberry-blond in the bright light pouring down on it. What was she doing sleeping in their living room? Temple's living room?

When the glasses appeared and pasted themselves to the bridge of her nose, he realized that this was not Temple. She wore contact lenses now.

"Max!" Not-Temple exclaimed in a hushed, hoarse voice.

"Yeah."

"What are you doing here?" they each intoned like a chorus of two.

"You remember me," the woman said. "Aunt. New York. I'm the one who stuffed my sexiest nightgown into Temple's overnight bag for your Manhattan reunion. Like it?"

"It didn't survive the reunion. That nightgown was *yours*?"

"I'm flattered, however vicariously. I haven't lost lingerie to an encounter in twenty years. Remember, it comes with full visitation rights."

"Never forgot that for a moment. So is Temple here?"

"Inner sanctum. Midnight Louie's out and prowling. Your path is unobstructed."

"Except for you."

"Oh, don't let me stop you. Not that I think I could. Or would. I'm an ex-actor. We all shared close quarters in my heyday. Want me to yell hey when the day is dawning?"

"You are an unnerving woman."

"Thanks! Now I need my beauty sleep, which you won't notice the results of unless we meet in daylight. Ta-ta."

The woman stretched out an arm to turn off the lamp and roll herself into the sheets. Max was now night-blind. Again. He felt his way to the bedroom door, which was indeed shut, and eeled inside.

Temple was asleep. His frazzled nerves suddenly smoothed out. She always loved being awakened in his own special way.

He slipped into the sheets beside her, managing not to awake her. His fingers barely touched the familiar contours of her face. It turned toward him, in her sleep, the way a sunflower follows the sun that names it.

She was rousing now. In the sense of awakening.

"Max," she muttered.

"Yes," he said. *"Shhh."*

"I had a dream. You were falling!"

"Falling here. Into your arms."

"No! A long, long way. Max!"

She was way too lost in some nightmare. He pulled her into his arms, but she was still falling, her arms and legs jerking and flailing.

"We'll crash," she cried. Under his fingers, her face was a spasm of furrows.

He couldn't erase them. Eradicate the dream. Overcome her fears with the mere nearness of his presence. Not anymore. His fingers felt her eyelashes batting like bird wings.

She struggled up in the bedclothes, sitting.

"Max? You're really here?"

She still sounded drugged with sleep.

"Really."

"There's something I've got to tell you. What? Oh. Yeah. That white witch is at the New Millennium."

"White witch?"

But he knew whom she was referring to, and he had known for some time that Shangri-La had hooked up with the Cloaked Conjuror, although their professional alliance hadn't gone public.

Temple just didn't know that Max knew so much more than she did about Shangri-La. Another thing he knew: Shangri-La hated him for some unknown reason. A lot of women seemed to. The late Kathleen O'Conner, Molina. Thank God for Temple.

"CC calls her 'Shang.'" Temple yawned. "Thought you'd want to know. I can't seem to reach you anymore."

He leaned back with her, against the pillows, uneasy about carrying a concealed load of knowledge and keeping it from her. "It's okay. I know now."

She was still murmuring sleepily. "Shoulda grabbed her by those horsey locks and demanded my ring back."

"She can't give it back. Molina has it now, remember?"

"Right, Molina. Another wicked witch. Don't let the wicked witches get you, Max."

"Speaking of locks, aren't yours a whiter shade of pale?"

"The teen reality TV show mavens made me dye it platinum. What started as an undercover job stuck me with a dye job."

He chuckled as she nuzzled into the pillow of his chest, drifting off again.

"I want a different dream, Max. No falling . . ."

So did he.

Temple tossed and turned onto her side. Away from him. Still stressed in her sleep. Dreaming disaster. Hurting.

Max felt his jaw clench. Pushing anything physical now wouldn't be sexy, but intrusive. When she'd needed him lately, he'd been committed to his various secret lives. Now that he was here and ready, she'd obviously been up late drinking wine with her aunt. Maybe talking about him. Complaining. One sure thing was that he'd lost his last magic midnight touch. He didn't want to be her bogeyman. And he sure as hell didn't want to be her sleeping pill!

Max slipped away, like the dead part of night. He even made it past her guard dog of an aunt undetected this time.

He still had his skills, if not his will for using them.

He'd gone over to the Dark Side. For the time being. Best to leave the creatures of light and hope to themselves.

He'd phone Temple tomorrow. In daylight. Maybe. If he had time. Meanwhile he had other promises to keep. Bad ones to dark forces. All in the name of ultimate light.

Chapter 11

Spider Men

An hour and a half later, Max was literally out on a limb.

He was garbed in magician's black: spandex tights, turtle-neck, black gloves, black-masked spandex face to match his black hair and bleak expectations.

He was suspended high over the New Millennium exhibition area, a spider on an invisible web, clinging to the network of rosin-treated cables that formed a high-tech web over the entire space.

He felt like a cyberspace creature, some gaming entity loose on a hidden grid.

He'd entered this bizarre, deserted world by the lighting service tunnel. Painted matte black, light hoods studded the ceiling like black holes. They were cobras, poised to strike with shafts of illumination when turned on, ready to run through their preprogrammed schedule once the show began.

The Cloaked Conjuror wasn't here now, nor the pupae of his spinning web diva, Shangri-La. Spiders had thousands of spawn. Max pictured Shangri-La as a sort of White Widow Spider hanging from an invisible tensile line, spinning her web, changing shapes as she changed venues.

She knew him. Knew he was in Las Vegas, in the equation. She hated him. He didn't know why. Didn't care. E equals mc squared. Enemy equals mega-competition squared.

This was Shangri-La's territory. He was intruding. He moved along the taut wires, slid his gloved fingertips along the bungee cords ready to cut loose and plummet down almost to the top of the mock-onion dome far below that would shortly encase the Czar's scepter.

Guards would soon blanket this exhibition from ground zero to pinnacle. But the high-flying performers would be the last to be suspected: the Cloaked Conjurer, whom Max both trusted and dismissed; Shangri-La, for whom he made neither assumption.

Assumption.

That was what this White Russian act was all about. It took place in the flies, to use a theatrical phrase. In the heavens. Above the crowd, as in the circus. The Greatest Show on Earth. The greatest shell game.

Max felt his way, fingers and feet leading, along the hidden web, tensile rope by tensile rope. A low hissing sound intruded on his concentration, but he ignored it. This unsensed network had been strung up here to create an illusion.

From an illusion, it morphed into an intrusion.

Max stared down, almost seeing the glittering Czar Alexander scepter in place. Twenty-seven-inches long. Diameter: two inches along the shaft. The orb at the top that held the fabulous jewel? Four inches. A phallic sort of thing, suitable for giants, easily concealed upon the persons of mortal men.

Or women.

Max, hanging by his long, flexible limbs, calculated the

possibilities. Capture before transfer from the bank vault to the exhibition. Substitution during installation. Virtual removal shortly after with all the eyes-in-the-sky cameras confounded. Abstraction during exhibition hours in front of dazzled tourist gazes.

How do I steal thee? Let me count the ways.

Everything below was empty now. Of treasure. Of people. It was all possibility and, for now, very little risk.

As Max meditated on this, the line of his supporting web vibrated with sudden shock. Glancing upward, he thought he saw one of the black-painted service hatches concealed in the ceiling shutting.

Max scrambled spider swift to spring onto another support rope, to cling at his concealing height. He froze while the scanning cameras cruised past him. Surely that betraying tremor, whatever it had been, had subsided enough to keep his figure safely in the dark.

Apparently it had, for no alarm sounded.

For the moment.

And in that moment, Max noticed what had brushed by his supportive wire network. He stared down on a black-clad figure beneath him, dangling by one extremity. In this case a crucial extremity. The neck.

The figure spun on its only support line, a noose, invoking the reverse image of the slender white filament that had been the rehearsing pale silhouette of Shangri-La.

This figure was no artful flutter of tattered robes, but the double of Max himself: black-clad, male, athletic, and dead.

Just as the audible alarms blared their shrill mechanical warning, Max swung from unweighted line to line, back to the claustrophobic shelter of the lighting conduits.

One line was like the deadly third rail on a subway system, one line he didn't dare touch. That was the tense vee of wire dipping down to the glistening empty onion dome, bearing the pendant of a dead man like a human jewel. His limp black feet almost touched the tip of the scepter's soon-to-be housing.

Was this some gruesome obstacle the Synth had set up to

make Max's test all the harder? A warning that he had better succeed?

Maybe.

Or maybe more than one cabal of thieves had its eye on the scepter.

Chapter 12

Who Do You Trust?

Lieutenant Molina was good to go: she wore her spring khaki pantsuit and her Glock 9 millimeter in a paddle holster at her right rear hip. Her feet were pushed into tan suede loafers that didn't make any insecure male officers or detectives suspect she might be taller than them by more than a smidge.

She carried several pairs of latex gloves and one colorless lip gloss in one side jacket pocket, her shield and sunglasses in the other.

And she was sitting on the arm of the living room couch, tapping her loafer sole on the carpet because America's almost 'Tween Idol, Miss Mariah Molina—just thirteen and out to prove that age was justifiably unlucky for parents everywhere—was still lost in the jungle of electric cords and tubes, jars and bottles the bathroom countertop had become.

"Hurry it up, *chica!*" Carmen called, checking her leather-banded wristwatch. "We'll both be late."

"Just a minute! I only have to do *one more thing.*"

Carmen shook her head. From tomboy to teen in one crazy dangerous stint of reality TV. Mariah appeared in the living room archway, flushed and still chasing her sequined flipflops down the hall to push her feet fully into them.

The Teen Idol hairdresser had chopped Mariah's dark basic bob into a ragged, flipped-up look that was surprisingly appealing except for chunks of highlighted blond here and there.

Try to keep a Latina from going blond nowadays! Even African-American women had jumped on the blond bandwagon. Asians too. Soon the only natural brunet left on the planet would be Midnight Louie, Temple Barr's pesky black tomcat.

"Look okay?" Mariah ran to the small oval living room mirror for further verification. She eyed only her lightly made-up face (that battle was a goner), not the blue-and-green plaid of her Our Lady of Guadalupe uniform.

Manly men could be a pain, but girly girls were catching up to them fast.

"Terrific," Carmen said, standing. "Now, let's roll."

Mariah grabbed her fully loaded backpack. At least her grades were pretty good. But Carmen missed the long, glossy brunet braid down her back, so ready to be tweaked on their way out to school and work in the mornings.

Tweaks were as out of date in maturing modern mother-daughter relationships as braids. Shoot.

Molina hit her office in the Crimes Against Persons unit feeling more naked that morning than packing a Glock should permit.

She'd come out of the closet a couple weeks back at the Blue Dahlia restaurant and cabaret. Mariah, Temple Barr, and one of Carmen's colleagues from work had met her occasional alter ego for the first time: torch singer Carmen, a continuing attraction in her vintage velvet gowns that matched her vintage velvet contralto voice.

"Morning, Lieutenant," a colleague greeted her.

No worry. It was just Detective Morrie Alch. He didn't know she had a closet to come out of. His genially furrowed face under its black and silver spray of thick hair reminded her of a faithful old Scottish terrier.

"Morning. What we got?"

"Trouble at the New Millennium."

"Who died?"

"We don't know yet, but he was found twisting in the air-conditioning above the fancy installation stuff they were putting in for that upcoming Russian exhibit. Kinda like a caterpillar in a cocoon. Hanging from a couple of bungee cords. Cirque du Soleil gone homicidal."

"Murder, then? Or accident?"

"Hard to tell. Was wearing this black spandex cat suit, but his face, get this, was painted white."

"Classic clown stuff. Accident, murder, or suicide?"

"Triple play. You got it, Lieutenant. Place is a mess. Workmen and hotel execs all over it. Not to mention T. B. and shady security. Su and I are up for it. Are we a go?"

"Sure. If it's odd, you're the perfect odd couple to handle it."

Morrie made a face not unlike Mariah's when reacting to a really stupid, horribly embarrassing suggestion from her *moth*-er.

Detective Merry Su was a pit bull–shih tzu cross. Tiny and ultra competent. Relentlessly cute and just plain relentless. A smaller, Asian edition of Temple Barr, PR woman to clients with a bent for providing the scene of the crime for murder.

Speaking of which . . . T. B. "Temple Barr—?"

"She sure looked different, but real cute, at that Teen Idol gig." Alch's chuckle was both paternal and, to Molina, annoying. "She's just like my daughter used to be . . . before she grew up and found out she'd become a wife and mother: you'd never know what they'd be up to."

"I'm not looking for domestic reminiscences, Morrie."

He shrugged. "Dispatcher gave me her name. Seems she's handling PR for this Russian thing at the New Millennium."

He actually sounded *happy* about that.

Molina hit the paperwork on her desk, her khaki blazer hung on her chair back, her short-sleeved khaki-and-white cotton blouse sticking to her shoulder blades despite the air-conditioning.

The paddle holster was in a drawer and her pen was tapping paper. What the heck was Temple Barr up to her hooker-high heels in now?

A set of knuckles brushed her door ajar. Dirty Larry was peering puckishly around it. He could afford to be puckish around the office. His street role as an undercover narc had him playing down and dirty. 24/7. Hence the nickname.

Molina regarded Larry with a twinge of regret. She'd let him bulldoze his way into her private life. She wasn't sure she knew his motive, although he'd certainly taken his opportunity. *Why?* A woman doesn't work her way up in a police department as an officer on a career track without questioning everything, especially herself.

Larry led with a question. "Kid come down off of Teen Idoldom?"

"Somewhat. They never get their feet fully on the ground at this age."

"Me neither." Larry sidled in. "So. You still having second thoughts?"

"About what?"

"Your big 'reveal' at the Blue Dahlia."

"*Reveal.* I loathe that reality TV word! It's so bogus."

"Like you aren't? Well, aren't you?"

Larry had taken the single plastic chair in front of her desk. He didn't sit so much as lounge. Molina suspected he had a spine like a Slinky.

She didn't really trust him, but something about him was oddly winning. No doubt that served him well when he was risking his neck among the Dangerous and the Depraved.

His close-cut hair still blared "dirty blond." He seemed the eternal hard-bitten kid you'd glimpse from railroad yards as the train pulled away from the worst neighborhoods in town. Any town. His face would haunt you like a Depression-era photograph until you saw a blurred green ribbon of bushes and trees beyond the moving window, not hovels and kids with nothing better to do than stare at themselves in passing train windows.

"I sense regret." Larry picked a square notepad block off her desk to play with.

"You're a narc. Regret is the sludge in which drugs grow."

"Stay a narc long enough, you can't come in out of the dark."

"So, how's accident reconstruction treating you?"

Larry came down from his dangerous game by taking on innocuous assignments for a while.

"Great. Instead of blood-spatter patterns like the crime techs fixate on, I've got shattered-glass patterns. Instead of crack houses, I get to go to toney nightclubs like the Blue Dahlia in my off hours."

"Toney? Please."

"I get to see and hear 'Blue Velvet.' " His smile was suddenly boyish, radiant. The passing train was a glittering, rattling string of diamond-mirror glass shattering the night.

Molina frowned. The song was one of her best. But the matching vintage gown, à la Topsy, had "just growed" in her closet, a single unsuspected moonflower in a midnight meadow. Or something sinister, like mold. Midnight blue mold. She didn't remember buying it.

Everything was coming at her so fast, the Cannonball Express. Her daughter blossoming into dangerously empowering girlyhood. Herself revealed. Part professional huntress. Part . . . moonlighting torch singer.

"Any luck on that off-time assignment I mentioned?"

Larry pulled a narrow notebook from his linen blazer pocket.

"You sure are one paranoid lady, but I suppose it goes with the job. First a rogue L.A. cop, then this. You've sure got me guessing." He quirked her his crooked grin, but his eyes were suddenly hotter than she liked to see on the job. Who was using whom here was still not settled, but it was unsettling.

"Get on with it," she said.

Larry settled even lower on his Slinky spine in the unfriendly plastic visitors chair, blue-jeaned legs crossed over his lean thighs. Undercover narcs tended to be super-casual, but he was taking a holiday from the drug wars in the Traffic Department for a while. So he was handy for her "black projects," like keeping her private life, such as it wasn't, private.

"This is hit and miss, you understand," Larry said. "When I have a moment. Gotta say this is not a shit assignment: nice neighborhoods, low crime, and the best tail I've tailed in my career."

"Save the sexist chitchat for your brother apes on the force."

"You are way too easy to rile, you know that?" He grinned again. "I just meant it was nice to do a wholesome bit of tailing for a change. Not very interesting . . . subject goes from home base to major Strip hotels; the New Millennium lately. Um, detour to a couple of real funky little joints on semi-shady blocks across from the worst section of Charleston Avenue."

"Really." Molina sat up to take notice.

"Yeah. By the Blue Mermaid Motel. Names of . . . Leopard Alley, the Bee's Knees, and, uh, a real kinky one, the Indigo Albino."

"Sounds like a list of sleazy clubs."

Larry leaned forward, forearms braced on knees. "Vintage shops," he whispered. "I even spotted a bong in one and an opium ring in another."

"An opium ring? What's that?"

He reached into his baggy jacket pocket again. Linen was like that, shapeless and prone to wrinkle. Molina hated it. For her own wardrobe. On guys it looked good: fashionable but not like they cared that much.

He pulled out a slender silver object, a tiny curved, sterling pipe, with a ring band just under the etched bowl.

"I got you it. Can't say I never gave you a ring."

"How exquisite." Molina turned the lightweight object in her fingers. It might make a good pendant.

"Ladies used 'em back when a little naughty drug use was a fashion accessory, kind of like cocaine spoons today. The twenties, I'd guess."

"I'll actually keep this," she told him. He raised his almost invisible flaxen eyebrows. "History of crime artifact."

But she was . . . what? Taken aback. Pleased? Larry had not only done her off-shift tailing bidding gratis, but had thought to bring her a pretty neat souvenir.

"I'll have to visit those vintage dives someday." She frowned. Her supply of vintage velvet gowns wasn't shrinking, but expanding. Maybe she had a magic closet. Yeah.

"You ever want a guide to the dark side of trendiness," he said, "I'm your man." His eyes glittered at the unsaid implications of his phrase.

Molina tried the ring on her right third finger. It would glitter if she wore it at the mike at the Blue Dahlia. She seldom wore jewelry, but this was exotic and just slightly sinister. She discovered she liked the exotic and just slightly sinister.

"Thanks," she told Larry. "Anything else?"

He shuffled through the notebook. "A couple of Strip shopping expeditions with the middle-aged chick who's staying with her."

"Oh, really? You know who?"

Larry gave her a rebuking look. "Talked to the landlady. "Aunt from New York City. Same type, just more miles on her. This is interesting. Aldo Fontana seems to have come and go privileges at the Circle Ritz these days. That black Viper of his is a regular in the parking lot."

"Oh, the Fontanas are fans of our subject from way back."

"This is Aldo, solo. And he seems like a real fan of the aunt, who must be fifteen years older than him, at least. Though she hasn't got a bad tail either."

Molina was thinking too hard to object to his terminology.

"So, she has an aunt in town who's hooked up with the Fontana Brothers? Odd. Where do they go, Auntie and Aldo?"

"Everywhere hot, loud, and expensive. We could do a double tail some night."

"I don't like heat, noise, and throwing money around."

"Anything for a collar," he said.

"Anything more on the real object of this investigation?"

"Temple Barr? Naw. Cruises by the Stuart Weitzman store in the Caesar's shopping arcade at every opportunity. Um, visited one of those older gated communities not quite near Henderson. Stopped by a veterinarian's on the way home for some suspicious-sized bags of something called Free-to-Be-Feline. Do you think it could be fertilizer?"

"If cat leavings are volatile, yes. Never mind. Just leave me the list."

"What're you looking for?"

"Something suspicious, but she's obviously just been a diversion for you during your off hours."

"Not much. Now tailing you—"

Molina felt her right hand clench under the bizarre accessory of the opium ring. She'd been some places lately she wouldn't want anyone to know she'd gone.

"Forget it. You're off this detail. Temple Barr is the same simple, shallow girl I always suspected her to be."

"What did you expect to get on her?" he asked, pocketing his notebook.

Max Kinsella, she answered herself. She had expected to find his fingerprints all over her and her life. Why wasn't he there anymore? Maybe he had other interests now.

Bastard! But weren't they all, given half a chance?

Molina thought about the men in her life: past, present, and future tense. Very tense. Rafi Nadir. Haunting. Unsuspecting parent and patriarch. Failed policeman. Successful ghost and potential blackmailer. Dirty Larry. New kid on the block. Brassy, pushy, sexy, suspect. Max Kinsella. Mortal enemy. Mysterious. Taunting. Murderous?

She didn't trust one of them. Except Morrie, who was too decent to count on for the ethical pinch she was in.

Carmen began to get an idea of what her blooming adolescent daughter was up against.

Larry left, both pleased with his report and puzzled by her behavior, her goals.

She regarded the opium ring. She really liked this little toy, and his thoughtfulness in buying it for her. Nobody had bought anything for her for a long time. Nobody had ever bought her anything interesting and beautiful. Maybe there was more depth to Larry than street smarts. Maybe this . . . bribe, was supposed to make her think so. Turn her into a silly woman believing a man, believing in a man like Max Kinsella, as Temple Barr did.

Not her. Not Carmen Molina.

Not ever.

Chapter 13

Depend upon It

"The police?"

Temple was astounded by what Randy told her when she buzzed by the New Millennium to check on things and ran into him in the lobby. He looked frazzled.

"A body was found about five A.M. this morning. On the damn exhibition site," he whispered, hustling her back to the area. "There's no way we can duck the disastrous publicity consequences."

Temple didn't contest the word "we."

Randy paced when they reached the entry area, then pounded his forehead with one palm. "This exhibition opening is starting to feel like a season debut of *CSI: Crime Scene Investigation*."

Temple thought for a moment. "Not necessarily a bad thing. Maybe we can get a 'curse of the Romanovs' rumor going. Did a lot for King Tut."

"We're supposed to support rumors of vivified czars strutting around nights stringing people up?"

"Not as creepy as mummies, I agree. What do you think it really is? A botched robbery?"

"Why? Not one priceless artifact has been taken out of the vault and displayed yet. This is not encouraging for that ever happening. The insurance will skyrocket."

"It does seem . . . premature. Why would anyone with designs on the artifacts tip his hand like this? Security will just get tougher."

"Maybe someone likes a challenge."

"Or needs a distraction," Temple suggested.

"Or maybe someone wanted to warn us. Because someone sure has."

"Or maybe someone wanted to short-circuit a heist."

"Why?" Randy asked. "Who?"

"Almost a million new whos arrive in Las Vegas every week," Temple said. "You should put casino security on red, white, and blue alert. What do the executives say to do next about the exhibition?"

Randy shrugged. "This is Las Vegas, a twenty-four-hour town. The show must go on. And it's our job to see that it does."

Temple sighed. How dismaying to think that the pristine white exhibition space, before it had been used for the first time, had already been the scene of someone's death, even if he had been up to no good. Was it her presence on the job? Did Death have a yen for good PR? Was she the Typhoid Mary of PR women? What else could go wrong?

"I'm afraid," Randy said, "you need to see the scene of the crime too."

"What's to see?"

"The body's still hanging there. Obviously dead, so the CSI people want to examine every square inch above and below it, and probably every cell of the air around it."

* * *

Temple thought she was cool with seeing the body.

She'd had a habit of tripping over murder victims. Maybe it was her red hair. Unlucky. Fey. But it wasn't looking red these days. So she could rule out the hair.

Yellow crime scene tape kept Randy and her by the cushy stadium seating ringing the exhibition area.

CSI techs in latex gloves were swarming like worker ants over the sleek cone of the spiral exhibition space and up in the dark flies above it. They were laying out grids, like archeologists, preparatory to recording every element of the huge crime scene.

It was the single limp figure in black suspended halfway between the literal "heavens" of a stage set and the milk-white curves of the high-tech exhibition mounting that riveted her glance and then her emotions.

Trouble was, she'd nearly had a heart attack, seeing that black-clad body dangling from a bungee cord cradle high above. It was so Max: solo, daring, dangerous. Thinking ahead, she knew she couldn't blame Molina for thinking the same thing when she saw the death scene photos. Well, she *could* blame her, but that was hard to justify.

Temple hadn't been able to reach Max by cell phone recently, but what else was new? He'd been putting her off for weeks, telling her he was working up a new "act." She had a muzzy memory of him visiting her bedroom, way late. She'd been unusually loopy on wine and Tylenol PM. Not a good date prescription. The hour had been too late for her to wake up enough to take advantage of that hit and run visit of his. Something was eating up every spare moment of his time, night and day. Something too consuming to be the easy suspicion of another woman.

If Max *was* making a comeback as a magician, it would take months of secret preparation. On the other hand, if he was planning to knock off the New Millennium's White Russian exhibition, he'd be on the same impossible schedule.

"Art Deckle," Randy said out of the blue. Or the white haze, rather.

The bizarre name echoed in the huge New Millennium exhibition space. Randy shrugged after saying it.

"They found an ID on the body."

"That's the real name of the dead man? Not a *nom de huck-ster*?" Temple asked, still envisioning Max twisting silently in the air-conditioning wind, although this man looked far shorter than Max's limber six foot four.

"Could be an alias. He has a record under it."

"Not the music industry kind, I take it?"

"Thief. Would charm the lonely lady tourists, get to their rooms and run off with their credit cards."

"Doesn't sound very profitable. They'd be onto him pretty early the next morning."

Randy smiled. "In a twenty-four-hour town you can buy a lot of bling with a credit card between two and ten A.M."

"So he played the happy winner. Hitting big at the tables and buying the girlfriend a big gift? On her card."

"Right. A lot of these gambler guys owe everybody. And some of them do hit once in a while."

Temple gazed at the vaulted space above the exhibition area. "A con man, but not a world-class art thief."

"His reach exceeded his grasp. That's what the police think."

"Including Lieutenant Molina?"

"Who?"

"You haven't met the homicide queen-pin yet?"

Randy shook his head. "So you've an in at the LVMPD?"

The initials referenced the Las Vegas *Metropolitan* Police department, as opposed to the separate and smaller North Las Vegas force.

"I did think so," Temple muttered.

"What're we gonna do about the media?" Randy asked her.

"Smother them with sound bites on how high security is on this show. The flypaper caught a fly, didn't it?"

"You mean he killed himself."

"Can the police prove otherwise?"

"Not . . . yet."

Temple sighed. "I better run home and get my full address book of general contacts. I can prepare e-mails and releases from the computer setup here once I have that. I, um, know some magicians and high-wire acts around town. I'll look into what they think really might have happened here."

"Could you? That'd be great. We could get a local story about their opinions on it. If they suit us."

"Let me talk to them first and see."

"Right. No spills from uncontrolled leaks."

Temple doubted that Max had ever been uncontrolled in his life.

At least he wasn't maxed out in a black spandex body suit, twisting in a deadly vortex for all to see. And whoever had killed Art Deckle, improbable name, had blown the whistle on the exhibition as a serious target for someone.

She returned to the Circle Ritz one downhearted frail, as the blues songs called sad women. *Ick!* She didn't want to even think of Molina the torch songstress.

So running into Danny Dove bouncing out the back entrance to her building was not the upper it should have been. He looked puckish again, though, instead of as shrunken and sere as an autumn leaf.

"Why, Miss Temple. Imagine meeting you here."

"Are you renting at the Circle Ritz after all?"

"Almost." He doffed his sunglasses, revealing eyes still blasted with strain. "And how are you doing? Looking a little peaked for a Teen Idol contender, *hmmm*?"

"Please, Danny. That was undercover."

"Speaking of *undercovers*—"

"I wasn't," Temple said severely. Danny was like a favorite old-fashioned uncle, always trying to fix her up with a steady beau.

"Well, I'd think you'd be dying to see our friend Matt's new improved look."

"I didn't think he could improve on it."

"Not personally," Danny said, rolling his eyes with some of the old spirit. "I'm talking about his . . . decor."

It occurred to Temple that she could learn everything she wanted to learn about that right here and now. From Danny, if she worked it right.

"You've been helping Matt out," she said in a leading way.

"*Au contraire.* The dear boy has been helping *me* out."

Temple remained silent, the key to good interviewing technique.

Danny looked down to watch himself swinging his fragile designer sunglasses by one bow. It was a new quirk, as if he were measuring the seconds the concealing tinted lenses were away from his face, his eyes.

"He's a damn good counselor."

Temple smiled, proud of them both. It must be an uneasy alliance: a celibate ex-priest and a gay man bereft of his partner. Somehow they had bridged the cultural and religious divide, and it said a lot for both of them. It showed her hope, and her anxieties about Life in General lifted a little.

"He doesn't have the slightest notion," Danny added.

"About what?"

"Anything, my dear one." He leaned close, voice lowered. "I've brought him kicking and screaming into the twenty-first century as far as decor goes. Someone else will have to drag him in the rest of the way. Not my type, if you know what I mean."

Temple did, and tried not to blush. "So, what worked?"

"You."

Oh. She'd hoped Danny didn't know about that.

"What a little motivator you are." He took her arm, walked her farther out into the parking lot.

"I'm engaged," Temple said. Firmly.

"You're between engagements, as far as I can tell. Honestly, Munchkin. You know he's—well, divine. He needs guidance. Be still, my . . . heart. You're lucky I'm bereaved, or I wouldn't answer for myself here. And, he's depressingly straight. What's holding you back?"

"You know." Temple couldn't quite keep her voice even.

"I know even you can't keep up the pretense that you're sufficiently spoken for to keep the strings of your heart from zinging in another direction."

"Danny! This is none of your business."

"It's all the business I have left."

Temple couldn't meet the blaze of anger and loss in his eyes. Nor could she argue with his accurate diagnosis. Still, she said, "I am not your matchmaker project. Not even if it would . . . ease something for you right now."

"Matt has become my project. Such a dear boy. Reminds me of myself before I dared come out, even to myself. There are such standards for a boy, Temple. Being manly. Being hard and callous. Being tough. Being a braggart about women, even if they're not your thing. Demeaning everything honest and soft and true for fear you'll show a weakness some boy who's even more uncertain than you will kick a hole through, just to prove *he's* all right."

She felt tears sting her eyes. Danny was talking universals. She remembered how girls had to hide too, pretend to be blithe and uncaring in the face of relentless bitchiness. To pretend when your heart was breaking.

"Awful years," she said, thinking that pretending and heart-breaking could track one for many years afterward.

"No argument. We must speed him through them."

"We?"

"It'll take both of us. Now, I've civilized him in the decor department. It would help if you would . . . bless my efforts with your approval."

"Just how much approval are we talking here?"

"Follow your heart and your healthy libido. At least back up my efforts."

"You make a very odd advocate," Temple said.

"I'm only following the path you trail-blazed. That red suede Kagan couch is to die for."

"It's a Goodwill find."

"I can guess who found it. And you let him have it?" Danny frowned playfully. "You were caving even then. I'm afraid my domestic improvements have been more upscale. Was that naughty of me?"

Maybe frowns were catching because Temple was doing it now. Despite the grisly crisis she had to hie back to at the New Millennium, she was dying to see Matt's new "home improvements." She would also die before asking him to show her personally. Maybe she could talk Electra into a private preview . . .

"I see it was," Danny said. His thoughtful expression had turned bleak again.

"Oh, dammit, Danny! I'll, ah, say . . . I don't know what I'll say."

"I already said it. I told him he needs a woman's touch for the final fillips. Linens, silk flowers—nothing allergy prone in the bedroom and *none* of those beastly throw rugs you women are always having underfoot."

Temple thought of the faux goat hair rug under her coffee table and winced.

"You *don't*!" Danny sighed. "I see I must offer my discerning services in your quarters next. A girl who would let somebody else have a fifties Vladimir Kagan couch! *Tsk.* You are an angel on earth."

Danny donned his sunglasses, bussed her cheeks with Italian film star gusto, and left in the silver Spyder convertible that made her Miata look like a Barbie car.

Chapter 14

Louie's Choice

Of course, I am lounging under the oleander bushes circling the parking lot when my Miss Temple and Mr. Danny Dove have their little tête-à-tête, as we Francophiles call it. (I had thought Francophiles had something to do with 1930s Spain, but apparently not. Those French do get around.)

I confess that I am deeply worried about my usually reliable roommate. It is those female hormones that produce that unreliable state called "heat."

At least in my species it is a come-and-go sort of thing (much to my regret). However, human females have a 24/7 case of it, which is appropriate to Las Vegas. Perhaps it is only in Las Vegas that this condition occurs, as in other aberrations of the human species.

I can usually find some way to assist my Miss Temple in matters of crime and apprehension but now my apprehension is directed at the fact that I do not know how to handle this pesky situation.

It appears that I need female advice. The dedicated operative is never too proud to consult experts no matter how uppity they might be. I decide to make the rounds of my acquaintanceship. So, while Miss Temple is safely on the job at the New Millennium, I vow to scour the city for useful suggestions.

First, I go to the empty lot opposite Maylord's Fine Furniture, which is looking a little seedy since the shocking events at its opening revealed a business plan that involved discrimination, harassment, felony, and murder.

The lot is empty of everything but trash, so I know Ma Barker and her clan have left and are working their way toward the Circle Ritz, as I had advised.

Now, I only have to find out how far they have gotten.

This is like tracking a tribe of Paiutes on the move on the wild Mojave Desert in the nineteenth century. It requires that I think like a scavenger rather than a sophisticated dude about town. So, I hopscotch northwest back toward the Circle Ritz, eyeing Dumpster environs and the empty concrete corridors behind strip shopping centers. I am not talking about the big boys and girls—Strip Shopping Centers—here, just the small fringe one-story layouts that surround the flash, glitter, and cash of Las Vegas Boulevard, to use the Strip's formal moniker.

If my Miss Temple knew how I was sanding my pads to the bone for her wayward heart . . . !

I catch up with the crew behind the Shanghai Noon all-you-can-eat buffet. They are dozing unseen, natch, in the noonday sun, but Ma Barker has posted two goons on guard in case any mad dogs or Englishmen show up.

"Hey, it is just me!" I say as Tiger and Tom jump out of nowhere, fangs bared and whiskers and nostrils flared. "I need to check with Ma Barker."

"Ah, he needs his mommy," Tiger snarls, his tone dripping mockery.

"Not to teach you manners," I reply as I box the sneer off his mustachios. "C'mon, Tigue. I need a morning workout."

The way I work it out is I duck as Tiger lunges, and Tom ends up giving Tiger another facial with his shivs. Heh-heh.

My mental comment is echoed by two short meows behind my back.

The lady in question has been roused by our set-to. In this case, this is no lady, it is my mother, my esteemed dam, my . . . ow!

She has boxed my ears. "That is for making jackasses of my guards." She boxes the guards' ears. "That is for being taken in by a smooth operator. Now." She turns to me.

"What can I do for you besides rearrange your silly mug?"

No one can accuse Ma Barker of being anything but even pawed.

"This is private," I tell her.

She jerks her head over her black-like-me shoulder and leads me to an overturned hounds-tooth-pattern loveseat that looks as if it last served as a rat condominium.

However, it is cool under there, and quiet.

"You are sure this Circle Ritz place we are headed for has lots of sheltering shrubbery?" she asks me for the fourth time.

"And even more soft-touch humans."

"*Hmph.* I am not fond of a parking lot view."

"Very low traffic, and the vehicles are mostly late models with few oil drips."

"It is taking a lot of my street cred to herd this group uptown. It had better be worth it."

"I will be able to keep an eye on you there."

"Not a plus. On the other hand, I will be able to keep an eye on you."

I give Ma a good onceover. She has recovered somewhat from her solo match with a marauding raccoon, but one eye is still swollen half shut and her black coat is full of claw tracks. She licks her ragged bib into shape and sinks back against the spewing stuffing, half sitting, half reclining like a sultan.

"So what advice do you need, grasshopper, other than to not make a fine point of it with my guards?"

I smooth my whiskers and satin lapels, both of which her boys had mussed. But not much. "It is about the human species."

"You ask me? Who has had as little to do with them as possible?"

"It is about the female of the species."

"Anyone I know?"

"My associate."

"You mean your sugar mama."

"Please! I give Miss Temple so much more than she gives me."

"That is always the way with our kind, and what do we get for it?"

I am not about to go into an Us and Them riff with her. "They have strange mating habits."

"You noticed?"

"Although the females are ever capable of being in heat, they attempt to ignore the fact."

"Which the males do not."

"No. This creates a certain tension."

"Tell me about it."

"Anyway, the humans aim at solo long-term mating."

"Like some birds. Dodo birds."

"And wolves."

"Wild dogs! They are no role model for the superior species."

"Right. Anyway, my roomie has found herself in a perplexing situation for the breed."

"She is with litter?"

"No!"

"Then you have no rivals in the offing, at least."

"This is not about me, Ma. It is about understanding her. Which seems to be the goal of the human males around her too. Mr. Max was her long-term squeeze, but now it looks like Mr. Matt is edging him out."

"Sounds like a horse race rather than a romantic quandary. At least she gets to choose. I had to take all comers, which is why you had a calico sister and a gray brother."

"Had?" I ask gingerly.

Normally, we street kits are cut out from the litter so fast by chance, death, and animal control that we would not recognize a sibling if it stood up and sang "O Brother, Where Art

Thou?" right in front of us. I am one cat in a million for know-ing who my ma and pa are, but I am one cat in a million any-way, just for being alive after a street birth. That is without mentioning my entrepreneurial success with an investigative operation.

"I do not know where they go," she agrees, "or even *when* sometimes. Motherhood is way overrated. It was a boon when the Cage Ladies arranged for a tubal ligation."

I do not ask what this "tubal ligation" is. It sounds like doc-tor or lawyer language, and one usually does not wish to deci-pher what they are talking about, which is why they end up with all the money and yachts on Lake Mead.

But I do wonder if a "tubal ligation" might be the answer for Miss Temple.

I ask Ma. Who laughs.

"She does not have my problem. Tomcats do not tiptoe around what they wish to be up to, like your roommate's suit-ors. One would think that she could easily accommodate only two, but humans are a mystery."

I cannot help sounding a bit whiny as I lay out my case to my esteemed dam, known as a "queen" in fancy cat breeding circles. Which are where they matchmake pedigrees and put dudes and dudettes into forced breeding arenas. Barbaric!

"I am afraid I am a wee bit selfish at this point," I admit. "I fa-vor Mr. Max because his various mysterious ways keep him from coming around too often, and I get full bed privileges in his absence. On the other hand, Mr. Matt offers Miss Temple more constant attention, but I fear he will boot me out of both bed and bedroom, and where will I find another roomie as at-tentive and even-tempered as my Miss Temple?"

Ma Barker shakes her venerable, raccoon-scabbed head. She is one tough cookie.

"You have become the fourth leg in a love triangle involving two alien species, Louie. Face it, you will never win. You have been trying to live in two worlds: wild and domestic. You will have to make a choice."

"That is just it! I can tip the balance, if I feel like it. That is a lot of responsibility. I lean toward Mr. Max. He is wild and free and wily and noble. But Mr. Matt really needs a good home. Mr.

Max and I know we are two of kind, and there is no love lost between us, but there is the kind of wary respect we both crave. Mr. Matt would not shove me aside on purpose, but he is a domestic born, loyal and true, and I share his quest to find a safe place in the world."

"Louie, Louie, Louie." Ma shakes her head. "I blame it on your coming from a broken home, but then most of us do. You have been a good boy. I realize that you want my gang moved uptown so we can live out our declining years under the watchful eyes of you and your humans. What you worry about is that your humans have feet of clay. They are not as stable as you had hoped. You will just have to see that they do the right thing, and then everybody will be happy."

Argh! Seeing that everybody does the right thing so that everybody is happy is the one thing that does not make this world go round. In fact, reality is just the opposite.

I bid Ma Barker adieu and move on.

Miss Midnight Louise is sunning herself in front of the canna lilies that fringe the koi pond that used to be my office view and private fishing hole.

The koi are as fat and wet as ever, and come pucker-lipped up to the pond edge trolling for tourist bread crumbs, as if Midnight the Merciless had not suddenly cast his shadow in their sunshine once again.

I plough a paw through the water just to make my presence known.

"Be nice," Miss Louise admonishes.

"Why?"

"This is my territory now, and I get plenty of legal fish and lobster from the house chef. You must learn the difference between game and decorative fish."

"They are all game to me," I announce, sitting on the water-dewed stones and curling my longest extremity around my toes.

"You are a girl," I tell her.

"Obviously."

"You have had the operation that makes this condition moot."

"Obviously."

"Do you miss it?"

"Miss what?"

"Being the object of male attention?"

"Not a bit," she says. "That was always a nuisance. It is such a relief that a small surgical procedure can put an end to tomcats harassing one. A puss needs a tomcat like a fish needs a bicycle."

I frown. "Fish have nothing to peddle with but fins."

"Tomcats have nothing to peddle but fishy lines."

"So, why does a modern woman need a man?"

"She does not." Louise's yellow eyes squint into gleaming slits. "Ah. You inquire about that human hussy you are shacked up with."

"Miss Temple is not a hussy! That is the problem. She is only able to deal with one dude at a time. I do not understand."

Miss Louise sits up and actually smoothes my agitated ears with her tongue. It is a daughterly gesture, which I know by the fact that she is fixed and has no reason at all to give me more than five in the face.

"Poor Louie. They are a strange breed. It is always a risk to try to depend upon such a fickle kind. I know you thought you had a permanent arrangement—"

"It still is!" But I am no longer so sure.

"Yet," says Miss Louise, patting the tip of my tail in a most patronizing way, "they will go off and leave us without a thought. Move. Advertise for new homes because of . . . change of address. Change of circumstance. Babies. Is that it?"

"No! No babies. Yet. It is just that I sense she is having a change of heart. That is a very mysterious process and alien to our kind."

"Yes. We do not give our hearts lightly, but when we do it is eternal. That is why I will never consent to being owned."

"I am not owned! I own. I am in a position to bestow favor on one or another of Miss Temple's suitors. I lean to picking the one who suits my habits best, but realize that is perhaps not as noble as I could be."

"The way to be noble, Louie, is to let others be as noble as they can be."

I gaze into Louise's gilt eyes. She is not quite my spitting image (except when she is mad, often at me) but she is a sassy little kit and I would not be loath to call her my daughter. If she was my daughter. Which is still up for grabs. Like my Miss Temple.

I move on.

I return to the Circle Ritz (because it is en route to the last way station and I am loath to confront the most iffy female on my list).

Karma crowns the Circle Ritz like an invisible diadem of New Age mumbo jumbo. The penthouse is her territory, and the ambiguously phrased declaration is her bread and butter. But she is female and deserves consultation.

I claw my way up the old palm tree onto the high patio, and then through the French doors into the shrouded environment.

Miss Electra Lark is away, so I have full interrogation rights here.

First, I have to find Karma, who usually hides.

She is not under the couch. Or the chairs. Or the bed.

She is under the sink, in an area reeking of wet wood and lemon wax.

Her blue Birman eyes shine red in the dark. She was made for color-correcting cameras.

"Pssst!" her voice warns me.

"Chill," I tell her. "I am conducting a survey."

"You? A census taker?" The shock draws her out onto the kitchen parquet.

"A personal survey," I say.

"And?"

"If you had your druthers, would you rather live with a human with a devoted roomie of the opposite sex, or a come-and-go boyfriend with interests abroad?"

"Are you working for *Cosmo* now, Louie?"

"Naw. This is a private poll."

Karma slinks all the way out from under the pipes.

"An interesting question. Does it behoove us felines to have domestic stability or romantic uncertainty in our own love lives?"

"Uh, I am not talking about *my* love life. I am talking about my domestic situation, which is another kettle of fish entirely."

"Your roomie is a mermaid?"

"No. She has two legs and no scales, except in her bathroom. I am just wondering which dude to encourage her to glom on to. In a way that would benefit her. And me."

"Are you sure that your interests are matching?"

"No. That is why I am conducting this poll. Look. I know that a girl has gotta do what a girl has gotta do. I just wonder how I come out in all this. I have certain needs."

"Like what?"

"Um, to come and go as I please."

"Check."

"To have a litter box on the premises, even if I do not deign to use it."

"Check."

"To be consulted as to my position on the bed."

"Aha! That is where your territory overlaps with the men in question."

"Right."

"And you have been her main squeeze of late?"

"Pretty much."

"Then you are obligated to claim lounging rights no matter who has been or is sleeping in her bed. Assert yourself!"

"I can handle keeping my claim in the current digs. But what if she moves in with the guy upstairs? Or they buy a house? Then it will be a free-for-all in claiming territory. And I may not want to move and leave the Circle Ritz. It is an ideal location and I am just now engineering moving my aged mother into an adjacent situation."

"Louie! No wonder you are troubled. I was not aware that you actually knew your mother, and I am most impressed by your loyalty to her."

Karma, being full of slightly schizty psychic cheer, cannot yet grasp what kind of cat dear old Ma Barker is.

"Do you see any glimmers of who my Miss Temple would be best off with?"

"And she is—?"

"Cute little redhead, now temporarily blond. Feisty. Her main job is public relations but she is a darn good gumshoe too."

"Ah, she has visited my retreat on occasion. My companion person, Electra Lark, tries to keep intruders out so that my delicate sensory apparati are not clouded, but she is not always successful. I do pick up vibes from humans who haunt the Circle Ritz. But they seem vague, like spirits to me."

Karma seems vague to *me*!

"Tell me of the rivals for her love."

"One is long, dark, and sleek like me."

"Him! I have sensed him before. He is a creature of air and high places, an overseer, a guardian, like myself. He is wise but troubled by a past he cannot elude. Your redheaded miss is a fire spirit, a spark of energy and ability. The air spirit will fan her flames, but will also exhaust her emotions."

Okay. This does not sound too far out. For once, something Karma says makes sense.

"And the other man?"

"He lives here too. He's got looks to rent out and still win a pageant. He has been stuck on meaning well for so long he can hardly move sometimes, but he is getting over it."

"Ah, yellow haired?

"Right. Blond, the humans call it."

Karma nods her head, which is also masked in darker fur like the Siamese breed, only her dark hose end in white satin gloves and spats.

"I have seen him."

"How?"

"Sometimes my mystical communion with the stars and moon require me to emerge onto the balcony. He is a water spirit, that one. I have seen him drawing himself powerfully through the deep blue pool below. His life has been struggle, but he has become good at it. I sense a new lightness in his dogged laps to and fro, as if he has sprouted wings that lift him above what weighs him down in the water."

"Water and fire, not a good match, right?"

"To the contrary, Louie. They balance each other's destructiveness. Water needs fire to produce steam heat, you know."

I gulp. I think I do know. And, worse, I think that Miss Temple and Mr. Matt know now too.

A lot of help Karma has been.

But I cannot help asking, "Which element am I?"

Her Lieutenant Molina blue eyes, which is to say a body-armor-piercing shade of electric blue, nail me to the wooden floor.

"Earth," she says. "You are a creature of the streets who trusts your pad leather and your eyes and ears only. A born loner, you are, plodding and practical, and you always get your man. Or woman. You are not airy, or fiery, or even misty, but you are not one to leave any job undone. As for your own love life, I see many options, none of them very immediately rewarding. For now, you are better off meddling in human matters. You seem to have some minor gift for it."

On that unhappy prediction, Karma makes the royal circling wave of dismissal with her foreleg.

I back out, careful not to salaam, and run my rear into the side of a mohair sofa in the main room. Dude, but those buzz-cut bristles sting like a radiator brush!

I cannot wait to escape onto the balcony and then piton my way down the rough trunk of my faithful palm-tree bridge to the Circle Ritz's various floors.

My pads touch hot asphalt at last, and I reflect that solid ground is indeed my medium.

Unfortunately, my current case is an air-bred one, and I am off to the New Millennium to reconsider just who and what is going on there to put my Miss Temple's stilettos in a sling.

As for whom I wish to back in the Circle Ritz bedroom sweepstakes, my mind is torn between the elements of water and air. One fellow can drown in, and the other can break a dude's neck.

Looks to me like my little doll had better watch her backside.

Chapter 15

Old Acquaintances
Not Forgot

Back at the scene of the tragedy, an airport metal detector now provided a nice paranoid touch at the entrance to the museum area. A young uniformed guard was manning it.

Sure enough, Temple "tinged" when she walked through. She had to remove her emerald ring from Max and the small studs in her ears and go through again. *Ting.*

"Sorry, ma'am," the guard said. "I'll have to wand you. Maybe it's something metal in your clothing." His eyes skimmed and nervously deserted her bust area.

An *underwire*? He'd thought Temple was wearing an *underwire* bra? And her a measly 32B since high school? Bless him! The notion was flattering, but Temple couldn't bask in it for long and still get on with her sad business.

"Are you kidding? You have *no* future in lingerie sales. Look. It's probably a steel arch in my shoe."

Temple went back though, stripped off her Beverly Feldman spikes, and this time waltzed through without producing any rude noises. By then the barely twenty-one-year-old screener was redder than cranberry sauce on Thanksgiving.

"They should have an ID badge ready for you," he muttered.

But when Temple pawed through the plastic-laminated cards, hers bore the image of her old curly redheaded self, not the straight and sleek-locked blond temptress with the Little Orphan Annie chest measurement the Teen Queen show had recently made of her.

"Old photo." She sighed, then proved it by flashing her driver's license. "New look."

"No problem, ma'am, just step up to that tape mark and I'll have this new photo ready by the time you leave."

A computer captured her digitally and the guard nodded to indicate that the shot was taken. "Nice change," he added, auditioning a shy smile.

Maybe blond hair magically inflated the viewer's perception of bust measurement. Temple sighed again as she walked into the museum proper and turned about six male heads.

She had to dump this bleach job if she wanted to get any work done! Maybe a temporary rinse close to her natural color; anything that would cover platinum blond.

Crews were still finishing work on the display structures and connecting electrical gizmos for light and security when they weren't ogling her. Temple eyed them back, which she'd normally never do. Any one of them could be a shill checking out the art installation for future tampering.

Uniformed guards stationed around the perimeter added an air of seriousness to the central chaos. Scaffolds ringed the area too. Temple's eye was drawn up to the dark dangling *V* of line still pointing like an arrow to the top of the scepter's translucent housing.

He'd been turned to show a clown-white-faced man wearing a greasepaint mask, black spandex tights and leotard like an acrobat, apparently strangled by the hammock of bungee cord that spanned one side of the museum ceiling to the other.

"Awful to think about, isn't it?" an unearthly voice said behind her. Think James Earl Jones as Darth Vader.

Temple spun around, gawked, looked up. And up. And then decided that the men had not been ogling her and her electric blond hair, but the awesome oncoming form that had just now caught up with her.

He was well over Max's six foot four and robed like a Klingon crossed with an Egyptian lion-faced god.

Towering over her five foot zero in his built-up boots, he was clad in superhero spandex all in black, the better to emphasize health-club muscles. His head was a mask of two-tone black tiger stripes and a mane of dreadlocks. Add the funereal basso and you had that always anonymous but never shy performer known as the Cloaked Conjuror.

"I almost didn't recognize you with the hair redo," he said. "You were the little gal involved in getting that bad guy at TitaniCon a few months back."

When Temple gaped at him for even remembering her after the chaos of that night, he added, "I never forget a face."

"Yes, well, your own current face is pretty unforgettable too."

He didn't comment but joined her in gazing up at the place where the dead man still hung.

"One of my stunt doubles died high up in the stage flies at TitaniCon," the Cloak Conjuror's disguised voice rumbled. "Good man. They never determined if it was an accident. Or murder."

"This one also iffy?"

"I suppose. Could have been some nutcase working up a publicity stunt. Could have slipped and died with no one around to help. Could have been murdered."

"Las Vegas leans to aerial murders," Temple mused, remembering the dead bodies in the ceiling at the Goliath and Crystal Phoenix hotels, both of them connected, perhaps circumstantially, to men she knew and loved.

There! Her subconscious had tricked and kicked her into a

reality check. She was a total romantic schizo! Her outer blonde and her inner redhead were of two minds and hearts as well as two Lady Clairol shades.

Temple didn't think she should be having an emotional epiphany right here amid the rubble of museum construction, but there it was.

" 'Aerial murders'?" The Cloaked Conjuror was struck by the phrase. "My guy was killed up on the catwalk up top." The ponderous head tilted to view the black-painted upper third of the space.

"Is there a catwalk up there too?" Temple asked.

"Of course. To service the lights and the magic act rigging."

"Which is pretty Cirque du Soleil."

If a mask could grin, the voice behind this one did.

"Imitation is sincere. No one in this town can put together a new act without taking Cirque into account nowadays."

That made Temple wonder again what Max was dreaming up in that direction now that he had recommitted to a performing career. She knew the discipline was fierce and all engulfing. Something else occurred to her.

"Are your big cats involved in this museum act too?"

"Of course they make an appearance. I need to limit their time up there. Too risky. Even for magicians." He chuckled. "But I've a got a new cat*woman* in my act, so that provides the feline presence so effective in magic shows."

"A catwoman?" Temple feigned ignorance all the better to pump CC on his fishy new partner. "To your Batman/Catman? Interesting. I'm supposed to be skewing publicity toward the high-end art audience, but I could probably get some pop culture media interested in your new partner. Where'd you find her? In one of the Cirque shows?"

"Nope, though she was right here in Vegas. Did a little act at a place called the Opium Den. Shangri-La's the name, so I guess she's a Siamese kind of cat herself."

A thieving kind of she-cat! While Temple was struggling mightily not to go Scarlett enough to outright swoon with fury, he added, "Even has a Siamese cat she used in her old act. Damn agile and clever little thing. Hyacinth. Those two communicate like a witch and familiar. Ought to be a few publicity angles in that."

Temple could just see the headlines: EXTRA! READ ALL ABOUT IT! LAS VEGAS PR WOMAN GOES CODE RED IN CZAR EXHIBIT.

The Cloaked Conjuror was walking away to chat up Randy. Temple guessed that she had held up, as any delicate blossom must when she hears her most fatal female bête noir is on the scene of a very ugly possible crime. She already knew Shangri-La was a thief. She'd taken the diamond and opal ring Max had bought Temple at Tiffany's.

Temple at Tiffany's. Hey, that sounded even better than *Breakfast at Tiffany's*.

The Opium Den was a third-tier theater off the Strip. She and Max, and Matt and Lieutenant Molina had all gone there for different purposes a few months back. Temple had been asked up on stage; somehow stripped of her ring and lured into a cabinet that deposited her in the building's basement, from whence she was whisked as a prisoner. Along with Midnight Louie, a cat who had a habit of trailing her like a dog at the most perilous moments. She and Louie had been bound, boxed, and rushed out of town in a semi full of magician's boxes and designer drugs.

Max had taken the whole cargo apart to find them in the trick cabinets, not too much the worse for wear, except Louie was literally spitting mad. Sometimes having a magician boyfriend was a boon. Sometimes not; say, when he vanishes for a year without a word.

Temple didn't want to dwell on her worst moments, or months. Max was back and he'd had a damn good reason for ducking out: contract killers on his tail. They still were. And Max was still ducking out, for days rather than months at least. Although Temple was finding that harder and harder to take.

But it was disturbing to think that Shangri-La had shown up again. At best she'd been an accessory to a drug deal. True, no one at the police department had ever been able to connect her to anything. And, believe it, Molina would have tried. Hard. Molina viewed anyone who had anything to do with Temple with suspicion because of Max. Except maybe Matt Devine, who was hard to view with anything but admiration, or . . . lust? Gorgeous ex-priests with an ethically sincere approach to romance were not a dime a dozen even these days, God bless him and his Catholic conscience!

Back to Shangri-La. At worst, she'd wanted to hurt Temple for some reason. Or maybe just use her as a distraction, but how did Shangri-La know who Temple was, or, rather, with whom she associated?

Temple cricked her neck at the pendant dead man, a macabre human chandelier in this vast, airy space.

People wearing latex gloves were laying a plastic drop sheet beneath him. The inevitably paint-spattered step ladders were being brought in, their aluminum feet shod in plastic baggies so as not to contaminate the drop cloth.

Temple couldn't help shivering in the 72-degree air-conditioning that chills every Las Vegas venue.

"He's the only one in this room who *can't* hurt you. He's thoroughly dead," observed a dry, slightly accented voice behind her.

Temple turned, glancing up, as she usually had to. *Surprise!* The woman was her size, maybe only two or three inches taller. Temple was wearing her three-inch corporate pumps and this woman wore—Temple always checked shoes after faces—snub-toed Mary Jane ultra flats. With a strap across the instep. Not evoking all-American Mary Jane but . . . Detective Merry Su. Yet this wasn't the same woman.

The face was way more interesting than the footwear.

Pale but unfreckled; unlike Temple's, the eyes boysenberry dark in a pasty oval cameo of a face—rice powder, maybe? Eyelids and eyebrows tilted up at a sharp angle, with the epicanthic single eyelid of Asian physiognomy. Oh. Temple's earlier shiver hardened into an overall alert; she froze against allowing all motion. She could guess who this was.

The woman wore a fluttery off-white chiffon top and handkerchief-hemmed skirt, her white tights stark against the black satin Minnie Mouse flats, a disingenuous Alice in Wonderland look. Dull black hair was pulled back hard from her face into a ponytail as coarse and lavish as a show horse's.

Could Temple be gazing not on beauty bare, but on the bare face of that almost mythic, duplicitous illusionist and ring thief and CC's new partner in magic, Shangri-La? *Yes.*

Temple thought her heart had stopped and restarted about three times, but it might have been four. Or five. This was the mysterious enemy to all things Temple: Max, Louie, Tiffany opal-and-diamond engagement rings. Ring, solo.

"Temple Barr," CC was saying by way of introduction. "She's doing PR for the hotel on our new show. This is my petite performing partner, Shangri-La, less formally known as Shang."

Temple nodded to acknowledge the introduction. Shang nodded with almost deliberately clichéd Asian inscrutability.

What an actress! Temple thought. Could the woman have failed to recognize her? Shangri-La had stood next to Temple onstage, then had conjured the ring off her finger, pushed her into an onstage box and down a dark rabbit hole into a coffin-like box ready for transport and who knew what else?

Surely she didn't forget a victim.

Oh, wait! Temple was still a flagrant bottle blonde from her last assignment, not a natural redhead. It threw off her most intimate friends, particularly the male ones. Why not a woman?

"Nice to meet you," Temple said, happy that the woman was disinclined to thrust a saber-nailed hand at her for shaking. "You're quite right that this poor man couldn't hurt anyone now, if he had ever wanted to. But he can hurt the public profile of this exhibition."

"Bad publicity is the best kind nowadays," Shang said, eyeing the hanged man.

They all stood around staring, like crowds come to see an execution in the bad old days of public hangings.

"We must embrace such facts," Shang added, looking up into CC's stoic mask. "And you and I must triple check our equipment once the authorities have freed the scene."

"Any notion of who he might be?" Temple asked, knowing the answer but wondering if they did.

"Nobody," Shang said coolly. "Nobody having anything to

do with our performance. Just a supernumerary. An extra."

Temple quelled another shiver.

CC moved off in the custody of his much smaller partner, like a mastiff dominated by a terrier.

Temple had to admit that it had occurred to her more than once that Shangri-La, that down-scale lady magician in extravagant Asian theatrical face paint and razor-slashed hair and kimonos, might have been a secondary persona of Kitty the Cutter.

Having met the lady wearing what was as close as she might ever get to civvies, no way was she a Black Irish superpatriot and stalker. That woman was well and truly dead, and no one mourned her. Except maybe Max, in the temple of his heated adolescent memory and forgiving Catholic soul.

Temple. She'd thought she was that for a while, with him. A permanent refuge from the international war of terror and counterterror going way back before 9-11.

"Get these civilians out of here," a new voice ordered.

Temple shivered again.

Just who spoke this time, she didn't have to guess.

Temple turned. It was her red-letter day for unhappy encounters.

"Ah, Miss Temple Barr," the voice continued. "I took you for a chorus bimbo from the back."

"They're usually your height, not mine, human giraffes almost six feet tall."

"True." Lieutenant C. R. Molina was tall, dark, and semifemale. She was also not a friend, although sometimes an associate. "I see you're keeping Zoe Chloe alive."

"Do you have any idea how hard a bleach job is to undo?"

"No, and I never intend to. Now shoo. This is a crime scene and snoops aren't needed here."

"I'm doing PR for the exhibition. Naturally, I was informed."

"The New Millennium doesn't float its own flock of flacks?"

"Not with a fine arts background," Temple said as snootily as she could. She hated snooty people and hoped Molina did too.

"You?"

"Guthrie Repertory Theatre in Minneapolis. You know, Shakespeare and Congreve and Oscar Wilde."

Molina sighed. "You never cease to amaze. Now . . . back."

She could have been a lion tamer and Temple a housecat.

"Let my people work in peace."

Molina turned vivid blue eyes up at the blacked-out exhibition ceiling above the acres of off-white walls. Temple suspected she didn't realize that she had sighed.

"You understand," Molina asked, "that there is one and only one likely suspect for aerial deaths in this town?"

"You said you'd give Max a free pass if I masqueraded as a teenybopper on that reality TV show to protect your daughter. I kept my part of the bargain. Just look at my hair!"

"I don't have to." Molina kept her eye on the slightly twirling corpse not-so-high above. The crime scene technicians had reached it and were carefully freeing the lines from which it was suspended. "All of the men in this room are doing it for me. Men can be so shallow, as we know, and your girlish, gilded head is a distraction, so . . . out."

"Why would Max have anything to do with this dead body?"

"Because it's there?"

"That's not fair. You promised."

Molina smiled. Like a shark.

Temple froze again, this time to hear herself sounding just like the lieutenant's whining teenage daughter, Mariah.

"Mother" Molina had one last bombshell to lay down. She wasn't smiling now.

"I promised that I'd lay off going after your elusive significant other if he didn't flip a smoking gun in my face. I think he just may have. All bets are off. This is Las Vegas, after all, and the odds on anything can turn in the wink of an eye."

It was some comfort to Temple that Randy insisted she be present when Molina held an informal convocation with the New Millennium management an hour and a half later.

By then, the body had been removed. The police presence had retreated to a pair of buff young uniformed officers guarding the entrance to the exhibition. In their khaki shorts they looked rather like Boy Scout docents. Temple was thinking that she and the hotel could live with that if they were stationed there throughout the exhibition.

Besides, they were eyeing her with great interest. Apparently, she now could wrap men around her finger as easily as she could curl a strand of her blatantly faux blond hair around it.

This realization was sobering. Jessica Simpson *knew* something, although it wasn't Chicken of the Sea tuna fish. Even Midnight Louie would never get confused about whether fish were chicken. In fact, he probably had a higher IQ than Jessica Simpson, but alas, he wasn't blond.

Temple realized that she was going beyond the bend, but Molina and hotel executives negotiating when and how a crime scene could become a public attraction again were too bloody boring to bear.

Chapter 16

Siamese If You Don't Please

Unfortunately, they rush the body out before I can do some shamus-class sniffing around on the scene.

I do not dare show myself anyway, but lurk up in the blacked-out flies. This is a sky-high hodgepodge of catwalks and ledges trimmed with deceptive mirrors and electrical wires and bungee cords, where all the magic show equipment lies in wait for the unwary. Or the gullible observer below.

Speaking of below, far down and away I spot the bright blond blot that is now my Miss Temple. It is sad how they tart up these showgirls for the ring nowadays. Yet I understand that she underwent this transformation for the Greater Good and the high purpose of rooting out a killer. Too bad she will have red roots for a number of months now.

I also watch Miss Lieutenant C. R. Molina prowl the scene like a big black leopard with bright blue eyes. She is a man-hunter, that one. Not for her personal use, of course, but in the name of crime and punishment, which would be admirable if she were not hassling my Miss Temple at the moment.

I must lay low (in this case, high) and take it without defending MMT, but I growl out a low grumble of frustration.

It is answered by a bewitching *merrrrow?* of respectful interrogation.

I turn to find that a parchment-pale frail has pussyfooted out onto the long lean line of ledge on which I perch. Precariously.

Every muscle in my body tenses! Yes, every one. I have not glimpsed hide nor hair nor polished nail of the feline fatale attached to the magician known as Shangri-La for some weeks, even months.

Yet I know that hip-swinging long lean stride, so like a high-fashion model on a catwalk. I know those blazing blue eyes. Rather like Miss Lieutenant Molina's human version (only with a feline pupil as impetuously vertical as an exclamation mark). I know that gray mask and gloves and hose. And tail.

She is pretty poison, Miss Shangri-La's performing partner from the storied land of Siam, now Thailand, who goes by the name of Hyacinth. Yet I am glad to see her again. Curare-painted nails and all. She stops to sit about two feet away, then curls her sinewy train around her gray-booted tootsies. I love boots on ladies!

You would never guess we were both balancing on a high-wire line sixty feet above a floor thronged with cops and major hotel executives.

She purrs. "They have taken our twirly toy away. I see you miss it."

That is my Hyacinth. Heart of steel.

"I miss getting a good look and sniff around," I say.

"You do not like to play with your food?"

"I am all work and no play, missy. I am a professional."

"Performer?"

"Detective. You do remember me?"

"Oh! A shamus. You do not look Irish."

"I am not! I am all-American, unlike you, lady. And we have met before."

"Not to my knowledge. And I may be happy about that, if you are going to be so rude."

"Look here, Hyacinth—"

"I am not Hyacinth. My name is . . ." Here she sighs. Pauses. Paws the adjacent ledge as if burying something stinky. "Squeaker."

I am knocked speechless. Not only is this dame a double for the deliciously evil Hyacinth, down to her undercoat, but she has a moniker I would expect to find on a cat toy at Petco.

"Squeaker?" I repeat.

"I am told by my trainer that I was adopted from the shelter because I was a dead ringer for the commercially viable Hyacinth. But I was named because I had a"—another sigh— "'screen door' mew."

"Screen door? What is that?"

"I do not know. Only that it has scarred me for life. At least my shelter name was feminine, Fontana."

I do a drop back and ticker-clutch pose to convey my shock. I know ten cool cats named Fontana, and not one is a feline. But the little doll is still airing her grievances in the human nomenclature game, and I cannot blame her.

"Do I look like a 'Squeaker' to you?" she is demanding.

I do some heavy little-doll-aimed back-peddling. "Nope. You could be a . . . Cleo, or a . . . Sirena . . . or even a Britney, but not a Squeaker. No way."

She sniffs. Mollified. Maybe she is Irish. "And you are—?"

"Midnight Louie. Dude about town. Private investigator. At your service."

"Well, you go get that twirly toy back. I am so bored up here."

"Not possible. The Las Vegas Metropolitan Police have taken it home to take apart. They are very possessive, trust me. So, why are you up here?"

"I am to become part of the act, but only as a body double for my adopted sister Hyacinth. I did not want to do it but you know Hyacinth."

"Not as well as I would like to. Sorry, Squeaker, but Hyacinth is hot."

"And I am not? We are identical twins. What is the difference?"

What can I say? Squeaker seems the nice, shy, domesticated sort.

Her stepsister Hyacinth would carve your heart out with a toxic toenail and eat it. She is irresistible. The male of the species is pretty stupid. Of any species. But somehow we survive.

"So what is your part in the upcoming show?" I ask.

And she tells me, sweet trusting soul that she is.

I am getting a sense of the high jinks that are going to unwind up here. The dude on the yo-yo string is just the beginning. An unscheduled beginning. But I love getting in on the ground floor. So to speak. Or to Squeak. So I ankle over to my new partner in high crimes and misdemeanors and we talk further. Among other things.

Chapter 17

A Heist Hoisted

"Déjà Vu," Max said. Glumly.

"Double-jointed assistant at the Treasure Island," Gandolph said, nodding, "worked under that name in the nineties I remember her well. Indian. Eastern, not Western. Best little sawed-in-half lady in the business. Great stage name: Déjà Vu. Those were the days."

"Never knew her. I was speaking generally."

They sat cloistered in the daylight darkness of Gandolph's former home, now Max's digs. The darkness came from metal security shutters at each window and door. The place was a fortress.

"Max. I know it's a pain to be upstaged by a corpse."

"It's not a pain. In my case, it's a habit."

"We just have to wait until things settle down again."

"Which will be in what century?"

"Sooner than you think and sooner than the media and the police will like. This Russian show is way bigger than a worker's unfortunate . . . accident."

"You think?"

"Or suicide."

"Or murder."

"See. So many to choose from. It'll confuse the authorities."

"You never used to be callous."

Gandólph sighed. "I never used to be so close to mortality myself. You understand it's crucial that you steal the Alexander Scepter. This is one lost life. What you can do inside the Synth could save dozens."

"Somehow quantifying tragedy doesn't do it for me anymore, Garry. At least the IRA has officially pulled its own teeth, though it can't guarantee the shadow factions. But the rest of the world is running willy-nilly toward the same ugly, blind, political stewpot of tit for tat at any price. And who pays? Not the old, cold warriors. It's the troops and the civilians. The casualties. The numbers, not the names."

"You want to bow out?"

Max twirled a tall glass of tomato juice on the kitchen island's stainless-steel top. It resembled a bloody carousel.

"I want to see some good results. We're chasing phantoms here in hopes of catching a vague mastermind, or the money behind the madness."

Gandolph pulled a computer printout from his always-concealed pockets. This unassuming man in black had always seemed made of hidden resources.

"Your ladyfriend is thorough, I'll say that for her. I like her Table of Unresolved Events."

"Did she call it that? Really?" Max tried to see, having forgotten the details.

Gandolph wrested the paper away. Teasing. Tempting.

"Yes, she did. It's all laid out right here. The sad history of unsolved murders and related conundrums in Las Vegas since you and she hit town a couple years ago." Gandolph's plump middle-aged face wrinkled with mock consternation. "You two have not been lucky charms for this old town."

"Tell me something I *don't* know! 'This old town' hasn't exactly showered us with roses and rice."

"*Tsk.* I see my cover as a corpse is not blown." Gandolph put the paper down so Max could read it, which he eagerly did, although he'd seen it before. Still, a refresher course was always welcome in Life 912B.

WHO	WHEN	WHERE	METHOD	ODDITIES	SUSPECT
dead man at Goliath Hotel	April	casino ceiling	?		Max
dead man at Crystal Phoenix	Aug	casino ceiling	?		?
Max's mentor, Gandolph	Halloween	séance	?		assorted psychics
Cliff Effinger, Matt's stepfather	New Year	Oasis barge	drowning		2 muscle men
Cher Smith, stripper	Feb	strip club parking lot	strangled		Solved
Gloria Fuentes, Gandolph's assistant	Feb	church parking lot	strangled	"she left" on body in morgue	?
Prof. Jeff Mangel	March	UNLV hall	knifed	ritual marks	?
Cloaked Conjuror's assistant	April	New Millennium ceiling	beating or fatal fall	masked like CC or a TV show SF alien	?

" 'Roses and rice,' " Gandolph echoed his words. "Max, you're thinking of the normal life you could have had, if you hadn't been what you were forced to be, and if we hadn't done what we did, and had the times not called for us to do it again."

"Damn it, Garry. You're the closest thing to a father I've had since high school. You know I want to get out. You know I need to give Temple something better to do than make tables of unsolved deaths and lists of my possible prosecutable delinquencies."

"Just this one last game."

" 'Last' is the operative word." Max crumpled the paper. "I'm losing her."

He was this close to saying no more games, no matter how noble the objective. This close to saying, "I deserve a life, and so does Temple." Hadn't she adapted to every suicide curve on his undercover trajectory? Wasn't she as true blue as her eyes? What did he think he was saving, the whole world? And losing the most important person, to him, in it?

Garry nodded, poured himself a bit more of a superior Beaujolais. Filled Max's glass, which was only down a sip or two.

"I have no family," Garry said. "No lost lovers. Just you, my boy. I truly do think that if we expose this Las Vegas connection to international terrorism and thievery, we will disarm a significant force in today's miserable world."

Max sighed. Sipped. Raised his eyebrows in tribute to the vintage. "So now we have to get back inside the New Millennium with half the LVMPD homicide department crawling all over the site."

"You mean . . . with the lady lieutenant alerted to the signature of a Max Kinsella Production."

"Woman. She's no lady. And politically correct on top of it. Molina is not to be underestimated. At this point, the burr under her saddle to get me will warp even her professional judgment."

"Warped professional judgment might work very well for us."

"For you." Max pursed his lips.

He had certain advantages. The Cloaked Conjuror relied on him. Shangri-La hated him and was looking for his signature on the scene. Expectations were more often blinding than forewarning.

Same with Molina.

Only thing, it might best suit their plans to make him look damn guilty, even to Temple. He hated the idea of deceiving her. When he had been forced out of town by the hitmen at the Goliath two years earlier, he'd deceived her by omission because he didn't dare contact her until his trail was months cold and no one could follow it back to her and the Circle Ritz. But this time, the deception would be deliberate. How many times could Temple's loyalty defy the odds of how things looked on his behalf?

Funny. Everyone . . . Gandolph, the Synth, Molina . . . thought Max Kinsella was the major player, the center, the man to get, one way or another. And he knew the key to himself was and had always been Temple, because she was pure of heart. And far from simple.

Max pushed the glass of fine wine back toward Gandolph and sipped the tart tomato juice. What he really cared about had become nobody's concern but his. But this world wouldn't be fit or free for anyone to live in, including Temple, if he didn't follow his fate card to the final shuffling of the deck. If he wanted Temple, free and clear of any past shackles, his or hers, he'd have to finish this final charade.

He'd need his wits, and his iron wrists, and his ever-calculating nerve and his indomitable Irish soul on this job before it was over.

Chapter 18

Dudley Do-Right

"Say, who's spinning the major new wheels outside?"

Matt was shuffling through the coffee and cookie line in the sterile meeting room, picking up stirring sticks and packets of sugar and powdered creamer to dilute the sludge-strong coffee in the big aluminum urn.

Someone answered the question. "You mean the chick magnet? Not me, brother. I've got kids to support."

Matt already felt a little awkward. He'd hadn't attended a meeting for area ex-priests at Maternity of Mary Church's community rooms in Henderson for months after his first visit.

Everything here was the same, as plain as a convent: beige vinyl tile floors, inexpensive folding tables, metal chairs, Styrofoam cups, even the echo from no carpet or drapes. Holy Mother Church frugal. The show was saved for vestments and mass. Priests were the church's underpaid but cock-of-the-walk peacocks, and he wasn't one anymore. He wasn't even the same as he had been a few months before.

"Silver is the coolest car color," another man said.

Then Matt realized that it was *his* car, *his* relatively new silver Crossfire two-seater, they were all talking about. And blushed.

God! He was a real boy now. He wanted to sleep with a woman without benefit of matrimony. He shouldn't lose it like this back on the old stomping grounds. Actually, he didn't want to sleep with Temple without benefit of matrimony; he'd gladly marry her first. Except she wanted to sleep with him and wasn't sure she was ready for matrimony. What's a good Catholic boy to do?

Matt turned from the table to the filling room, knowing he looked sheepish.

"It's mine. The car."

He was going to add an apology when Nick, whom Matt characterized as the Progressive Cleric, ex-version, came over and pounded him on the back.

"Good going, Devine. Losing the lust for a simple Honda Civic provided through parish donations is the first sign of becoming a civilian. What's it do?"

The same first question Temple had asked. This time Matt didn't hesitate.

"One forty."

The men in the room nodded sagely. Who would have thought it? Priests could be guys who talked cars and speed. Their first names and thumbprint IDs began to come back to him: Jerry, the Really Nice Guy, with acne scars and thick glass lenses; Paul, the Earnest Thinker, already in trifocals and thinning hair; Damian, the Theologian, bald and distant; Nick, the Coach.

They were a mixed bag as to age and home state, all the city of Las Vegas had to offer in terms of resident ex-priests. LV wasn't exactly a Mecca for the religiously inclined, at least not along the Strip. It had one of the country's largest numbers of churches of all denominations in the residential areas, including Molina's home parish of Our Lady of Guadalupe. It even hosted one of Temple's Universalist Unitarian churches, housed in a shopping center. Okay, he'd looked it up, thinking if they got married soon . . .

"The first and last time you attended was a zoo," Damien noted with a chilly quirk that passed for a smile. "What brings you and your fancy new car back now?"

Damien was an ascetic. The disdain in his voice echoed the stern voices from Matt's seminarian past. The original Father Damien had founded an island refuge for lepers when they were truly pariahs. Matt felt right now that he'd kinda like to go there.

"Lighten up, Damien." Nick pulled Matt into the circle. "Attendance here isn't mandatory, like Sunday mass. You're just jealous of the wheels."

This was so absurd that everybody laughed, including Damien. A little.

"I forgot about that," Matt said as he took a seat in the circle. "They were offering such good deals and the mileage is pretty good—"

"God, Matt, are you going to plead guilty for avarice or energy consumption, make up your mind! Religious or secular sinner?" Jerry joked.

Matt sighed. "Probably both."

Nick leaned back in his chair, the natural leader. "Let's introduce ourselves and our life states," he said, looking around at two new guys, both older.

They went around the circle. Phil and Tom were new in town, Phil a college instructor, Tom an administrator for the local National Public TV station.

"That means I'm working my old con: raising money."

Everyone laughed. Parish priests were renaissance men in every respect except husband and literal father.

When Matt's turn came, he merely said he was a radio counselor at a local station.

Nick didn't prod him to say that he was *the* radio shrink in town, Mr. Midnight, syndicated nationally and a frequent national talk show guest. A man who had an on-air popularity. A man who made money. Even ex-priests could get jealous, and the group's driving force was support, not rivalry.

Matt decided that he should have asked to drive the old Probe he'd passed on to Electra tonight. That anyone would look at his car had never occurred to him, although Temple sure had, and sure had looked good in the passenger seat. He felt a shiver that was surely confessable just thinking about that. The questions he wanted answers to were so corrosively personal that his hands were sweating, as they had in the dark St. Stanislaus's confessional in Chicago when he was eight and was trying to decide whether to declare a "bad thought" to commit murder, or not.

That was then. This was . . . so now. His unthinkable, unsayable sin didn't involve bodily harm to his hated abusive stepfather, but bodily delight with his beloved Temple. Definitely a better class of failing. Only she wasn't his. She was hers. And there was the rub.

"Matt," Nick said, regarding him with kind eyes. "You've obviously come tonight because you have something the group might be able to help you with. What is it?"

There it was. The pastoral role of the priest. To succor the sick, uphold the shaken.

He didn't know these men well. He feared they might, would, judge him. And Temple. He couldn't stand them judging Temple. Still, he needed . . . something. Help.

"I'd mentioned before I'd met a woman," he said, "but she was claimed. I don't think she is anymore."

Nick smiled. Jerry smiled through pursed lips. Damien lifted an intellectual eyebrow. Tom nodded. Phil sighed. Paul frowned.

It was Eve and the Garden all over again.

"You've got guts."

Nick pulled Matt aside as the men shuffled out, the hour near eleven P.M. Matt needed to get to the radio station for his midnight show.

"Listen, Matt, we all have our way of integrating into the secular world. No one way is right."

"The church says—"

"You the definitive expert on the subject?"

"No, but I know what's expected of us."

"Perfection. Right. Listen. The love of your life—don't deny it, I can tell—the love of your life grew up in a different church, with a different standard. I admire the UUs. Their hearts and minds are in the right place, and so is yours. Look at it this way. The woman you love is eminently lovable, good, kind, and true."

Matt nodded. He loved Temple for her heart and mind. The body came after. But, oh, boy, did it count.

"She's also imperfect, as we all are."

"Maybe."

Nick laughed. "God, I envy you that first dawning of total love. I had it. I'm happy and so is my wife, but life dulls the edge. The point is, Matt, that her experience, her standards, are valid to her. You have to respect that. Falling in love isn't a conversion assignment. You're not among the pagans, looking for babies. You give. She gives. You love. She loves. If you love her, you accept her. As she needs to be accepted for the moment. *Capisce?*"

"Are you the godfather, Nick, or the Godfather?"

"I'm Italian. I'm Catholic. I'm both, you'd better believe it. And do as I say."

"Which is love, unconditionally."

"Is that so hard?"

"No. In this case, not at all."

He left with a lighter heart, knowing now what he had to do.

Chapter 19

Rushin' into Trouble

"Any idea," Temple asked Randy after meeting him in the New Millennium lobby the next day, "why the honchos called this top-secret meeting?"

"Other than murder?"

"Shhhh!" Temple eyed the hotel's Spaceport entry now behind them. It looked like a flying saucer, the fifties' riveted-silver-metal variety. Crowds of squealing people were still pouring through the doors that goosed them with a whoosh of air as they decompressed into the hotel's interior.

Silver-skinned and clad robot types directed the tourists to various areas, including an upward-flowing water slide that would take them to the external roller-coaster ride that circled the hotel's solar system every half hour.

Between the exotic elements snaked the usual lines of bag-toting tourists checking in and checking out.

"Shhhh!" she repeated. "In Vegas hotels, even the crystal chandelier drops and robot valets have ears."

"We're meeting in one of the high-roller suites. Those have the least access and the most security."

Temple was glad she wore what passed for a power suit in Vegas: white silk suit with a cropped and fitted jacket and slim skirt, with high-heeled gold sandals. With her red hair the outfit was spectacular. With her hair blond these days, it was stellar.

"You look very Heather Locklear today," Randy commented in the private elevator. Temple didn't consider that a compliment. At least the gilt woven-leather tote bag on her shoulder proclaimed her as another kind of working woman. She normally didn't wear metallics but was finding that blond hair dictated a certain style. No wonder they all looked alike.

Her heels clicked on the marble lining the halls on the suite level. They weren't going to sneak up on their bosses.

Randy had donned a tie for the occasion, a sure sign that this was a serious pow-wow. They both had better report positive ways of spinning the recent murder.

The suite's entry mimicked a real front door, like Temple's Circle Ritz condo, but this one had double doors, stained-glass sidelights and transom, with entry torches shining even during daylight hours.

Randy rang the bell.

The door took its own sweet time about opening, probably because there were so many honchos inside, no one was lowly enough to tend to practical matters.

The door opened into a wall of dark navy polyester suit and black shirt with a white tie. What did the museum muscle think this was, a touring company of *Guys and Dolls*?

"Da," he said.

Temple was almost tempted to answer "da," as in Da-da. Or Dada, the art movement. Or da-DAH, the theatrical presentation syllables.

All of these creative possibilities were lost on Boris, whose broad peasant face never showed its teeth. He stepped back, drawing attention to his unimaginative brown shoes.

She and Randy crossed a foyer paved in a mosaic of multi-colored marble and stepped down onto the living room's thick off-white carpet. A wall of distant windows framed the very tops of the Strip's highest landmarks against a background of vivid blue sky.

The pale cream grasscloth walls hosted paintings from the hotel owner's private collection of French Impressionists.

Such huge and luxe suites went for $30,000 a night, or more, but were often given gratis to major domestic and foreign high rollers called "whales," visiting ex-presidents and film stars. A lot of Las Vegas insiders had never seen such a layout, and Temple was making her debut as one who had.

The usual suspects had gathered in the huge dining room under a pair of vintage Lalique crystal chandeliers. Natasha, the muscleman whose Prince Valiant haircut grazed the bottom of his rear suit collar, stood guard by the granite-topped sideboard loaded with various samovars, plates and napkins, and finger food so elegant it defied description.

Temple always avoided that kind of spread, not wanting to discover mid-mouthful that she was eating an exotic pet . . . like a snake or a tarantula. One could never trust high-end chefs in their race to be edgy and unexpected, especially since the *Fear Factor* reality TV show had made the public mass consumption of living vermin its main dish.

Being an animal lover, although not a vegetarian, Temple often walked a fine-line foodwise: raw unadulterated body parts were off her list, so none of the no-doubt pricey varieties of caviar on the buffet were for her. But truffles were all right. Also chocolate. And Strawberries Romanoff. Deviled eggs were iffy.

Everyone nodded at the new arrivals and continued eating voraciously. All had red-rimmed eyes and furrowed brows. Obviously the higher-ups really had been up . . . all night, discussing whatever crisis this was: bungled theft, tragic accident. Or murder. She'd been up worrying too, and not only about the public relations fallout of sudden death. She was haunted by her first impression that the dark, dangling body was Max's. His midnight visit the other night proved that he was out prowling somewhere in the service of counterterrorism. Could this Russian exhibition be connected to his shad-owy current concerns? The Synth? Shangri-La?

The lowly flacks had just been called in for the post-decision duty roster.

Randy shrugged at Temple, having come to the same con-clusion, and attacked the buffet with gusto and little or no conscience for the contents of the platters.

Olga Kirkov, the ex-ballerina turned exhibition director, al-ready sat at the boardroom-long dining table with its mala-chite top and pale beige travertine stone base. Correction: she sat at the *head* of the table, in one of the cream leather cap-tain's chairs.

Gradually, they all took their plates and cups and settled at seats flanking her down the fifteen-foot expanse. Temple and Randy chose seats opposite each other, in the exact middle, so they could parry questions from each end.

Dimitri Demyenov, the Russian government representative, was backed by his bodyguards now that door duty was over. Temple watched him, thinking that he wasn't as ignorant of the English language as he appeared to be.

Ivan Volpe, the Parisian descendent of fleeing White Rus-sians during the nineteen-teen Revolution days and curator of the exhibition, remained standing, the obvious spokesman. Temple began to realize that this ritzy secret meeting was for her and Randy's benefit. It was a pre–press conference strat-egy session.

"Mr. Wordsworth, Ms. Barr," the aristocratic curator began, "we are faced with a terrible crisis. We haven't invited the emissaries from the co-sponsoring corporations, or the art media that are covering this installation and debut. Given the uncertainty about the nationality or motive of our personal Hanged Man, who had the rather bizarre name of Art Deckle, are we to forge ahead or admit to the tragedy and say it was . . . a personal act, having nothing to do with the exhibi-tion? I report directly to the owner and executive board of the hotel consortium, which promises to do anything necessary to safeguard this exhibition and see that it continues its mission to foster international culture and accord."

Temple had withdrawn her reporter's notebook (slim and

lined) and made notes on the last bit of gobbledygook. Volpe always spoke as if every syllable was quotable, so he would appreciate attentive underlings.

Opposite her, Randy was assiduously doodling in a way that passed for rapt recording.

So, if this was "Murder on the Siberian Express" . . . how much dodging and burning could even the most pompous museum curators do to hold back the inevitable tide of media interest? Temple may have been a bit hard-headed on this subject. She'd faced the disruption of murder on more than one assignment. Between living in one of the fastest-expanding areas in the U.S. with an annual tourist influx pushing toward forty million a year, the odds in Las Vegas for serious crime, including murder, were staggering.

It was a miracle the place was as safe and secure as it was. And it was, basically, thanks to hotel-casino security forces backing up local law enforcement. The city was Oz on the Mojave, and the "palace" guards were rigorously trained and employed to make sure it remained safe for Dorothy Tourist and the Gang. No Wicked Witches ruled here, if you excepted Shangri-La and her performing Siamese, Hyacinth. But Temple was a little biased on that account.

She dared to ask a question. One she regarded as fairly safe.

"Sir," she asked Volpe during a pause when he downed the steaming contents of one samovar that smelled slightly festive. "Murder will out, but this death is clearly ambiguous. It could be just a tragic accident."

The aristocratic white fuzzy eyebrows lofted while the dark eyes beneath sized her up. Oh, God. She couldn't help that she looked like the Sugar Plum Fairy as a blonde.

"You're right," he surprised her by saying. "The death is indeed ambiguous. The police and coroner haven't declared a cause, and the coroner's office, thank God, is far behind on its case load. So we may be lucky enough not to get a determination until after the exhibition moves on to the Frick.

"However . . ."

Temple stopped basking in her good-student mode and held her pen poised above a blank line, ready to record the nitty-gritty that was about to issue from those pale, wrinkled Russo-Parisian lips.

"The excellent police in this city have identified this man, at least under his alias, and have informed us of his criminal career here. We do not know his real identity and, whatever the cause of death, we feel we need to know if he was connected with someone else. Perhaps they may discover an international connection, even with such as Chechen rebels. I merely mention the more dire international possibilities."

Temple's pen hit paper, making a period on the notebook sheet.

She was inclined to object that simply being a Chechen made anyone a "known" criminal, but there was no doubt that Chechen rebels had been making it as hot for the Russian government as unknown anarchists had for the czars in the bad old days a hundred and more years ago.

A possible dead Chechen swinging from a bungee cord in the New Millennium wouldn't be just a would-be jewel thief but a possible political gauntlet slapped across everybody's face. And as a PR problem, he would be a top-drawer nightmare. It would take a pile of artful public relations to salvage a situation like that. No wonder she often ended up solving crimes as well as creating press releases. It was the only way to protect her clients from the law's delay. She had to do it herself.

Well. A big cold, slimy salty mouthful of dead fish eggs might be just the thing to snap Temple out of the serious PR funk Monsieur Volpe had just put her in.

Chapter 20

Maximum Insurance

Temple kept her own counsel until she got home to the Circle Ritz.

Who would have ever thought that a PR person for a major exhibition would have ever *welcomed* the idea of plain and simple out-and-out jewel thieves?

Especially since the only model that came to mind was Cary Grant in *To Catch a Thief*. Who wouldn't want Cary Grant on one's case? Speaking of art thieves, there was always Pierce Brosnan in the remake of *The Thomas Crown Affair*. Not too shabby either. Every female PR freelancer should be so lucky!

Except. Here. Now. A Russian exhibit blending Czarist and post-Soviet politics with Las Vegas capitalist commercial sizzle. A marriage made in hell, for sure. And if a Chechen rebel in black spandex accessorized with bungee cord turns up dead on the scene?

Oh, hell indeed!

Temple speed-dialed Max on her cell phone. It was the relatively early hour (for a magician) of 1:00 P.M., but she hoped he was out there. Somewhere.

An answer!

"Well. Hello, Miss Teen Hottie. You still a bad, bad bottle blonde?"

"Yup. Sorry I was so out of it when you paid your respects the other night."

"I hate to disillusion you, but those weren't respects."

"Hmmm," she responded.

Max was doing his best to sound Max-errific, but Temple could tell that he was . . . simply . . . tired. Just awakened. Getting his bearings. Pretending to be perfectly alert, perfectly all right.

Just as she was. Pretending, that is. *Rats!*

"Listen, Max, I have that New Millennium Russian exhibition PR job and I need your input."

"The Millennium? You're doing the public relations for it?"

"Yes, duh. That's what I do for a living. This is my biggest commission yet and it's already going south."

She outlined the exhibition and her role in it, surprised he didn't already know. Max's job was being preternaturally informed and his avocation was keeping an eye on her, wasn't it?

"So, how can I help you?" he said.

"So . . . if it turns out that this death means that terrorists are stalking the exhibition, what's a savvy PR person to do to prevent more mayhem, murder, and, worst of all, bad publicity?"

"Watch her back?"

"That's all?"

"And front." Max chuckled. "Now that you're a platinum blonde, everybody else will be. It's a knee-jerk response."

"And unwanted, but I can't just wash that dye job out of my hair."

"Nor me either."

Temple warmed to the conviction in his voice. "Max, this is

way out of my league. I'm supposed to be getting goodie-goodie artsy coverage, but all the media will want is gory details."

"That's all the media ever wants these days."

"True, it's all sunk to *National Enquirer* level. Maybe I should become a . . . I don't know, an etiquette columnist. Miss Manners is looking rather wrinkly these days."

Max laughed until he sounded like his old self. "You as an etiquette dominatrix? Brave New World. Don't worry about the New Millennium job. I've got a feeling it'll work itself out."

"Max, I know I wasn't at my best the other night. But I *did* tell you that *she's* there, yes? On the scene."

"She?"

"That treacherous bitch." The phrase even surprised the usually ladylike Temple. "That awful female magician who napped your ring right off my hand on stage. Shangri-La."

A long silence, then Max said, "The ring that Molina found near the murder site of Gandolph's former assistant, you mean."

"Right. That one. I swear, Molina would never be girly enough to have a hope chest, but her custody of that ring of yours, of ours, is as close as she'll ever come to one. It's evidence of something, though I don't have any idea of what. Do you?"

Max was silent again.

"Shangri-La is Asian, supposedly," he finally said. "This exhibition is pre- and post-Soviet Russian. She may be involved merely as the Cloaked Conjuror's co-performer. Even treacherous bitches have to work."

"Yeah, well, I don't know what *his* real game is either. He's masked, isn't he? A conundrum. And so is she."

"Masked magicians are an ancient tradition."

"You always performed bare faced."

"Maybe I was just a good liar."

The last word hung suspended in the ether that connected their voices, but not their faces.

"I'm not a good liar, Max," Temple said.

"That's why I love you."

Oh. *He still did.* And she still did. And that combo still

made her heart sing. But. She knew she'd been treading toward lies of omission with her new, closer relationship with
Matt. If only Max would sweep her off her feet again into
surety, security.

*Give me a rope, Max! You who are so good at spinning over
the abyss. Give me something to hang on to besides faith and
fairy tales. Be my prince, not my pauper.*

"I don't know where you are," she said in a little lost voice.

"Neither do I."

Temple recognized truth even when it came wrapped in
three little words over a cell phone line. She sighed. "We need
to really talk, Max. Face to face. Soon."

"We need to do much more than that. Agreed." Pause. "I
can't now. Later, though."

"Later," she agreed.

"Don't worry." His voice was already fading.

She thought he'd added, "I'm on it." But it could have been
anything murmured in passing, some good-bye formula that
meant nothing.

She snapped the cell phone shut, torn between taking comfort from Max's certainty that everything would work out all
right, and an odd worry about *why* he should be so certain.
She had the unpleasant feeling of having been sweet talked.
Max knew better than to offer her Splenda instead of simple,
high-calorie sincerity. Didn't he? Didn't Max, more than anyone? That was her mantra, her faith, her story.

Maybe she'd been reading herself into the wrong book.

These new divided loyalties were tearing her in two. Why
was she still putting her heart and soul into a relationship that
had been perfect at first but had become more and more tenu-
ous? Even Matt, Mr. Patient, thought Max had deserted her. He
wouldn't be tempting her with romantic gestures and the
sweet, crazy idea of an opt-out trial civil marriage if he thought
her relationship with Max was the done deal it once was.

Temple took guilty refuge from her quandary over Max by
mentally replaying her most recent intimate moments with
Matt. He had sure found his inner Casanova. That combined
intensity of tenderness and sheer engulfing sexual hunger
loose for the first time was pretty overwhelming. So. Over-

whelm her. That would surely erase this miserable sense of loss and increasing distance every time she saw or talked to Max now.

She shook herself out of her sad, sexy reveries and examined her familiar homescape.

Midnight Louie was lounging on her living room sofa, one long foreleg sticking out over the edge as stiff as a shotgun barrel, yet oddly graceful.

It was the pose of a bored, indolent cat, but Temple didn't believe it for a second. Any more than she'd believed Max's offhand, indolent reassurances.

"A Chechen rebel," she told the cat, only because Max had signed off and wasn't there to hear, and regard, her. "That's crazy. What would they gain from disrupting a pretentious Las Vegas circus-act-cum-art-exhibition?"

Would Louie shrug her off, like Max? No. Cats didn't shrug. They just yawned, and blinked, and fanned their toes.

As Louie was doing right now.

Men! They were all alike.

Even when they were wearing fur.

Chapter 21

Playing Chechen

Max came out of the back patio's scorching sunlight into the house's cool dark shadows.

Garry, aka Gandolph, was in the kitchen, literally whipping up lunch. Max sat on a stool to watch his mentor in magic and counterterrorism whisk egg whites into a bowl-topping foam. The process was tricky, so he nibbled on some red grapes and kept quiet.

Gandolph finally looked up from under his salt-and-pepper eyebrows, now shaggy and quizzical when in his youth they had been devilishly peaked and cynical.

"Working two nighttime undercover jobs is putting maroon circles under those baby blues of yours, my lad."

"Working two nighttime jobs up in the rigging, period, is putting circles under my eyes. One blink too many and it's splat."

"You are fanatically precise about the care and feeding of your equipment."

Max grunted. "There's been an ugly turn in the New Millennium situation."

"The dangling dead man wasn't enough?"

Gandolph turned to put the dish into the preheated oven. Cooking was his form of meditation, and he was damn good at it.

"Now they're speculating the victim could be a Chechen rebel, or at least someone tied to them."

Gandolph's pudgy form (with time and retirement from the stage, the gourmet cooking had won the battle for Gandolph's physique) whirled around to face Max.

"And you know this from—"

"A little bird."

"Ah, *your* little bird, the redheaded PR chick."

"Blond, temporarily, as you recall. She couldn't know that I knew she was working on this PR assignment so I had to act, surprised. Damn! Why did she have to get hired on a project that I'm being forced to muck up? She is very proud of this New Millennium exhibition, thinks this could be the plum PR assignment of her career, and is afraid that things might turn really ugly and political."

"And she went right to you for advice. Good thing for us!"

"Possibly."

"What's not to like about a tip-off?"

"One ugly fact. Not only has the murder drawn higher hotel security and the LVMPD's attention to our little heist site, it implies that we've got a lot more to worry about than some greedy low-end would-be jewel thief. This might mean that if terrorists plan to use this exhibition for a political statement, we'll have the FBI all over the place as well. I'm supposed to nip a large and valuable cultural artifact from under the noses of hotel security, the Vegas cops, hidden anarchists, the FBI, and God knows who else?"

Gandolph set the oven timer and hopped up on another

stool like a chubby adolescent bellying up to a soda fountain. He grinned.

"We always did our best work against impossible odds. You love 'em."

Max grinned and ate another grape.

The grin faded fast as he considered how much this last, demanding, double-edged masquerade to infiltrate and topple the Synth was imperiling his long-held and deep love for Temple.

Maybe, he thought, it was high time to love impossible odds less and to spend his energy loving Temple more. Only a month more, surely. Once he was an inside man. Which he wouldn't be without stealing the scepter. Which would damage Temple's job performance.

Damn, sometimes there wasn't any which way to go, including loose.

Chapter 22

Better Bred Than Red

Hot news is hot news even when it is hot mews.

I allow my Miss Temple to mistake me for a stuffed pillow (a role I had more than enough of during one of our previous adventures), but the moment she leaves the condo, I bestir myself. I also desert the Circle Ritz, my home away from homicide, for the New Millennium, my homicide away from home.

I cannot tell you how all my hunting instincts sit up and take note when I hear that the dead man in the exhibition area may be from Chechnya (or could be connected to some rebel cause there?). I have relatives in Chechnya. (In fact, I have relatives all over the globe. Those of us who do not cling to limited pedigrees are truly universal. Some call us "mongrel" but it might as well be "Mongol" as not.)

Global politics is not normally my bailiwick. (Bailiwick is a good old-fashioned word for "arena of operation.") My arena of operation for the nonce (another good old-fashioned word) is the New Millennium and the White Russian exhibition. By now, I have found a handy ground-floor entrance: the back area where they download the Big Cats every day for rehearsal.

I merely hop through the bars of their cages—all right, I have to shimmy-shimmy my midlife male middle through the iron uprights—then I can hunker down between their extended forelegs and pass as a shadow. We are all big black dudes, after all.

Kahlúa is cool, but I have to watch Lucky, as he is new to the act and at times does not realize his own strength. Sometimes when he yawns, his lower jaw knocks my skull sideways. But a few blows to the cerebellum does not stop the streetwise shamus, as all the noir detective novels point out ad nauseam.

By the time the boys are transferred to their holding cages up top I am freewheeling and hard on the trail of crime and punishment. First, I need to know if the Big Cats have any insight on Russian politics.

Zip. Nil. Nada. These guys are huge and brawny and cooperative, but not much in the little gray cell department.

So I slink about the upper area, blending into the matte black paint job as long as I keep my eyes slitted almost closed, looking for some high witness I have missed interviewing. See, the guy was found dangling just above the apex of the exhibition area. That was sixty feet below the magic show staging zone. I figure somebody up there was not only watching, but pulling the strings.

CC and Miss Shangri-La are not on the scene yet, so I edge to the rim of a ledge to gaze down at the busy work below. It is way higher than an elephant's eye up here and is in no way a beautiful morning, so I am not surprised when a cold bolt of fur and claws bowls me over and has me hanging by my flimsiest nail sheaths from the wooden platform.

I gaze up into celestial blue eyes rimmed in predator red. Before I can blow my cover and whimper "Squeaker," I watch those Babyface Nelson—blue eyes blink.

"You!" Miss Hyacinth hisses. "I would help you up but my curare claws might bring you even farther down. Now we will see what upper foreleg strength will do for a common street fighter."

She steps back out of sight, leaving me to heave myself up on semi-solid ground sheath by sloughed sheath. I hear their tiny clicks hitting hard surfaces below like invisible hail.

Panting, I have regained my footing and stare my sudden tormentor down. That is just an expression. She remains with me up here, on this pseudo–crow's nest perch. I wish one of those big-beaked black birds were up here. They would teach Miss Hyacinth a thing or two.

While I catch my breath, she eyes me up and down, no doubt regretting that my "down" was not fatal. That is always the thing with these feline fatale types: they have to establish their street cred.

"Midnight Louie," she acknowledges. "I thought you had taken a few days off to bury your impertinent daughter after our encounter at CC's estate."

"Hmph," I say, "more like *her* burying me. I see you survived her onslaught."

"Easily."

I look into those crystal blues and know she is lying. Her set-to with Miss Louise is why a body double is in this new show. And . . . she might have enjoyed the superiority of helping me back up on the platform, except I can sense a certain delicacy in the joints on her part.

For a moment a soupçon of sympathy vibrates through my vibrissae (that is whiskers to you!). A domestic-size cat is always at a disadvantage on stage. Hyacinth is struggling to keep up with the Big Boys despite suffering a world-class catfight a few weeks back against my purported daughter, Miss Midnight Louise. I would have to say Louise may indeed be my spawn, for she won that one, pads down.

So, Hyacinth had thrown her weight around on me because it is her best weapon at the moment, curare-painted nails or not. Besides, she probably has a soft spot for me, anyway. Who would want to off the only reproductively harmless macho housecat in Las Vegas? The Big Boys would have her for lunch, or elevenses, if it were left to them.

"I did not know you were interested in high-wire acts," she says from her usual defensive crouch, which emphasizes the sharklike sharpness of her shoulder blades. Her coat is the same pale cream shade but her dove-gray trim shows slight scars.

"Me? An aerial act? Bast forbid."

"You do look a little bottom heavy."

"Physique has nothing to do with it. I am an earth sign."

"Oh, really? Which one?"

"Well, I do not believe in that astronomy stuff so I cannot say. Maybe, uh, Taurus."

"Ah. The bull. As in slinging lots of it. Why are you here? This is *my* mistress and *my* new gig. Intruders are not welcome."

"I am not an intruder."

"Then what are you?"

For one thing, fast on my feet with a good story. "Ah, I represent the boys."

"Boys?"

"Yeah. The Big Boys. I am their agent."

"I do not have an agent."

"That is because you have a verbal contract with your mistress. Never a good idea. You need someone between her interests and your interests."

"My only interest is serving her."

"Tsk." I sit down and slick down the hairs between my nails. "An admirable, self-sacrificing attitude but short-sighted."

"I am not short-sighted," she declares, so angry that she crosses her pale blue eyes, thus proving my point.

"Every performer of every stripe should have a personal representative. An agent. Are you willing to take humans at face value? At their so-called word? There is no more slippery species on the planet. I give you Enron, Worldcom, Tyco."

"I know no cats of those names."

"Of course not! These are predatory humans called CEOs. I think it stands for 'Cruel Evil Owners.' They make man-eating tigers look tame! Of course there are way more of them than there are man-eating tigers left in the world."

"So. Are you one of these 'representatives'?"

"Yeah. I could be yours, if you were looking for something in the representative line. What kind of contract do you have with Miss Shangri-La?"

Hyacinth hunches sourly into her shoulder blades again. "She owns me and I pretend to let her think she 'trains' me."

"That is it? No terms on length of contract? No bonuses for good behavior? No hazard pay for high-wire work?"

Where physical threat stands no chance against a spitfire like Hyacinth, she positively caves under the burden of legal language.

"None of that. Should I have it?"

"Absolutely. What about disability pay when you are side-lined and a double like Squeaker subs for you?"

"That namby-pamby, wishy-washy no-papers excuse for a Siamese! She is Melanie to my Scarlett. If I hadn't strained my spine recently . . . er, during rehearsal, of course."

Of course *not*. I know precisely when she sprained her spine: under the tender attentions of a spitfire masseuse named Midnight Louise.

Her eyes cross again as another thought occurs. "'Pay'? Did you use the term, 'pay'?"

"Pay. That's what I got when I did a couple of TV commercials for some cat glop. All specified by contract, seven pages of contract."

Hyacinth's forehead furrows. It looks like bleached moss. "Maybe you should be my agent, Louie."

I see my opening and I take it. "Sure thing, Princess. My cut is only fifteen percent."

She rouses herself from her troubled reverie and snicks out eight purple-enameled shivs from her forepaws, plus two scimitar-size dew claws. "Your cut is ten percent, one for each of the trails I will leave in your hide if you try to cheat me."

I see that even her strong, long lavender-enameled nails are flexed for quick action. I cannot swear that curare is mixed with that nail polish, but I would not want to test the theory on my own hide.

"Ten," I agree. Besides, I am not in this for the commission. "Being your agent will entail my hanging about up here—secretly, of course. We never want to warn humans of impending legal obligations—and observing what you contribute to the operation and what would be just compensation. Grandfathered in, of course."

"What does my grandfather have to do with this? He is retired from stud duty on a farm in New Hampshire."

I am astounded that she knows the whereabouts of her grandfather, but most of these purebreds have nothing better to do than tote up their family tree back to Bast, no doubt. For all I know, my grandfather may be the Cheshire cat.

" 'Grandfathering in' is a legal expression, meaning, um, your compensation must be paid retroactively." I am not at all sure about this, but when in doubt, sound confident.

I watch her baby blues cross again. It is a rather fetching habit.

I am on a roll. " 'Retroactively' means it goes back to when you first began working with Miss Shangri-La."

"You mean she would owe me?"

"Indeed. I think she owes you quite a lot. You are the only performing housecat in the magic game."

"How would I be paid?"

"Any way you like. Fancy Feast coupons. Bejeweled collars. French nail enamel. It would all be specified in the contract."

"And could I trust an agent who maintains sleeping arrangements with a human who rubs my mistress the wrong way, and vice versa?"

"Business is business. A commission on a hot act is a commission."

"Well." Miss Hyacinth (formerly the evil Hyacinth, but a dude needs to show proper respect for a client or how will he get any for her in negotiations?) rises, stretches with only a trace of painful hesitation, and bares her fangs at me, in a friendly way. "I will show you all my hidey holes, for when I am having an artistic tantrum over the choreography. Perhaps not all, Louie. A girl needs her secrets."

She is back to her flirting, fickle self and I feel pretty relaxed myself.

One does not wish to get too cozy with a deadly enemy, especially if one is using her for a higher purpose, but I have declawed the one creature up here who might blow my cover.

Now, she will be busting her gray velvet garters to conceal my presence. I will be able to spy for my Miss Temple and make sure her project goes as smooth as spider silk. She can cover the infighting on the ground level; I will handle the high jinks on high. Plus I may be able to collect a sweet commission. In one form or another.

Chapter 23

United We Stand

Temple wasn't unduly religious. Not when she'd been brought up as a Unitarian Universalist. It was the one area where her usually staid midwestern family had kicked over the tracks.

Slightly.

There were only about 800,000 registered UUs in the U.S. of A., including four U.S. presidents, which made them a pretty significant insignificant minority, to turn a redundancy into a contradiction in terms.

The universality and unity implicit in the name pretty much described the doctrine: inclusive. A UU didn't even have to believe in God (as a sort of straight Leonardo da Vinci in a long beard and antiquated robes) or as anything other than an innate kindly bent in human nature.

Backsliding in the practice of Unitarian Universalism was very difficult to do. They stood for such large, all-embracing concepts and had so few narrow, excluding ones. But Temple had managed to do it. Simply by not going to church.

So making an appointment with the local UU minister for an office "consultation" felt like stealing. And operating under false pretenses.

But Sue Hathaway had been perfectly willing, even eager, to meet and talk with Temple. Temple had a good feeling about a woman with a position few other women in the country held listing herself as "Sue" instead of the more formal "Susan."

It felt UU and even MU: Midwestern Unpretentious.

And Temple needed all the good feeling she could muster for slinking around, just when the going got tough, to a church she'd ignored for several years. But when she'd told Max that they needed to talk, Temple knew she needed to talk to an expert first. A UU minister named Sue.

"Come in." Sue answered the door herself.

She was only three or four inches taller than Temple's five-foot-nothing, a high point in her favor. But she was the opposite kind of woman: wiry short hair, no makeup, blue jeans, linen blazer over a sky blue silk camp shirt; Birkenstock shoes, flirting with either side of forty-five. She was plain but reassuringly savvy seeming and competent, perhaps because of her plainness.

"Temple Barr," the woman, uh, minister, said. What should Temple call her? "An interesting name. Come sit down. Some espresso? Tea? The obligatory glass of afternoon sherry?"

"Why don't we wait and see what's needed," Temple said.

Sue laughed and nodded.

"By the way, I'm not usually a bottle blonde. This is just part of my last job."

"You're an entertainer?"

It was a natural question in Las Vegas.

"Nothing so exciting, or lucrative. I'm a freelance public relations representative, but sometimes in Las Vegas—"

"*Always* in Las Vegas. Say no more. What can I help you with, Miss Barr?"

"Temple, please."

"Miss Barr" was how Lieutenant Molina invariably addressed her. Temple did not want to think about the homicide lieutenant while on this particular, and highly personal, mission. "I was reared UU."

"Not in Las Vegas."

"No. In Minneapolis."

"But you haven't been active."

"No. So I suppose I really shouldn't be here."

"To the contrary. Welcome back. At least for a meeting. What can I help you with?"

"I need a religious professional's viewpoint on something."

" 'A religious professional.' I'd never quite thought of it that way, but it's true."

Temple sighed, big time. Then she plunged right in with the immediate problem. "I've been seeing an ex-Roman Catholic priest."

Sue Hathaway was a pro. Her expression remained supernaturally noncommittal. And she said nothing, so Temple had to go on.

"I've learned a bit about that religion's position on a lot of things, which are way more . . . definite than I grew up with."

Sue smiled.

That forced Temple to blunder on even further. "Anyway, although he's wonderful—smart and kind and well, hot looking—I once made this flip remark that modern girls don't want to discover sexual compatibility or incompatibility on their wedding nights like in the olden days."

"One does tend to get flip when nervous," Sue said.

"And now he's come up with the darnedest compromise between his religion, which is way anti-premarital sex, and what I sort of said I expected. Which was a"—Temple cringed—"a free sample."

Sue laughed. Hard. Until the tears came. "How long was he in?" she asked when she could. "The church, that is."

"About seventeen years."

"Ouch. Why and how'd he leave?"

"It's complicated."

"If it wasn't, it wouldn't be real life."

Temple sighed again, much to her surprise. She was astonished by how hard it was to talk about her personal ambiguities even to encouraging strangers of the same gender.

"I told you he was smart. He figured out he'd entered the priesthood to be the perfect father because he was born out of wedlock. Then his mother married the most imperfect stepfather she could find."

Sue's encouraging expression had curdled with instant understanding. "Poor woman."

"Girl. So there was"—Temple wouldn't give away Matt's name. Talking about him behind his back even with a stranger was bad enough—"my friend, dealing with all that. He says the attraction of celibacy was it was the only way in his church he could be a hero for not having children, which he's still pretty conflicted about. He knows kids from abusive families can . . . abuse children."

"And you?"

"Children? I don't know! I'm single. I'm thirty. It's hard enough to decide who you love, much less whether you want to add . . . cats-with-souls to the mixture."

"So, the immediate issue is—?"

"He's mentioned marriage."

"Very serious."

"Being a good ex-UU, I get that! He's offered, actually proposed that we get a civil marriage here in Las Vegas. As a . . . test run. Then, if we're compatible, we can remarry back wherever—my home, his home in Chicago—in a religious ceremony, probably ecumenical."

"And your question is?"

"My question is a lot of things about marrying a devout Catholic and what it would mean to me, but I'm here to ask what this crazy idea means to him. I've never had to answer to a demanding religion like he has. I could get married here by Elvis and feel married. Or do a church thing and feel just as committed. But . . . I'm not sure where his plan puts him, in terms of his religion."

Sue leaned back, tenting her fingers. "I can tell you that he's seriously sincere."

"I've always known that. It's one of his best and most aggravating qualities."

Sue chuckled. "You like him. You really, really like him."

Temple nodded. "It's my Sally Field Oscar moment."

Sue was old enough to recognize the reference. "You could love him."

"Yeah. Except I'm not mentioning my long-term boyfriend, who's being pulled in directions he can't help."

"Which don't include you."

"Probably not."

Sue inhaled deeply, lowered her head, then lifted it and asked, "Sherry?"

"Yeah."

The glasses were tiny and exquisite. The sherry was the color of watered-down blood. Temple killed hers with one swallow.

Sue chuckled again. "At least you're trying to figure this out. Listen. This man, the ex-priest, I don't think he's fooling himself. No, this civil marriage plan is not a way out for *him*. It is for *you*, if you don't mind having a Reno divorce on your record. His church would never recognize the validity of a civil marriage. He'd have sinned. But both you and he could start over again, fresh. You'd be a Reno divorcee, not odd at your age. And he would have sinned but he wouldn't have committed himself to a real marriage, the only kind his faith recognizes, a Catholic one."

"All this for a free sample?"

"That was you, not him."

"Oh, God. Oh."

Sue shook her head and refilled Temple's glass.

"You two. You're like a pair of blind people trying to meet in some nonexistent middle." She leaned forward. "You don't have Doubt One about your sexual compatibility with this man. You have doubts about your religious compatibility."

"It's strange. I don't want to think about some of these things in advance. I'm okay with sex, marriage, and what next? Who knows what I'll want in three years? But my not wanting kids right away, or ever, would be a big religious no-no for him and his church. Yet he's the one with a legitimate reason to worry about that."

"There are options. Natural family planning, for instance, is accepted by his church. You know, it means abstinence on presumed 'fertile' days. It works a lot better these days than when it was take-your-temperature-and-hope forty years ago."

"I don't want to think about that. It sounds so . . . clinical. I want to think about who I love and could spend the rest of my life with."

"What about who loves you?"

Temple smiled, shakily. "I'm lucky. I know two guys do. And I guess I . . . love them both. Is that possible?"

"Maybe, but it doesn't work very well. I can see you'll be conflicted no matter which way you go."

"That sucks! Excuse me, Reverend."

"The truth often does."

"He said . . . my ex-priest friend, that he never wanted to confess anything that happened between us."

"Nor should any seriously sincere person, no matter his religion. I'm afraid, Miss Temple Barr, that you also are a seriously sincere person. It doesn't make life easy. But it will make it rewarding. Eventually. That doesn't help, I suppose."

"You've confirmed what I was afraid of. Ma— The ex-priest was thinking of me, not himself, when he came up with that civil marriage stunt. He'd still be in trouble with his faith."

"You gotta love a guy like that." Sue smiled.

"Yeah. But the other man has always looked out for me too, even risked his neck. It's just that he's been so . . . absent lately. I know he has good, even noble reasons."

"Sounds like you can't live with one man's religious values and the other's man's job."

"I can't live with liking, needing, wanting, loving two men at the same time!"

"A lot of women claim they can't find one good guy nowadays. You have two. Can you spare one? I'm single."

Temple, on the verge of tears, found herself laughing instead.

"Yeah," Sue said. "I'm a fine one to give advice. Love isn't for sissies. I think something will happen to push you one way or the other. It'll just happen, and you'll know what's right."

Temple nodded and got up to leave.

She had no doubt that Max was another one of Sue Hathaway's "seriously sincere" persons. Maybe the answer was not what she couldn't live with—subdivided loyalties, conflicting love and lust—but what, or who, she couldn't live *without*.

And maybe she'd recognize *that* when she saw it.

Chapter 24

Police Work

Now that Temple was a bottle blonde, Morrie Alch was salt-and-pepper putty in her petite little hands.

She would bet that his only child, a grown daughter, had been a taffy-haired honey of twenty-two months at one time.

"Thanks, Detective Alch, for handling this so discreetly."

He gazed up at the empty area above the peak of the exhibition ramp, where men in coveralls sat on boards suspended on paint-spattered ropes.

"Thank the New Millennium," he said. "They have clout in this town. We poor flatfoots do our job and bow out."

"You're not a flatfoot; you're a detective. You don't fool me. That poor dead man. I'm still trying to find out if he could possibly have been hired by the hotel."

"Waste of time. All that fuss about him maybe being a Chechen rebel. He has a Slavic look, but 'Art' was a petty crook. A hotel hanger-on, all right, but more used to hanging paper around town than hanging dead over the site-to-be of a priceless artifact. It takes a superior criminal mentality to engineer a major art heist."

"I don't doubt it." Temple tried not to think of the superior criminal mentality she knew intimately. "We've tripled security."

"That ought to make somebody very unhappy."

"You think the exhibition is still endangered?"

Alch shook his grizzled head. "Security is out of our hands. Homicide's the name of our game. The LVMPD will offer some officers to watch things around here, but it's up to hotel security now. That's the way they want it."

Temple checked her watch. It was one of those easy-read dials big enough to cover her wrist. Nothing Paris Hilton would wear, but it kept her on time in a field where split seconds could make all the difference in the world.

Randy Wordsworth had arranged for her to interview the Cloaked Conjuror in his dressing room.

This was a biggie. The New Millennium kept the name of their headlining masked magician a state secret and his safety Job One. When you live and work in a magical kingdom where illusion adds up to a billion-dollar-a-month industry, your hide can become wall worthy when your whole shtick is outing the opposition. Death threats combined with the masked mystique to keep CC pretty much out of reach of the media, except for a few controlled appearances outside the New Millennium, like judging the TitaniCon science fiction costume contest at the Hilton Hotel a few months before, where Temple had first encountered him.

One of his body doubles had fallen to a suspicious death from the flies there, so CC's security had tightened even more after that. But since Temple's job here was partly spin control, management was letting her play sleuth in hopes she could head off more disastrous events spelling bad publicity.

Temple was pleased to think that she was gaining a reputation for PI as well as PR work in Las Vegas. They made a useful combination.

She wasn't surprised she had to sign in with a guard at the entrance to the backstage area. And to show her special New Millennium ID card. God, she hoped she could keep it when this job was through. Between her new blond bling look and the softening Glamour Shots effect of teeny tiny security card photos, she looked hardly as old as teen queen Hillary Duff. And thirty was already beginning to feel over the hill.

"You the one going to be working with CC?" the guard asked a bit shyly. He was the usual sedentary Social Security geezer who was content to watch the world go by, especially if it had good legs.

"Gosh, no!" Had he really mistaken her for Shangri-La, the lethal mistress of Asian illusions? Not so strange. "Shang" almost always wore makeup, so who knew what the woman really looked like? A handy asset. "I work PR for the hotel."

He waved her onward, down some bare concrete steps into the significant bowels of the backstage area.

. If Las Vegas shows were overly glitzy behemoths featuring casts of dozens and stage effects that mimicked natural catastrophes almost as well as a Spielberg flick, the underbelly that supported such overweight extravaganzas ran even deeper, wider, longer.

That meant a creepy underworld of dim-lit halls lined with fluttering ghosts of a zillion costume changes. Of crowded chorus dressing rooms haunted by disembodied heads in Marie Antoinette–high wigs and moving bits of glitter everywhere, even when the rooms were empty. Of high heels hitting jackhammer hard on concrete and echoing into eternity, as Temple's were now.

This was no brightly lit yellow brick road, but she did have her Toto on board. A small black form was trotting ahead of her. Not fluffy, but sleek. Not canine, but feline.

She ought to have known.

"Louie!"

For a moment, she wondered if Max could shape shift. Because Louie had certainly been dogging her footsteps lately, as if subbing for her missing significant other.

Temple winced mentally. Did a woman who smooched a close neighbor still have the right to a significant other?

Another guard could be seen on duty a long way down the hall. Standing at attention, his beer gut leading the way. Louie was not to be seen, but the hems of some gowns on a nearby rack were fluttering suspiciously.

Temple reported to Guard Two.

"Need to see your driver's license too."

"My driver's license?"

"Rules."

Temple sighed and dug it out of her tote bag. Finally. The guard then rifled through the bag while she worked to pry the license from behind a permanently sticky clear plastic window with her still too-long pageant fingernails.

"Sharp," he commented.

"A fingernail file."

"Have to hold it."

"I'd get through the Cloaked Conjurer's crocodile-tough costume with a fingernail file?"

"Orders."

"Why don't I just go to McCarren and go through airport security there, then come back here?"

He sniffed. Allergies. "Patience, little girl."

That was better than the usual "little lady"?

"What's this?" He held up her little motorized instant flosser.

"A birth control device." She was kidding.

He dropped it back in the bag like a hot potato. "So, okay. You can go in now. You can collect the nail file on the way out."

At that moment Temple felt the softest tease of motion at her ankles. She resolved not to look down.

"Thanks, Sir."

And she turned toward the next tunnel of gray hallway, nothing visible ahead but various closed doors and the convenient ranks of costume racks.

The greasepaint in her blood made her inhale deeply. No matter how fancy the theater or amphitheater, below stage it was the same bare, functional, fascinating, weirdly enchanting wonderland.

She was off to see the Conjuror.

His dressing room soon became obvious. The single star had a peephole in the middle. Talk about paranoia!

Temple knocked, realizing that both peephole and star were positioned for a man who wore elevated platform boots and reached close to seven awesome feet onstage. He'd probably be unable to see her.

Apparently, the guard had called ahead, for a deep voice asked, "Miss Barr?"

"Here!" Temple piped up, waving her fingers before the peephole.

The door opened a crack, while she was inspected. Then it widened just enough to admit her.

On the other side stood not the Cloaked Conjuror, but a man who embodied the description "bruiser." All this for little her. Imagine if somebody suspicious had come calling unannounced. . . .

A figure bigger and broader than the silent doorman was sitting on a squarish couch at one side of the room. The dressing table and mirror, directly across from the door, were not only unoccupied but looked oddly vacant.

Then Temple realized what she was missing: the clutter of tins of greasepaint and powder, of tubes of makeup. Because CC wore a voice-altering masking headpiece, he didn't need to touch up a thing. The mirror was useless, except for reflecting the beefy bodyguard now backed up against the door as if holding off a horde of Huns.

"Sit down," CC's weirdly altered voice, rather like Darth Vader on cough drops, said. "Randy Wordsworth said you needed to interview me for PR reasons."

Temple did as invited, feeling like a bug on a log alongside a large, leathery, tiger-faced toad.

"We need to defuse the publicity on the . . . unfortunate death," she began. "If the exhibition got the reputation of being jinxed—"

"It'd bring the crowds out in droves."

"Maybe, but the art museum is already nervous about the

risks of showing such rare works in a Las Vegas hotel. Showing them over some poor man's dead body is even worse."

"You think I don't care? I do. Believe me. Few know this,
but I lost a crewman during TitaniCon. Up on the catwalk.
Fell to the floor sixty feet below. Dead. Wearing a costume
much like mine. You think the *museum* is spooked? You
haven't walked in my shoes, Miss Barr."

Temple eyed the footwear in question. Possibly a size thirteen, built up like a Klingon's seven-league futuristic boots.

"I don't think walking in your shoes would be possible for
me," she said. "Sleeping in them, maybe."

The large head with its narrow eye slits had to move far to
eyeball Temple's size five Via Spigas. CC laughed, an operatic
sound that combined both basso and tenor.

"Sleep indeed. Let's just say I don't like the coincidence of
two men working the flies on an act of mine dying for it."

"When do you actually go up there?"

"Later in the act. My female assistant goes on first. She's a
midget like you, no bigger than a mayfly, and she does this
ballet-acrobatic routine, like a silvery cocoon spinning and
lifting and lowering. Very classy. Then she bursts out of her
chrysalis waving filmy wings of fabric."

"I know. I saw the tape. Her act reminds me of Loïe Fuller."

"Louie who?"

Temple smiled. "A pioneering modern dancer at the end of
the nineteenth century who wielded incredible lengths of
white silky wings."

"Everything recycles."

Temple was thinking that Beauty and the Beast was one of
the more enduring fables to recycle, from French seventeenth-
century fabulist Charles Perrault to Walt Disney. And that's
what an act comprising the Cloaked Conjuror and Shangri-La
would be. Beauty and Beast. How clever. How marketable.

She recalled, with a pang, that once Max had kidded her
about joining his act. She was no acrobat or illusionist, but she
understood the innate showmanship of it, petite little her, supernaturally strong and elegant him: fairy girl and superhero.

"And then, of course," CC added in his commanding faux
voice, "there are the cats. Now that Siegfried and Roy are

tragically removed from the scene, mine is the only act to feature big cats, and one very small one."

So, the amazingly agile performing Siamese that Shangri-La had worked with at the Opium Den would be appearing here as well! How had these two far-removed performers ever hooked up?

Temple asked CC that question in much more elegant terms.

"She hit on me, in the professional sense. Showed up at my ... home with an offer I couldn't refuse. Amazing woman. I notice small-statured women are particularly insistent. And Shang had her Asian background to both overcome and assert."

Temple flashed for a second on half of Molina's prize homicide team of Alch and Su: detective Merry Su. Teeny, wiry, implacable. Given the historic low regard for women in her culture, from exposing girl babies to the lethal elements in the bad old days to aborting them in the bad new days, those Chinese women who went West and thrived were veritable Dragon Ladies.

Normally, Temple admired women of steel. In Shangri-La's case, she made a significant exception. The woman was associated with an incident involving a semi-load of stolen designer drugs. People often forgot that Las Vegas catered heavily to the Pacific Trade. Asians were fevered gamblers, and had become treasured high-roller clients of every major hotel-casino along the Strip.

With that came the Asian mafia, the drug trade, and every evil flower of crosscultural international corporate/gangster contamination. So, what was Shangri-La's game here? Besides spinning like an entombed butterfly above a fabulous treasure trove of Russian artwork? She couldn't ask the Cloaked Conjuror such blunt questions, but she could skirt around them.

"Your solo act was a huge hit, exposing magician's tricks. Why add an element?"

Even through the cumbersome mask, CC's laugh was rueful.

"My shtick is great. I'm big, I'm anonymous, I'm half man, half mystery. Even the death threats work into my mystique.

And the big cats. Audiences are all unconsciously waiting for that Roy Horn–Manticore moment, though they'd never admit it. Ask NASCAR drivers. But look at me. All this disguise paraphernalia weighs me down. My act needed a certain lightness of being. Shangri-La and Hyacinth provide that."

Temple was surprised to hear CC use a literary phrase, but she nodded. "Yin and yang. Always appealing, always commercial."

"And this blend of fine art and illusion is another yin-yang combo. Very potent. Very exploitable."

"Very volatile maybe."

"For that dangling dead man, yeah. I earn millions per year, Miss Barr. I pay my crew a rock star's ransom. The hotel has millions sunk into my act. But there's a person in here behind all this theatrical bluster. I don't want anyone else to die on my set. Ever."

"You think the death of your TitaniCon crewman and this unidentified stranger are connected." Temple did not put a question into her voice.

"I do."

"Part of the magicians' vendetta against you?"

"Maybe. But I suspect it's even more than that."

"Why?"

"Instinct? In this getup, that's what I rely on, more than my senses."

"It must be hell, being a literal prisoner of your success."

The huge head was eerily still for several long moments.

"I didn't understand," the mask said in its altered voice, "when I got into this thing." CC's gauntleted hands struck his Batman-molded chest. "It seemed like a straight drive to success after years of fringe action. So what? James Earl Jones's voice got fab reviews for *Star Wars*. Let me tell you, Darth Vader is not a cushy part."

"Surely at home you can ditch the equipment."

"And wouldn't everybody think that way, and go after me there? Tabloid photographers. Blackmailers. Hired killers."

"Maybe. You really think that if they solve the murder of this poor guy they might close that TitaniCon case?"

"Probably. But I'm not sure 'they' will have anything to do with it."

"Who, then?"

CC couldn't smile, grin, grimace, or change his expression a scintilla in the lordly leonine mask with its tiger stripes. Temple had heard of lion-tiger crosses: tigons and ligers. The Cloaked Conjuror was his own rare breed.

His leather-gloved forefinger tapped her on the breastbone, his intended gentle tap nearly pushing her over.

"Why not you? You're enterprising, small, mobile, curious, just the kind of cat who could sniff out this murderer."

His suggestion was interesting but not alarming. Enterprising, small, mobile, curious. He could have been describing Temple's sometime secret shadow on the scene of a crime, Midnight Louie.

Still, she was highly flattered to hear this huge, menacing man express such confidence in little her. Max had, but he wasn't around much anymore for ego boosting.

"Maybe I'll do just that then," she said, sounding impish but feeling dead serious.

It was her job as well as CC's to run a steady ship on this show and she disliked lost lives as much as he did. Besides, Temple was more than ready to wade hip-deep into anything that might unmask Shangri-La and any ulterior motives that mysterious creature might have.

Chapter 25

Dead Man Falling

It is always a pleasure to watch My Miss Temple talk her way into—or out of—any situation.

Unfortunately, talking is not an option for me.

So, I follow her as discreetly as I can, past growling guards who would be neutered overweight Dobermen in other lives. I cling to the walls and the concealing curtains of the costume racks, etcetera, until she vanishes into the Caped Conjuror's dressing room.

I am perfectly content to trust her to handle a seven-foot-tall icon. She has managed Mr. Max Kinsella for these two years, and he is only six four, not to mention way more challenging than poor old CC in his dead Big Cat mask.

My role here is to investigate the hidden underbelly of the act.

Which underbellies may be decidedly feline. I am thinking of the evil Hyacinth, with whom I have crossed nail sheaths before, and the new kid on the block, this seemingly innocent "Squeaker." Both, however, are Siamese, if you please (and if you remember the song from the classic Disney dog fest, *The Lady and the Tramp.*)

I would never call a lady a tramp, but then I am talking felines here, not dogs.

I know why my Miss Temple is so disturbed by the recently dead dude in the webbing above the exhibition site. There was a dead man falling at TitaniCon, where both she and I were active in allowing Miss Lieutenant C.R. Molina to capture a murderer on site.

Both air-borne murders link to our mutual acquaintance, the Cloaked Conjuror. I have nothing against the dude. He is the usual Larger-Than-Life Las Vegas attraction. It started with Elvis, or maybe Frank. No, Elvis. That guy is so much more larger than life that many folks think he is still living.

Me, I would like to think that too. We have a passing acquaintance, Elvis and me, and he was always first and foremost the "Memphis Cat." We share a certain misconception with the public. I had a dead twin myself, as a matter of fact. Not everybody knows that, thank you verra much. We back-alley cats do not have a high survival rate.

But Elvis has left the building and the New Millennium was not even here when he strode the old town. I will have to deal with the younger generation, which is alarmingly female. Not that I am alarmed by the female. *Au contraire.* Still, these New Age babes do make me rush to relevance. I remain convinced that they know more than they are telling me.

So. Where are they likely to be housed? I slink past CC's dressing room, where My Miss Temple is handling things in her own inimitable way. I am looking for the ladies in the case.

My nose does its duty and soon it is snuffling under the door of another dressing room. *Perfume, smerfume. Pheromones, sharemones.* I can track my species anyplace on earth, and especially among a tsunami of humans, who generally stink, in my view, most often of preparations intended to make them *not* stink.

I must duck under a frill of peasant petticoats on a neighboring costume rack when an attendant busts open the door to the dressing room to deliver an anchovy pizza. But I slither in on his departing heels to find myself alone with the nuked fish, the sodium overload, and a distinct odor of feline femininity.

Which wench is it, though? Hyacinth and her curare toenails, or Squeaker and her strained high notes?

"Louie?"

Her voice was ever soft, sweet, and low . . . for a purebred Siamese. I ankle up to Squeaker and settle beside her to dispatch a selection of previously dispatched anchovies. I do love fast food.

She says not a discouraging word, but nibbles on fish and cheese as if to-the-pizza-oven born. You would never know she was recently a shelter cat.

"So," I ask after washing my whiskers, "are you alone by the xylophone?"

She giggles charmingly. "There is no xylophone in our act, just a lot of New Age music."

"The same sort of thing. Where does the headliner, Hyacinth, keep herself these days?"

"Oh, I am not allowed to room with her. She is a star. Plus, she might nail me with her poisonous claws. Stars are very insecure, did you know that, Louie?"

"Not being one, no. And I am not sure those claws are as lethal as advertised."

"Have you never been a performer, then?"

"I did some commercial TV work for a while, but I am mostly employed as a dude-about-town. An . . . investigator, as you know. Death. Crime. Conspiracy."

Miss Squeaker furrows her blond brow, her blue eyes crossing slightly with concentration. What a charmer! "Are you now investigating the dangle toy on the exhibition floor?"

"*Above* the exhibition floor," I point out.

"I saw the workers take him away on a stretcher with wheels. I recognized him, having seen him out and about."

"Part of the crew?"

"I do not think so."

"So." I dust off the itsy-bitsy spidery tail of an anchovy; these are squinky critters, let me tell you. "Where did you see him?"

Here, Miss Squeaker settles down on her haunches to play with her food. One delicate nail-tip hoists an anchovy over to my side of the cardboard circle. I love a dainty eater, especially when she is not eating but letting me hog it all.

"What do I know?" she says listlessly. "I am only worth anything for my resemblance to the great and powerful Hyacinth."

I bite my tongue. The great and powerful Hyacinth is one hot chick but not an empowering role model, I fear.

"Louie," she goes on, "I cannot sleep a wink at night, dreading our opening, my debut. Fearing that the web of lines we must work upon will fail and cause me to fall. So, I go up alone to walk the wires."

"Without a safety net?"

"There is no safety net for this show. In rehearsal, yes, but once the run begins, it will be naked claws."

I shudder despite myself. This is no way to introduce an amateur to a circus act. "I admire your devotion to your job, and survival. So. No one knows you are up there putting in rehearsal time?"

She ducks her head, then nods. "If I am to do well, I must seem to be a 'natural.'"

"Which is why you are."

She flashes her fangs. This is the equivalent of a feline smile, nothing predatory. "Have you ever hung sixty feet above a concrete floor, Louie?"

"Just on a case, and then not happily. The only thing I think should be hanging that high is a piñata."

Squeaker blinks wryly at me. "And those are usually made in the form of donkeys. A very meek and mild creature."

"I often thank Bast that our kind does not have four hooved feet for then we would all be enslaved."

"Some of us still are."

I cannot argue. Squeaker was "rescued" but into servitude.

"What did you see up there that no one was supposed to see?"

"I see why you are a prime investigator," Squeaker says, hunkering down.

What sexy, sharp shoulder blades she has! A born sweater girl.

"There have been," she says, her whiskers tickling the vibrissae near my ears most lasciviously, "several mysterious humans up there with me."

"Humans are always mysterious."

"But not always . . . sneaky."

"No. 'Sneaky' is a word often applied, unjustly, to our breed. So. Who was hanging out under the ceiling with you?"

"Two men."

"Not part of the crew?"

"No. Strangers in black."

"Suspicious. Not my natural kind of black, I take it?"

"Not fur, no. That second skin that humans wear."

"Spandex?"

"Yes. I had not heard the word until I left stir for show biz."

"Understandable. What kind of men?"

"Men. They are big, clumsy. They speak, smell. They would easily trod upon one's tail and never notice if one fell at forty miles an hour to the concrete below."

"They would easily never notice that one had a tail."

"Exactly."

"So, they are not part of the crew?"

"Many men who are not part of the crew hang around the set and exhibition."

"You mean hang around but not lethally. Did you see the victim?"

"I cannot be sure. He was a man and wore black spandex. Some call it a cat suit, and now that I have met *you,* I see why."

She bats sea blue eyes at me.

Merrowphhh, I do recognize when a nubile doll is making cow eyes in my direction. Squeaker makes her slinky sister Hyacinth look like a hooker on Zoloft.

"Tell me, my acrobatic charmer"—can I help it if she giggles with a sort of throaty purr?—"how could that cat-suited man have managed to die when you have been able to survive, and thrive?"

We nose the dressing room door open and she leads me through a circuitous backstage route and up into the flies via a webbing lattice that only those of us gifted with claws might manage.

The setup is clear once we are high above the exhibition area. The magic act is laid out on an invisible web. You always knew every illusion comes with strings, did you not?

A single tightrope stretches straight and strong across the chasm below. It is steel cable, a half-inch circumference of metal filaments, both flexible and taut. If one has the impeccable balance for the job, it is a royal road of stability. A human foot, trained to curl, can toe dance across . . . as long as the body above those feet is lean, schooled, and attuned for infinite balance. No magic, just rosin and gutsy skill. The feline foot, clawed by birth, is even more flexible and clingy.

That is not to dismiss the heart and skill it takes for any living thing to perform sixty feet above the ravening crowd.

Black bungee cords are all over the place, swagged against the side walls like anorexic curtains. The way they are arrayed, you could grab one and swing down from any point on any of the four walls, which narrow into a funnel at the very top.

There is a ledge about twelve feet from the top. Squeaker (I will have to find a pet name for her, and soon!) points out black sliding panels that allow humans to enter and exit the scene and the black platforms where the Big Cats perform.

Of course, from a vantage point far below, all the machinery blends into a solid firmament of black, against which any wires, cords, platforms and escape hatches become invisible.

"So," I ask myself as much as my guide, "the dead man had to have come out here, willingly or not, before he could get entangled in a bungee cord and garotte himself."

"Or before someone could ensnare his neck in a bungee cord and push him off one of the launching platforms."

I study these platforms. They are built for strength. The act's Big Cats are of the leaner, smaller variety: black leopards. They weigh maybe a petite 250 to 300 pounds. The Cloaked Conjuror in all his gear runs perhaps 250 himself. Shangri-La, 110. Hyacinth, maybe 7 or 8. I am a bruising 20 pounds myself, and not even the tightrope trembles at my few steps upon it.

"Louie! Do not toy with the tightrope. It takes a trained professional to walk it."

"I am a trained professional."

"On the high wire?"

"When this joint was brand new, I busted into it through the neon planet sign on the roof."

"Really!"

"Really, S. Q."

"S. Q?"

"A nickname, compliments of Midnight Louie. Short for 'Cute-with-a-Q.' Or the more common 'Susie Q.' Do not thank me, S. Q."

"I was not about to, M. L."

She is especially cute-with-a-Q when she is mad. "Tell me," I ask again. "How do two black cat dudes, no matter how outsize, show up against all this black matte paint when they perform?"

She uses her elegantly pointed tail to indicate the doused stars in our artificial sky. "Pinpoint spots. Plus, their coats are dusted with iridescent powders. Kahlúa with black diamond, and Lucky with rainbow platinum."

I nod. Such serious shimmer will keep all eyes on the cats while their human partners do-si-do with illusion and misdirection.

"What does Hyacinth do during the show?"

"Her personal brand of acrobatics. She even has a fur-colored harness and does several high dives from a bungee cord."

If I could whistle, I would. Instead I manage a high-pitched wheeze. "That Hyacinth is no shy violet."

Squeaker sighs. "Do not remind me. They want a stage name for me, even though, as a body double, I will get no credit in the program."

"You mean that will be *you* bungee jumping your little heart out?"

"I hope not, Louie. It is more than possible that Hyacinth will be strong enough and will not require a substitute. But if she does, I need my heart right where it belongs when I do these stunts."

I look down, eyes narrowed. Human workmen in white paint-ers' overalls blend with the pale travertine floor below.

"So, you're the bungee cord expert up here?"

"Along with Shangri-La herself. She did not want to risk her treasured companion in rehearsal."

"The Cloaked Conjuror?"

"Hyacinth."

I should have known. "So what does CC do here?"

"Stays safe high above, on the platform. He has never been an acrobatic performer."

No, not weighed down with those height-enhancing boots, that heavy face-concealing, voice-altering device that makes him into the magician in the iron mask.

"Wait a minute! Have you seen the whole act?"

"Of course not. None of us has. Only bits. It is secret until the grand opening."

"Then maybe . . . just maybe, CC needed a secret body double himself. Maybe the double needed secret practice. Maybe that was the guy who got a little too friendly with a bungee cord coil and dove. And died."

"Maybe." Squeaker's big blue marble eyes light up, even in the shadows up here. "So . . . CC might need a replacement. Who could he get on such short notice?"

I put a testing foot on the high wire again. Something in me would like to prove I could still give Death a run for my money. But I am older and out of practice.

I wonder if Mr. Max Kinsella faces the same dilemma.

Only one man—magician—in Vegas could step into the dead man's shoes on short notice. That is a pun. Mr. Max Kinsella is six feet four of muscled tensile nerve. This would be a perfect way to secretly swing his way to a comeback if he wanted to.

And did someone else figure he could, and would, want to? Did someone want the incomparable Mystifying Max up here for some reason? Did CC's body double, if he was one, die to make room for Mr. Max?

I look down. My poor Miss Temple's common blond head is again on the scene with no idea that her faithful roommate is up here, above it all, watching her back and ruminating and contemplating risking his neck. Mr. Max Kinsella and I have way too much in common nowadays for me to be entirely comfortable with it.

"Louie?" S. Q. sounds sweetly uncertain, but she is another one being forced into a situation where risking her neck is the only way to save her hide.

"Yes?"

"What do you think of Fontana?"

"Which one?"

"*The* one. For my performing name. 'The Flying Fontana.'"

I am picturing the Flying Fontana Brothers as a trapeze act and work so hard to smother a laugh that I almost overbalance into instant oblivion. But this will be the only comic relief I will have for some time, I fear.

"Great," I tell her. "Whatever makes you happy."

What I have learned up here does not make *me* happy. I sigh and step back from the hypnotic highway of the upper air. No tightrope walking for Midnight Louie. I am here to stand on solid ground with the Big Cats, and find out who is playing fast and loose with illusions and fine lines and fine art and lives. Both human and feline.

Chapter 26

A Moving Experience

Temple returned to the Circle Ritz parking lot from a long day of spinning press releases into gold only to find a huge furniture store truck blocking her favorite parking spot under the shade of the lone palm tree.

At least it wasn't a Maylords truck, she thought, remembering her last PR assignment with a shudder. Not only had murder been involved, but one of the victims had been a good friend's significant other.

And not only was the behemoth truck keeping her from preserving her brand-new red Miata from sun damage, but a trio of laboring men were preventing her from entering her own building.

Well, not *her* building. Electra Lark was the landlady.

Electra herself was standing in the parking lot just like Temple, blocked from entering by the humongous cardboard package the visiting apes were wrestling into the Circle Ritz's narrow fifties-vintage back door.

"Quite some carton," Temple said.

"Don't tell me!" Electra said. "I have no idea how that box is going to get up there. The elevator's a thimble and the service stairs turn more often than a corkscrew. And there are two more cartons: box spring and frame. I'm afraid you're stuck in a holding pattern, dear."

"I'm not in a hurry. What on earth is all this?"

Electra, a chubby, cheery figure in a flower-patterned muumuu, her white hair sprayed to match each vivid tropical tone, eyed Temple oddly.

"I can't complain, I guess. He's been such an ideal tenant. Not a speck of inconvenience to anyone. Like a ghost. Until now."

"Who? Mr. Simpson on four?"

"No, Mr. Devine on two. Hold on to your pillbox hat, honey, that mammoth installation is going in right above you. I'd prepare for something going bump in the night, if I were you."

"What do you mean? Matt's above me."

"Well, that's his new bed, from what I can read on the boxes. And I tried to catch every word and number."

"New . . . bed?"

Electra nodded. "I don't know what's gotten into him. He's always been such a quiet tenant. The only significant piece of furniture he's ever imported was that vintage red suede sofa you talked him into. You didn't sweet-talk him into a huge new bed any time recently, did you?"

"*Me?* No!"

Electra turned at Temple's vehement denial to eye her.

Temple had protested too much.

"Is it a waterbed?" she asked quickly to derail Electra's curiosity.

"Nope. The old-fashioned kind. A waterbed would have been easier to lug up two floors, although the frame would be hefty. As far as I can tell, it's the usual king size with some fancy bedstead that must have cost a fortune."

"King size?"

Electra eyed her again. "None of my business, of course, as long as the woodwork isn't damaged. But it's a far cry from that funky old-fashioned twin Matt bought when he moved in."

"A twin. How quaint."

"Poor boy. Just out of the . . . you know, what they call those priest places. I'm glad to see his horizons are apparently expanding."

"Big time," Temple said. "Really, don't worry about everything getting in. The building is old, but my . . . our . . . California king size made it in."

"Of course Max would need a California king size," Electra said. "Such an extravagantly tall fellow like him. And I suppose even Midnight Louie is a yard or more when he stretches out."

"Easily," Temple said quickly, happy to have the bedroom talk shift to her cat as opposed to her significant others. *Other!* Singular.

"I'm pleased, actually," Electra said, wincing despite her words as a workman braced the glass door open with his sweaty back. "Matt deserves a more . . . active social life, don't you think?"

"Absolutely. He deserves anything he can get. Within reason. And . . . within the rules of his religion, of course."

"*Hmmm.*" Electra watched the two beefy deliverymen wrestle the huge cardboard box into her building. "That bed setup doesn't look like it's within the rules of any religion except the *Playboy* philosophy. But that's none of my business."

By which she meant utterly the opposite.

Temple nodded, afraid to say another word.

About fifteen minutes later, Temple was allowed up into her own rooms. Above them came the expected thump and pound of a major furniture installation.

Temple started like a nervous gerbil at every sound. Matt and a king-size bed was not good. Not good for her peace of mind. He'd just semi-proposed to her a few nights ago. Good thing Kit was out flitting about and not here to ask awkward questions.

Temple still didn't know what to make of the proposal, much less a new bed. Beds were way more stressful, actually. Especially when she knew about them. It. Big. Expensive. Not kidding around. The whole enchilada.

Speaking of beds, Midnight Louie was staking his usual claim to hers, which used to be theirs when Max had still lived here. Louie had beaten her home, as usual. That was getting rather uncanny, if she had time to get rattled thinking about it. She would have loved to have a word with him about his New Millennium presence, but, unlike a human roommate, he never explained himself. Maybe that was a consummation devoutly to be wished.

Temple smiled to view Louie's luxuriating black feline form making a swatch like an Asian letter across her zebra-striped comforter. Beds were for stretching and sleeping, Louie announced in his catlike way.

Don't get paranoid about beds, Temple admonished herself.

Then her doorbell rang.

What didn't she want to know now?

By the time she reached the door, she was prepared to be perfectly blasé about any improvements her upstairs neighbor was adding to his apartment.

Blasé went out the window when she found Danny Dove on the threshold, leaning like a lazy imp against the door jamb.

"Danny! How are you? Come in. What a surprise to see you again."

"And these are your Circle Ritz digs. Charming. I adore this building."

Temple recalled that he and Simon had been enchanted with the idea of establishing a pied-a-terre here. Danny Dove, being a major—if not *the* major—Las Vegas choreographer, had a huge house in an older section of town. It was an empty big house since the death of his significant other, whom Temple had met only days before his demise.

So, now their happy chatter about the Circle Ritz resonated like a dirge.

"It's rather small and quaint," Temple said, trying to take the gloss off a rose that had wilted beyond revival.

"That's what we . . . I love about the place." Danny paused in her living room. "May I see the rest of it?"

"I . . . suppose so."

Choreographers are similar to generals. They see and direct the big picture. They push ahead where they're not wanted. Danny headed right for Temple's bedroom.

"Delightful. So *you*. Your cat comes with the decor, I suppose. A touch of black enhances any room. My, these rooms are small! Very difficult to happily integrate such modern necessities as the significant bed or home entertainment system. It appears that each unit in this most admirable building is utterly individual."

"Yes, they're all different. Danny, are you still planning to move here?"

"Maybe. I have to tour the premises first. Oh, look at the shoes! So you, munchkin. You really need a top-drawer display rack for them all. Just like a department store. Shoes Are *Us*."

"Are you . . . getting into interior design?"

He turned and regarded her seriously. "I learned a lot from Simon. Interior design too. I'm happy to share that with my friends. It's a pity to know something and never pass it on."

Temple nodded with a lump in her throat. She didn't fully understand the why and wherefore of Danny's visit, but recognized that it was a kind of catharsis for him.

Danny, meanwhile, was playing the ideal home decor maven. "The cat, I suppose, is not a built-in accessory. He adds a great deal to the ambiance, you know."

Temple couldn't help smiling. "I know. Louie is the mascot of the whole Circle Ritz."

"Master I could believe. *Mascot,* never. Well, thanks for the tour."

"Wait! Danny. Don't you want a . . . cup of tea? Something?"

"Gracious no. I have work to do upstairs."

"Work? Upstairs?"

"I am still consulting, and just now I'm masterminding the choreography of the master suite, of course."

"Matt's?"

"Is there anyone else residing directly above you? I hope not. The dear boy gave me to believe it is to be a bachelor pad, as they used to say before you were born."

"There was a lot they used to say before I was born, such as 'Excuse me?' Matt? A bachelor pad?"

Danny came closer. Despite his curly blond hair, which made him look like a cheerful cherub when he wasn't behaving like a chorusline Nazi, Temple saw that his eyes were sunk in blueberry stains of fatigue.

"Well, that's not a permanent condition, I understand. Why don't you pop up and have a look once the delivery apes have finished destroying the pieces and have clumped their way down the service stairs?"

"No. I can't. I have a huge new client."

"Darling, everything is huge in Las Vegas. Except some well-advertised personal accouterments."

Temple ignored the racy reference. Hard. "It's the New Millennium and their White Russian exhibition."

"That *is* huge." Danny found the idea so intimidating that he plunked his wiry frame down on her Big White Sofa. Busby Berkeley at home, Temple thought recalling the sublime Hollywood choreographer of the thirties. "How'd you nab that account?"

"I know the New Millennium PR guy, and he has his hands full, plus."

"I would think so. White Russians can be so terribly autocratic. Almost as bad as the bureaucratic Red Russians."

"You make Russians sound like varying bottles of wine. You know something about them?"

"Ballet is theirs! Easter eggs are the Ukrainians but they're only peasant paintings. I prefer the Fabergé eggs the Russian czars commissioned."

"The exhibit will have the bejeweled eggs, including some borrowed from the Forbes collection."

Danny whistled. "You're going to need major security."

"Not my responsibility. I just have to make sure that the media I attract aren't jewel thieves in disguise. Of course the real prize is the Czar Alexander scepter."

"How are they going to display that?"

"In a bullet-proof clear plastic Lexan box."

"Last I heard it was worth eight million."

"That's not replacement value. It's priceless. Alexander was the grandfather of the last of the czars, Nicholas Romanoff. My problem is that the sheer worth of these pieces will turn off the national high-culture press."

"Sure. Those arty pencil pushers adore things like yak-spine paintings from the caveman days."

"Reporters are as likely to use PDAs these days as notebooks and pencils."

Danny shrugged. "Speaking of priceless objects, you want to pop up and see the divine Matt's new crash pad?"

When Temple hesitated, he added in a seductive singsong, "He's just come back to view the formal installation and has no one to show it off to."

Temple still wanted to dither, but Danny was looking animated for the first time since Simon's death. Flexing his creative muscles, even on something as trivial as the redo of a friend's decor, was a good sign.

An acquaintance, rather. And not just a room, a straight guy's *bedroom*. A straight guy acquaintance's *bedroom*. The *bedroom* of a straight guy acquaintance who happened to have formally declared an interest in her, Temple Barr.

This was really crowding her comfort zone.

"Dear one, do tell me that what little I can do is worth at least a look," Danny said.

Danny was dear, devastated, devious, devilish, divine.

She caved.

Chapter 27

Bedtime Stories

Temple trudged up the stairs one floor, skipping the elevator to give herself time to think.

She was a friendly neighbor, interested in supporting Danny's recovery after a dreadful loss and Matt's graduation into a fully secular life. Cheerful, helpful. So Doris Day it would make your teeth decay from fifty feet.

She was not a curious, edgy, way-too-turned-on possible partner inspecting a hot new venue: Matt's investment in a big new bed after sleeping on a monklike cot for God knew how long.

That was the trouble. God did know. What would He think of her?

Temple paused in front of the familiar door, then knocked. Of course Matt was here. Danny had just left and told her so.

They hadn't spoken since their incendiary "prom" night on the desert. She hadn't seen him since then. Too late to take the knock back? They weren't ready for this.

She wasn't ready for this.

"Temple." Matt stood in the doorway, looking surprised, then as uncertain as she was.

"I saw Danny on the way out."

"Right. He just left."

"I didn't know you were working with him."

"He insisted."

"On counseling?"

"No, on . . . redecorating." Matt shook his head. "I guess one man's counseling is another man's therapy. It's helped him, I think." Matt's smile was rueful. "He feels sorry for me."

"Do they call that transference, or what?"

"No, not that. I figure if it gets his mind off the past, who am I to refuse to spend big bucks?"

"Well, let's see what big bucks buy." Temple peered past him, which was hard, into the rooms beyond. Matt was wearing the usual soft warm colors that made his blond hair and brown eyes pop, although he didn't know it. Khaki, beige. Like vanilla caramel pudding. Warm vanilla caramel pudding. "This is the first I've heard of a therapist having to spend big bucks to help a client."

"Danny isn't just any client."

"Then that's good because you aren't just any therapist."

"I'm not a therapist at all. I'm a radio shrink."

By then Temple had crossed the threshold. She blinked to see a despised throw rug in front of the fire-engine-red sinuous Kagan couch.

Funny, she'd always pictured . . . never mind.

The gray melamine discount-store cubes in front of the couch had been replaced by mirror-bright stainless-steel cubes.

"Same effect but way upscale," she noted.

"In case you haven't noticed, everything Danny Dove does is way upscale."

"The big production number, the chorus of glittering

dozens. It's his trademark. These improvements do make the room live up to the couch."

"I'm glad you approve. This has forced me to upgrade to a gold card."

Temple turned to Matt. She'd been shy about looking at him because the last time they'd been together had been pretty overheated. He always looked good enough to top with hot fudge and eat slowly with a long-stemmed spoon. Caramel-blond hair, milk chocolate eyes, toasted vanilla skin. He was one way to break your diet without gaining an ounce.

She had to admire Danny's discipline. Dancers had that in spades. Not that Matt was fair game, but Danny's instinct was to move beyond the surface to a genuine impulse to help the man who had helped him.

"I don't know what he's talked me into," Matt said. "It doesn't feel 'me.' "

Matt's "me" was in a state of evolution, maybe even revolution. Temple suddenly realized that she really, really wanted to be there.

"So," she said, not letting her gaze eel away into social evasion. "Show me the new bedroom."

Matt shrugged and opened the door. "It's not that big, Danny said."

Temple refrained from reading anything Danny said (or Matt innocently repeated) the wrong way, but she gasped as the opening door revealed the room beyond. She'd glimpsed this room before, a spare space with jerrybuilt student bookshelves and a barracks brand of simplicity.

The walls were now glazed shiny meringue white. A brushed stainless-steel king-size bed frame with touches of imperial gold thrust four sinuous posts toward the ceiling, where a Casablanca ceiling fan (the brand or the film variety; take your pick of the fantasy) made lazy circles against the daylight-washed curved ceiling.

The mirrored blinds on the window sliced the people on the scene into tantalizing slices of motion and distorted the bedposts into the disconcerting illusion of movement.

"I've never seen Art Nouveau Victorian before," Temple said at last.

"Is that good? Or bad?"

"Depends on what you like." Come to think of it, Matt's bedroom experience *was* a combination of Art Nouveau and Victorian.

"My credit card company likes it a lot," he said.

Temple laughed and turned to look at him, and at a mirrored unit that occupied the wall alongside the door and reflected them both against the sumptuous background of The Bed.

"What's that?"

Matt tapped a pressure hinge and the mirrored doors opened to reveal a big plasma TV screen, speakers, sound system, equalizers. DVD recorder, and possibly an alien spaceship launcher.

"I guess Danny didn't think the living room was big enough for an entertainment center," he said.

"Do you have cable?"

"Cable? Is something falling down?"

"Cable TV."

"Uh. No. Why?"

There would be time later to explain the facts of bedroom life. Maybe. At any rate, Matt was wired for sight, sound, and definitely not Disney entertainment.

"Danny," he said, "suggested that I needed some help with, you know, bedspreads and sheets and things."

"They're gonna run you a fortune."

"Why stop now?"

She glanced at him. The question had a certain edge. It could be about them as well as the room.

Temple escaped by approaching the bed. She absently ran her palm up one serpentine brushed-steel post. Cool. Smooth. Glittering with fugitive gold. The frame was a work of art. How had Danny convinced Matt to pay what it cost?

Of course. It was therapy for Danny. Cost would be no object. Matt had money. He just lacked the lust to spend it. So, Danny made him pay through the nose for a monument to . . . what? Lust? Love. Marital arts?

Matt was her would-be fiancé, and she hadn't given him an

answer. He came up behind her. He might be naive. He wasn't stupid.

"So, what kinda sheets and stuff do I get? And where?"

"Tuesday Morning. Great discount linens. Fabulous stuff. I think . . . this room is basically off-white, silver, and gold. Maybe Greek Isle blues, from indigo to cerulean to teal to turquoise. Come to think of it, that's too big a job for Tuesday Morning. We'll have to hit the boutique bedwear shops in the upscale malls."

"Yeah?" Matt was smiling down at her. "I'd really much rather shop with you than Danny. I like that blue idea. Matches your eyes."

"I've never been a true-blue eye-color person. Just sort of blah gray-blue."

"Silver-blue. That's the way they look in here."

And maybe they did. Danny wasn't beyond establishing a flattering color scheme that would paint Temple right into it.

She was wavering. This was a room where whatever a woman wore would slip down or ride up. Where a man didn't fade into the woodwork but seemed like a Great White Hunter taking a break from the noonday sun.

Max could do this room justice in a New York minute.

Matt would take a while to get into the groove. But he would. And getting him there would be all the fun.

"Temple. We haven't talked."

She didn't talk then.

"Since," he added.

Since.

He'd made a proposal then. Literal. Marry him. On the maybe plan. Civil ceremony. Civil opportunity to undo it all. Not a bad scheme for an ex-priest hooked on a fallen-away Unitarian with a pretty serious ex-Catholic boyfriend.

She had a proposal too.

She reached up, cupped his face in her hands and pulled it down into a kiss that did justice to the room, to Danny's romantic hopes, to her burdened heart, to Matt's expanding psycho-sexual ambitions. She was the experienced one. She shouldn't take advantage of his situation, his dead-serious feelings for her. He'd be so easy to seduce that he . . . was seducing her.

This felt like heaven. The sweet, seriously escalating way he kissed her, his hands clinging to her like she was his personal life raft. The hell with it! She just wanted to sleep with him. Full speed ahead. Damn the torpedoes. She felt him respond heatedly to her mouth, her hands. Want met need met love met sexual steam heat. Ah . . . the Perfect Storm.

She broke away. *She* did. Put a *shushing* finger on his lips.

Somebody had to run for safe harbor before the storm broke and drowned them all.

Chapter 28

Afternoon Delight

Now that Temple's personal life was in a sensual shambles, the art and magic extravaganza at the New Millennium was starting to pull together.

She may have enjoyed a brief encounter, an intimate interlude that had ended in a draw: she and Matt had both drawn back, shaky, from a brink that was still awaiting them with a sweet, edgy certainty. Hesitation only intensified the Danse Romantique.

But crass reality didn't slow down life crises for a second.

The media, like a Roman coliseum audience having had a dead body thrown to it, had buzzed around like flies. Then they'd accepted the notion of a petty thief caught in his own inept web and moved on to other, more gruesome crimes. Hanging was so bloodless.

And Art Deckle's rap sheet was too penny ante to present a serious threat to such a major event. He was a fruit fly caught on adhesive paper meant for a far larger pest.

Temple felt rather bad about that. She considered that if she *really* wanted to really feel bad, she'd make sure she and Max rendezvoused soon so they could seriously examine the state of their union.

But she didn't feel quite up to that yet after her brief but warm encounter with Matt yesterday afternoon.

So, she lingered at home for a change, brooding over her four P.M. energy-boost coffee and yogurt smoothie while Kit padded back and forth from the living room to her office bathroom with an ex-actor's heavy-lidded dislike of mornings.

"You must have been up really late," Temple said as her bath-robed aunt sleep-walked past for the sixth time. "I'm sorry this New Millennium project has put the kibosh on our running around town and having fun."

"Don't be." Kit paused beside Temple at the kitchen counter stool and yawned. "I *have* been running around and having kinky fun anyway."

"But Vegas isn't a place to see all by your lonesome."

"Who said I was lonesome?"

"I thought we'd do all these girly things, like the hotel world-class shopping malls."

"That will be fun." Kit hopped up on the adjacent stool and poured coffee into a clean mug.

"There's Splenda in the dish."

"No thanks."

"Cream or milk in the fridge."

"No thanks. I want this cup as hot as hell, as black as sin, and as strong as the devil."

"Goodness, Auntie!"

". . . has nothing to do with it, as Mae West remarked. I didn't come in until four A.M., but you were slumbering like the babe you so clearly are in my memory. Glad I didn't upset your dreams."

"Four A.M., Aunt? What were you doing?"

"None of your business, Niece."

"Have you picked up some gambling jones while I wasn't watching? Mom would never forgive me."

"Why should she? She never forgave me."

"Forgave you for what?"

Kit's pale blue eyes, now half open, eyed Temple over the mug's thick rim.

"Let me count the ways. For being her younger sister. For majoring in something as impractical as theater, for leaving Minnesota when I was twenty-two, for never marrying, for actually getting acting jobs in New York, for never having kids, for becoming a writer on top of everything when I got too old to play thirty-somethings."

"Kit. I thought you and mom were . . . okay with each other."

"There were just two of us, Temple. Two sisters only a couple years apart in age. That's an awful lot of sibling rivalry for one family. Didn't you ever wonder why you were her *fifth* child?"

"That did seem like a lot of kids for Protestants in Minnesota, but my oldest brothers were already in high school when I came along and seemed more like . . . cousins or young uncles. Come to think of it, somebody did once suggest to me that my family was so large because my parents wanted a girl."

"That may have been part of it, but who wouldn't have wanted you?" Kit smiled fondly as she stroked Temple's blond hair. "You were adorable. I was almost ready to escape back to New York with baby you. Yeah, I think Karen really, really wanted a girl. Because she was the older sister and she always thought they hadn't raised me right. But then you turned out to love all the things I had. Theater. Writing. Fascinating guys who aren't about to settle down to nine-to-five jobs and backyard barbecues. With lutefisk yet. Life isn't fair."

"Oh." Temple had never seen her family like that, through the opposite end of a telescope, far and wee, as a whole unit of time and distance and many different personalities. She

was that little red dot, there, on the fringes of the four boister-
ous older brothers and her harried parents. Like a little red
wagon left out in the rain.

She was supposed to be Kit, only doing the right Minnesota
thing: staying in the home state, marrying and having kids,
driving a minivan, and not worrying about dead men hanging
from bungee cords. Or what her magician boyfriend was really up to, or whether she should marry an ex-priest at a Las
Vegas wedding chapel, maybe even with Elvis officiating. . . .

"Oh," Temple said. "So that's it. That's the vague something I always felt. I was a disappointment."

"Not to me, kiddo." Kit chimed mug brims with her. "Just
don't go all Carpool Mom on me now. I was out until four. So?
I don't ask what your ex-live-in does when he comes creeping
in at three A.M., do I?"

Temple felt her face flushing, not a good complement to
ice-cool blond hair.

"Listen," Kit said, "I am very carefully not prying into your
love life, although your landlady has told me 'The Tale of the
Bed' one floor up in lavish detail."

"Things are a little . . . unsettled lately," Temple confessed.

"No kidding."

"So . . . what about *your* love life?"

Kit lifted her cup in a toast. "Viva Fontana!"

"What? All of them?"

"I'm flattered by your question, but no, alas. I'm not as
young as I used to be. Aldo and I have been doing the town."

"Aldo?" Temple rapidly pulled up a mental image of a
lineup of Fontana brothers. They had such an impact en
masse: tall, dark, handsome guys in pale designer suits with
an air of concealed Berettas and expensive cologne possibly
named Vendetta. Nine in all, not counting their brother Nicky,
the clan's white sheep, who owned the Crystal Phoenix Hotel
and Casino. They had always treated Temple like a kitten
among a litter of adolescent Dobermans, protective and play-
ful and ever so careful to see that she never got hurt.

They were like fairy-tale brothers, she realized. Not rough
or teasing and distant like her four real brothers, but courtly
and happy and good to have on her side and really cool to be

seen with. Now her own aunt Kit was poaching on one of her idealized foster family.

"Isn't the age difference—?" Temple began.

"Math was never your strong suit, right?" Kit asked.

"No," Temple said meekly.

"Figure it out. Ten brothers. Even a Mafia matron could hardly crank 'em out faster than one every eighteen months to two years. The eldest Fontanas are pushing fifty."

"No!" Temple felt a cherished assumption melt like cardboard in the rain.

"Well, forty-five anyway," her aunt temporized in the face of Temple's horror. "Cheer up. That's mid-life, a stage that lasts a whole lot longer these days. Anyway, I'm not exactly robbing the cradle."

"Oh." That meant her aunt was *sleeping* with a Fontana. "But you must be—"

"Don't go there, kid, or I'll call your mother on you."

Sixty, Temple was thinking. Her mother was way past sixty, like sixty-three. Kit was almost there. She was cool, yes, and didn't act her age. Just like the Fontanas.

Oh.

"So what's going on with you?" Kit asked, pouring more coffee.

Kit's eyes were wide open now. She had a pretty square face with strong, camera-loving features: sharp jaw, small nose, high cheekbones, deep-set eyes. She looked, with her attractively faded reddish hair tousled and her glasses off, maybe . . . forty-something.

More like Temple's big sister than her aunt.

"Not much lately," Temple admitted after sipping straight black bitter coffee. She was too listless for some reason this afternoon to rustle up the fake sugar and watery milk that usually adulterated her morning coffee. "Max and I don't seem able to coordinate our schedules these days."

"Maybe more than bad timing is the problem. What about Mr. New Bed upstairs?"

Temple groaned. "I don't know."

"What don't you know? You don't really dig him? He has bad habits, like cleaning his toenails with a beer opener? I would think an ex-priest would be incapable of being unfaithful, but then I would have left my kiddies with one before the headlines came out."

"None of that, Kit. There's nothing wrong with him."

"Nothing? He's a saint?"

"Almost. Well, his faith might force him to have kids."

"Faith equals force. You gotta love it."

"I guess that's it. Faith is important to him. He's working his way through what kind of life he can live with it."

"And you come second."

Temple stirred her coffee so *not* in need of stirring with a nearby fork while she thought. Not so much thought, but worked out her emotions. "Doesn't look like it. Looks like I could call the shots. And that's a lot of responsibility. Who wants to supplant the Virgin Mary?"

"No modern woman. Doomed to lose all she cared about and be married to a eunuch."

"You are so irreverent. Do you work at it?"

"Daily, my dear. It's a requirement for living in New York City. So. Matt sounds serious. What are you going to do about Max? He's not chopped liver either."

"I don't know! But Max hasn't come up with the *M* word lately, and Matt has. That means I'm running out of time. I have to give Matt an answer."

"You don't have to but it would be merciful." Kit sighed. "Got a little flavoring for this coffee? It's seven P.M. in Manhattan."

"What goes with coffee?"

"During a major-life-decision discussion like this, anything eighty proof."

Temple pawed through her lower cabinets until she brought out the battered bottle of Old Crow. She poured some in her aunt's mug, then more when ordered to. She kept her own mug alcohol free.

"Okay." Kit took a long swallow, then spoke, her slightly husky voice so like Temple's. She was really more like Temple's mother than Karen.

Temple now understood that had always rankled her mother.

Things ran in families: talents, voice quality, looks. Sometimes in just the wrong members of the family.

"You have to," Kit said, "find and follow your heart. Which direction is it going?"

"Both! Honestly, Kit. I was crazy in love with Max. Then he vanished for a year for pretty good reasons. That gave me just enough time to really get to know Matt. He was playing catch-up with life. I know what he feels for me started because I helped him when Max was gone. But . . . he's all caught up now, and he wants an answer. He wants me."

"And—?"

"It's mutual but I still love Max. I don't get it. How can I feel this way?"

"You're such a chick out of the shell here."

"I'm thirty, for God's sake. I should know what I want and what I want to do."

Here Kit laughed uproariously, and she'd only had one swallow so far of the doctored coffee.

"You think you will ever know exactly what you want? Let me clue you in, Niece. Thirty. I'm almost twice that . . . no, I won't get more specific. None of your business.

"Want to know what issues I'm dealing with? For one thing, all the men my age are facing prostate problems."

"Mom has mentioned that some men—"

"*All* men. Cancer is just the poisonous icing on an unpalatable cake. The aging dough is . . . how shall I say it to a tender blossom of thirty? Well, the songwriter Leonard Cohen said it best, 'I ache in the places I used to play.' "

When Temple remained stunned and speechless, Kit shrugged. "I guess you have to hear it in his own post-midlife growl. Anyway, a younger man makes a lot of sense to an aging single woman. And I haven't told you what starts happening to women at forty or so."

"Forty!" Temple felt her jaw drop. That was only a decade away.

Kit leaned closer. "Your mother didn't tell you?"

Temple leaned closer and reached for the bottle of Old

Crow. "They don't talk about things like this in Minnesota. At least not to me."

"Peri-menopause," Kit intoned as if naming some hideous harpy from a Greek tragedy.

"I've heard about menopause, but this peri-thing . . ."

"No one tells you it starts in your forties. First, you feel as frisky as a sex kitten. But that's just a last gasp. Then, you hit the dry period, then the hot and sweaty and sleepless period, only you have nothing really good to do while you're lying awake all that time. Then, the earlier 'symptoms' settle in for a nice long stay, and you hit the emotional roller-coaster period. And no one can stand to be around you. And then you have no periods. And then you're over the hill and sixty is looming."

Temple saw Sixty Looming. She saw far ahead on the road of life over the daily hills and dales to a big sign by the side of the highway: sixty miles per hour. The speed limit. All she could do. And her oil was dry, her air-conditioning was inoperative, her ragtop had turned gray . . . and that was *only* thirty years away.

She looked back down the highway as far as she could see. There was a tiny sign. She'd made the trip this far in the blink of an eye . . . she looked ahead. She would hit sixty in a blink as rapid and unexpected.

She eyed her aunt, who nodded soberly.

"On the other hand," Kit said, "there are vitamin supplements that are claimed to be effective, and a younger man can work wonders."

In her mind, Temple deserted her car, her darling zippy new little red Miata, and ran screaming down the highway.

But . . . which way?

Chapter 29

Little Black Dress

The Circle Ritz's sole elevator ground through its rare, mysterious movements in the middle of the night like a cranky architectural bowel. This was past the middle of the night. Past two A.M.

Temple thought of the timeline documentaries PBS liked to present: if all human history was a clock and it was one minute to midnight, we, the people, would not even exist. Dinosaurs would rule the earth. As if dinosaurs had ever had political ambitions.

On the other hand, all politicians had dinosaur tendencies.

She next heard the slow approach of footsteps on parquet flooring, a dull *tick-tock, tick-tock,* like a clock. Her heart was off beat, pounding triple time.

A shadow filled the opening to the short hall that led to the unit's front door. The covered light by the door was an old friend to her by now; she'd been here for more than half an hour, but the light was new and blinding to anyone who emerged from the main circular hall. Even a resident.

The shadow had stopped to try to figure out what, or who, she was. The shadow was a bit wary. She bet its heart had speeded up too, but not enough to match hers.

It moved toward her again. Not afraid, just puzzled.

The light hit Matt's features. "Temple?"

"I heard your radio show tonight. It was good. You were good. You always are."

"Thanks. But—"

She didn't say anything else, just let him come closer.

"Is something wrong?" he asked.

Matt lived to fix things that were wrong, you could hear that on his radio advice show. That's why he was such a success, why droves of people called in, wanting his attention, his help, his wisdom, his caring, his voice, his touch. . . .

Except Temple knew now that he wanted her attention, her help, her wisdom, her caring, her voice, her touch. . . .

"Temple?"

It was like some damn jazz ballet in *West Side Story,* slow, dreamy, stagy, romantic as roses. It was driving her crazy.

He came closer. "What are you doing here?"

And then he saw her in the light. What she was wearing. Her explosive silence. What this meant.

His hand reached out, touched the small black buttons down the middle of her dress, the same fitted knit dress, long sleeved, long skirted, closed by black plastic buttons from throat to hemline, that she had worn to his awful stepfather's funeral, a sort of sexual cassock. The very dress she'd worn when he'd melted down afterward. He'd ordered her to keep it. Matt. A man to ask, not to order. To wear it for him at some future time, when the time was right, ripe, for their separate truths and overheated instincts.

She'd unbuttoned the top eight buttons, not being a sadist.

He took in her, the dress, the hour, the place, the words not spoken, and acted.

She was in his arms, in a deep kiss, a tight embrace, as he unlocked the door and pushed their entwined bodies through it. He spun her back against the interior door and their union pushed it shut.

He turned the deadbolt with one hand while pulling her closer and walking her, backward, unerringly through the sinuous path of living room furniture to the bedroom door, which was shut.

There, he kissed his way down the undone buttons and undid a few more, and pushed the bedroom door open, then waltzed her through and kicked it shut behind him and shot another deadbolt—on a bedroom door? Perhaps a wise security device . . . for privacy at any rate.

There she managed a gasp and a few explanatory words. Like they were needed. "I thought it only right that you shouldn't have to inaugurate your new bed by sleeping alone."

"You're after sleeping, are you?"

"Eventually."

They fell together onto the bed, where he ripped the remaining buttons from their tight threaded nests. Temple heard a small plastic rainstorm of hail on the bleached wooden floor.

The bed was a ghostly galleon on a cloud-swept sea as they rocked together in the heart of a storm of their own making, and there was no going back to shore.

Temple tiptoed back to her own condo at five A.M. holding her buttonless dress together fairly unsuccessfully.

Her aunt Kit was awake, sipping cocoa at the kitchen counter.

"You're out later than I was," she observed. "Most impressive, but you *are* younger. Forgive my waiting up. An unexpected maternal spasm. Are you all right? That dress sure isn't."

"I can't talk about it," Temple said.

"Then to bed, as they say in Shakespeare, but you look like you already have been."

Temple toddled into her bedroom, shut the door in Aunt Kit's face, and let the dress fall to the floor. Her underthings and her emotions were in a twist, but the deed had not been done, despite mutual satisfaction on a scale most teenagers would consider quite satisfactory.

She'd gotten cold feet.

Her. Not him.

He'd told her everything. How hooked he'd been on her way, way back when. When they'd first met. His hands and voice had trembled, but she had too, because it was too much, this Perfect Storm. It could eat her alive.

There was nothing blasé about him.

This was the central event of his life. His love. Because he did. Love her. Always. Only. Had burned for her from the first, not understanding why he could think of nothing, no one else. Trying to pull his outward personality together. Trying to respect her wishes, her past alliances. Refraining from undermining Max. Trying even to relate to other women. Recognizing his sexual drive and still coming back, always and only, to her.

She'd never been so touched, so shaken. So . . . okay, Max was a great lover, but this was beyond any experience or anticipation. This shook her to her soul, which she apparently still had. And a conscience too. This maybe was the thing she couldn't live without. Except . . . was she worthy?

The responsibility was numbing. She knew what to do, how to do it, where to do it, but not where it would lead. And it had to lead to something significant, something . . . holy, or it was a lie and cheat and she would die before she would be part of it.

So. She'd chickened out. Matt thought he needed a license, or to offer her the option of one.

She didn't. She needed to believe in what he did. Herself. She'd blown it. Stopped the music when it was the most sublime and irresistible. Still, there was something to be said for coitus interruptus. Like increased desire. The Scarlett in her smiled in hapless helpless kittenish anticipation. Temple tumbled into bed, reliving every instant and enjoying it more with every rerun, even as she shied away from the ultimate truth.

She was headed for the dreaded sixty: better enjoy thirty while she could. But glib answers weren't for her. Or Matt. Or

Max. That's what made them all worth something to each other. My God, they were an awesome triangle! That tripod couldn't keep its balance forever. Could it? At some point, it would be only two, and one would be so alone, and off-balance and hurt.

Temple fell asleep, next waking in the morning light sifting through her bedroom miniblinds. Midnight Louie was snuggled up to her hip, black hair shiny and soft, clawless feet pummeling her back, all dark embracing domestic pet.

She remembered Max and burrowed under the dark of the covers and wept for an hour. She remembered Matt and wept for another hour. She was an equal opportunity wuss.

Until she realized Kit was knocking tentatively on her door, promising coffee, and she knew she had a life-changing decision to make PDQ and a disintegrating status quo to deal with ASAP and a job to do at twelve o'clock high. STAT.

Chapter 30

Cat in the Hat

Is my work cut out for me!

I have not been in such an early morning downpour since my mama done left me by a drainage ditch when she was swept away by one of Las Vegas's tsunami rainstorms. She would not have left by her own druthers, of course. But these gully washers sweep druthers away like dreams.

So there I was, a kit with my ears still wet and getting wetter by the instant. My littermates were leaves in the watery wind. My sire at that time was just a whisper on the desert dust devil.

It was survival of the fittest and I was not very fit at that young age.

My Miss Temple reminds me of my abandoned younger self, and for a moment I could cry cat tears with her. Save that cat tears have never changed anything but the saline composition of my eye fluid.

So.

I could shake the sheets and some sense into my Miss Temple. Like tomorrow is another day and there is always another fine dude in the offing. But she would not listen in her present state, and I cannot blame her. We dudes are sometimes more than somewhat dense.

However, it is clear to me that what she most needs at the moment is not moonlight and roses and regret, but someone steady to untangle the many webs being woven at the New Millennium.

And I have the claws to do it!

I shimmy-shimmy off the zebra-print comforter. I have personally never taken much comfort in stripes of any sort, including tiger. We solid guys are the ones to rely on: solid black cats and . . . black panthers.

Faster than you can hitch a ride on a roller coaster, I am inside the New Millennium and rousting the resident Big Cats in their cages.

They blink and growl and hiss loud enough to fill the sails of a nice little ketch. Where, they ask, is Miss Louise?

While I am tongue-tied—for Louise is holding down the fort at the Crystal Phoenix—I feel an airy feminine presence brush by my side. Feline, of course.

The Big Boys growl in tandem, which—let me tell you—is ear inspiring. Also deafening.

"This is not the valiant daughter of Louie the First," they thunder.

I see Squeaker's narrow tail tremble slightly.

"*You are that sssspolled houssssecat, Hyasssscinth,*" they add hiss to growl.

Well, I am about to be outa there, seeing as one of their mitts would make a giant Freddy Kreuger–like razor-nailed glove, AWOL from Elm Street and in my own back yard. But Squeaker weaves back and forth, tail high and tickling their baseball-mitt-size noses.

"You big dummies," she begins.

I cringe.

"You cannot tell a lilac-point Siamese from a chocolate-point one! Have you ever heard of Siamese fighting fish? You cannot keep two in a bowl, for one will eat the other."

"Eat?" Lucky asks. "I am not into rampant indiscriminate carnivorosity. I am on a strict health regime. I do not eat what I do not know."

"How unfortunate," Squeaker says, "for your social circle."

Kahlúa tries to clear things up. "We do not eat our trainers."

As with dames of all species, explanation is a fatal move. I feel forced to put my body between hers and the Big Cats.

"Give the little lady a break, boys," I urge. "She is new not only to show biz, but the crime beat. Have you two seen anything suspicious?"

"Everything is suspicious to us," Lucky says. "We work for a masked man, and we see workmen crawling around up here where only bats and tree frogs should hang out."

"And then there is the woman," Kahlúa said.

"Shangri-La?"

"Shangri-La-ti-dah," Lucky growls. "She has no time for leopards, but dotes on that skinny, snooty housecat of hers. No offense," he adds in a polite aside to Squeaker.

"At least she is small, as humans go," Kahlúa adds. "Our master has no business risking his neck up here, as he is so large and slow, like a lion."

"And his mask emulating the look of our kind impairs his vision," says Lucky.

"Which is weak and human to begin with." Kahlúa looks out toward the performance area, his vertical pupils instantly adjusting to the change of focus and light, making his point. "One wrong step on those suspended platforms out there and any one of us could come crashing down."

I sense their sincere worry for their master. Now that I hear them discuss it, I realize how dangerous a show this is for the Cloaked Conjuror and his Big Cats. What it offers is a showcase for the lithe Shangri-La and Hyacinth. And the lithe Shangri-La has been involved in criminal shenanigans before this. I wonder how she talked her new partner, CC, into doing this stunt. The New Millennium sure wouldn't want their major attraction executing a swan dive from sixty feet up.

Could the Cloaked Conjuror be blinded by love, or lust?

"She is always telling him what to do," Kahlúa says with disdain. "We are a better-known attraction in Vegas, and Lucky and I do not do more than demur with a friendly growl now and then."

"Really? Shangri-La rules this roost then."

Lucky sniffs and lifts his upper lip to bare truly awesome fangs. It is an expression of total disgust among our kind.

"I could not sleep the other night and I heard them arguing. Well, I heard her arguing, her voice is high and harsh. Our master's voice rumbles deep like a purr. He never says boo back to her."

"The other night?" My ears perk up. "When was it?"

Lucky rubs his huge black nose with an even huger black mitt. These guys are *big*. "Three, four nights ago?"

"The night before the police came?"

"Yeah. Maybe so, now that I think of it." Lucky yawns. "I have a bit of insomnia."

"After what they tried to do to you, I can bet you do," says Kahlúa. "If Miss Louise had not taken things in hand you would not be here and your new name would not be 'Lucky.'"

"Hey," I say, "that was my case, fellas. I had something to do with Lucky's rescue too."

Lucky was purring, so loudly the boys apparently did not hear me. "That Louise, she is a plucky little thing for someone who could be an appetizer for us."

"We would not snack on one of our own species," Kahlúa says quickly.

"Unless we were starving," Lucky agrees.

I back away, just in case the meat truck has been a little slow today.

They have forgotten me anyway. Apparently, they only have eyes for Louise.

I am chewing over what I have learned, anyway, and find it pretty disturbing stuff.

There is a very good chance that *Shangri-La* was the last person to see the late Art Deckle alive, that she wasn't arguing with CC but with Deckle, and that she helped him dive off the platform to his death.

Chapter 31

Accursed

"Well, don't you look like something the wet cat dragged in?"

Randy Wordsworth did a double-take to examine Temple's expression. "Don't tell me there's more bad news about this accursed exhibition."

"Don't call it that. 'Accursed' is the kind of word that takes on a life of its own if the media get ahold of it."

"Maybe you will call it that too when I tell you what the higher-ups learned from the police and told me, confidentially."

"And you'll tell me?"

"They don't know what to do with it and I have a feeling you might."

While Temple mulled that over, she studied the assembling skeleton of the exhibition spaces. Worker ants in white coveralls climbed an elliptical yet narrowing structure, reminding her of slaves laboring on Cheop's Great Pyramid in Egypt.

The pinnacle was the clear Lexan plastic onion-shaped dome. Lexan was Lucite on steroids: impact proof. When the Czar Alexander scepter was suspended above its stone base and a bright pinpoint spot was aimed at all that high-carat jewel fire, the effect would be spectacular.

Already the exhibition's lower levels glittered with period gowns and high-polished furniture, interspersed with islands of imperial silver and gold and more gemstones.

"This should be a knockout, Randy."

"This information should knock you out more."

Temple gave him an inquiring look. Her usual slightly sandpapered voice was raw gravel this morning, thanks to serial sobbing into her pillow. Even Visine had only softened the bloody tinge of her eye whites. Having an emotional meltdown as a blonde was way too risky. Normally, her natural red hair would have deflected interest from her eyes.

"Tell me," she said. Even bad news would take her mind off . . . things.

"The dead guy may have been a petty con man, but he had experience topside in this kind of show. He was, get this, Madame Olga Kirkov's brother. Got his start performing in her traveling ballet company, then came here and got an American citizenship years ago."

Temple allowed herself to look shocked. "Art Deckle had been a Russian ballet dancer?"

"Andrei Dechynevski. He made the leap thirty years ago. Did you know Madame Olga herself had defected from Russia twenty years ago? Back when you couldn't leave the Soviet Union without an escape pod and help from the CIA or an underground group?"

"So, this White Russian exhibition in the white-hot center of American tourism would mean a lot to her. Could she and her brother have been in it together? Why would a respected elder stateswoman of the ballet world want to steal the Czar Alexander scepter?"

"Dunno. Maybe some clever person with a reason to interview the old dame should ask her. You know the ins and outs of this museum/performance fine arts stuff."

"That's true. I do," Temple said. She winced at her last two words. "I will." That wasn't much better. Why did she have vows on her mind? For reasons of breaking or making them?

Concentrating on the weird death—and now strange family history—of Art Deckle might take her mind off . . . other things.

After inquiring, Temple was directed to the second-floor meeting room that served as exhibition headquarters. She found her way to the same oblong room wrapped around a very long conference table littered with architects' floor plans and elevations.

It was her luck that Madame Olga was the only one here. The old woman was sitting cross-legged like an elf atop the table, studying the pale blue lines of the drawings. The prominent veins in her hands and arms were even more vivid than the sketch lines.

Still, her back and spine were ruler straight. That she maintained that ballerina's combination of flexibility and ramrod posture was amazing for a woman of her age. Maybe Aunt Kit was mistaken about inevitable female decrepitude. Just a little.

"Ah." The woman looked up with a grateful sigh. "My eyes are seeing double on these drawings. Just the one to make it all come clear. Miss Barr, is it?"

"Yes. Why are you sitting *on* the table, may I ask?"

"Why not?" The age-faded face wore a pixieish grin. Madame Olga reminded Temple of an octogenarian teenager, a total contradiction in impressions. "Come. Join me, child. You can't see anything right unless you're in the middle of things."

Or the muddle of things. That's where Temple was right now.

"I don't know if I can—"

"Not in those high heels. Leave them on the floor."

"But . . . I'm not wearing stockings." She didn't feel that bare-foot odor was suitable for the woman's turned-up yet aristocratic nose.

"Excellent. Stockings only cut off circulation. High heels are the average woman's equivalent to toe shoes. They strengthen the line of the leg and intensify the curve of the calf. Very sexy, my dear. Do you dance?"

"Only socially. A little."

"Pity. You have dancer's legs. I noticed that immediately. I always judge people by their legs. A clumsy leg betokens an idle mind and crooked legs signify a twisted soul. Your legs are slender and straight. You can be trusted."

Temple hoped Max would agree with that evaluation.

"Why are you here to see me? You *are* here to see me?"

"Um . . . yes, I am." Temple gazed at the architectural renderings papering the wooden tabletop. She felt she was at the Mad Hatter's Tea Party without tea, and with only one very old, eccentric, and formidable guest.

She eyed the old lady next to her, who seemed her own height.

"It's funny," Temple said. "I always feel short but I don't now that I am sitting next to you."

The black eyes in that pale, blue-veined face crackled with energy and amusement.

"The best ballerinas, my dear, are petite. We reach for the sky, or the flies, when we go *en point,* our arms high above our heads. We then become one elegant attenuated line, as if suspended from an invisible thread of spider silk. There is nothing like it in the performing arts. We are the centerpiece. The male dancer is but a suitor, a slave, a mere prop to our strength and certainty. We are queens. We are the Alexander scepter of the stage. We are czarinas. We defy gravity."

Temple was reminded of Mariah Molina's performance song at the recent Teen Queen pageant. "Defying Gravity" was from the Broadway hit *Wicked,* based on the imagined lives of the good and evil witches from *The Wizard of Oz*.

The confluence of ideas and images confused Temple. Just as they did in her personal life. Everything seemed weighted now. Significant. Painful. Liberating.

Was she consorting with a wicked witch, White Russian style?

Madame Olga had no doubts. "You have not come to me for affirmation, but confirmation. Am I right?"

"You must always be right," Temple said with a grin.

"I am old enough to give that impression, but my early life was struggle, disappointment, frustration. Uncertainty. I deserted my homeland because it was in the hands of venal bureaucrats. I left my family because they were broken and accepted it. I abandoned my one true love because he could not change. I gave myself to my art because it was cruel and demanding, but it gave me wings."

The old woman's knotty but strong finger speared a point on a nearby drawing. The sketch of the Alexander scepter's installation.

"This is the nexus. The link between the Old World I loved that nurtured my family line and my art, and this New World that makes art into spectacle. Still, that is a kind of immortality. They draw on the same energy, *River Dance* and *Swan Lake*."

"A peasant form and an aristocratic one?"

"They are the same. If you do not understand that, you do not understand art. That is why I embrace this American potpourri of commerce and art. Why I lend my name, which is all the power I have left."

She flexed a bare instep, drawing it almost into the image of a bound Chinese foot, all exaggerated curve of arch with the toes curled into crippled insignificance underneath it.

Temple winced to witness that ingrained deformity. Were her own means of borrowed height that disabling? No, she wore heels only for short periods. If she could have gone *en point*, maybe she wouldn't have worn them at all.

"What do you want to know?" the old woman asked.

What not?

Temple tried to fix herself in here and now, job and profession. She wasn't a czarina, but she was a media mistress.

"The dead man was your brother?"

"Yes, a long-lost one. I had no idea until the police confronted me with evidence of his identity. He was the only family member besides me who left for America. I sought art, he sought profit. Still, I had a soft spot for him. Is that the expression? Yes. He wished to seize this world and make it his, as I did. He had a crooked leg and insufficient art, thus he took the name 'Art.' He had a certain nerve and desire. I liked him. He was the peasant, asking for more than crumbs from the indifferent table.

"Early on, I found employment for him among my company, but he had higher ambitions and lower means. He left. I never saw him for, um, perhaps twenty years. Until he hung dead over this exhibition and of course had become unrecognizable to me. That clown-white painted face was both a disguise to the end and an editorial comment."

"You don't think it odd that the person who threatened this show, this exhibition, should be a shirt-tail relative of yours?"

" 'Shirt tail.' So casual. So American. No, I don't think it odd. I think that this exhibition brilliantly combines Old World and New. Old troubles and new ones."

"Had he become a terrorist?"

"Andrei? He had not a political bone in his body. He had no bones at all. He was a tool, not a terrorist."

What a pitiless assessment of a life. A death.

"And what of Ivan Volpe?"

"What of him?" Madame Olga asked with supreme indifference.

"Might he have a motive for disrupting the exhibition or stealing the scepter?"

"He has a motive for self-advancement. He is one of those sad, professional displaced Russians, consoling themselves with exile in Paris. His whole family was of the same, spineless stock. First to leave, and last to lament the great, grand old days. I would not be surprised if he would some day soon produce another candidate as offspring of the mystical Anastasia."

"Czar Nicholas's daughter who was rumored to have escaped the family slaughter."

"People love legends that never die. Why else does *Swan Lake* persist, and the paintings of Van Gogh. And sightings of Elvis Presley? Even those who are not Russian need their icons."

Icons referred originally to the gilt-touched paintings of

Russian Orthodox saints. Like many specific words, it had been adapted to apply to modern idols as well as holy figures: to rock stars and Hollywood legends. Even to a blue-collar boy from Tupelo, Mississippi. Just as the word "diva" had been plucked from the operatic world to revert to pop music stars.

Things always went from the sublime to the ridiculous, Temple reflected. Maybe even murder.

Temple nodded her thanks to Madame Olga for her time and her insight. She skittered across the tabletop, pushing papers away like leaves, and hopped down onto solid ground to push her toes back into her usual high heels.

She wasn't sure she needed to feel taller anymore. Just grounded.

Chapter 32

A Bottle of Red, a Bottle of White Russian

He scared her.

She'd asked for this interview, but it scared her.

She wasn't the police. She was a PR person with a license to snoop. She was messing in what could turn out to be an international incident, but she had a pressing need to know. For her job. For her peace of mind about what had happened on her watch.

So she was scared, not because he was a scary guy, he was just so totally different. He was a living legend. A Russian aristocrat who'd become a French citizen. The aristocrat and French parts were paramount.

Temple recognized that Ivan Volpe was a rare breed, someone a midwestern mutt like herself would ordinarily never have crossed paths with. Except in Las Vegas. She also recognized that he traded on his unique, blue-blood-drenched background to make himself into a high-flying standard of the Jet Set.

Madame Olga was an aristocrat of the stage. Temple could recognize that honor and deal with it. Danny Dove was a commercial version of Madame Olga. Their common tongue was "theater, dance, art," and Temple spoke that, albeit humbly.

But "Count" Volpe. He flummoxed her.

She had been an essay contest finalist once, back in college, for one of those "one-year editorships" at a women's fashion magazine. Several months of demanding editorial entries had culminated in a group of twelve finalists spending five days inside a Manhattan whirlwind learning experience. The two midwestern finalists were like token blacks: in for the appearance of equity, out for the reality.

She had met him before. *The* Ivan Volpe, a Russian émigré with an Italian last name. Her, a tiny girl in a little black cocktail dress (the magazine had corrected her self-description to "after-five" dress) introduced in a Manhattan penthouse to a tall, aristocratic Russian émigré, a consulting director, impoverished but possessed of major snob appeal, at a cocktail (Temple hoped that designation was chichi still) party catered totally by blacks in black tail serving platters featuring gross and relatively raw truncated parts of animal life.

"Do you speak Russian?" the anorexic magazine editor who'd introduced her to this *blanc eminence* had asked Temple over the beef tartare.

Heck, no! Why should she?

Probably because it was the current trendy major at the Eastern women's colleges. Minnesotans like Temple majored in English. Duh.

"No!" Temple had dead panned in a Russian accent right out of *Ninochtka* (the thirties movie with Garbo; if you're gonna steal, steal from the best). "I do *not* speak Rrrrussian."

A dead pause.

When Volpe had laughed, long and hearty, the snooty editor had been required to produce an anemic snark.

Temple hadn't won the competition, although she'd seen signs that her entries had been winners. A deadly dull girl from an Eastern "Sacred Seven" college and an über-wealthy and aristocratic family had won. And to think all this American aristocracy had started with that dinky scruffy ship called the *Mayflower*. Temple had never heard of any of her group of twelve again.

But here was Count Volpe, twelve years later: tall, straight, white-polled, intimidating.

"I do not speak Rrrrussian," Temple declaimed in her best Garbo voice.

His white lashes blinked. He visibly scanned for the first recording of their meeting, and found it, though he was past ninety now. Then he laughed again.

"*Ninochtka!* Hah! Your hair used to be Communist red. I remember. Now you are White Russian blonde, but you are still spirited. They were all such bloody bores, weren't they?"

Temple grinned.

"And look at you! A player on the Las Vegas scene. How can I help you? Dinner, of course. Later. I must discover how you have got here, along with that most . . . interesting hair. I, alas, must take whatever 'gig' my advanced age permits. Like reality TV. I have always been a showpiece. Blue blood is very rare in the modern world. I hope not to shed any more than I can spare. But this exhibition seems to require human sacrifice. I remember the last czar, can you believe it? I was an observant and prescient infant. And my memory has always been my meal ticket. Dinner. Will your hotel pay?"

Imagine!

She, Temple Barr, taking a Russian count out to dinner. On her expense account. An account for a count. For which she expected a full account of what was going on at the White Russian exhibition.

"I have become a professional consultant," he explained as

they awaited their cocktails in the Pluto Pavilion restaurant. Pluto was the farthest out planet in the solar system, and this restaurant was the New Millennium's farthest out in menu and prices.

"Why not?" he asked rhetorically. "I am quotable, suitably distinguished, old but still mobile. I am camera ready. I have nothing to lose."

"I guess your family lost it all in the revolution."

"Yes. You Americans are just now getting a glimpse of how much can be lost so quickly. But I do not talk about the bad old days. I radiate their lost glamour. I bow and kiss hands. I assiduously ensure that I have not lost my heavy Russian accent and overlay it with a fine soupçon of French. In the old days, in Russia, my very, very young days, I had been born a prince of privilege. Here, at the beginning of another century, I have become a prince of media. The celebrity photographers rejoice to 'shoot' me arm in arm with Paris Hilton and her puppy dog. I would say 'just shoot me,' but I am too old to object to being still valuable in any arena, even that of mockery."

Temple frowned as much as she was capable of, which wasn't a lot. She was still too much of an optimist.

"When we met," she pointed out, "you were playing that same role for the fashion magazine."

"Of course. Trot out the old dog to do new tricks. I was being used as much as you were, my dear."

"I really, really wanted to win and live in New York on their pittance of a salary and shock them all and become a famous writer or fashionista, but an original."

"And so, what have you become?"

"You've seen it. A freelance public relations person. At least I work for myself."

"*Ummm,*" he said in a dubious British way. He had an international air, man without a country. "Then why are you probing the whyfores and whereabouts of our entire cast of culture vultures, as I believe we are called by the hoi polloi, during the time in which that rather vulgar fellow fell to his rather careless death?"

"It's not enough to wait for the coroner and police to come

to a conclusion. I need to know what might be behind the death so I can deal with the press. The opening is only days away. If the Czar Alexander scepter is stolen, it will ruin the exhibition and the hotel's new museum. They won't be able to book an exhibition of sweat socks after that."

Volpe lifted one expressive eyebrow. "No? Sweat socks sound like the essence of Modern Art to me."

By then their White Russian drinks had arrived and Temple was taking some solace in sipping a cocktail that tasted more like dessert than some Nouveau Cuisine blueberry aspic flan with seaweed garni.

"The key to a robbery," she said, "is who would want the scepter."

"It's a priceless artifact and quite beautiful. Who would not?"

"But what would anyone do with it?"

"There are always the rogue collectors, my dear. I find them fascinating, and am sure that I've met a few. They are fabulously rich, their walls are papered with Old Master paintings, and yet you suspect that somewhere in some bank vault of a room they harbor some of the century's missing masterpieces for their own private delectation, almost like an upscale pornography collection."

Temple made a face. People like that were true culture vultures, accent on the word "vultures."

"It is pornography or greed that inspires your obvious distaste?" he asked.

"That kind of greed *is* pornographic."

"Nothing I can exercise, in case you're wondering." Volpe shook out his French cuffs, displaying his gold-and-malachite cufflinks. "I earn a decent, vulgar salary with consulting positions like this, but I earn my living as a professional guest and 'interesting person' on three continents. I could never afford to underwrite a major art theft, much less sit on the monetary results of it. And, as you say, the scepter is too rare and valuable to merely sell."

By then the salads had come, frills of greens obviously hydroponically grown on Mars. Temple had seen curled dandelion stems (as a child, when that had been a game) that looked more edible. A bowl of dressing with little black specks that looked like nits floating in it sat alongside her plate.

Volpe noticed her dubious summation and called the waiter over. "Russian dressing, if you please."

"This is the house recipe—"

"And most tasty upon a house, no doubt. But we celebrate all things Russian here." As the waiter whisked away the offending bowls, Volpe leaned over the table, and said sotto voce, "A bottled mayonnaise–heavy abomination, I foresee, but better than that green mess with the measles."

Temple laughed. "So. If a spoiled billionaire didn't order the scepter stolen, who else would want to take it?"

Volpe folded his arthritic yet graceful hands under his chin, resting it on one pointed forefinger. "You think too reverentially, in terms of Great Art, or Great Decoration, in this instance. Have you considered Eastern European politics, my dear? Such a ripe field for treachery. All those barbarous Asian states nestled up against Mother Russia's far eastern flanks. Terrorists of the Muslim persuasion? Oh, the global ramifications, plus the jewels wrested out of their frame, worth enough to fund any amount of lethal mischief anywhere. Osama bin Laden isn't made of all the money in the world. An influx of imperial Western wealth would be welcome to aid in its downfall."

"That would make more sense of Art Deckle's involvement. Terrorists might recruit someone dubious like him. And terrorists of all stripes now attack Russia, including Muslim Chechen rebels."

"How history turns. So amusing. I remember when our Russians were rebels against their countrymen. Now, they are besieged from without. 'Art Deckle,' by the way! The man had gone utterly show biz. A sad fate for Olga's brother, once a promising ballet dancer."

"That would make him adept at upper-air acrobatics, though, the kind necessary to attack the scepter from above."

"True. But his injury had been devastating: the leg shattered from ankle to thigh. He would have been mad to attempt such a feat."

Temple nodded. Max could do it. Maybe had done it, who

knows? He didn't seem to be confiding in her anymore. She swallowed a lump of regret, remembered her own torn emotions, tried to think more generously. And who was to say this recent death hadn't been a tragic accident? Maybe Art-Andrei had been trying to prove to his sister that he still had the chops to perform, if not in this show, in another?

Their entrees arrived while she mused, and she shook off her speculations to find Count Volpe's dark eyes focused solely on her face.

"You pity that dead man," he said.

Yes, and all the performers who meant to fly and who are then deprived of that freedom, the Mystifying Max included.

"It must have been a diminished life."

"And a diminished death. Trapped like a fly in amber in that net of elastic cord. Olga would never admit it, having long ago become the Iron Woman the ballet demands, but she felt the shattering of her brother's leg long ago in her own imperious limbs. She cannot be as indifferent to his final death here, and now, as she pretends."

"She pretends?"

"Don't we all, Miss Ninotchka? We White Russians who . . . decorate . . . this mummer's show pretend we are content in our remade Western lives, but we ache for the old days we barely remember. We weep to see our people consuming two quarts each of vodka a day, and being known for a gray, laboring life in the shadow of a Kremlin that is scattered and attacked and, sadly, second rate now in world affairs."

Temple felt for the old woman and her cataclysmic times.

She ached for her own old days that she could so readily remember and wept inside to think of Max trapped and reduced, and herself safe elsewhere. Happy.

Chapter 33

The Wrath of Carmen

The house was empty.

Molina slapped her car keys onto the high counter that divided kitchen from living room.

When had Mariah's schedule gotten tighter, busier, more demanding than hers?

Band practice. Soccer practice. Cheerleader practice. (Boys still dominated basketball, but there was a fledgling girls' team. Not for Mariah. Too short. Hence, a cheerleader.)

The striped cats, Tabitha and Catarina, came twining around her ankles, mewing, plaintive. They were suffering from *Home Alone* syndrome too.

Carmen unloaded a couple of cans of cat shish kebob or

whatever onto some saucers and put them on the floor. The cats settled down to eat, feet neatly tucked.

That reminded Carmen to kick off her leather loafers, murder in this hot weather, and lift her legs one by one to peel off the knee-highs she wore with them. Sure, Temple Barr could clatter around bare legged on her perky mules or whimsical high-heeled sandals. She was a PR woman in the entertainment industry. Dignity was not a job requirement. Carmen padded barefoot on the cool laminate floor to the fridge to extract a Dos Equis. Kid not home; mom could chill out. As much as mom could ever chill out.

Female homicide lieutenants did not ever want to look bright and breezy. Carmen shook her head. This was a tourist town where the street cops wore summer uniforms of beige Bermuda shorts, but casual was not an option for her.

And that was okay. She wasn't a casual kind of person. Casual doesn't cut it working your way up on the force, being a single mother. *Aaaiiy!*

She sat heavily on the off-beige sofa covered in a wide-woven jute fabric. Fairly cool. The shoes and socks had left welts on her arches and ankles. So had the ankle holster she'd taken off first.

She'd left her guns on top of the eating bar. Mariah wasn't here. Cats don't have opposable thumbs to handle firearms. She'd stow them in the bedroom gun safe after she'd cooled off with half a beer.

Condensation dimpled the brown bottle. Dew for the drinking woman. The beer tasted effervescent and stinging.

So. Mariah was off social butterflying. Maybe Larry was off. Carmen felt like some adult company. Tabitha ratcheted up the side of the couch to one arm, then blinked solemn yellow eyes at her. *Me? Snag upholstery?*

Cats were born hostile witnesses. Mum to the max.

Max.

Carmen made a face. Her deal with Temple Barr was going south before the ink was barely dry. That swing-style death at the New Millennium had Max Kinsella's imprint all over it. The only oddity was that it wasn't Kinsella himself throttled and hung out to dry.

Maybe someone else felt the same way as she did, and had missed his or her mark. Carmen stretched her bare toes into the only sand available to her . . . the sandy beige nubbles of cheap wall-to-wall carpeting.

Maybe the place could use some updating, but with Mariah's college tuition looming . . .

Carmen sipped beer, then stowed the bottle on a terra cotta coaster on her coffee table. Now that she'd wound down a little, she was aware of a tiny distant sound.

Outside? Some neighborhood low-rider twenty blocks over?

And there was a smell.

She eyed the cats, the usual source of unlikely smells. They had moved away from their half-demolished dishes to tongue-scrape their whiskers, faces, and feet clean.

Good children with bright shining faces.

The distant insectlike buzz of semi-music was putting her to sleep. Like she didn't lose a lot of it in the night. And the scent. Heavy, come to think of it. Sweet. The way death was sometimes, in the earliest stages, before the sour . . .

Molina shot to her feet, bare toes digging in so she could charge in any direction. She eyed the black, dead bug–like silhouettes of her guns on the pale kitchen countertop.

She ran to grab them, secured one in each pocket of the hot polyester-blend blazer she'd still kept on. In this climate, linen and cotton wrinkled like your grandfather's forehead from sitting at desks and in cars.

The cats leaped onto the abandoned sofa, claiming her vacant spot. They always wanted to be where you were, where you had been.

Maybe somebody else did too.

Her cell phone was on the coffee table. It wasn't like her to strew her belongings around, but the day had been hot and Mariah was gone again, and maybe she'd felt a false sense of solitude and security in her own home.

A homicide lieutenant should know better.

She snatched up the phone, pressed it on, hit . . . Larry's number. Didn't hit TALK.

She was carrying a 9-millimeter Glock and the Colt Pocket Lite. If she couldn't handle vague buzz and sniff without backup, she might as well use her shield for a beer coaster.

The house was older than she was. Laid out like a thick-waisted hourglass. Kitchen, dining, and living areas off the attached garage; long narrow hall with bedrooms and bath leading off that.

Modest house. Modest neighborhood. Fairly safe unless the Hispanic gangs were at it on your front doorstep, which they usually knew better to avoid in her case.

And so she walked into her own hall with the 9 millimeter cupped in a two-handed grip, elbows braced, body sideways.

Mariah could have left her bedroom stereo on. The sound was still soft, but louder here. A Latino station celebrating *la vida loca* in ways Ricky Martin had never thought of.

The odor hit her as sharply as vomit the minute she crossed into the hall's eternal shadow. Houses in Las Vegas demanded interior darkness. Cool. Shelter from the sun.

She looked down, took a moment to focus.

She stepped in the smell, and made it sharper. Sweet.

Carmen bent to touch the dark red ovals that dotted the bland hall carpet.

Velvety. Thick. Saturated with scent.

Rose petals. Crushed to release scent. Each a separate blot on the carpet, like gouts of blood.

Sweet. Sick.

She followed the trail, knowing this was intended, her stomach twisted with anxiety. Mariah's room on the right. Was that where the muffled music was coming from?

Call in? Call backup? Call Morrie? Call Larry?

Someone had been playing games with her for weeks. Leaving things in the house, announcing a bold come-and-go presence. At first, she'd doubted her own senses.

Not anymore.

Oh, God! And if Mariah wasn't out as announced? Wasn't doing teenage overtime on the social circuit? If she was still here, in that room where the rose petals led and the music was just a shadow of itself . . .

She came almost abreast of the door. Ajar. And the radio sound. Louder. And the rose petals, crossing the threshold.

The door banged against the wall, askew on its hinges. Her semiautomatic's sleek, sweeping muzzle had the whole room covered.

A life-size poster of Johnny Depp as a pirate had nearly bought it until she recognized another familiar media face in the male photograph on the opposite wall. Had looked like a long-haired druggie at first flash. That beard sure begged for a 9-millimeter shave.

She had to wade through teenage effluvia, kicking away several stuffed animals, to reach the closet and rip that door open.

Just more girly clutter on the floor and unmoving ranks of clothes old and new. She used the gun muzzle to sweep the hangers back, her bare foot to feel and kick the clutter off the floor.

Nothing there. No one.

Back to the wall, backed up by Johnny "Pirates of the Caribbean" Depp. Big help. She needed to re-enter the hall, but someone might have followed her down, or preceded her down. Be waiting for her now. Or have been waiting for her all along.

The bathroom. Shower curtain. Oh, great, Janet Leigh at the Bates Motel time. But too small to conceal much. Then, her own bedroom.

In the hall, she pointed the Glock left, then right. Someone might have been lurking in her bedroom and returned to the living room while she investigated Mariah's room. The rose petal trail smelled like a trap. There were still rose petals at her feet and they led into her bedroom.

If she goes on toward it, she bottles herself up in an architectural cul-de-sac. Just how well does Whoever know her house? Very well indeed. The music must be coming from the radio alarm clock in her bedroom.

No wonder it sounds so tinny. They never put decent sound systems into those cheap dual-function things.

At least Mariah is out, and safe at . . . someone's house. Try to keep track of a kid nowadays. *Try to remember the kind of September*—this is *May*! Concentrate.

Carmen eyes the hall back where she came from. The perp could be out there, escaping. Or poised to bottle her in. Or . . . not.

She edges along, back to the wall, ready to move, or fire, in either direction.

What if this is just the misguided prank of some besmitten teenage boy, trying to get Mariah's attention? Carmen overreacts, and disaster.

But she's the one who's had strange vintage velvet gowns showing up in her closet. Alien gift boxes left on her bed. She's the one being stalked.

Carmen nears the door to her own bedroom. That door is ajar.

It always is. This is a two-female, two-cat household. The cats bounce between her bedroom and Mariah's every night. Several times every night. And their litter box is in the bathroom under the sink with its four chrome legs circa the fifties.

Normal is open doors.

Abnormal is someone lurking behind them. Someone more solid than a poster. No posters in *her* bedroom. She spots a male figure . . . it's surrender or shoot.

Her own house has come to this. Ticks her off. She adjusts her hands on the metal grip, the trigger guard. She's got her forefinger resting on the guard, not the trigger. She moves it slowly and carefully to the trigger itself. Her palms are damp. They just stick to the warming metal better.

Her grip is sure.

She kicks her own bedroom door open and backs into it fast, so the door can't rebound, hiding half the room.

Everything is so damn familiar. So damn static. But this room has a closet. And a gun safe in that closet.

There are a couple more guns in there. The standard issue .38 she got on her first patrol job in L.A. Another .38 she accidentally took during her flight from L.A. when she was pregnant with Mariah. Rafi Nadir's, with his fingerprints all over it, like they were all over her past. How do you return an accidentally abstracted police department issue gun to an ex-lover you never want to see again? You don't.

He'd never see the daughter he'd tricked her into bearing, he'd never see his gun again. Bastard.

She's mad now. A match for anything.

She takes down the room foot by foot, piece by piece. Her own sanctuary, a crime scene.

After twenty sweaty minutes, she has nothing.

The gun safe is secure. Locked. The alien blue velvet dress still hangs among the other vintage velvet gowns for her secret off-duty role as Carmen, just Carmen, the blues singer.

She sits on the bed, her bed, holding the gun, her gun.

No one is here. She'd barged back out into the main rooms, shocked the cats, looked behind and under and over and into every nook and cranny. Nothing.

The bedside alarm clock radio drones on.

She can't be sure she forgot to turn it off this morning.

There've been a lot of mornings like that lately, tainted by serial worry. About her job, her daughter, her stalker.

Then the alarm goes off—buzzing, buzzing—on her bedside table.

She slams the button down. And listens.

The radio, the damn radio is still playing.

From under her pillow.

She tosses the pillow aside like a lightweight Hollywood rock.

Something remains.

A vintage transistor radio.

A flat box, like nylon stockings used to come in. With a note.

After she dons latex gloves, she teases the box open with the muzzle of the gun at arm's length. As if that would do any good against an explosive device. Just red tissue paper. She doesn't really expect a literal explosive device. Her stalker is too subtle for that.

She expects an explosive message.

She gets it when she eases the enclosed gift card out of its Barbie-size white envelope. The note reads, "This is what you should have been wearing for a midnight rendezvous in the Secrets' parking lot."

The box holds one of those sleazy sub-Frederick's of Hollywood outfits: black garters and red satin and white lace and underwire bra and filmy chiffon.

Only one person knows about Secrets' parking lot. She puts

the safety on the Glock but not her emotion, which is sheer fury. Max Kinsella with his sick cat-and-mouse games has invaded her home, her privacy, and threatened her child.

This is war.

Chapter 34

Home Invasion

Temple heard the knock on her door. Too demanding for Matt Devine, the only one diffident enough to ever knock. And maybe that would stop now.

Max just broke in, born second-story man that he was. As long as it was her second story. Temple used to think that was cool. She was starting to resent what she had loved before.

She opened up.

Whoa. Lieutenant Molina, looking navy blue official, like a nun or a military man. Was there a difference? Wasn't *your* guilt and anxiety always to their advantage?

"Excuse me," Temple said, trying to stretch to at least five four on her three-inch heels.

"I'm here to gather evidence," said six-foot-something C. R.

Molina. "I don't have a court order. You can kick me out. But then I'd have to put it all on the record. If you want that, fine."

What a witch! Temple so resented this woman breaking into her life, her condo, her sense of privacy and security.

"What do you want here?"

"Not much, and everything. Something he has touched. Besides you."

Temple had already been backed up until she dug her heels into the faux goatskin rug under her coffee table. Make that cocktail table, because she could use about three right now. Plus her aunt Kit.

"You have no idea," Temple said.

"You have a crime scene bonanza," Molina contradicted Temple. "You believe in Max Kinsella. Okay. Just let me gather my evidence."

"What evidence?"

"What would still have his fingerprints? *Hmmm?*" Molina produced a latex glove and snapped it on.

Euww! So like a gynecologist. Temple's home was a laboratory? Like she had a yeast infection named Max?

"You—" Temple began.

"You give me what I want, I'm outa here. Scared?"

"Of you, no. Of your unadmitted obsessions? Yes."

Molina marched on. Later, Temple would wonder why Molina did this take-down solo, with no paperwork. But Temple had been caught head-on, like deer being shined. No time to think.

"You live in Las Vegas," Molina said. "You bet on this town for your livelihood. For your luck. Just something. One thing he has touched. An innocent man leaves no trail but trust. Yes? One little thing."

They were in the bedroom by then, Temple quavering, thinking madly but not well. She didn't want this woman in here, tainting the truth of her past and possibly even the present.

Temple's eyes gave her away. They flashed on the second stereo system. Small but mighty. The rack of CDs. Vangelis, of course, a magician's musician. Soaring. Dazzling. Mystifying.

"You gaze longingly at the sound system. Music is the food of love. And delusion." Molina's latexed fingers snared one

CD. Old. Not played recently. *Cosmos.* Not dusted. Not wiped free of fingerprints, just Max all over it. The music, the mood, the intimate moments.

Molina read Temple's unreeling memories and anxieties in one glance. The CD was sealed in plastic, ready to be raped of all its secrets.

Temple took that image, that notion, way too personally.

Temple sat sweating in her air-conditioning after the homicide lieutenant left.

She was dazed. Molina had only recently promised to leave Max and her alone. Now she was muscling into their intimate lives, sneering at the implicit details of their love life. Making it criminal to care. To defend and protect.

Or, was she just too tired to be Max's personal pit bull anymore? Was she weakening because she was distracted by Matt and his needs, his attractions? Was it getting easy to give up the ghost? Max, her maybe lover?

Temple knew she should have done more to resist Molina, but she also knew that this humiliating breaking and entering wouldn't have been necessary if Max had done less. If he'd been here rather than anywhere else. And the fact that he needed to do what he did didn't make it one damned bit easier. For him.

Or for her.

Chapter 35

High Anxiety

Max's stint as the Phantom Mage at Neon Nightmare was the ideal training ground for this job at the New Millennium.

"Job" in the sense of pulling a heist.

In the deepest dark of night, against the ceiling of the black-painted area above the exhibition, he'd installed his own web of deception.

He and Gandolph had spent many wee morning hours after Max's Neon Nightmare shows tunneling a secret entrance above the suspended platforms and electronically operated mirrors and the web of bungee cords the Cloaked Conjuror and Shangri-La had rigged for themselves, the two black panthers, and her acrobatic Siamese cat.

The tangled nest of electric cords and circus gadgetry had

evolved into two levels of treachery. The machinery of illusion could always be dangerous. Two hidden hands, two different purposes made it doubly treacherous. As was Shangri-La herself.

Max had erected a secret shadow rigging above the original installation.

He planned to tangle CC in a falling net of cables, then swing down in his stead, wearing a duplicate costume. In front of a transfixed audience (the way he always liked 'em), he would use the heavy boots to kick away the Lexan pyramid-cum-onion dome protecting the scepter, which he and Gandolph had rigged to give. Then he'd swing up into the black nowhere, prize attached to utility belt.

No matter that the alarm system screeched its worst.

The guards would believe their eyes and waste time lumbering upward to corral a sputtering and stunned Cloaked Conjuror.

Max by then would be shimmying through eighty feet of narrow aluminum tubing installed like a long, long, skylight tunnel. CC's mask and heavy shoes and cloak would remain behind, as deflated as the hat and robe of the melting Wicked Witch of the West.

What a world, what a world!

The Synth would have proof of his loyalty and daring and would at last admit him to their inner sanctum of secrets. Gandolph, presumed dead and therefore not suspect, would keep the scepter for producing later, when the Synth and all its murky works would be known to Max and the world and be broken.

Max would gladly retire his growing poker hand of identities. Maybe he could break the Synth in a couple of months, then come back as his original performing persona, the Mystifying Max. He was in superb physical condition again. Maybe the Crystal Phoenix would renew its offer, particularly with Temple as his . . . agent. They could stop playing hide and seek. Get married. Buy a house of their own.

But all that was later. This was now. The biggest problem for his successful escape was Shangri-La. He carried a lariat of steel cord. If he could encoil her on the way down, her long tatters of costume would become her prison.

Now, he hung under the ceiling like a big black spider, feet and hands in the holds he and Gandolph had screwed into the unseen joists. He breathed deeply, trying to relax in the trying position.

The music was revving up to introduce the Cloaked Conjuror and Shangri-La. Across the chasm below, he could see into the staging area hidden from the audience. The low-level spotlights that dotted the black ceiling gleamed on the steel bars caging in the big cats across from him. Their eyes gleamed in the dark as they growled softly with anticipation. They saw him and spotted prey, but no one would heed them. That would be invisible to the audience looking up from the pool of brightly lit white exhibition cubicles and pedestals far below.

They sat in a semicircle of sleek white stands on the museum's far walls, chattering with opening night excitement. Buzz. Temple would be happy. Even though the press wouldn't be allowed into the exhibit until the following week, he knew that she would be down there, making sure all the VIPs were at ease and ready for the big preview night. But he didn't dare shake his concentration to look for her.

He hated to ruin an event she had worked on, but she was endlessly clever at turning bad publicity into good.

Max eyed the equipment installed for the true performers. They had tested it many times for stability and strength, as he had his own gear. This mock-robbery stunt was nothing more, or less, than Cirque du Soleil had so elegantly reinvented for Vegas, a spectacular, arty circus act.

Max inhaled long and slow. Launch time was only a few minutes. He would swoop down, looking like part of the act. He would leave the real CC and Shangri-La hanging uneasily, shocked.

He would take the prize and retract his presence as swiftly as a spider reeling in web silk. And he, like Robert the Bruce, had studied their swift and efficient ways on the back patio of Gandolph's house, now his. Not his and Temple's. Someplace new for them. Fresh. Free.

No. Think the job. Only the job. Not the rewards.

The music swelled into the introduction segment, forcing

the upward-staring faces below to turn down as they settled into their seats.

Like a bird of prey, he swiftly eyed all the platforms: CC's, Shangri-La's, the big cats', even the tiny one reserved for the Siamese cat named Hyacinth.

She was really too small for an aerial show. She wouldn't be very visible. But Max understood Shangri-La's loyalty to an animal partner. He'd worked with some himself and knew that they came to love and crave the spotlight. Praise and adulation and applause could seduce any species, a sad commentary on how often it was missing in young human and animal lives.

Max blinked. He wasn't wearing his colored contact lenses tonight: not the Mystifying Max's feline-green ones, not the Phantom Mage's brown ones. His eyes were their natural hue, blue, rather like the Siamese cat's.

But he wasn't seeing a Siamese cat on the small, half-hidden perch reserved for it.

He was seeing a small glimmer of ultra-feline green, as vivid as his own false lenses. He didn't see much else there, just disembodied eyes, like the isolated toothy smile of the Cheshire Cat from Wonderland, implying a total cat, but winking out.

This was a kink in the perfect plan. Hyacinth hadn't suddenly made her blue eyes green. With a shudder of premonition, Max looked harder. A dark feline form was moving onto the platform poised like a diver's board on the edge of nothing.

It was, of course, Temple's eternally meddling tomcat, Midnight Louie. While he posed there, invisible to everyone near and far but Max, he glanced up. Directly. At Max.

Great. Outed by an alley cat.

Then Louie pounced farther out onto his podium, as if chasing phantom prey.

Max's mouth opened to shout a warning no cat would heed. *Stop!*

But Midnight Louie had already leapt back into the shadow of what passed for wings up here, besides bungee cords.

And the entire platform buckled and fell vertical to its support members. It dangled there as if held by an invisible thread of remaining support.

* * *

Sometimes seconds can take minutes. It required enormous muscular strength for Max to cling to the ceiling. His body craved the release of a bungee freefall, of stretching long to fly and then liberate the prize, seize it, rebound upward toward ungiving ceiling, then cling and skitter out the escape route.

That release was gone, Max realized. While he and Gandolph had been rigging their secret web above it all, someone else had sabotaged the actual performance platforms, and probably the bungee cord anchors too. Everything was too weak to hold . . . even an alley cat.

Who? Why? Didn't matter. Everyone involved in the show, everything, including the cats big and small, were in peril of fatal plunges to the hard marble floor below.

Max glanced again to where Louie had appeared. His place on the brink of the disabled pedestal had been taken by a small, pale-coated cat tipped dark brown on all its extremities. Hyacinth.

A piece of moving darkness showed that Louie was now balancing at the entrance to the big cats' divided platforms. Their huge forms shifted in the dark, the spotlights glancing off huge white fangs as they panted with pre-performance excitement and off the bejeweled green of their shining eyes.

Louie apparently intended to turn these bruisers back. Single pawed. Max saw Louie's back hoop in the classic feline offensive/defensive pose. He could almost hear the hiss of a housecat hitting those large, rounded, jungle-sharp ears.

Max could do nothing about the cats, wild or domestic. Who ever could? His eyes flicked to the two opposing platforms where CC and Shangri-La would appear very shortly.

Great. Two booby-trapped platforms waiting for the weight of one footstep from their human victims.

One observer, with only a reach and strength so long, so fast. Who to rescue?

Shangri-La weighed maybe a hundred and ten pounds in her airy costume. Easy save. Like Tarzan and Jane. Except . . . she was an enemy.

The Cloaked Conjuror was a confrere, a kind of friend. Max

didn't envy his hidden life and the masked face that kept him isolated, however wealthy and famous. Maybe he'd welcome a spectacular death. A Page One passing. Anyway, the man, costumed in Klingon-style platform boots and mask, must run two-fifty. Max weighed one-eighty sopping wet, which he was now, with dangerous perspiration. Bad for his grip.

The introductory music swelled to a climax to blast out the entrance bars. Echoing here above and down below. In Heaven and Hell.

The most certain save was the most personally distasteful. The most unlikely save was the most preferred. Gallantry said rescue the woman. Personal druthers said preserve the fellow magician.

Time for thought was done. The spotlights brightened on each platform, forty feet apart. A lithe figure in fluttering white stepped forward. A massive Darth Vader–like persona in black stepped forward.

Max swung out from the ceiling, dark but neither light nor heavy.

He swept out and down, catching Shangri-La's torso in one arm, and rappelled off the side wall to deposit her in the niche where Midnight Louie held the big cats at bay. Maybe she was too light to tip the balance.

He pushed his feet against the wall again and caught up with the Cloaked Conjuror just as the platform broke and plummeted from his booted feet to the floor below. The crowd roared with fright.

He'd snagged CC by one arm. Their combined weight pulled Max's bungee cord down, down, down toward the Lexan onion dome that both revealed and guarded the newly installed scepter.

Drop CC and the prize was his.

Instead they fell together like a lead weight, until the top of the spiral staircase leading to the scepter was just below.

Max let CC go. He dropped perhaps four feet.

Max kicked off the onion dome, swinging over the installation.

In an instant, he had seized the scepter and ricocheted from the base of the installation. The piercing whine of an alarm ran up and down the scale as the bungee cord rebounded up to the ceiling, making him a Spider-man about to go comic book *splat!*

Max caught at the collapsed platform that had been CC's downfall. His body bruised into it, but his grasp held long enough to slow his rebound.

Then the platform sagged and broke free, falling down into the heart of the screams and scattering audience members below, including Temple.

Max had no time to look back. He bounced off the looming ceiling, slowed, in control again.

The big cats, cowed perhaps as much by the unscripted chaos as Midnight Louie's fierce stand, had backed away from the treacherous platforms they'd been trained to mount on the music's cue. If Midnight Louie could intimidate two panthers who outweighed him a hundred-to-one, Max guessed he could pull Shangri-La to safety.

She was using her considerable acrobatic skills to take her weight off the disintegrating platform beneath her feet, which were hampered by arch-deforming ballet toe-shoes. They produced a graceful image for an airborne magician-acrobat, but they were useless for establishing any foothold on a disintegrating web of wooden platforms and elastic bungee cords.

Max sailed down, the scepter in his belt flashing in one of the hidden mirrors above. He glimpsed Shangri-La's makeup-masked features, her exotic beauty and grace, dismissing her ambiguous role in shady events past and present. Her life and lifeline made her as fragile now as a blown-glass ballerina.

He caught one wrist as she was slipping away. It was sharp and thin, a bundle of razor blades. Every sinew in his arm strained, but he had only to dive low, release her over a safe landing point, then fly up like Peter Pan dropping Wendy back at home.

But CC's rescue had strained his synapses as well as tendon and bone. He could barely hold on to her. . . . Then a fiery cactus exploded on his back and shoulders.

He heard a martial arts yowl, cat style.

That damn Hyacinth, thinking to protect her mistress, was

dooming her instead. Max's fingers tightened, flinched, then felt skin and bones slipping through his grasp.

They were still thirty feet above the hard marble flooring.

The white butterfly fluttered free below him, spinning and glittering in a graceful, fatal trajectory.

Max, freed from the dead weight, rebounded against the ceiling so fast it took all of his remaining strength to slow the snap, to grab disintegrating platforms on his rebound, to become an unseen spider in a lethal web high above.

The cat slid off his back and fell, a tangle of bungee cords serving as its precarious cradle. It swung there, its shrill voice mimicking the relentless, heartbeat-stirring siren of the alarm.

The canned music hid the sound of whatever impact there had been. The scepter installation site looked as if it had been hit by a tornado.

Below him, people—heads of all colors—gathered, unthinking, around a shining reverse-Rorschach ink-blot pattern of fallen white on the pale floor far below. No one else seemed injured.

Max had no time left to linger, look back, regret. He unsnapped his trusty bungee cord, the only safe one because whoever had sabotaged the magic act had not known about his own arrangements. Then he ditched the boots, cloak, and CC mask, and his spider self slipped from the ceiling handholds and down the narrow escape tunnel he and Gandolph had made.

The Cloaked Cònjuror and the big cats had survived to perform another day, thanks to Max—and Midnight Louie—being on the scene. Shangri-La definitely and possibly her cat Hyacinth were among the collateral damage.

"Damn," Max hissed to himself over and over as he elbow crawled through the passage, its existence now publicly betrayed.

He struggled to keep the invaluable scepter from scraping on the narrowing ductwork. His spectacular theft had turned into a botched heist and a messy, semifailed rescue operation.

A woman lay dead on the exhibition floor. Temple's assignment as well as his own were both terminally damaged. The Cloaked Conjuror's show and career were tainted, perhaps beyond redemption, like his own.

He had let down everyone who depended upon him, whether they knew it or not.

And . . . the Synth would not be pleased. Or maybe those manipulative shadow figures would be delighted with the carnage, and the publicity.

Poor Temple! Her career was at stake, and he had not only meddled in it, but devastated the site of her greatest PR triumph.

Damn!

His back burned with raw fire, the badge of a cat's tragically misguided courage. Otherwise he could have saved a human life, no matter his suspicions about its purpose. Shangri-La had been a mystery, maybe a criminal, but until tonight, she had been living. Her life had hung from his hands and slipped away.

He felt sick, as sick as when the IRA pub bomb had turned his boyhood best friend, his cousin Sean, into exploded bits of flesh and blood.

How could he face his uncle and aunt, his family?

He couldn't then.

He couldn't now. He had to go away, run far, find some way to make reparations. Leave home. Leave Temple. Leave Las Vegas, leave life and death behind him. Again.

Damn!

Chapter 36

Cat's Cradle

Triage is not a skill you usually find in PIs, or the apparently humble pussycat.

But I gaze down from the lip of the Big Cats staging area about as horrified as I have ever been in memory.

Shangri-La lies there, a mangled white butterfly on the white marble floor, a small pale form, framed by pieces of black platform that circle her like flotsam from a shipwreck. A shipwreck in the sky.

What to do? Where to go?

The Cloaked Conjurer is stirring at the mouth of his staging area where Mr. Max deposited him with superhuman strength. For even he cannot fool Midnight Louie. I would know those moves anywhere.

I glance at the Big Boys, who have realized that the act has turned deadly wrong.

"Return to your cages and sit tight," I tell them. "Someone will come for you when they think of it."

They retreat as meekly as the Cowardly Lion after Dorothy has slapped his nose. I am afraid I had to unsheath my shivs and do a little nose whacking myself to force them back from the deadly, drop-off edge.

I dash around their cages and to the connecting hall, taking a left and another left in the ill-lit maze all backstage areas are, the better to keep audiences from seeing in.

I have guessed right. CC is pushing himself up to his knees and leaning over the edge in an attempt to view the same horrible sight I have seen. He is shocked and groggy, so I am forced to take a stand in his path. I hiss and growl and slash him back, as if I were the trainer and he the cat act.

"I must be hallucinating," he mutters during his retreat. "Lucky and Kahlúa have shrunk? And Shang and Hyacinth too?"

When I have herded him ten feet back from the edge, I hear the scrabble of rescuing hands and feet in the maze of service chutes honeycombing this sky-high stage.

Not Mr. Max's. He is long gone and that is one party in this tragedy I feel no need to follow. Worry about is something else. He tried for a two-fer save. Had not the misguided Hyacinth scourged his back, he might have made it. I sincerely hope her boast of curare-painted nails was all bravado. I watch her struggling in her bungee cord cradle. I shall never hear the truth from her lips. Shangri-La has made her eternal peace with solid marble, but Hyacinth will never make peace with me. I cannot help but think that they were two of a kind: unhappy, scrappy souls. Only Hyacinth remains now, but for the intervention of a few threads, and Shangri-La perhaps has brought her end upon her.

Still, my Miss Temple is somewhere far below, by herself, trying to salvage order from tragedy.

I duck into the entrance/exit tunnel designed for Hyacinth . . . and nearly swallow my own tongue to see her silhouette waiting for me.

Maybe nine lives are literal with her kind of cat. Maybe she is some immortal emissary of Bast and I have failed to save her. Maybe I too will soon be floating like a butterfly and landing like the QE II. . . .

"Louie! We must get to the floor below."

The silhouette says Hyacinth but the voice says Squeaker.

"Are you okay?" I ask, astounded.

"No, of course not. I witnessed everything, as you did. Hyacinth, as you saw, felt strong enough to perform herself. And then some. Poor misguided creature! She had no idea her interference was what doomed her mistress. If only there was something we could have done."

"Not without leaving our hides on the exhibition floor."

"I saw you warn Lucky and Kahlúa. And the Cloaked Conjuror is safe?"

"Yes."

"Who was that masked man?"

I am certain that Squeaker, fresh from a shelter experience, has not logged the hours I have in watching high-number cable channels with ancient TV show reruns, so I only say the truth.

"I think he came to steal the Czar Alexander scepter but discovered that someone had got here before him and rigged the whole suspended performance area to collapse."

"We all could have been killed then, if he hadn't been here?"

"Sure as shootin'," I cannot resist saying, thinking of the Lone Ranger's silver bullets.

"At least CC and the Big Cats are safe."

I nod modestly. Mr. Max and I work well together, even when we do not know about it beforehand.

"That masked man would have saved Shangri-La too, if Hyacinth had not gone postal."

Squeaker is not as sheltered as I had suspected.

"Louie, I do not wish to be found up here!" she says. "I am very sensitive about facing humans. I was not treated well by them. Call me a coward but I must find a way out of here. Quick! Before they catch me and put me in a cage again."

"No problem, Princess."

I peer out Hyacinth's entrance niche. Everyone below is focusing on the emergency personnel who have made a circle around Shangri-La's form. The rescue parties are swarming up the tunnels behind us.

"We will have to risk a little Tarzan swing up to that tangle of bungee cords under the ceiling."

"I fear man but not the works of man," Squeaker says. "You know where you wish us to go. Lead and I will follow."

Suits me. This leap is kit's play compared to the acrobatics I use to scale the Circle Ritz most nights. I lunge, hang over empty air for a split second, and tangle sixteen shivs in Mr. Max's special ceiling cradle of bungee cords. It still holds firm.

Squeaker glances over her pale cream shoulder at the approaching hordes of inquisitive humans, then blinks her baby blues at me. Or maybe she winks, but I personally think that she is too shy.

She launches her lean form like an Olympics gymnast and in a moment my webbing trembles from the impact of another sixteen-point landing.

"Unlatch yourself and follow me," I say, swinging into the barely visible open black mouth of Mr. Max's escape hatch.

She manages the transfer like one running for her life.

When we are both safely situated, I lean out and slash a key bungee cord free. The whole mess falls free, then snags on a piece of dangling platform twenty feet below.

Squeaker's velvet gray muzzle wrinkles with puzzlement at my action.

"The masked man is a sort of friend of mine. Besides, the longer they do not find his escape tunnel, the longer we will have to escape."

With that we turn and make our easy way through an anaconda-size twist and turn of giant piping. Sometimes, even I wonder how Mr. Max Kinsella does it.

But I am glad he did it.

Chapter 37

Brass Tactics

"Is she . . . dead?" Temple asked Randy.

He nodded, his face paler than his ash-blond hair. "I'm pretty sure. You don't have to see for yourself."

"I do."

"Then I'll come too. They'll only let us so close."

But he hadn't reckoned there'd be the sober ring of Fontana brothers circling the death scene like white-suited angels from a 1940s movie fantasy.

Despite their light-colored garb, their serious and handsomely swarthy faces lent the somber air of a Mafia funeral to the occasion. They posed with their broad defensive backs to the victim, legs splayed apart as if for a last stand, hands clasped in front like an honor guard with the muzzles of the black Berettas in those hands aimed at the white marble floor.

Temple could already hear a wave of rising consternation from the casino as emergency technicians and police forged their way through the crowded aisles to this cul-de-sac of tragedy at the very back of the huge hotel.

Probably there was a nearer, more discreet entrance, but emergency crews couldn't gamble on finding it. This entire museum wing was new and had never required a siren run before.

"Well?" she asked the nearest Fontana brother. He looked down at her, his expression stern as a Marine's.

"Not pretty, Miss Temple."

"This is my job scene."

Ralph nodded and shifted to one side.

She saw the form aptly described as "crumpled."

The painted face was turned toward her, almost accusingly. The traditions of Chinese opera face painting made American clown-face colors elegant: white face accomplished with fine rice powder, not heavy grease paint. No enlarged fire-engine-red lips, but the crimson petals of a mouth echoed in a red blush over the cheekbones and around the eyes, delicate as a pale rose petal. Slashing black lines exaggerating natural eyelashes and eyebrows.

And a crooked trickle of blood drooling out one corner of the perfectly painted crimson bud of a mouth. A pool of that blood engulfed the horse tail–long strands of dull black hair, probably false, haloing the figure.

This woman had stolen Temple's ring as part of a stage magic act and probably participated in her kidnapping. So Temple shouldn't bat an eyelash to see this stagy figure melted into white marble like her darker sister, the Wicked Witch of the West, right?

Temple batted two eyelashes, thick with tears of shock.

Aldo stepped in front of her to conceal the body again.

"Cheese it, the cops," he muttered, while an adept hand gesture made the Beretta vanish.

The Fontanas had broken rank and melted bonelessly into

their ice cream suits, backing into the watching crowd of murmuring hotel and corporate honchos.

Randy pulled Temple aside as a gurney crashed through the mob faster than an Olympic sled. They were called over to the fringes by the murmuring executives.

"Thank God the press was barred from attending," Pete Wayans noted. "What about the formal opening next week?"

"How soon can the damaged set pieces be replaced?" Temple asked.

Madame Kirkov's papery skin was a duplicate of Shangri-La's painted mask. It had been paste white since the first death on the exhibition site. She waved a beringed, shriveled hand that would have seemed natural to a mummy.

"The crew built the set and can rebuild it. The question is, why did it fail?"

"The question," Temple said, "is who rigged it to fail?"

"If that was the case, 'who' is obvious. That man who came plunging down from nowhere. Obviously, another thief. First Andrei, now this. The scepter must be recovered. Nothing can replace it. The exhibition is lost."

A murmur of deep men's voices escalated into muted squeaks of despair. The scepter was the drawing card for the entire exhibition.

"This has been a pretty obvious heist," Randy pointed out in his patented Sominex tones. "Maybe there are also some pretty obvious clues to who's behind it. Once the authorities give us leave to go, we can adjourn to the conference room to plan the next steps. It looks like this death was accidental. Even if someone rigged the machinery to fail, that's going to take at least a day to determine. All of us down here saw the same thing."

"The security cameras," Temple added, "are the witnesses the police will want most."

"Security cameras," Madame Kirkov said sharply. "Up there, too?"

"I'm sure of it. They'd provide a constant overview of the exhibition, and the hotel would recognize the performance tunnels as a risk. Unless," she added, thinking of someone who was supernaturally security wise, "they'd been disabled too."

* * *

The police took names and phone numbers and made cursory inquiries, but clearly didn't think a shocked crowd made for very reliable witnesses.

Temple left them interviewing the Fontana brothers, whom they thought would make reliable witnesses for some reason, or perhaps reliable suspects.

Temple had informed the sergeant in charge that the Fontanas were special security hired by the hotel, which had made him snort and say, "We'll see how special they are."

Temple couldn't afford to worry about the flock of Fontanas, or even Aunt Kit's Aldo. She had to hustle off with Randy for a late-night emergency session with the people bankrolling this event.

And then . . . then she had to break her string of bad luck in communicating with Max to find out where and how he was before Molina got on the warpath again.

Because everything about that chaos in the upper air had the mark of a Mystifying Max operation, except for the death.

Chapter 38

My Baby Tonight

Max wasn't answering his cell phone. Temple hoped it hadn't fallen during the struggle above the exhibition. Talk about leaving a telltale clue behind. She was pretty sure he wouldn't weigh himself down with anything unnecessary during whatever he was attempting, but it was hard to be absolutely sure about anything involving Max lately.

The thing was, she'd always assumed that Max had an unseen motive for everything he did, because of his long-time role as an undercover operative, a counterterrorism agent long before the world had felt the true potential of terrorism. She'd aided him now and again in that noble pursuit, and now the furies of lawful and unlawful pursuit were harder on his trail than ever.

She drove to his house in the aging development that had been new when Orson Welles lived out his last years there.

There were protocols for approaching Max's house, most recently inherited from Garry Randolph, Max's magic and counterterrorism mentor, known as Gandolph the Great before his retirement years ago.

Protocol one: Temple parked the Miata four houses away. She moved quietly to the home's front door. Protocol two: she rang the bell twice. Protocol three: she waited.

She waited for so long she almost slunk away into the three A.M. darkness, recalling that Matt would be just home and unwinding from delivering two hours of instant empathy to all comers. She felt a strange pit-of-the-stomach craving for Matt that it was better not to examine right now.

Only streetlights and house security lights lit up this residential part of the city. It could have been Anywhere, U.S.A. Except it was Anywhere But Here. And if Max *was* home, he might very well be unwinding from botching a high-end heist and failing to save the life of a woman they both distrusted but neither knew. Poor Max! He hated failure, even in an iffy cause.

Finally, the door cracked open.

"You're crazy; get out of here," Max whispered through the crack.

"*I'm* crazy? I've got to talk to you, and not just about tonight."

The door opened a begrudging foot. Temple eeled through anyway. Max sealed it behind her with the sophisticated security system that made this mild-looking house into a fortress.

There was enough light, barely, in the hall to follow him, and then only because he was shirtless and his bare, muscular back reflected a bit of light. His bare and cross-hatched back.

"Max!"

He turned as they reached the living room, which was lit by pools of lamplight like spotlights in the dark.

She stopped him to examine the long, jagged claw marks festering on his pale skin. "Those'll put you at the scene for sure."

"If anyone can find me to see this. Besides you."

"You've got to get them treated. Even so, the marks will be visible for weeks."

"Fine. I don't intend to be."

"You're not really magic, you know. You can't actually disappear, like the Cheshire Cat, until only your scratch scars are visible."

"I'll have to. Drink?"

A bottle of Bushmill's Irish whiskey sat on a wooden end table beside a juice glass filled either with cider or whiskey neat.

"Didn't feel like breaking out the best crystal," Max said, noticing her surprised look. "Nothing to celebrate. I'll get another glass."

"I'll get some rubbing alcohol, antibiotic cream, gauze, tape . . . from the bathroom. Cat scratches can be virulent. You never know where those claws have been. Especially Shangri-La's cat's claws."

"These claws already have been virulent," he said from the kitchen. "They made me drop her and they sting like they had chili peppers on them."

By the time Temple had assembled the first aid materials, Max had poured her a fruit juice glass of straight whiskey. No coasters. He was really rattled when he skipped the small civilizing touches. Details were his livelihood and his safety line and his passion.

Temple sat down and had a good belt, then made him sit forward in his chair and tended his back by lamplight, feeling like Florence Nightingale.

"You saw, I suppose?" he asked.

"What there was to be seen. I don't know *why* you were there, or *what* you thought you were doing, or *how* those set pieces collapsed like that."

"Why, what, how are the mystery. We know when and where. Answer the first three and the five key questions of a journalist are covered."

"Max! I'm not asking this as a journalist. I'm not even asking this as someone who's responsible for the exhibition going smoothly and has had her ground cut out from under her by her own boyfriend. I'm asking this as someone who cares about you. And your bloody back."

Max bolted more whiskey but never quivered a muscle as she flooded his back with raw alcohol, then patted it down with a towel.

"A Max Kinsella Production gone very wrong," he said at last. "Some other unexpected stage manager had gotten there before me and booby-trapped the entire set. Everything alive up there was meant to plunge to the floor below."

"Including you, the mystery guest?"

"I'm beginning to think so. Maybe me most of all, and the others were just a cover."

"Why?"

"Sabotage on that scale usually has more than mere greed behind it. Maybe a geopolitical motive."

"Russian stuff?"

He eyed her. "More likely the Synth."

"They're a logical suspect for a plot to destroy the Cloaked Conjuror who's been betraying their trade secrets nightly, but why would renegade magicians have a geopolitical motive?"

Max shrugged, then winced at the pain the automatic gesture caused. "For years, Gandolph and I found the role of magician handy for international tours in the service of counterterrorism work. Why wouldn't the opposition discover the same thing?"

"Magicians are entertainers, not political fanatics."

"Fooling all the people almost all the time can get to be a power trip. Maybe the profession is uniquely vulnerable to political recruitment. I was."

"You'd lost a close friend and relative to terrorism. Why did your mentor Gandolph become involved in counterterrorism?"

"He'd become disillusioned with hucksters who used their talents to delude and defraud gullible people, false mediums and the like. When he was approached to use that gift to foil spies and bombers, he was ready for a more meaningful role."

"Could you go back to it full-time, just being a magician? Just being entertaining?"

"Maybe. I won't know until I infiltrate the Synth and break it, or vindicate it."

"Why were you there? Did you have some idea that the cast would be targeted?"

"No. No heroics. I was there on behalf of the Synth. A sort of initiation ritual."

"Some kind of frat boy stunt? Intrude yourself into the aerial show and upset everything and vanish? No harm done?"

"Right. No harm done. That was not on the menu. Not mine, anyway. Now I'm wondering if they haven't seen through my deception and if my so-called 'assignment' wasn't an attempt to off me. My 'entry fee' for the Synth was stealing the Czar Alexander scepter. They wanted me out on a limb; they wanted to have something on me before they would accept me."

"A very sick initiation ritual." Temple resumed her seat, dismayed.

She'd suspected the Synth had become Max's mission, that the Synth had put their relationship on the back burner. That situation was even less likely to change now that it had impacted her work.

"And you couldn't argue, of course," she told him, "when their target turned out to involve my job and my reputation. You're clever, Max. Couldn't you have talked them into ripping off some other hotel that hadn't given me the best PR contract of my life?"

"I'm clever, but they made it clear that it was this or nothing. Of course, I didn't know then that you'd been hired for this exhibition. When I found out, it was too late to pitch another treasure. It would have looked suspicious, and they already have their suspicions about me."

"Just asking you to do this pretty much blew your cover. Who else besides you could have engineered that death-defying aerial ballet of thievery, rescue, and tragic death?"

"God!" He drank half the fruit juice glass in one gulp. "I could not hold on to that lightweight woman one more second. Her cat landing on my back, all four feet splayed out, and scratching me to ribbons was the last claw."

"Everyone could see that you—Zorro, the masked man, the superhero—saved the Cloaked Conjuror and almost saved

Shangri-La. And still snagged the scepter. Maybe saved it too. Frankly, I'm toying with spinning it for the press as a Robin Hood sort of feat. The earlier death proved someone was interested in robbing the exhibition and the booby-trapped platforms tonight show that some kind of plot was still live and lethal."

"The masked man stole the scepter to save it?"

"Something like that."

"*You're* the clever one, Temple." His expression, bleak until now, softened into a smile. It quickly vanished. "Watching those white robes flutter like a leaf to vanish into the matching marble floor below were the longest moments of my life. I wished—I really, really wished—that I was a real magician, that I could have waved a hand and kept that from happening."

Temple kept silent. A death not prevented was a life lost forever, for no reason. She tried a different tack.

"Maybe *she* was always the target of the falling set pieces. Shangri-La did work the shady side. She must have at least been complicit in the kidnapping of me and Louie and the truckload of designer drugs we were spirited away in. Who knows who put her up to that and maybe wanted to punish her for failing?"

"She still didn't deserve a fatal fall to a cold stone floor. She was no friend to either of us, but at least we know she wasn't in on this caper or she'd have saved herself."

"She was working with the Cloaked Conjuror. The Synth would have considered her a traitor."

Max nodded and sipped again. "Maybe they meant to off all three of us in one blow. I'm still not sure that my 'test' wasn't a way to get rid of me."

"What'll they do now?"

"What can they do? Welcome me into their ranks as promised. I did steal the scepter, whatever the cost. From their viewpoint, Shangri-La is no loss and rescuing the Cloaked Conjuror is no feather in my cap to them. . . . I'll say I needed him out of my way to complete the job of stealing the scepter, so I was 'forced' to save him."

Temple shivered a little at the idea of justifying saving someone. "If it was obvious to me that it was you up there, you know that Molina will be right on that and go after you for this."

"She'd be going after me for something else anyway."

"No. I negotiated a deal with her during that Teen Idol charade where I was locked up in a mansion with a TV crew and her daughter and twenty-eight rival unnatural blondes. If I watch-dogged her daughter Mariah, she promised she'd lay off you." She squirmed, knowing that the deal was off because Molina now suspected Max of being her stalker, but she figured that Max had enough on his plate at the moment. He was surely wary and wily enough to elude the Blue Ice Queen.

Max's own blue eyes paled in the lamplight as he studied her. "I didn't hear much about that caper. Sorry I couldn't be there."

"It worked out. But Molina can't ignore that there are very few people at large in Las Vegas who could stage that surprise guest appearance at a floating magic show. This is the second death at the White Russian exhibition. Major Las Vegas mojo will come down on the police to solve them both. You are the prime suspect."

"Good. I'd hate to give up my crown as the town's perennial Number One Suspect."

Max leaned forward, took one of Temple's hands. "Whatever the Synth is, they're formidable. Forget you ever heard of them, Temple, as you ought to forget me. I've got to get out of sight again."

"I won't say anything about you. You know you can count on me. Ducking out of sight for a while is wise. But . . . for how long?"

"Maybe . . . forever."

"Max! What are you saying—?"

"A woman is dead, Temple, one I never meant to hurt."

"It was obvious to anyone who saw that you were trying to save her!"

"Or trying to kill her? Both actions resemble each other. Don't they?"

"You caught the Cloaked Conjuror and saved his life."

"Or a snare that only by chance, or mischance, kept him from falling."

"You risked your life to catch Shangri-La and would have saved her if her cat hadn't attacked you."

"Or I always intended to drop her, and the cat merely got in the way. Besides, how many people saw way up there as clearly as you, my dear defense attorney? I disabled the cameras. There's no record. I sealed my fate, or my reputation, at least."

Temple was silent.

"Every eyewitness sees what he or she is bred to expect, or want."

"What saved the big cats from going out on those booby-trapped platforms?"

Max bit his lip instead of shrugging and swigged more whiskey. He was a fast adapter.

"A sixth sense?" he suggested finally. "It was so black over there and I had a lot to think about, all simultaneously."

"It's a wonder you managed to save CC. He must be your weight and half again."

"And don't it make my biceps blue? He okay?"

"Fine. Shaken up about losing his partner, of course."

"Yeah. I know the feeling."

"What?" Temple sensed sudden alarm bells in the pit of her stomach.

Max regarded her with far too limpidly innocent eyes. "Gandolph, I meant. What other partner would I have lost? I suppose my cousin Sean was a sort of partner for the summer."

Max reminding her of his losses made Temple want to swear, *"Not me. I'm not the next one you'll lose."*

But she couldn't say a word. Not if it meant repudiating Matt. She was already half lost, which made her feel all the more adamant about defending Max. Supporting Max. Paying Max back for her wayward heart.

"It's best you stay as far from me as possible," Max was saying, urging. "Not that I don't appreciate first-aid. Or your opinions."

"Right." She sipped a little more whiskey, then stood.

He was *telling* her to go. Pushing her away for her own sake.

Pushing her toward Matt, when she'd already leaned way too far in that direction for her conscience's sake.

What should she do? What could she do? Max wouldn't fight to keep her. Didn't he see? Or did he, as usual, see all too well? Damn you, Max!

He'd never tell.

She had to drive home. She had to pull herself together. She had to picture Max colored more than the usual invisible, but absent. But she didn't have to stop believing in him, his innocence, even if hers was compromised.

"I'll stick to my job at the New Millennium," she told him. "And I'll find out who really did this, because that's my job and because there was another man killed earlier on that same scene, and I think that there's a criminal operating there who's closer at hand than the Synth."

"You may be right and if anyone can prove it, you can. That'll keep Molina on her toes." Max rose to escort her out.

"Molina in toe shoes, now there's an image to stop the heart."

"Don't underestimate her. She's aching to stomp on someone who's gotten away with something for far too long, and it's a dead heat between you and Rafi Nadir who'd make the best fall guy."

"Nadir had nothing to with this."

"No," Temple admitted, "but if I could make Molina think he did, she might blink and you'd be able to eel out of her sights."

Max drew her close to him at the door and kissed the top of her head. Her artificially blond head.

"Always a superb strategician." He pulled her closer, hugged her almost to death. "I'm sorry, Temple. More sorry than I can ever say and you can ever know. There are some things I only realize now that I just can't control."

Temple couldn't decide whether to take that as a confession, a farewell, or a prediction.

Chapter 39

Triple Threat

Nobody much notices what us cats get up to.

That is why we make such good detectives and sneak thieves. There is not that much difference between either role.

Anyway, there is nothing I can do for Mr. Max eeling away like the snake that dropped the apple at Eve's tootsie tips and then remembered a pressing appointment elsewhere. Nor can I help my Miss Temple in performing whatever acts of Public Relations legerdemain that she finds necessary with the press and the forthcoming police.

Nor can I do much with the Big Cats, who have been sealed up in their portable tin cans and carted away. So much for brawn when the chips are down.

So.

There is only Squeaker and me gazing down on the aftermath of one nasty bit of carnage. And contemplating the ignored but wriggling form of Hyacinth clinging to the unseen back of a dangling platform twenty feet below.

"They assumed she fell," I note.

"Erroneously," Squeaker notes in turn.

"She was a witch bat out of hell."

"*Is,*" Squeaker says, quite accurately, "and I do not like her either. She could be very sharp with me."

I examine the tiny blood-red scabs visible around her throat and neck. "She no doubt did not like competition."

"I was just an anonymous body double. I offered her no challenge."

"That is challenge enough for one like Hyacinth. Oh, well. Hide-ho. I suppose we might as well consider how to rescue her."

"You are a noble breed, Louie."

"Naw. I just do not like to leave one of my own kind on the ropes. I do not know how we will manage it, though."

This last statement wins the applause of a feline hiss. I gaze at the empty carrel of the two black leopards and find a pair of old gold eyes with green backlights gazing back.

"Louise!"

"Moonlighting again," she says, "without a net. When will you wake up to reality, Pops? Who is the caramel-cream popcorn?"

"Ah, Squeaker, this is my partner in crime solving, Miss Midnight Louise."

"Oh, I see the family resemblance. You must be Mr. Midnight's sister."

What a ditz! I hear Miss Louise purring while I smother a growl of protest.

"I had heard," Louise goes on, "that my pals Lucky and Kahlúa were performing marvels of levitation at the New Millennium, so I decided to drop in on the proceedings. Little did I know that others of my acquaintance would have the same idea."

Miss Midnight Louise, of course, is quite familiar with the onstage shenanigans of Mr. Max Kinsella. At all costs, she must not mention this to Squeaker because the fewer beings, four- or two-footed, who know about his brief but spectacular presence here, the better.

"We have a more immediate problem, Louise," I say.

"Yes, I see my former sparring partner is hanging by a hair, what little of it she has."

The antipathy between the longhairs and the shorthairs of the cat kingdom rivals that between the Gelphs and Merovingians. I do not quite know who these funny-named dudes were, but I have heard their names mentioned on PBS, along with other individuals of supposedly liberal biases, so maybe they are libertarians or librarians or something.

"We cannot leave one of our kind just hanging," I venture.

"Speak for yourself, Johnny Snappleseed," Louise retorts. "I cannot wait to watch the scrawny little witch drop. Considering her attempts to end your life, liberty, and pursuit of haplessness, I would think you would be counting down the seconds too."

"Oooh!" Squeaker's eyes could not be rounder. "Your sister is most outspoken."

"She is not my sister, but she is right in that Hyacinth has been a bad girl."

I look down at the cat in question's long dangling gams in their plush gray stockings. Bad girls are minor failings of mine. Those long, painted showgirl nails won't stick to hardwood for long.

"So," says Louise from her higher perch, "it is decided. We all have suffered at the claws of Hyacinth and hate her arrogant, destructive guts. Who wants to go down and peel her treacherous claws off the board, and who wants to stay up here and make sure we all get back up safely?"

"I will go down," Squeaker says promptly. "I am her body double and have been rehearsing acrobatics on these fallen pedestals."

"And we are the lightest," Louise concurs, joining the rescue party.

"What is left for me to do?" I ask.

"We need a reliable counterweight, Daddy-o, to pull us all up. Now, I will hop onto this snarl of cable that the Mysti . . . that the mysterious stranger in black used to disable and save the Cloaked Conjuror earlier. We should go down like an elevator. You hop on as I pass your perch, Miss Caramel Cream. And you, Big Boy, grab on to the trailing rope as we swing low enough to reach that piece of traitorous feline fur."

"I can slow and stop you two girls," I protest, "but once you have Hyacinth on that cable netting, you three will outweigh me."

Louise is now head rescuer and not to be gainsaid. "Hopefully, we can all scrabble back up the rope while you hold everything steady. You do know how to hold the rope steady? You just clamp your two paws together on it and pray."

Before I can get out a quick ejaculation to my favorite Egyptian goddess, Bast, the impetuous Louise has extended shivs on every limb and leaped onto the pile of limp cable, pushing it and herself out over the looming gulf that is now dark and empty, although cordoned off with crime scene tape.

If this does not work, there will be much speculation in the Las Vegas papers tomorrow about how and why four formerly cool cats should choose to leap to their deaths like lemmings, a vastly inferior species.

Before I can blink or get a go-ahead from Bast, the disabled snarl of rope and Miss Midnight Louise flash past my puss. Squeaker leaps aboard, grappling hook shivs sinking into the cable.

So far, so good. We now have three ladies in dire peril.

I throw a full body slam at the long rope rising up as they sink down and pin it to the mat . . . or to the platform that supports me. If this thing goes, we are all pancakes.

My move was made just in time. The falling cage of cable jerks to a halt opposite Hyacinth's clinging spot.

I feel the rope fibers fighting to slip through my shivs but tighten everything I have, and it holds.

I watch while Squeaker leans out and prods Hyacinth with a delicate shiv. Shangri-La's partner seems dazed and lethargic. I guess seeing your main human go smash on a marble floor is not a life-instilling experience, even if Shangri-La was bad to the bone from the word "Shazam."

Maybe this rescue attempt is misguided.

Squeaker has overcome her timidity to reach out even farther and sting Hyacinth's long, lean dangling form with a spurful of shivs. Getting her own back, in a way, prodding the other cat to a life-affirming leap onto the already hefty mass of rope I am anchoring.

Louise and Squeaker have started clambering up, making the whole rope quiver like a bowlful of Santa Claus belly. This is not helping me maintain my grasp. And Hyacinth is still playing the swooning southern belle. In moments, the whole kit and caboodle will plummet down, unstoppable, and I will be the sole survivor. Or the counterweight.

It is not in my code to let the women and children sink with the ship.

Belle. *Hmmm.* Bell!

I embrace my rope and swing out over the abyss.

Whomp!

I descend like a dude who has been presented with custom-fit concrete booties.

My move works like a charm. The Medusa-mass of entwined rope and feline hitchhikers snaps right up to the ceiling pulley, allowing Louise and Squeaker and Hyacinth to drop off on a secure platform and lay there preening their nails.

It does, however, also leave me swinging out over the abyss like that ugly bell-ringer guy from France. Not my favorite position in front of the ladies.

"Louie!" Miss Squeaker cries in heart-rending fashion.

Miss Midnight Louise is mum, and I can see that Miss Hyacinth is still comatose and that she is the only one *not* licking her ravaged nails, which might give some credence to that curare-nail-polish boast, which means my Miss Temple's Mr. Max is in dire danger of blood poisoning.

But it does not behoove me to reflect on the imminent danger other dudes may be facing. I have done my survival of the species thing and saved the ladies.

Who will save Midnight Louie?

You can bet it is not going to be the ASPCA.

I take a deep breath and suck in my gut.

Someone has to reach for the falling star; I guess it is up to me.

First I go limp. Second, I let go.

A chorus of wailing disbelief from above cannot stop me.

I swing down onto the platform that Hyacinth claimed and snap my shivs out so I slide down it. It gives under my flailing weight and sinks like an elevator. As the momentum gets suicidal, I release every shiv, and catch hold of the thin bungee cord that Shangri-La fell from before Mr. Max made a superhuman effort and caught her by one wrist.

I am hanging by two nail sheaths, but the bungee cord has enough elastic left to stretch gently under my slighter feline weight. I am still downward bound and can see only the furtive glimmer of security lamps on the geography below.

The bungee cord is getting tired of the down escalator and is tensing its fibers to rebound up again.

I let go and close my eyes, calling on Bast.

I see a transparent pyramid coming up at me fast, planning to transfix a very tender part of my anatomy on its sharp, onion-dome tip. I execute a Greg Louganis triple-twist-and-turn dive to make a one-point landing—stomach down—*oooof!* There goes my Salmon Supreme with Smoked Oyster Sauce—and I am sliding down the steep smooth invisible roof, searching in vain for the 365-carat diamond on the Czar Alexander scepter to wink at me. It is gone for good and I may be a goner for good too.

I have engraved four lines into the pyramid side before I slide off onto the viewing platform surrounding the scepter area. I land on all four feet—whew, that stings!—my head unbloody and unbowed, but my pads burning like Hades and my head aching like Zeus's before that upstart Athena burst out from his brain.

"Way to go, Daddy-o," a voice calls from high, high above. Midnight Louise, of course. "I never knew that you had won a Purple Heart in Olympic air skiing."

My heart is not all that is gonna be purple from this little stunt.

Chapter 40

Deadhead Curtain Raiser

"Sorry," Detective Alch told Temple way too bright and early the next morning, "but I've asked around this entire end of the hotel, and you're the only one who'd seen Shangri-La without makeup. So, you'll have to do ID duty."

"She was right down here with me the other day, on the main exhibition floor. Dozens of people could have seen her."

"But they didn't. You say you did."

"I thought I did."

Alch scratched his thatch of salt-and-pepper hair, more from habit than necessity. "At least we'll know if the Asian woman you talked with was the dead woman, or not."

Temple sighed. Deeply. "You mean I have to go the coroner's facility."

"Not a formal autopsy. They have a viewing chamber."

"I've heard of it," Temple said quickly, recalling Matt's description of IDing his dead stepfather.

"Ordinarily we could use a photo," Alch said, "but this is a pretty critical ID since the victim was anonymous, in a way. Can't take any chances. Sorry."

Everyone was telling her he was sorry these days. Except Matt, for a change. A big change. But now *she* was sorry. She hadn't told him about Max's latest gig as Suspect of the Week.

"You've got a lot of catch-up work here at the New Millennium, I know, Miss Barr," Detective Alch said. "I'll drive you over personally and have you back ASAP."

"Where's your partner, the petite fleur of the Crimes Against Persons unit?"

Alch guffawed at that description. " 'Petite fleur' with dragon-claw thorns. Sorry, no Su on board. Naw, they always send me on these unpleasant runs. Figure I'll ease along the poor civilian who has to gawk at dead bodies."

"Quite a compliment," Temple allowed. "Molina knows I wouldn't do it if she asked."

"Now of course you would. You're a good citizen. Clear up this thing with a solid ID, and who knows what suspects we could find other than your boyfriend."

"You know?"

"It's my job to put two and two together, and you two have been a duo for a long time."

"A long time," Temple repeated.

By then Morrie Alch had her out the door and was ushering her into the front seat of an unmarked police car. It was a nondescript vehicle except for the flat computer screen and keyboard and two-way radio enthroned on the console.

"This Shangri-La," Alch mused as he spiraled the car out of the shadowy hotel parking ramp into the sunlight glare of jammed near-Strip traffic. "I hear she snookered you once."

"We talking pool?"

"I'm talking sweet-talking you out of the audience and onto

the stage, where she relieved you of a valuable ring. Some magic trick. The lieutenant happened to be there."

"I remember. But the police couldn't find any way to charge Shangri-La with anything, ring snatching or drug smuggling. So, now that she's dead months later, *I'm* a suspect?"

Alch chuckled like a befuddled uncle. "Maybe. If you really liked that ring, and what's not to like about a Tiffany ring from your best beau?"

Temple could see why Alch pulled escort duty to the presumed bereaved so often. She appreciated the quaint old-fashioned way he phrased her romantic situation while pointing out her potential for revenge for her traumatic past encounter with Shangri-La.

"No, you're not a suspect," he reassured her. "Not to me." And panicked her. "I'm just saying you had opportunity to study her close-up in her stage costume. And if you saw her bare faced—"

"I did. I was shocked. I'd assumed, as you had, that she showed her face to no one."

"Musta caught her off guard. You think that ring thing had any hidden personal meaning?"

"No. She just wanted a distraction for her stage trick."

Alch made a face that was half frown and half pout. On him, it looked good. "We found no evidence at all that she was involved in the kidnapping that followed. So. Innocent bystander, huh? Not so lucky last night."

"None of us was lucky last night, Detective."

" 'CC' was. Cute how they abbreviate 'Cloaked Conjuror.' Guess it must be a pain to refer to him daily by such a klutzy pseudonym. I can't get over all these anonymous magicians around town now. Like that new guy at Neon Nightmare, the Phantom Mage. Does all that new-fangled bungee work too. Used to be that breed kept their feet on the ground and lived for the limelight. Like Siegfried and Roy, bless their hearts, or this Mystifying Max my boss has on her hit list."

Temple didn't know how to reply to this comment, so she didn't say anything. Avuncular Morrie Alch might seem as comfy as chocolate chip cookies with milk, but he was a detective with a disarming Columbo-like way of seriously nosing around.

Temple yawned. "I'm sorry."

"Must have been up pacing all night," Alch said with a quick glance. "Trying to figure out how to get this hot tamale out of the fire. I notice the hotel press release refers to an 'accident.'"

"I didn't write it. Randy Wordsworth did. But isn't that the best public conclusion for now? The stage machinery was defective but nobody fell without a mighty effort to prevent it."

"Then you're of the school that the guy in black was trying to save Shangri-La, not torpedo her."

"Is there any other school among the witnesses?"

Alch concentrated on easing them into a parking spot outside the coroner's low-profile facility on Pinto Lane. "Not among the witnesses, no."

Temple knew that he was referring to Molina and her grudge match with Max.

Pinto Lane was a two-block street north of busy Charleston Boulevard and south of Alta Drive, where Our Lady of Las Vegas Church Convent School could keep an eye on the quick and the dead at the Clark County Coroner's office. Like most public buildings in Las Vegas, this one was pale, bland, and entirely overlookable, if that was a word.

The lobby resembled the waiting room for a dentist's office.

Alch ambled up to the reception window, flashed his shield, murmured a little, then beckoned Temple to a plain wood door.

A buzzer belched it open. They passed into a nondescript hall. A nose-tickling odor of oranges grew stronger but vanished as Temple was led through another door into a cubicle. The process reminded her of nothing so much as getting a mammogram, except for the male escort. And in fact she'd had her first one recently at the University Medical Center just two blocks away. Turn thirty and all sorts of strange and serious things come at you face first.

There had been a full-length curtain on that cubicle door. Here, they faced a shorter curtain on the opposite wall. Temple was reminded of a motel window with the drapes drawn.

"You know what to expect?" Alch asked, a hand on the drapery pulls.

"She'll look like she's 'sleeping.'"

"No, young lady. I well know the temptation to get smart in the face of something unpleasant. She will look like she's dead. You need to compare the pallor and stillness you see here with the healthy and mobile face you saw a few days ago. There will be changes but not significant ones."

Temple swallowed, remembering that Matt had performed this very unpleasant service for his dead stepfather. How domestically bizarre and living-roomish it was to open the chintzy, short drapes just to see a draped gurney with only a dead head revealed.

How weird to see a person lying down never to get up again. How bizarre to imagine that graveyard-pale, makeup-masked Shangri-La persona as still as death.

"They washed off the makeup, of course," Alch added.

Who was "they"? Temple wondered, bracing herself. Barefaced. Temple recalled the taut, angry, raw features she'd glimpsed on the exhibition floor when she was too surprised to realize that it was Shangri-La until the woman had moved on.

"How tall was she?" Temple asked.

A rustle as Alch consulted his lined notebook. "Five four."

Temple nodded. Her impression exactly and height was always a prime issue with a shorty like herself. She knew where the top of her head hit on Max, for example, in heels and out of them, and now, on Matt. What a fickle girl! She deserved this moment of penance and repentance, only she didn't believe in all that breast-beating stuff. Did she?

You don't gaze on a dead person everyday. In funeral parlors they're tarted up for the afterlife. Here, it was the naked and the dead and no escaping that reality in the comforting rituals of church and state and custom.

"Ready?" Alch didn't sound ready himself.

Temple nodded.

The curtains hissed open on their rods like hula-dancing snakes. The sheet was so white it made the body's skin tone look dingy, like yellow-gray laundry. In a way, Temple felt she was viewing a gray-and-white movie still. She saw mostly profile, but there was no denying the small, stubby nose, the large flat cheekbones, the jet black eyes. Nothing could return the taut muscular facial animation that had made all these features bold and vibrant and rather scary.

"That's her."

"Sure?" Alch's forehead had creased like a raised mini-blind, all furrows. Must be from working for Molina.

Temple nodded. "The animation's gone, of course, but the features were quite striking. Unforgettable. And, we were a similar height, I saw them close-up. Do you have any idea yet who she really was?"

"We know exactly who she was." Alch came to stand beside her. "Fingerprints. Ran them internationally."

"Internationally?"

He shrugged. "Her Asian origin, the fact that the exhibition has a Russian connection. You never know what will turn up."

"And?" A minuscule part of Temple's reptile brain, the sheer primitive instinct part, still wasn't sure this wasn't Kitty the Cutter with plastic surgery and a spirit-gum extreme makeover.

"This little lady was on an international wanted list."

Kitty? My God. Maybe she'd had plastic surgery years ago when she was on the run from both Interpol and the IRA, like Max. He'd just popped in some green contact lenses and disappeared into a bold performing persona. Maybe Kitty had remade her face and created a veiled persona. But wait! Matt was the only one to see her face-to-face as Kathleen O'Connor, and she'd been a black Irish beauty then. How could she—?

Alch was watching her wheels turn way too carefully.

"What could a young Asian woman do to be wanted internationally?" Temple asked.

"She defected fifteen years ago from a mainland Chinese company of acrobats touring Las Vegas. Was never seen since. Until now. Name of Hai Ling."

Temple would have gasped but she held her breath instead. That would explain Shangri-La's on- and off-stage makeup disguise. She was a political defector using her acrobatic prowess in a new career, magician.

That would *not* explain why this wanted woman who apparently had no love for Temple, sight unseen, had shown Temple her true face on the floor of the exhibition hall only two days before her death.

Chapter 41

Who, What, Why?

Okay.

The Synth was big, bad, and in this caper up to its vanishing cream in perfidy.

Temple knew that. She also knew, somewhere deep in her foreshortened bones, that more was going on here at the New Millennium than Synth games.

Andrei-Art had died first, during a possible attempt to steal the scepter.

That meant that someone had torpedoed his scheme as artfully as Max's. Not just anyone. If she believed in Max, at least as a wily super-criminal—and she did, until death or disinterest did them part—his role was the coda of this operation, not the prelude.

Speaking in musical terms, could Olga Kirkov have used her disabled and disowned younger brother to fulfill a long-delayed lust for a priceless piece of her White Russian past?

And what about Count Volpe, an urbane aristocratic gigolo living on the decadent Western cult of personality? He had consulted himself into the trivial notoriety of the *Vogue* and *Vanity Fair* party-photo pages, a grave that would ultimately be unmarked. Unless he recovered the Czar Alexander scepter for his family, his past, his legacy.

Then there was Dimitri, the government functionary nobody much liked. And his big guard dogs too. Two. What couldn't the three of them accomplish if up to no good . . . up to no Boris Godunov? Temple imagined that the New Russia was no more immune to the lure of Big Bucks than the old imperialist model.

So. Who had planned what would have been a spectacular distraction? *Up in the sky! Look! It's a bird, it's a plane, it's super-destruction—!*

Had Max not been there on Synth business, the Cloaked Conjuror, Shangri-La, the two black panthers, and Hyacinth, the performing housecat, would have all plummeted to their deaths.

In that chaos, with everybody present focusing on the carnage on the floor, any ground-bound predator could have easily nipped the scepter.

Max had admitted that he'd prepared the Lexan cover for lift-off. Someone else might have observed his operation and planned to take advantage of it.

Had the scenario gone as planned, the crushed body of Max Kinsella, aka Mask Guy, would have joined everyone else on the killing floor.

But the plan had gone wrong, thanks to the hypersensitive sixth sense and super-physical strength of said Max Kinsella.

Temple paused to smile. Even when she was mad at him, she knew he was a hero. Her secret smile faded. It was hard to be a hero's helpmate, was all.

And . . . there was something Max wasn't telling her, as usual. He had gone very vague when she'd asked what had kept the leopards from plunging to cat heaven sixty feet below.

He'd had nothing to do with it. Couldn't have.

And what the heck had happened to Hyacinth anyway? After she'd left the wide-load tracks in Max's back? Shouldn't she have been DOA on the floor far below, along with her mistress?

Nobody had asked Temple to ID a cat.

Not even her own.

Hmmm.

Since she didn't think interrogating Midnight Louie, wherever he was, would do her one whit of good, she decided to start with the wandering Russians.

Madame Olga was to be found wandering the lower levels of the installation, a study in melancholy. The exhibition was roped off now, of course, but it was not the scene of the death and insiders were still allowed access.

"Such a pity," Madame Olga said when she saw Temple catching up to her. "Such glory. All fallen."

Temple eyed the fittings from the Czars's private apartments; exotic woods inlaid with mother-of-pearl and green-veined malachite and capped with gleaming gold ormolu decorations.

"So exquisite," Madame Olga murmured. "Hard to believe that anyone lived like that. Our *Swan Lake* tutus were real swans' down. Genuine diamonds studded our tiaras. Our strained muscles and bleeding toes were our own, however. We last dancers of the Old Regime. Oh, not myself, Miss Barr. I was too young for that. But the tradition lingered on. Even today, I am watched. Not that they can stop me. Even though I defected twenty years ago, and it is now legal, old habits are stubborn and they fear bad press. They fear an ancient of days and dance like myself. Mighty Mother Russia, who feared no one, not even Napoleon! Now my home is a bankrupt republic and its rulers are the Russian Mob, not the liberated mob of the people. Bullies will always be bullies, only some will be refined."

"Is wrong ever refined?"

Madame Olga finally glanced at Temple. "Perhaps not. So.

My brother, poor wounded swan, is dead. He was poetry in *Swan Lake* once. Now I could not knit a missing wing for him to fly one short distance with."

Temple instantly recognized the fairy tale of the maiden indentured to weave wings for her seven brothers before they were turned into . . . what? The proletariat?

"Someone," Temple said, "wanted you to help steal the scepter for your brother's sake."

"Ah. A young woman with imagination." Madame Olga lowered her imperial receding chin to focus on Temple's face instead of the glittering artifacts surrounding them. "And a knowledge of folk tales. Yet you look so . . . Paris Hilton. Perhaps it is just an American affectation of corrupted innocence."

Temple cursed her bleached blond locks for the eighth time. Goldilocks was not a useful role model for modern women. Nor was Scarlett.

"It's the look of someone who wants an answer," she said. "There was more to your brother's fall from grace than you let on."

The old woman pinched the top of her Roman nose as if clearing her brain of blood. Strong nose, weak chin. Always a deceptive physiognomy in a woman. Temple tended to believe the nose, not the chin. Some of the feistiest breeds of lapdogs and the boldest belly dancers were zilch in the chin department. The recessive chin, in fact, was a snare and delusion for men who needed to think they were in charge. Her own was neither leading nor retreating, but just right, like Baby Bear's bed. Which was still a bear's bailiwick and very dangerous to be caught sleeping in.

Hmmm, speaking about being caught sleeping in . . .

Madame Olga laughed. "You have not lived in a totalitarian state, *ma petite.* Your face is a mirror of your emotions. I read guilt and it will cloud your judgment."

"You called me '*ma petite.*'"

"Are you not petite?"

"Did you live in France for a time?"

"*Mais oui.* We all did. We Imperial Russian entertainers spurned, our artistry despised by the New Order. We fled to France, always a haven for the artistically disenfranchised.

Your Negro musicians, for instance, and dancers. Josephine Baker, the divine *Afrique*. Erté, the gay blade of Art Deco designers. My poor brother took a pseudonym from him."

"'Art Deckle,' a play on the Art Deco style. I always think of the paper when I hear the name. Deckle edged."

"Yes. He was a man of culture at the beginning, anyway, which may be why he used white-face for a disguise that night. Then he was a man of any way he could make a living. Being an exile does that."

"And you?"

"I suppose women have it better. We can always settle for decorative. I became a dressmaker's model for a time. Everyone sketched me. I was quite famous for a mystery woman."

"Still, that must have been a fabulous time."

Olga leaned her Roman nose hard against a Plexiglas barrier, staring at a mannequin wearing a Russian court dress with a glittering white train as long as a snail's trail at dawn.

"My brother's body was broken, I was impoverished and forgotten. Our history was . . . considered trivial and decadent. We went our ways. His were secret and demeaning. I was eventually . . . rediscovered. Asked to teach master classes in Paris, London, New York City. I never saw him again until I came to this"—she sighed, looked around the vast museum-within-a-hotel-casino space—"this proletarian paradise. What hath Lenin wrought? Las Vegas. Anyone can win. Or lose. A people's paradise."

"Someone won possession of the Czar Alexander scepter," Temple heard herself saying. *Hypocrite!*

Temple felt horribly guilty for playing dumb, but she still needed to determine whether the earlier death was part of a separate plot. Damn Max for putting her in this position! For the first time, she understood Molina's fury at being sure he was guilty of something and being unable to touch him. And now Max had really become a thief. Was it possible he had killed Andrei? The idea was unthinkable, but Max had been doing a lot of the unthinkable lately. No wonder Temple herself was contemplating the formerly unthinkable.

"Not I," Olga said in her measured way. "And certainly not poor dead Andrei."

"Were you working together to get it, though?"

"No. Never working together. Not again. Not dancing together. Not for decades. Working apart to the last."

She eyed Temple askance through her crepe-paper eyelids, so like an aged serpent's.

"Someone had enlisted him for this cursed venture. I discovered his participation too late. He never dropped me. Not once. When we danced. Until here. And he did not drop me here either. I dropped him, I suppose. It is the perfect pitiable end to *Swan Lake* that a ballerina should be the cause of her supporting prince's fall. Brother, lover, it does not matter. Do not cause any man's fall, my petite interrogator. It is not something one ever lives down."

Chapter 42

When, Where, Why For?

Temple fled from the nihilism of Madame Olga to the urbane charms of Count Volpe, even though he reminded her of some rapacious object of Molière's wit.

He was always ready to oblige a young woman, an attractive young woman, as he told her freely.

"Are there any unattractive young women in your opinion?" Temple asked.

"Not really," he said, after a moment's consideration. "Why are you worrying yourself white about these exhibition-area deaths? It was obvious that someone would attempt to steal the scepter and someone did. Quite dramatically. Pity about the acrobat. I don't believe the thief intended to drop her, although that fact did slow down the pursuit."

Volpe's urbane Old World sexism and New World frankness almost undid Temple. She supposed if she had seen an old political order perish she might be somewhat cynical too.

"I've just come from identifying the body."

"My dear girl! Pardon my blasé pose. It's expected of me. Here. Sit down. Why would the police impose on you for this sad duty?"

"I'm the only one around at the moment who'd seen Shangri-La out of her concealing makeup."

"Surely the tiger-faced fellow—?" He waved a veined but exquisitely fluid hand.

"The Cloaked Conjuror had never seen her face-to-face."

"How bizarre, when you think of it. Two strangers performing life-threatening antics on wires and cords. It did lend itself to substitution, didn't it? Is it certain that the Cloaked Conjuror we saw before the fall was indeed him?"

"He was by the time the police got there." Temple sat up straighter. "But it may not always have been him, is that what you're saying?"

Volpe shrugged and produced a dark European cigarette. "If you permit. Nasty habit, but so is being the eyewitness to a violent death. Who's to say that was the mantled mage himself we saw caught in that cat's cradle of rope? This theft was a piece of legerdemain gone astray, I think. The man in the Cloaked Conjuror guise appeared to be improvising, but he did apparently make off with the prize." Volpe exhaled an elegant stream of blue smoke, scented slightly of licorice. "And why are you so involved, *petite chou?* Dragging you out to see a dead body! So retrograde. I thought they had television screens for that now."

Was Volpe probing?

"They do," Temple said. "But since no one else on the premises had glimpsed her face, I was elected to go to the viewing chamber. A room with a glass viewing window," she added in answer to his elegantly inquiring eyebrows, which reminded her of something. Someone?

"I wish I had seen her! She was an amazing performer, sinewy as one of the big cats yet delicate. Do the police have any idea who her almost rescuer was? He does appeal, doesn't he, to the dramatic sense? Part rogue, part rescuer, anonymous. That sort of swashbuckling type went out with the old-time movie stars, didn't it? Fairbanks. Flynn. The Scarlet Pimpernel in literature. Zorro. Irresistible to women."

"I imagine that would be hard to live with."

"Who said anything about living with? I meant loving with. Young women today are so distressingly practical."

Temple felt her lightly freckled skin flush. Why did she think she could domesticate the wild Max anyway, or even want to?

"I see his attractions are not lost on you. A fine hero for an opera—no, too ponderous. A ballet. He certainly had the moves up there. I almost thought he'd save her; I'm afraid he did too. It's a remarkable thief who interrupts a clever caper to save the innocent bystanders. Or to try to. I hope the scepter is worth it to him."

"I do too," Temple muttered fervently. She fidgeted under Volpe's keen dark eyes, then struck back.

"I think he was hired help."

"Really? Not a dashing entrepreneur, then, but some coarse theft-for-hire thug?"

She wouldn't let Volpe yank her chain any more. Time to turn the tables. If he was so blasé but observant, he might know something she could use. He had confessed a weakness for young attractive women, after all, and Temple could attract when she felt like it.

She smiled and nodded. "You've said exactly what I was wondering. The scepter isn't just some valuable artifact, it's a one-of-a-kind catch. Whoever wanted it doesn't need to sell it, or even show it off. It's a trophy. Who'd want it for that?"

"I would."

"You, Count, the toast of *Vanity Fair*'s photo layouts?"

"Theoretically, of course. I am a penniless aristocrat, I'm afraid, and could not even hire a pickpocket. I might, however, be tempted to by the Russian government's current scrabbling for money and recognition over the graves of my ancestors. Of its crawling like what you call a Johnny-come-lately to exploit the culture and glory that was Russia before the anarchists and Bolsheviks and drunken peasant party functionaries ravished its heritage and weakened its influence in the world."

"White Russians still have such strong feelings?"

"You Americans have felt the first wave of anarchy in your own, sea-bound land. Russia has always been the large, unmanageable brother of western and eastern Europe, the not-quite-tamed lumbering bear. We produced more art, music, literature, and grandeur than we have ever been credited for. The Czar Alexander scepter is a symbol of that, yes?"

Temple just nodded, slowly. "What about Red Russians?"

Volpe snorted and stubbed out his exotic cigarette. "Not much left for them these days but backpedaling. The economy is lame, the mobsters have emigrated from the U.S. to our shores, not literally, but their spirits have. A proud people who held off Napoleon and Hitler are now more noted for their shopping lines and vodka consumption than their technological or artistic achievements. Bah! I salute whoever took the scepter. He who has the nerve to claim it, deserves it. He is Russian."

Temple blinked. She didn't see Max as a White Russian icon, but stranger things had happened.

"He was hired, remember, in our theory? Even Red Russians can hire good help."

"*Touché!*" Volpe laughed, then grew broody. "Of course they could be behind it, the uneasy alliance of bureaucrats and brigands that rules Russia today. Are you a police spy, Miss Barr?"

Temple gasped. "I . . . the local police know me from my PR business around Las Vegas, that's all."

The dark eyes narrowed like a needle, ripe for stabbing. "I have seen spies and stooges and tools before. They were not to be trusted. Are you to be trusted?"

"I want the exhibition to go smoothly. I want the scepter back. I want the person or persons who killed Andrei and Shangri-La caught and tried and punished. I want to do my job in a crime-free zone."

"Your list of wants is ambitious and impressive. And what of your list of likelihoods?"

Temple stood, smoothing her skirt. "This is Las Vegas. I know it inside out. I figure my odds are at least fifty-fifty."

Volpe did her the honor of paling.

Chapter 43

Home, Sweet Homicide

I owe Miss Temple Barr the roof over my head, the litter box that I never use under the second bathroom sink, the copious treats of real fish over my Free-to-Be-Feline health pellets, several prime Circle Ritz lounging spots, including her lap and zebra-pattern comforter, and a lot of crime scenes that need tidying up and puzzles that need solving.

It is a pretty soft life, as Miss Midnight Louise would be the first to tell me, and I can even forgive the recent presence of Miss Temple's maternal aunt on my living room sofa.

I mean "maternal" aunt in the sense that she is Miss Temple's mother's sister. (Whew! These human relationships are complex. To me, aunts and uncles are nonexistent and cousins are aliens. It is bad enough that I know my own father and mother—and do not think that I do not regret it every day!). Knowing a possible daughter is . . . bizarre in the extreme.

Anyway, my Miss Temple and I go pretty far back for both of our breeds, far enough that I feel for her in her pretty nasty state of perpetual heat with two equally persistent toms on her tail. In my circles, the female is not crazy about the urge to procreate but must submit to nature and a domineering dude. In my Miss Temple's world, the choice is solely up to her, poor thing. Much too much stress for the female brain and delicate emotional structure. Obviously, Mr. Max Kinsella has been the top dude around here, but Mr. Matt Devine is coming up on the inside. *Hmm.* That sounds a little racy. Come what may, I am the dude in the middle . . . of the comforter and of my Miss Temple's delicate emotional balance.

I must do something. Since I cannot compete head to head, or whatever, with these human dudes, I guess I have to help her out in the sleuth department without nailing her main man as a perp.

What a dilemma!

Miss Midnight Louise has no idea what a narrow ethical tightrope a righteous dude like myself must tread. . . .

So, I watch my Miss Temple come home, sigh, drop her heavy tote bag by the empty couch (Auntie Libido is out with the top Fontana male again), and turn to me for comfort.

"Louie." Sigh. "Louie." Sigh.

I began to think I am a squeaky toy. *Whoosh. Whoosh. Wussy.*

This will never do. I happen to be in possession of a lot of insight from my hours hanging up top with Squeaker and the other cats big and small, like Hyacinth, high above the New Millennium exhibit space. Time to share the riches, and I do not mean the Czar Alexander scepter, only the likely disposition of who did whom in to get it.

I understand the rules of the game: Mr. Max must not be nailed. Pity. I am beginning to think he deserves it for conduct unbecoming to a progenitor of the species.

I get up and swagger into the office off the living room.

"Louie," she calls after me. (Dames are always calling after me.) "It is too late to work. Come back here and settle down! I promise Aunt Kit won't roll over on you again. Louie!"

Hah! Promises are cheap and my ribs are still sore. . . . Besides, I have something in mind, and something in store. Now. How to communicate with a professional communicator of the lesser species—? It will be a challenge, which is why I like hanging with my Miss Temple.

"Lou-ie!"

She is after me like a puma on catnip. What did I tell you? I got It.

By now I have hopped up on the bookshelf opposite her computer desk, having first dislodged a few annoying impediments.

"Louie!"

She is so cute when she sounds annoyed with me. Like I do not know she will come over forthwith and scratch my chin and tickle my tummy and tell me I am a bad, bad boy. I must admit that these humans have foreplay down cold.

"Louie."

She is crooning now, in the palm of my paw. I stretch out a foreleg, casually, and let her hold my, er, hand.

"You naughty boy! Why do you have to knock everything off a shelf before you lie on it?"

Because I *can!* And I am not "lying," I am telling a bigger truth than anyone has told you on this case. Read my lips. In this case, my hips, which have dislodged a big fat clue right onto the parquet floor. Read it and weep! *Read it!* Well, just notice it! And then think!

I tell you, leading these humans around by the nose hairs is a very fatiguing business. What? You say I am the one with nose hairs? I beg your pardon. These whiskers are vibrassae, a high-toned Latin-language accessory if there ever was one.

But, hush! My Miss Temple is noticing. And thinking. At last. *Shhhh . . .*

"Gosh." She sits on her heels and pages through a few of the paperback tomes I have cast to the floor to make room for my luxuriating torso. "I remember reading these books way back when while waiting up for Max to do his last show at the Goliath and come home."

Now she is sniveling! Not my desired reaction!

"Short stories by H. H. Munro, known as *Saki*."

"Sake?" I did not want her to turn to the bottle, although I can understand why she might want to.

"And . . . oh, my goodness. My favorite Agatha Christie."

Warm.

"I always loved the ones with exotic settings."

Warmer.

"This was my favorite. Reminds me of a Russian blue cat, in a way."

Skip the rival breed! I am an all-American alley cat. And black to the bone.

"A Russian blue is an exotic breed but basically . . . gray."

She sits up as if she had borrowed a swordfish's spine.

"Oh! That might be why . . . that might be it . . . that might be the answer!"

Duh!

Chapter 44

The Murderer in the
Gray Flannel Suite

Temple breezed in to the New Millennium the next morning and asked Pete Wayans for the use of the gray flannel suite.

"We are way past planning sessions, Miss Barr. In case you haven't noticed, our exhibition is ravaged, our magic show is compromised, and our joint credibility is zilch. It's not your fault, but you were a major hire. *C'est la vie.*"

"No. *C'est la key.* I'd like everyone involved in the exhibition convened there, this afternoon. May I order a round of hors d'oeuvres?"

"That would cost hundreds. If you deduct it from your contract."

"Of course, but if I solve your murders, the same amount goes to me as a bonus."

"A bonus? I'm sorry but the police solve murders."

"Sometimes. Sometimes I do if I must. A clean slate would give this exhibition and show a new lease on . . . death."

By then Randy had joined them. "What's up, chief?"

"Your little Miss Barr. She's making bail-out noises."

"Not me wanting to bail out," Temple said. "Me wanting to bail you guys out."

"We could use a bail out," Randy said. "I advise we listen."

"Your job is at risk."

Randy visibly braced himself. "Could things get any worse? I say we go along to get along."

"Crudités," Wayans snarled.

"A large happy carrot stick to you too," Temple said.

She couldn't help being upbeat, although Randy winced as Wayans stalked (get it, celery!) away.

"He's the big man, Tee. Our futures are riding on this."

"I'm feeling very futuristic. Can you make sure that all concerned show up?"

"Yeah, but why?"

"I have places to go and people to see. See you later, defribulator."

Randy clutched the area of his heart but headed out to do his duty.

Temple speed-dialed her cell phone. "Dear Detective Alch," she began.

He swore. Conservatively but colorfully and with a certain paternal certainty that she would absorb every rough syllable and still twist him around her little finger. . . .

The main thing was that Molina was *not* here.

This was a totally not-Molina operation.

Temple glanced at Alch. He knew that she knew he was bucking the command structure. She knew that he knew that she knew he had a soft spot for earnest young women with agendas. And that Molina no longer qualified. Too old. Too wired. Too seriously screwed. Too hung up on Max. Either way.

Temple eyed the full complement of White Russian exhibition professionals around the conference table, from the aristocratic elders to the brave new proletariat.

"Two people have died in the course of mounting this exhibition," she began.

Lips were bitten, heads lowered, crocodile tears shed, so to speak.

"In the course of mounting this exhibition, the prime piece on display, the Czar Alexander scepter, has been stolen in plain sight."

More feet shuffling under the long conference table, more downcast eyes. Temple stood at the head of the table. Several file folders shifted under her fingernails.

Detective Alch stood, back to the double–conference room doors, fading into a forgotten gray-suited figure. Another man in a suit had slipped in just before the conference room doors closed for good. Tall, angular, sharp, the opposite of Alch, except for the gray suit.

Those gathered around the table fidgeted like the courtroom cast in a Perry Mason television mystery. Some possible witnesses, some possible perps. The semi-anonymous Moscow muscle stood at the table's opposite end, bracketing Dimitri. He was sweating.

Madame Olga's neck was stretching longer than a swan's. Count Volpe's crepey eyelids sank shut like weary sails.

Swans and ships and sealing wax on bureaucratic documents, Temple thought. They were all suspects. Any one of them could have skewered the exhibition for any imaginable cause, old or new.

Except not *one* of them had done it. Had done anything. None of them had pushed Art-Andrei off a pinnacle platform. Had sabotaged the rigging before the dress rehearsal. Had taken the scepter. Had planned the operation.

Max, she knew, had been a wild card. The joker. The Fool in the Tarot deck. The unsuspected, unpredictable element. Ah, wasn't he always? Temple smiled in tribute, even as she doubted she'd ever tell him about this moment. About her triumph. That he'd ever be near her again to hear about it.

This was her solo act. Her debut. Temple without Max.

Her job at stake. Her heart at risk. Her pulse racing triple time.

It would be hard to reveal the scenario she suspected without putting Max into it, without revealing that she knew who had the scepter or what she knew about the Synth and its goals.

That was her trick to perform. To paint him as an anonymous confederate of whomever here in the room had engineered the exhibition disruptions on behalf of the real confederate.

"We have two very different deaths here," she summed up.

"One was man, one woman?" Dimitri asked derisively from his end of the table. His stooges cracked matching smirks.

"The first was a man, and there really wasn't much point in his death. It only alerted everyone to the fact that someone had a serious eye on the scepter." Unless that was the point, but Temple wasn't going to mention that. Her job was to defuse, not confuse. In fact, Andrei's death was a huge blow to anyone who planned to steal the scepter. It made any attempt harder.

"Therefore," Temple said, "it must have been an accident."

Alch shifted his weight unhappily against his door, though nobody but she faced him. Homicide detectives are not crazy about accidental deaths.

"What was Andrei doing up there, then?" Pete Wayans wanted to know.

"Scouting the setup, of course. He was the first one recruited to do what the man in black eventually did: steal the scepter.

"I see," Count Volpe said. "His accident . . . his fall from grace, forced the thief to hire a new person to 'crash' the performance and steal the artwork."

"But if," Wayans argued, "he was competent to do high-wire work, why would he fall?"

"I didn't say he was alone up there," Temple said. "I'm thinking a difference of expert opinion. Or he wasn't really willing to risk his bad leg on such a dicey stunt at his age. He was recruited or pressured because of his background. I think he argued with someone here, and in the course of it he over-balanced and fell."

"Someone here?" Wayans looked around. "These people are all directly involved in sponsoring or mounting the exhibition, except for the corporate sponsors, whom I'm pleased to see you are not subjecting to this humiliation, Miss Barr."

"It's better than death," she said.

"If someone on staff wanted the scepter," said Count Volpe, delicately adjusting the silk ascot that obscured his stringy neck, "look no farther than the political functionaries. They do not respect symbols of the aristocratic rule, and see only dollar or Euro or ruble signs."

Dimitri tried to charge out of his chair, but the boys in black held him down. For his own sake.

"And you worthless spawn of the privileged see more?" Dimitri demanded.

"Not only see it," Volpe drawled, "but we can read it."

"A nice show," Temple said, eyeing the combatants, "but it was all a magic act from the beginning. Who are you diverting our eyes from now with your posturings?"

They weren't about to look in any direction but their fingernails tapping on the exotic tabletop.

Temple eyed Madame Olga.

"He was your brother. You would have been able to persuade him to do the job. You helped design the installation. You would have been able to show him the literal ropes from a point way up high. You would have been positioned to cajole, coax, command him to do it."

"Steal the scepter? Why would I? Silly goose girl! It is a symbol of my roots. Why would I want it in crass commercial hands?"

"Maybe you thought this Sin City exhibition was a crass commercial venue for a Czarist treasure," Temple suggested. "Andrei wasn't meant to fall, to die. I think you had an argument. I think you reversed roles for once up there. I think Andrei the crippled con man didn't want to rip off one of White Russia's most amazing artifacts. I think you had to convince him to do it. What words, spoken harshly under the cover of night? Words escalating into gestures, broad gestures? Forgetting where you were? Turning, stepping—?"

Madame Olga's face grew paler by the instant.

"What a playwright you would have made."

"There's no room up there. Not for mistakes. Not for emotions. Did he demand a reason, wave his arms . . . then overbalance and, waving his arms, in the heat of anger and protest, fall, grab a bungee cord and struggle to climb up, save himself? And instead enmesh himself in it, his safety rope becoming a noose?"

"No, no!"

"And you watched, unable to do a thing, not even report it because that would betray the scheme. He hung there for hours after his death, a human pendulum, your own brother, who had taken a more noble stand than you had."

Temple had thought and thought about what could have led to Andrei's plunge from the platform high above the exhibition. She had theorized like a defense attorney on his mute behalf. And now she had made her case before the jury.

Madame Olga Kirkov shriveled into sobs of protest, hiding her quizzical old face in her time-veined hands.

"This is outrageous." Pete Wayans stood. "Madame Olga is the greatest ballet artist of her generation. She has volunteered her expertise in both arranging for and designing this exhibition. She is an old lady and her brother has died violently. This must stop. My God, she's an old lady!"

"Sit down," Detective Alch said mildly from the door.

Pete Wayans eyed him and the silent, unnamed man next to him. He sat.

The room's only sound was the choking sobs of Madame Olga.

"He had changed his mind about even planning the theft," she said at last. "Gazing down at the exhibition space he felt a pride of nation I had never seen in him before. He said he would rather die than take the scepter. Andrei! My crooked brother. I would never have asked such a thing of him, but . . . I had to. He was so shocked by my demand, so horrified. He backed away . . . from me, from the very idea. I never touched him. I couldn't save him. I could only watch, paralyzed, as he fell and . . . run away."

Volpe had risen to come and stand behind her chair, his knotted hands pressing deeply into its upholstered back.

"It wasn't murder, then," Temple said.

"Oh, yes!" Madame Olga's eyes surfaced from behind her hands. "I murdered his illusions about myself. I was the Sugar Plum Fairy, the good sister lifted twice daily by the prince in white tights. Pure Russian. Innocent! Andrei was no prince, and we both knew it. Until I tried to force him against his . . . his own honesty. Which humbles mine, in the end. Andrei! I not only let you fall, I let you take the blame for your fall. It was I. I was the snake in Eden and he was a better Adam than there ever was."

Temple's knees were shaking. She'd hoped . . . she *had* to . . . clear up a few mysteries, not peel back the top layer of human souls.

Old souls. Old wounds. New perfidies.

She was doing this for Max. One last obligation. He was the odd man out in all of this and shouldn't have to swing for it. She saw his rueful grin even as she thought that two-edged phrase.

If she convicted someone else, Max would be exonerated, even if only in her own heart. And she knew that this was where it would matter most to him, to her.

"Why did you have to persuade Andrei to take the scepter?" Temple asked the old woman. Gently.

The words came sharp and bitter. "Because my masters demanded it."

Volpe's hands moved from the chair back to her frail shoulders with a white-knuckled grip that shouted *"Silence!"*

Madame Olga had been used to commanding audiences, not being commanded. Not even by a confrere. She lengthened her swan's neck, hardened her fading features.

Temple decided to let that intriguing matter go for now.

"So with Andrei dead, who replaced him? Who was recruited next to steal the scepter?"

"You saw him," Volpe said. "We all did. "The man in the

mock–Cloaked Conjuror costume. He played Andrei's part: swooped down in masked disguise, disabled the installation case, and grabbed the scepter, escaping the same way he had come, from the magic show flies and wings high above. We don't know who he was, we don't know where they got him."

Madame Olga pressed her thin lips together. Temple knew that Count Volpe was seizing on Max's unexpected appearance to end these unsettling explanations.

"The police," Volpe added with a haughty glare at Detective Alch, "haven't any clue to who he is. I suppose with so many Cirque du Soleil shows in town, the place is crammed with unemployed world-class acrobats. Andrei had been unfit for such a caper, anyway, and too old."

"He could have done it!" Madame Olga said, her pride pricked again.

She was the one who would confess, because she was the one most offended by whatever forces had pushed them into this scheme gone wrong.

"The man who actually took the scepter," Temple said, "was obviously a last-minute hire. So much went wrong. It was a wonder he escaped with the prize. No, Madame Olga, there was someone much closer to the exhibition who was the ideal substitute for Andrei. Someone your 'masters' spotted and snapped up. Someone you, and Count Volpe on your behalf, felt obligated to protect, so that even Andrei's death didn't free you to wash your hands of the affair."

"A handy substitute," Wayans asked, sitting up. "Not the guy in black?"

"Were you aware of his participation?" Temple asked Madame Olga and Count Volpe.

He began to shrug, but she said No most definitely. "I'm tired of play-acting and lying, Ivan," she told him over her shoulder. "It's obvious we will not leave this room with our reputations intact. I see no reason to spare anyone else's.

"He was a complete surprise," she went on, addressing Temple and the room at large, "and he was completely surprised by the breakaway set pieces up there. He obviously saved the Cloaked Conjuror's life, and almost, almost—" She broke down in sobs, as Volpe knelt beside her.

"She's been through so much," he accused Temple. "You are putting her through more for no purpose."

"For the purpose of an answer so the show that you've all worked so hard on can go on and justice will have been done."

Pete Wayans was looking frankly puzzled. "You seem to know who this mysterious accomplice was. Why don't you just tell us?"

"Because I have a point to make and it's always better to let it be made by the suspects. This case is like, and very unlike, Agatha Christie's *Murder on the Orient Express*, where everyone did it. No one in this room is a murderer."

The silence was complete, and Olga let her iron control dissolve as her head sank onto Ivan's shoulder.

Wayans nodded. "This Andrei guy obviously died during an argument in a place where he shouldn't have been, a place way too dangerous for civilians. No one is allowed up in that performance area but the performers."

"And mysterious men in black," Randy put in.

Temple wished he hadn't. The less they thought about Max the better.

Time for her to exercise some iron control.

"Exactly, Mr. Wayans. Nobody was allowed up there but performers, and once Andrei was dead, the theft's masterminds had no literal fall guy."

"Except for a piece of wild luck and coincidence."

Olga and Ivan were now regarding her with mutual alarm. Temple knew they were involved, but she didn't know *why* yet. Or how deeply. Olga already carried her brother's death on her conscience, but something else deeply personal was still tormenting her.

Everyone in the room was quiet and still, as if any noise or movement would draw unwelcome attention. Dimitri and his twin bodyguards were as stolid as the red marble statues in the Red Planetary Restaurant (although they would look a lot less interesting nude).

The lawmen at the door were stone.

At the conference table, the elderly White Russians made a pair of rather frail mated doves. (And why had they concealed their obviously long-standing relationship until now?)

Temple had a few answers and they weren't pleasant, but she still had so many more questions that had to be answered before anybody here could move on from last week's events. So she spoke again.

"There was one person, already on the scene, who could substitute for Andrei. The perfect solution to the problem. So obvious yet hidden that only one careless moment was needed to give someone the awful answer to a criminal dilemma that led to grand theft and disaster and death."

Randy looked up at Temple with clear, disbelieving eyes. He glanced at Olga and Ivan. He saw where she was going.

"Shangri-La!" he said. "That twirling stunt right on top of the onion dome! She was perfectly positioned to knock off the scepter and bungee cord out of there. Of course, her performing career would be over—"

"As Shangri-La," Temple pointed out. "She already was a conundrum, as disguised as the Cloaked Conjuror in her own way. She could always have reinvented herself."

"Still," Randy said. "On a Las Vegas level? Comebacks are almost impossible."

Temple winced on Max's behalf but Randy was right.

"Why would she do it?" Wayans wanted to know. "This is a major venue. The money is princely."

Against their venal speculations, Olga's sobs were soft and continuous.

Temple looked over her shoulder at Alch. "Detective, would you mind telling everyone who Shangri-La really was."

He stepped forward. "Sure. Hai Ling. Member of a Chinese tumbling troupe that defected here in Las Vegas several years ago. They do that. Artistic types from Communist countries. Want the artistic freedom of the West." He stepped back into position at the doors.

"*We* defected," Olga said, her quiet voice clogged with tears. "Ivan. Myself. Andrei. All years ago, when that was the only way to leave Russia by free will. Andrei, he became drunk on Western freedom and destroyed his career, almost himself. Ivan and I met in Paris while I toured with the Russian Ballet. When Andrei and I defected, Ivan joined me in helping other defectors. After the Cold War ended, Russians could come and go, but not the Chinese or the North Koreans."

"We helped them," Ivan said, "the younger generation of defectors. Covertly, of course. We didn't want to cause international incidents. With Hai Ling, she had family back home she feared for. She wanted to work anonymously. We helped her in the beginning. Later, we'd lost touch. We didn't know her stage name. We didn't know Shangri-La was Hai Ling until she approached us, very discreetly, after we were all here preparing for the exhibition and show opening."

"She *thanked* us," Olga said, "for helping make possible her participation here. For helping to ensure her continuing career, so that she could perform as a star at this magnificent hotel in America . . . and because of us she was here to be coerced into becoming a thief and to die in a stupid accident caused by such a petty motivation as greed!

"She told us she'd been careless," Olga went on bitterly. "She was so eager to see the exhibition space going up she darted into the area without her constant concealing makeup on. The area was filled with workmen. How could she have known that our masters immediately spotted her. Defectors—their own or other countries'—were their business. They knew her instantly."

Temple was as speechless as everyone in the room. She had thought that only she remembered the few moments a barefaced Shangri-La had shown herself. And it wasn't due to bedazzlement at the White Russian exhibition, or any other naive girl reasons she had given to her long-ago sponsors.

It was because she had wanted to taunt Temple. She was already a thief, she had brazenly taken Temple's Tiffany opal-and-diamond ring from Max onstage. She was no shrinking lotus to quail at someone's suggestion that she steal a priceless artifact. She'd had some unsolved connection to designer drug dealers. She could turn on her persona as easily as she could spin on a bungee cord, and probably would, for a big enough cut.

Temple could have mentioned all that, but she didn't want to expose a personal life that led right back to the Mystifying Max Kinsella and the real thief of the scepter.

And she didn't want to disillusion a pair of heroic old people who revered their heritage and probably regarded Hai Ling as a foster daughter.

Hai Ling, aka Shangri-La, had likely laughed up her scalloped sleeve when she realized that showing herself to Temple had earned her a cut in a major heist. She at least had the grace, or balls, to make her former sponsors feel they had done a good thing all those years ago, and that she was an exemplary graduate of their school for defectors, and someone worth mourning.

Temple would leave her those two true mourners.

Pete Wayans was disrupting the silence by see-sawing a pencil on the lever of his fingers, one end and the other tapping against the tabletop like a metronome.

"So, just who are these 'masters' behind all this? As far as I know, these people don't have 'masters' anymore."

"You don't know much," Randy muttered into his double chin.

"Exactly," Temple said. "Who was putting the pressure on everyone to dance to their tune?"

Ivan eyed Randy. "Sometimes 'masters' are czars, or political functionaries, or CEOs. And even if one defects and is safe in another country—or one's family fled decades ago—the pull of power is a long and deadly one. You have your own masters to account to, Mr. Wayans, and you know it."

Pete cleared his throat and choked off the pencil.

"And sometimes," Temple said, "masters are mobsters."

"Wait a minute here!" Pete Wayans stood up. "That is such an old charge for enterprises in Las Vegas. Maybe the mob was a factor in founding Las Vegas. Maybe it ruled the roost in the fifties. And the sixties."

"And seventies," Detective Alch put in.

The other, unidentified man at the doors was unnervingly quiet.

"The mob has gone corporate," Randy said, "for the most part. It has to answer to . . . folks. It would never endorse a high-scale heist at a major hotel. Bad for business. Everybody's business."

"Agreed," Temple said. "But I'm talking about the Russian

mob." She smiled at Boris and Natasha, who did not smile back.

Ivan pulled Olga off her chair and to the floor.

Wayans gulped, grabbed Randy's arm, and pulled him down too.

The men at the door remained at attention.

Boris and Natasha pulled two ugly black guns with nasty long barrels that Temple didn't know what to call.

She did know enough to punch one button on the computer keyboard in front of her that was set to operate the gray flannel blinds that wore mirror shades on the other side.

The sound of them remotely being opened was enough to draw Boris and Natasha's attention in the same split second that the blinds reflected an infinity of Fontana brothers in off-white ice cream suits with black Berettas, all in copyrighted James Bond pose, legs planted and guns aimed and braced in both hands at Boris and Natasha's most precious bodily organs.

It was an infinitely split-screen stand-off.

Boris and Natasha lowered the firepower as the Fontana brothers to the ninth degree circled in on them like well-tailored sharks.

Dimitri sat still. "I am not a defector," he said, "but I am requesting the protective custody of the U.S. government. These are my guards, but not my bodyguards. I have been their prisoner since arriving in this country. They are mobsters intent on robbing the exhibition and I would like them extradited to my country for . . . proper punishment."

Temple sank onto her chair, her knees shaking, as the Fontana brothers wafted the two Russian mobsters to the doors, which opened to reveal the boys in buff (officers of the LVMPD) ready to cuff 'em, read 'em their Mirandas, and cart them away.

Pete Wayans was patting his forehead with his silk pocket handkerchief and sitting on a chair again.

Olga and Ivan were joined at the hip, although pale.

"Can we go?" Ivan asked.

"It's pretty clear," Alch said, "that a lot of folks were coerced here. We'll need a statement, but you two need to rest up a bit first. We'll call."

Temple was nearly putting her neck out of joint to see, but no Molina seemed to be lurking in the hall.

"So the only criminal still at large," Wayans was saying, "is the fellow who actually took the scepter. Do you think those Russky bozos will say who he was during interrogation?"

Alch smiled slightly at the paper tiger Wayans had become.

"Who's to say, sir? This is a pretty murky case, even with Miss Barr's masterful extraction of the facts from the victims of this scheme."

He quirked an eyebrow at her, and left.

"Great job," Wayans said, gathering up his automatic pencil. "The show will go on without the scepter. Too bad," he told Temple, "I like your spin that maybe someone took it to save it from these mobsters. Randy, do me a press release on all this. All's well that end's well. International scheme uncovered by the staff of the New Millennium and me. The regular."

He left briskly, except when he came up even with the remaining man at the door, and then he stalled a little.

The guy smiled like a shark. Maybe it was the sleek, gray sharkskin suit.

Wayans scooted through the door as Randy patted Temple on the shoulder.

"You're a better man than I am, Gunga Din. I would never have remained standing with the Fontana brothers and their Italian tailoring and designer Berettas the only thing between me and those Cro-Magnon mobsters."

"You didn't, Randy," Temple said, laughing.

"So this tangled web of theft is pretty much untangled, except for how all the magic show rigging turned into breakaway props. You can't tell me anyone up there was expecting that, not even Shangri-La."

Randy was right: Temple couldn't tell him most of what had happened up there, especially Max's involvement, or suspicions that the Synth had been trying to kill him. She had to come up with a good reason to overlook that issue.

"It's possible that Shangri-La rigged some of it to fail as a distraction, but was taken unawares by the extra rigging set up for the fake Cloaked Conjuror."

"Two forces working in secret opposition?"

"Something like that. The police will be working overtime to ID the thief and find him, believe me."

Especially Lieutenant C. R. Molina, she added mentally.

"Right. Well, I'll tell the press the equipment failed because the thief or thieves tampered with it. And I'll do as much for your role in resolving this situation in the press release as Wayans' ego will let me. *Semper fi.*"

Still, Temple's ankles wavered a little on her to-die-for Stuart Weitzman/Midnight Louie high-heeled pumps covered in solid Austrian crystals with a black cat image on the heel. They were way too dressy for this occasion but somehow it felt good to have Louie backing up her ankles, at least.

The only person left in the room was Mr. Stone Face in the gray flannel suit at the door. Obviously a Red State Republican. Obviously Law and Order, but whose?

Temple walked over.

"Nice shoes," he said.

"Thanks. I think I know you but I'm a little hazy just now."

"You should be." He took pity on her lack of instant recall. "Does Elvis Presley ever cross your mind?"

"Right! That Elvis impersonator competition. You're . . . Matt's FBI friend."

"Frank Bucek. We do want a go at those two Russian mobster guys. That's why Molina called me in."

"Molina?" Temple felt like cringing but didn't.

"She's peripheral to this. So. About you. Matt's Las Vegas friend."

"Right."

"Friend kinda doesn't cover it, does it? Not with Matt."

"Um, no."

"You'd never pass the physical, but I'd want you in the FBI anytime. That was a nervy little act you did there."

"Just doing my job. Public relations is a very demanding profession. If you do it right."

"So, how's Matt?"

"Great. He's becoming a major media . . . icon. Gosh. Speaking all over the country. His syndicated radio show. You're an ex-priest too, aren't you?"

She glanced at the plain gold band on his left ring finger. "Married?"

"Yup."

"Do you, like, ever talk to your wife?"

He cracked a smile, reluctantly. "Yup."

"What do you say?"

"None of your business."

"Well, it kinda is. Matt's asked me to marry him."

"That happens. What's the problem?"

Temple had been through a very stressful few hours. She searched for something decently vague to say, then couldn't help what came out: "I don't want to have thirteen kids, like more than Mama Fontana," she blurted, "considering how old I am now and how fertile I could be and no birth control and, oh shit."

Frank Bucek shut his eyes, gathering himself. "Only the Pope would have thirteen kids now, and he's exempt. I'll talk to Matt, okay?"

"That's just it. I think he's afraid to have any, and I don't know what I want. Yet."

"I'll talk to Matt."

"What about me?"

He smiled. "You need talking to, but by a superior officer. Thank God it's not me. Leave the Russian mob to the pros and go home and have a good belt."

Chapter 45

Mad Matt

"Ma! He's going to go to the Father-Daughter Dance next fall with me! It'll be so sweet to see the other girls' faces. I mean, Mr. Midnight. In person. With *me*!"

Carmen came up short on her daughter's teen exuberance.

Mariah had grabbed her in the kitchen as she entered from the attached garage and hugged her. *Hugged* her? Mean Bad No-no Mama?

No mother of a teenager expects anything but angst during that dreaded three-year transition period.

"*Whoa! Chica!* Who are we talking about?"

She'd had a big, bad day. FBI. Russian mob. Temple Barr.

That's when Carmen looked past the kitchen into the den.

Matt Devine was standing there, hands in chino pants pockets, looking slightly embarrassed. As well he should be!

And looking like . . . definite girl bait. Blond, diffident, and coolly hot: a total hottie according to teen parlance. Molina had seen the teen mags.

"I don't know much about it," Matt was saying.

Obviously, Matt had come to call for some reason and Mariah had seen, jumped, snagged, and overwhelmed. Girls today were so much more aggressive with boys than in her day.

So Mama was forced to give out the details. "Junior High formal dance. First one. Next fall. Mariah's way ahead of the gun—"

"Really?" Matt eyed her chubby-turning-tall daughter. "First dance? I'm flattered. But I'm not a great dancer, Mariah."

"You will be. We can practice ahead of time, right?"

"Ah, right."

Carmen smiled to watch Matt watch Mariah bounce down the hall to her bedroom, her inner sanctum of clutter and boy-band posters. He hadn't counted on rehearsals.

He eyed the mother in the case. "This meet with your approval?"

Molina sighed. "She doesn't have a father. A presentable father," she added at Matt's straight-shooter look. "You're a local celebrity. It'd make her day. Night."

"Done deal." He came closer.

Matt was attractive in the extreme. He was single. He was an ex-priest, which a Latina like her could certainly understand. She would trust him with her daughter, but not with his own personal instincts.

"Why are you here? I know Mariah snagged you for escort duty when you showed up, but that's just you being nice. Why are you really here?"

"Because I don't feel like being nice."

"Ah. Dos Equis?"

"Yeah. With lime."

"You feeling south of the border tonight?"

He watched her dive into the fridge. She knew the interior light uplit her face like a lineup photo. Not flattering.

He took the amber beer bottle she offered. "I'm feeling disappointed tonight," he said. It was a Catholic school line.

"With me? Sorry, Father. I don't go to confession anymore."

"You should. What you did to Temple was inexcusable."

"What? I did my job. I interrogated her. Finish."

"You bullied her."

"You can bully a redhead?"

"She's a blonde for the moment, and *you* could bully a shark. Listen, Carmen. I understand the limits and frustration of your job. I hear some of those same sad, self-hating voices over the radio waves five nights a week. That's who we deal with day after day, night after night. People who are losing, or have lost, hope. We're alike. The court of last resort for the self-esteem deprived. Excuses. Lies. And so human. So weak. That's not Temple. Why'd you have to treat her like that?"

"Because she knows what I need to know to close a case."

"A case? Or your own pre-conception of a case?"

"Kinsella is your rival. He's screwed the woman you love. Why defend him?"

Matt froze for a moment at the ugly truth coming from her mouth. She felt a little guilty. He remained a relative innocent in the world of he-she relationships. Love was still sacred to him. Screwing was still a word that twisted both ways: street vulgarity or mystical spiral of DNA, life, and love.

She felt way guilty. Damn priests! Guilt. That was their Job One, even when they'd left it far behind.

"He loved her," Matt said. "Still does. He's not my enemy but he is yours. Why?"

"He cuts corners, he hides out. He manipulates this town and this police force for his own reasons. He's gotta fall. He's gotta go down."

"For *his* sins? Or yours?"

"You're defending him?"

Matt nodded. Smiled. "Yeah. If he's innocent. What are you after him for now? Temple said you two had declared a truce."

"She's told you about the dangling dead at the New Millennium?"

"She's mentioned it in passing." He smiled privately as he sipped the beer.

Molina's nerves twanged. Something had changed there. What?

"Let's sit," she said, setting an example. It forced him into the role of a guest in her house, on her sofa.

"I admit," she said, "that dead bodies raining from the ceiling look like Kinsella's MO."

"Come on. Just one, isn't it? There was one at the Goliath the night his performance run ended more than two years ago. The only thing to tie him to that was that he vanished for a year. Why'd he come back if he was a murderer?"

"Sheer gall. That man stops at nothing."

"Probably true, but that's not a jailable offense. Neither does Lance Armstrong."

"Except Kinsella didn't beat cancer. He *is* cancer."

Matt pulled back, surprised. "I can't believe how much you really hate him. Personally, I mean. Why? I'm the one you think is entitled to despise him."

"See this house you're sitting in? See my teenage daughter run outside, fancy free? That man has been in here. When we haven't been. Prowling. Playing games with my wardrobe. My mind. The last time was really sick, but he got too cocky. His taunting little note mentioned something only he and I could know about."

"Carmen?" Matt had tabled the beer. The slice of lime lay on its pottery dish like a sick green grin. "You're being stalked? For how long?"

"A few weeks."

"And you're sure it's . . . Max?"

"Absolutely."

"What's the point?"

"Sickness. It's sexually . . . taunting. Items left in my closet, on my bed. Now a trail of rose petals to my bedroom, and Mariah's! Radios playing. The last 'gift' was a sleazy teddy."

While Matt looked blank, Carmen found herself laughing, giddy at leavening her tension with some unexpected comic relief.

"God, I sure know it's not you! Not a stuffed bear, like

you're thinking! A teddy is a sex-shop staple, a see-through . . . uh, bathing suit. Red, black, lace."

Matt frowned. "Sounds like a sort of valentine."

"A sick, threatening valentine only a stalker would slink into a woman's house to leave."

"Thanks for the tip." Matt was trying to lighten the mood, but his warm brown eyes were deeply concerned now.

She relaxed a little.

"So," Matt said, "you've been dealing with this on your own for how long now?"

"A few weeks."

"Can't you of all people sic the law on this?"

"No."

"You won't lose face by admitting to your peers that you have a stalker. I've seen those two, Alch and Su. They'd go to the wall for you."

She blinked back unlieutenant-like tears. So good to hear an outsider confirm her unit's loyalty. But police work was not like anything else. Loyalty would never overlook irregularity. And Carmen had done some damn irregular things lately while trying to keep her daughter safe and the creep at bay.

"*I* couldn't go to the wall for me in their places, Matt," she admitted.

He blew out a breath that indicated he understood the extent of what she was confessing. He was a hell of a counselor, quick to get it, slow to judge. Why hadn't she confided in him before? Too close to the woman in the case, Temple Barr. Just *how* close these days, anyway? He radiated a certain secret serenity she hadn't noticed before. She was pretty quick to understand too.

Had the scales in the eternal triangle tipped Matt's way in, say, the last few weeks? Had that made Kinsella go over the edge, and for Molina instead?

"You've always had your suspicions about Max," Matt said.

Suddenly, he was referring to a man he'd always called by his last name by his first. What was this?

"Surely," Matt went on, "your staff knows that, could make discreet inquiries."

"There is nothing discreet to be done when it comes to Max

Kinsella," she said, her voice as tough as Kevlar. She sighed, grabbed her beer and took a long, long swallow to rinse the recent words out of her mouth.

He raised sun-bleached eyebrows but said nothing.

"I can't call on anyone in the department because the note that nails him as my stalker refers to an . . . incident I'm not crazy to open up to anyone official. In fact, I must *be* crazy trusting you. You swear on the seal of the confessional—?"

"I'm not really a priest anymore, Carmen."

"But you'd hate yourself if you betrayed a confidence. Maybe there is still a little corner of Hell for someone like that, someone who'd betray a serious confidence?"

"A large corner. Unless someone else's life was at stake, or something."

"I suppose you think I'm just a neurotic woman, after all—"

"No. I think you're a rock, too much so. But I've noticed that something has been seriously bothering you. I thought it might be, you know, your ex."

"Him! Rafi. Some secret. Even you've met him. Sure, he'd be a likely suspect, but now his reappearance on the scene looks like child's play compared to someone stalking me and Mariah. And that someone can only be Max Kinsella."

"Why?"

"Because at the time that your adored Temple, crazy mixed-up kid that she is, went undercover to trail the Stripper Killer, I had Max Kinsella in my sights at Secrets's strip-joint parking lot. He was all hot to trot, saying that Temple's life was in danger at Baby Doll's. He wasn't going to assume the position and cuffs, no way. Much as I wanted him to give me a reason to shoot, he wasn't doing that either. He was unarmed."

"A stand-off."

"Right. What to do? I had to subdue him or lose Mr. Slippery again. And all I had was 'suspicion' of being the Stripper killer. But it was good enough to take him in for, with him right there on the site of a previous crime, and having been seen there earlier."

"So you radioed for backup."

"He was going to walk, daring me to shoot him."

"So—?" Matt was really curious now, sitting forward on

the sofa, a terrific audience for her defining, and dumbest, moment.

"So, I slapped my weapon down on the nearest pickup hood and we went hand-to-hand."

"Carmen!"

"I've been trained. The sexist watch commanders in L.A. set little old rookie me taking down three-hundred-pound brothers and drug dealers with Uzis in Watts. Loved that Latino-black rivalry. Adding a woman to the mix was even more amusing."

"Yeah, but . . . Max is a world-class strong man."

"He's not that tough. I did cuff him."

"Maybe he let you. So that's the problem? You cuffed him and what? Um, I know. He uncuffed himself."

"And me to the steering wheel of my car! Never arrest a magician. By then, the radio was announcing the takedown of the Stripper Killer, thanks to your pal Temple's meddling. I would have had to let him go anyway."

"But he would have escaped before then. What's so irregular about that scenario? You found and captured a reasonable suspect then freed him when fast-moving events proved him innocent."

"Don't ever apply the word 'innocent' to that man. Yes, he got away. Yes, no one knows about our parking-lot round but he and I. And that's how I know—I know now!—that he's my stalker."

"How?"

She took a deep breath. "When we were fighting, he thought he had the upper hand at one point. He came on to me. Seriously. Your lovely little Miss Temple was off the radar. He had turned my pursuit of justice into some sick psycho-sexual game between us. It was real, believe me. If she had seen it, she would have dumped him like that. I'm protecting her, in a way, from having her illusions sent to Sing-Sing for life."

"What did he do, say?"

"I'm too embarrassed to tell an ex-priest."

"Try me."

"Just that our cat-and-mouse game was substitute for what I really wanted and needed, a good screwing."

Matt winced. As much as he was adjusting to secular society and its rough edges, crudity still impacted his priestly sensibility. Suddenly, he looked at Carmen from under those baby-blond eyebrows, his penetrating brown eyes so unusual in one of his Polish coloring.

"Intense feelings can flip either way, love or hate."

"Don't say love."

"Passion or hate, okay?"

"You ever feel either one?"

"More than you can imagine, Carmen."

For a few fixed instants, she believed him. "Right. You hated your stepfather. I assume that's resolved now that he's dead."

Matt shrugged. "Nothing's ever resolved. It just evolves, or we do. I see your confidentiality problem. I see why you think what you do. What I don't see is Max Kinsella as a stalker. He's like Lucifer. He's got too much pride. So do you."

"I am the law!"

"No. You're a representative of the law. You may not realize this, and I can't say more because I do honor confidences, but Max is a representative of another kind of law."

"Another kind?"

"He's a seeker of justice."

"And I'm not?"

"He's an émigré from an abused minority."

"And I'm not?"

"So. You have a lot in common."

"No way! Matt, you've gone over the edge here. Stay out of it."

"May I still take Mariah to her father-daughter dance?"

"Yes." Said begrudgingly. For her daughter's sake.

"Sure. I will. But, you know, as long as we're being bottom-line frank here, I think her real father should do the honors."

He had gotten up and was halfway to the door.

"Are you crazy? Do you know what her father is?"

"I know who he is, but, no, I don't know what he is. Do you?"

And the bastard walked out of her house unscathed, as Max Kinsella himself had done not a day before having left his sleazy rose-scented threat behind.

Molina fumed, her teeth taking her frustration out on her lower lip, raking it with fury. It was a bad day when a former priest and a former magician could make her own home taste like bitter ashes in her mouth.

Chapter 46

Mum

Matt speed-dialed Temple on his cell phone before his Cross-fire had left Molina's curb.

She answered after five rings. Sounds of frantic activity buzzed behind her cheerful hello.

"I need to see Max as soon as possible."

"Matt? Hello to you too. He's not very accessible these days."

"Just get to him and tell him to get to me, fast."

"What's this about?"

"Him and me talking."

"About what?"

"I can't say."

"You can't say? Now you're sounding like Max."

"Maybe. Just get me through to him somehow."

"And you won't say why?"

"I *can't* say why."

"It's a secret?"

"Not mine."

"Max's?"

"Maybe."

"Who else's then?"

"I can't say."

After a silence, she said "Oh, that secrecy of the confessional thing?"

"Call it that. Call it 'don't ask, don't tell.' I really, really need to see Max, Temple. You've trusted him through a whole heaping helping of thick and thin. I'm asking you to trust *me* just this once."

"You know I'll die of curiosity."

"That might be better than the consequences if I don't speak to Max, fast."

More silence.

Then, "I'll call him. Leave a message and your phone numbers. Your local answering service signing off." The natural bounce had left her voice, and she hadn't said good-bye.

Matt's hold on the cell phone turned homicidal, then he realized he'd better not disable one of two thin threads of communication that linked him and Max Kinsella.

He hoped Temple would stress how important this was, how fast the contact needed to be made, before Molina got her "evidence" back, before Temple heard about this from the police. Before Max would be a seriously wanted man.

But the afternoon dragged on as he clung to his apartment at the Circle Ritz. The shadow of the lone palm tree in the parking lot elongated like a dark tightrope strung across the asphalt.

And nothing. Neither phone rang.

He heard the throaty little engine of Temple's Miata over the air-conditioning. Rushing to the spare bedroom window that overlooked the lot, he was just in time to spy a woman with strawberry-blond hair running out on high heels to get in the passenger side. The Miata spurted out of the lot, off for the evening, Matt sensed. Girls' night out. He grabbed his cell phone to call Temple, but . . . Max might call. He might miss it.

Matt tried to watch the TV news, some silly network programming. More news. The phone never rang.

The Miata wasn't back by eleven thirty P.M. when he had to leave for WCOO. *Listen,* he told himself. One more day won't make that much of a difference.

It was just the secret burning a hole in his pocket. He wanted to warn Max so Temple wouldn't be hurt. He wanted to confront Max, so he could find out if the man had done something to hurt Temple, something beyond forgiving, that would make her forever give up on him.

His noble and ignoble motives rubbed together like two worn coins in his pocket. Sometimes he felt one under his fingertips, sometimes the other.

For Temple's sake, he hoped Max had an answer, an alibi. For his own, and maybe Temple's in the long run, he half hoped Max didn't have an answer, an excuse. For once.

"Ooh, Mr. Moody Blue," his boss and sister DJ Ambrosia crooned when he walked into the broadcast booth. "You look just like Leo or Brad or Jude getting a pout on when you don't walk in smilin'."

The commercial breaks between her show of schmaltzy oldies and his "Midnight Hour" of schmaltzy talk radio were running. He seldom cut his arrival that close. But he had thought Max might call.

"Listen," he said, "I'm expecting an urgent call. You want to stick around and answer my cell phone off mike?"

Ambrosia's brown velvet face managed an expression that was both surprised and agreeable.

"I do love to hear you work that mike magic on those call-ins. Sure, I'll hang with you, bro."

Matt sighed relief. "Sorry I was almost late. Thanks, Leticia."

That was her real name, not her radio handle. Ambrosia was the scatwoman of the spoken word, soothing the airwaves with her voice and her songs for every emotion. Now she leaned into the foam-fat microphone to play one last number, her voice a low mesmerizing purr.

"I'm gonna leave you all to one last request, for a special colleague of mine. Don't let it put you to sleep, babies, 'cuz Mr. Midnight himself is right here, blinking his baby browns and getting ready to take over the seat I've kept warm for him all this time.

"Here it comes, 'Sentimental Journey.' Let me tell you, you will never go wrong taking a sentimental journey with Mr. Midnight."

She slid out of the upholstered rolling chair that her three-hundred pounds of leopard-spot caftan had literally made into a hot seat and patted the fabric with a coquettish look.

Matt couldn't help laughing.

"What do I do if your cell phone rings and a man answers?" she asked.

"Keep him on the line until the next break. I have to talk to him as soon as possible."

She cradled his cell phone against her Mother Earth bosom. "Trust me," she whispered before leaving the booth. "This will not be 'The Man That Got Away.' "

Matt sat on the prewarmed chair, rolled it closer to the table, donned the headset, wiped his wet palms on his khaki-clad thighs.

He had to let his anxiety go. It would show in his voice, the tightness in his throat, and he was here to ease anxiety, not spread it. Mr. Midnight, the radio persona, settled on him like a gossamer cloak. His body slipped into a posture both relaxed and alert. He kept a notepad and pen at his right to jot down the callers' names, issues, key words. That cool fat pen barrel between his fingers felt like an alabaster cigar. He doodled some loops. Temple's first name. That was the usual. He kept and destroyed the sheets each night. If they married and she took his last name, she'd sound like a place of worship. Temple Devine. That didn't strike him as out of place.

If they married . . . if Max had waltzed himself totally out of the picture with this last escapade—who was he kidding? Himself, of course. He wanted to talk to Max so badly because he needed to find out the man had done Temple wrong. Temple Kinsella just did not have the same ring as Temple Devine. Not that she'd take anybody's name but her own. Still. He wrote the new combo. He was literally loopy over her, had been for months, but hadn't felt free to feel it.

And so Matt did what he did with the disembodied voices who called five nights a week to ask him for instant on-air advice and comfort. He imagined how sad Temple would feel if she thought every loyal bone in her body had been devoted for two years to a creepy secret stalker.

And, loopy or not, Matt did not, deep in his way-too-honest soul, want Max Kinsella to be a guilty man.

Chapter 47

Riding Shotgun

"Hi-de-ho, honey!" Ambrosia greeted Matt as he stepped out of the glass booth at two A.M. She was lofting his cell phone like Perry Mason revealing Exhibit A. "This mockin' bird don't sing. Not one little ringy-dingy outa this cell phone. Daddy is not gonna get either one of us a diamond ring. No, sir. Is that bad?"

Matt reclaimed his cell phone with a sigh. "I'm probably taking this way too seriously."

"You do have that tendency, sweet cheeks. Hey. Ambrosia'll buy you a drink to wind down with."

"Thanks. Another time. I'm sorry I kept you up so late. I need to, ah, gather my notes. I'll leave in a bit."

"You vant to be alone," she accused in a dead-on Garbo

voice. "Sure thing. Curtis here is putting ole WCOO on digital autopilot until morning. Don't linger too long brooding, my man. It's bad for the face. Trust me."

Matt stood dreaming on the other side of the door to the waiting room long after Ambrosia had sailed out like Cleopatra's Barge heading over to anchorage as a famous restaurant at Caesar's Palace.

Talking to the people out there in Radioland had given him a sense of perspective. They were all trying so hard. Trying to stay afloat in this down-sizing economy. Trying to keep love in their lives. Trying to make sure their children didn't feel the losses they had, although that was always impossible. No matter how much a parent tried to "make up," there was always some new psycho-social stress to make kids' lives hard. Tragically, it was often caused by the parents' own anxiety.

Matt breathed deeply, and allowed as he didn't control a single thing in his life and the larger world beyond it. Just let go of trying to insist that God—or the Fates if you were a secular person—would ensure that things would go your way.

By the time he stepped out into the tepid Las Vegas night air, he was at semi-peace with himself.

His fancy new silver car shone like a slick magazine ad under one of the parking lot lamps. All alone. It had the same sleek mechanical beauty of the Hesketh Vampire motorcycle that had originally belonged to Max Kinsella, but Matt would have pushed his new car off a cliff if he thought it would make Temple feel one sixteenth of a scintilla better about the ugliness Carmen Molina was about to drop on her.

Turned out he didn't have to sacrifice his car.

A low, throaty growl drew his attention to something glinting outside the wash of parking lot lights. A motorcycle. Not the Vampire. Flashier but oh-so-familiar.

Matt edged over warily, like a kid to a high-end bike on Christmas morning. He knew that bike, that figure in glitzy leathers, that shining black helmet as round as a pumpkin on Halloween.

The rider revved the engine as his leather-gloved hands wrung the bike's handlebars. Matt approached. The rider tossed him a helmet that had been tethered to the back.

"Rock or roll?" he asked with something of a Southern accent.

Matt shook his head, not sure if he needed to clear it or to derail a rueful laugh. This was the motorcycle that had shadowed him during those dark nights when someone sinister had seemed to be on his tail light, his motorcycle's tail lights. When he'd ridden the Vampire he'd gotten from Electra after Max Kinsella had let her have it.

He'd had a shadow rider then. Two. One lethal, another riding ghost shotgun for him. That guy had looked and acted a lot like Elvis, who'd apparently called in to the Mr. Midnight show for a while there. An Elvis so real you thought you'd had breakfast with him one time that you couldn't quite remember: a pound of bacon and a dozen eggs. Elvis had been Atkins before Atkins was Atkins.

One mystery was solved. A persistent mystery of streets and night and pursuit. The voice over the air waves was a different matter entirely. Much harder to impersonate.

Matt donned the safety helmet and gazed at the night and its lights through the veil of its smoke-Plexiglas visor, darkly. He mounted the elongated seat behind the rider, curled his hands around the chrome rods beneath the seat, pushed his heels onto the chrome rods over the rear wheels.

The cycle charged into the night, leaning, roaring, shooting like a star.

Being a passenger on a meteor's tail took guts. Matt realized for the first time that he really, really wanted to be in control, not eddied along by his history, his inheritance, his losses.

The biker took the bike to a high point overlooking Vegas before his boot-heels dropped to asphalt and he let the machine tilt to a stop. All that massive weight, held up by a bike stand.

Matt hopped off, doffed the damn helmet. Waited.

The motorcycle man dismounted like a cowboy who loved his mount, fluid and easy. He took off the helmet.

"You were my guardian biker," Matt said. Accused. Thanked. "My ersatz Elvis."

"Maybe." Max Kinsella hung his helmet from the handlebar. The full moon reflected in its dark side, kind embracing kind. "Sometimes. Maybe sometimes it *was* Elvis. Dude had an aura, you know. You don't kill that."

"I know. Still, masquerading as a motorcycle cop that time—"

"Me? Impersonate a cop? Don't have that costume on tap. 'Fraid not."

Matt felt a chill trickle down his spine. That had been the guy who'd advised him to let the bike fly. If not Max, then who? Elvis for real?

"What did you need to talk to me about?" Max asked.

"You took me seriously."

"I take Temple seriously."

The words hung in the air, in their multiplicity of meanings. "Me too," Matt said. "What about Molina?"

"What about . . . her?"

"She's bound to get you for something."

Max shrugged. "Let her try."

"Fine for you, Mr. Invisible. Tough on Temple."

"Temple's tough. So, what's Molina up to now?"

"It's *who's* up to what against Molina."

Max walked to the overlook, trying to untangle that sentence. Las Vegas lay like a tea tray of white-silver glitz on the vast dark desert floor.

They were halfway up the Spring Mountains. Matt would have a long, exhausting walk back to civilization if he had to make it on foot power. How competitive was Max Kinsella, anyway? Very.

"You don't like me. You really, really don't like me." Max surveyed the distant glitter of the city where he had once been an A-list star, a magician to reckon with. "You particularly don't like me in Temple's life. Or bed. Still. You want to warn me. Why?"

"Because I don't like you in Temple's life." Matt made himself ignore the bed part. He felt guilty about being the other man. Given recent events, he was now supersensitive about beds and what did, or did not happen in them.

"That's why when you call, I listen. But I don't have a lot of time."

"You don't know how true that is."

"Tell me."

Max Kinsella never waffled around. Never shillied nor shallied. Matt admired that. He'd been reared to question everything, most of all himself and his motives. His motives here were pure, even selfless. Mostly.

"Carmen Molina's had a stalker for several weeks."

"Stalkers must be hard up."

"Not funny. I had one, one handed down from you."

"Stalkers must be hard up," Max repeated with sardonic humor. He turned back to face Matt. "Molina's a cop. Stalkers come with the territory. With her, I wouldn't doubt that it would come more often."

"She's got a right to be angry. The stalker has been breaking into her house. She has a young child there."

Max chuckled. "From what I heard went down at the Teen Idol reality TV show, that kid is hitting puberty big time. Maybe it'll keep Mama off my tail."

"I don't think so. This latest visit, the stalker left a trail of rose petals to Mariah's bedroom as well as hers."

"That's really sick! No wonder she's unhinged."

"And she's convinced you're the stalker."

For once, Matt had rendered Max Kinsella speechless.

"Me?" Kinsella said. Then frowned. "That's crazy."

"That's what I thought. At first."

"I don't care what you think. What has this got to do with Temple? That's all I care about."

Matt kept himself from saying "Me too."

Max was still on a tear. "Let Molina rant and roar and chase a phantom. She can't touch me."

"Maybe not. Maybe this time . . . yeah, maybe. But she's already touched Temple."

Kinsella's motorcycle boots crunched desert shale as he stalked back over to Matt, looming at six four with two added inches of boot heel.

Matt felt enough bottled fury, and a nasty edge of guilt, to take him on and take him out if he said anything dismissive about the threat to Temple.

But Kinsella never satisfied in that way. He cared about her as much, maybe, as Matt did. That knowledge was as bitter as an arsenic pill in his throat, but it was also why Kinsella was the first, and last, person he'd gone to about this.

"What did Molina do?" Max asked.

"Barged into Temple's place at the Circle Ritz"—Max didn't correct him on that. A magician was, above all, a realist, but it had once been theirs, that place, his and Temple's. "Took something likely to have your fingerprints still on it."

"Took? Without a warrant? Why didn't Temple—? Never mind. It was a lightning raid, wasn't it? What did Molina take?"

"A CD."

"Damn. Temple never did share my tastes, or like to run the VCR or even the multiple-CD player. So. Molina is now the only cop in the Western World with possible fingerprints on me. So what? She has nothing to compare them too."

"That makes anything she finds on that CD all the more likely to be yours. She already printed Temple way back when."

"I'm going to swear, Devine. You can put your fingers in your ears if you want."

"Go right ahead. On that I'm with you."

Max sighed, not a weak sigh, more like the hissing sound a weight lifter makes during ultra-heavy reps. "That damn . . . woman . . . will not leave well enough alone. If she had a decent sex life, she wouldn't have to mess with mine so much."

Matt shut his eyes. He didn't want to hear about this. Think about this. "That's what she said you told her in the parking lot of Secret's. That's why she thinks you're obsessed with her."

"Me. Her? Obsessed? *Get a life!* That's what I told her in that damn parking lot, while she was trying with all her might to keep me from going where Temple was in fatal danger. How has she explained her stupidity in fixating on hogtying *me* when a major capture of the Stripper Killer was going down with Temple playing the next victim?"

Max had grabbed his sleeves, was shaking Matt in agitation.

"Hey!" Matt slapped Kinsella on the leather lapels, forcing

him to back off. "That wasn't me standing in your way then, pal. Molina did give you a chance to fight her for your freedom from what she said."

"Couldn't shoot me cold. I wasn't carrying. Yeah, she had the guts to go hand-to-hand with me, risky considering how frantic I was about Temple. Guts were never her problem. She's not a lightweight. She's been trained. I finally had to play possum; live to fight another day, and get her in a situation where I could win without wasting time: handcuffed in her car. You know about magicians and handcuffs. Anyway, I let her grind my face into the asphalt, cuff me, and lead me away like Mary's little lamb. What more does the woman want?"

"That's all it was? Her not daring to shoot you dead? You two mixing it up? You letting her 'win' so you could escape faster to race to Temple's defense? Her hung up on catching you and losing you?"

"That was it. She'd got me cuffed and in her Crown Vic. I was already working on the handcuff's release mechanism when the call came over the radio that the cops had nailed the Stripper Killer while he was attacking a certain Miss Barr masquerading as a club costume seller. The minute I heard Temple was safe, Molina was wearing her own cuffs attached to the steering wheel and I was outa there."

"Interesting," Matt said.

"This stuff we're talking about is way more important than 'interesting'."

"I'm just replaying it. You're Molina's prisoner, then she's a police professional handcuffed to her own steering wheel, and not only that, wrong about you being the Stripper Killer."

"It might freak her out," Max said, a smile in his voice.

"It might freak her so far out that she'd violate Temple's space and her trust to take you to the cleaners."

"You know what I think?" Max's voice had lowered. It sounded dangerous in the dark. "You and Molina are a pair. You've got that blind Catholic standard that makes everyone else substandard."

"You were reared Catholic."

"I got over it."

"She said—"

"He said. It's a draw."

"Molina said you came on to her. She said you said all she needed was a—I guess you might be kinda conceited—'good screwing.' "

Kinsella laughed. "That's ridiculous. Not that it might not be true. I don't know what I said, did. I was fighting for my freedom to go and protect Temple. You might know what that feels like, someone you love in mortal danger. You might know what that felt like for me."

It was Matt's turn to keep silent. He did, way more now that he and Temple had become . . . closer.

"Carmen distrusts you," Matt said at last. "I guess she hates you. She might take whatever you said or did to get free of her as the God's truth. That you would have screwed her to make her let you go. That you thought she would have liked it."

It was Max's turn to be silent. "Maybe that's true," he said. "Maybe I found her weakness and it was me. Hate is fear, and sexual fear hides unadmitted desire. If that's what it would have taken. As it happened, I preferred to let her grind my face into the ground and feel she'd beaten me physically. Pride isn't worth a penny if someone you love is at risk."

"Nope," Matt agreed. That's why he was here, warning Temple's lover, instead of letting Max go down so he could have Temple all to himself.

"So," Max said. "Now *your* face is asphalt dust. Maybe you'll have to screw Molina to get her off Temple's case. No sacrifice too harsh."

"You can laugh. I guess it's a kind of defiance. But if Temple thinks you'd ever thought of betraying her with Molina—"

"Oh, shit," Max said. "Oh shit oh shit oh shit."

"Did you?" Matt asked, because he had to and because he actually enjoyed asking it way too much.

Matt couldn't believe how much he relished the idea of Max being unfaithful, how down and dirty he could get, for the right wrong reason.

But he had to know.

"Because, if so, I'm going to have to warn Temple, to tell her something. I'd like to include your self-defense."

"Sanity? Look. Why would I? I don't need this right now. I have no idea where this nonsense came from. And I don't need some do-gooder John Alden playing go-between for me and Temple. Even you should know by now you want her."

Matt felt a flush. Why? It was the truth.

Max threw up his long, bony hands, always clever, always strong. "That was a low blow. Sorry. I suppose you are a professional mediator of sorts. Mediate this."

"I won't use this against you with Temple. Or for me."

"Use it. I won't surrender Temple to anyone without the balls to take her."

Matt felt the old blinding rage he thought he'd buried with his stepfather surging into all his muscles. He stepped forward, balanced for martial arts moves. Max was more expert, he knew, but Matt had the fire in the belly in this case. It would be a long, bloody draw probably.

Max stepped back. "*Pax*, priest. Us tearing at each other will only hurt Temple more. That's one thing we're agreed on; the less damage to Temple the better."

"Is there anything you can say to defend yourself, to counter Molina's charges?"

Max had nothing printable to answer.

Chapter 48

Free to Good Home

I have pretty much figured out this whole murder-theft ring and given my Miss Temple the credit, or the main ideas, at least.

Now would be a good time for resting on my laurels, and this is exactly what I am doing in my crib at the Circle Ritz when I hear the scrabble of pointed nails, i.e., claws, on the French door–opening mechanism.

I am too worn out from my recent intense cerebral labors, not to mention the late hours I have been keeping, to do more than cock one peeper open. Sure enough, a furry snake slides under the crack in the frame. In a moment, the door pops open as sweetly as if my own supple touch had cracked it.

Much to my surprise . . . not! . . . Miss Midnight Louise ankles in.

"Sawing timbers in the Pacific Northwest, I see," she says.

"Who, me? Not on your life. I am for saving the forests. What I am doing is resting up my muscles after serving as a counterweight to three females of my acquaintance the other night."

"Big deal, Daddy-o. All you had to do was throw your weight around, which should come naturally. But that is why I am here."

"Oh, really. It is not because you wish to check up on the health of the senior member of the team?"

"Oh. We are a 'team' now?"

"Well, I mean that we are Midnight Inc. Investigations, which is a firm, and since there are only two members of said firm, I suppose in a loose sense we are a . . . team. But nothing personal."

She sits and tucks her long, luxuriant black train around her dainty forelegs. Show-off!

"Whatever," she says in the irritating manner of the younger set. "We still have a problem in the flies at the New Millennium."

I frown. "The show has been closed down for now, and even the police are through dusting the area with a mouse-hair brush and going over it with a flea comb."

"That is part of the problem."

"Tell me."

"I think you should see for yourself."

"Jeez, Louise! That is a long pad across some pretty hot turf, not to mention the climb at the end. I need to preserve my strength."

"On Miss Temple Barr's cushy sofa, of course."

"So. You want one, find your own sugar daddy."

"I do not need a keeper, but I admit I am an exception."

"You admit something. *Hmmph.* All right. I guess I can go and survey the scene of my latest exercise in crime deduction. Miss Temple has seen that the authorities know all about who was in on what and why and how."

"Exercise is the key word in all that hot air. You need some. Up and at 'em, Pop, before I sic Ma Barker's gang on you."

This opens my other eye and gets me up on my feet and humming "The Star-Spangled Banner."

"The gang is here?"

"Right. And your next trick will be letting the residents of this Building That Time Forgot realize they better put some grub and water out for them."

"I must see my troops."

"Forget it. No time to say hello, good-bye, you are needed first and foremost at the New Millennium."

I suppose it was Miss Louise employing the word "needed." I respond to necessity. I suppose I caved.

She manages to spur me away from the Circle Ritz without looking around to spot and welcome the feral gang. I mean that "spur" literally. Her foreclaws are as sharp as Ginsu knives on a three A.M. infomercial.

Of course, Las Vegas is the second City That Never Sleeps. We dodge traffic and tourists, but in due time trot our way back to the New Millennium. I am about to show her my secret entryway six floors up on the neon solar system, but she taps me on the shoulder—*ouch!*—and leads me to the service entrance.

Here we are greeted like old friends, or she is.

"Ah," says a slim dude of Asian appearance dressed all in white like a bride, or more likely, a cook. "The little lady with the Canton palate. And a gentleman friend. Some wonton soup this evening? Oh, you wish to study the menu?"

He admits us both into the kitchen area as if we were gourmands or something. I nearly swoon. I smell duck. Fish. Eel. *Eeew.* No eel. I do not eat snakes and lizards and other desert delicacies.

Miss Louise mushes me through the fragrant preparation area ringing with the cymbals of copper lids.

Before I know it, we are dodging the usual footwear bazaar in the main casino and edging around the darkened exhibition area to the access ladders and ramps at the back.

"Up again!" I protest, eyeing the climb. "I thought I had made all this moot."

"Scoot!" she says, with a prickly encouraging pat.

"The place is deserted," I protest, as I climb the long, dark, and winding road built into the access area for the magic show installation far above.

"'Up' is your motto," she replies, prodding from the rear.

I must admit it is more than mere weariness that makes me loath to repeat this journey. A man and woman died on these artificial heights. On these man-made mountains, my Miss Temple lost her Mr. Max to obligations she had no power to overcome.

And I nearly strained everything I had to rescue a feline assassin who probably deserved to kiss concrete as much as her human mistress did. There! I do think that there are villains, and villainesses in the world, and that they should meet their just desserts.

On the other hand, my just desserts are lingering in the kitchens we have just forsaken.

"Onward!" Louise matches gesture to vocal command.

Ouch!

We reach the top, and I am immediately struck by the emptiness of the area. The fallen structures still dangle there unanchored. I almost smell the recent death reeking in my sensitive nostrils. I picture the powerful persona that had commanded these black-painted perches on the edge of nowhere: CC, the Cloaked Conjuror, who had lost a performing partner.

The exhibition would continue but the sky-high magic show was suspended, like Siegfried and Roy, maybe forever.

Shangri-La, mystery woman, no friend of my Miss Temple and her Mr. Max, yet a sublime performer and a cat person. Hyacinth, her familiar, the performing partner who had inadvertently sealed her fate and caused her death. Loyalty carried to a lethal degree. How did she deal with dealing her mistress death when she meant only to preserve? I shuddered to think of being in her skin.

Of being in her skin. Right. Where was it? Now. Exactly. I gaze at Midnight Louise. I must admit the kit has climbed every mountain with me.

"Where is she?" she asks now, echoing my thought.

"Hyacinth?"

I do not know. We saved her from dangling death. We risked our own skins—me, Louise, and Hyacinth's shelter-rescued body double, the delicate and shy Miss Squeaker, aka S. Q.

"Hyacinth is not to be found?" I both ask and declare. She was a magician's familiar, an apprentice. She would not simply walk away. But she might . . . vanish!

Midnight Louise does not mince words. (When has she ever?) "She has not been seen since S. Q. and I threw ourselves into her rescue."

"And *moi*," I point out. "I was the counterweight."

"True. We could not have made it without you."

Yes!

"But I am not concerned about Miss Hyacinth," Louise says.

Why not? That is truly disturbing. Where can a pampered show cat like her go?

"Squeaker is missing also."

Oh. My blood runs cold until it chills out my super-overheated tootsies.

I recall the shy shelter cat known first as "Fontana," and later as "Squeaker."

No one recalled her when clearing out the paraphernalia of the abandoned magic show. CC had his Big Cats to remove. Who spoke for the late Shangri-La? Who for her performing partner, Hyacinth, and the lowly body double, Squeaker?

"Hyacinth?" I ask.

"She can take care of herself," Louise says.

That leaves Squeaker.

"She was shy," I say. "We need to check all the duct work. Especially that engineered by . . . Mr. Max."

Louise flashes me a twenty-four-carat okay from those orange-gold peepers.

About half an hour later, I am beginning to think that Midnight Inc. Investigations should be renamed Mummy Central. These ducts and escape routes are as empty and dry as King Tut's tomb.

Midnight Louise and I poke our kissers out of equally empty escape routes and compare notes.

"No Hyacinth?" she asks.

"No flowers of any description," I report.

I must admit that this ceaseless scrambling down narrow, dark ducts is wearing me out. Again. I lay back to pant out my frustration.

And then I hear a sigh.

A shaky sigh.

I push myself as erect as I can manage (my frame, not anything personal) and sniff around for a source. The odor is faintly lavender. As in lavender Siamese.

I edge forward until I spot some ruby irises in the dark. That always gives away a blue-eyed girl. I belly crawl the last five feet and am rewarded by the sight, sound, and sniff of Miss Squeaker.

"What are you doing hidden away down here, girl?" I ask.

"They have forgotten me, Louie. And if they remember me, they will whisk me away to the nearest shelter. I do not ever want to go back to one of those places."

"I have been there," I point out carefully. These spooked runaways are touchy. "I do not ever want to go back there either."

"Oh. I am sorry Hyacinth is gone. When she vanished, the others appeared to forget about me. But there is . . . nothing to eat here."

"No. As you can see, I do not approve of a state of nothing to eat. If you will inch forward, just a little, I believe that Miss Midnight Louise and I will find you a fine Asian buffet not too far from here."

"They will know I exist! And destroy me!"

Unfortunately, she is not too far wrong.

"Miss Midnight Louise and I have strings to pull in this town. Often those strings are wrapped around main courses for our kind. Just edge your smooth lavender stockings along this pipe, and you will soon be on your way to a free dinner."

I ease her out, step by step.

Louise is waiting at the end of the tunnel, all purrs and velvet paws.

Yeah. Like I should get that.

* * *

Later, the guy in the white pipe-stem hat is purring over how hungry Squeaker is for his appetizers.

Louise and I consult in the corner of the busy kitchen, trying to ignore a bunch of lobsters who are held captive for the main course.

"Where can we take her?" I ask.

"She is too sensitive for Ma Barker's gang."

"And then some. She is a very timid individual, due to early kithood trauma," I add.

"I had early kithood trauma and you do not weep for me, Argentina."

"Huh? I have never been to Gaucholand. Or Evitaland. Or Madonnaland. I am just saying that she is not accoutered for survival on the raw edges of anything."

"It is the raw edges of Ma Barker's gang, or nothing," Louise says.

"Maybe not," I say, looking like my usual inscrutable self.

It takes a lot of paternal persuasion, but Miss Louise and I get a well-fed Miss S. Q. easing on down the road.

I will not describe the rides we have had to hitch, or lies we have had to tell to coax our charge along, but at last we are hotfooting it through a very upscale part of town.

This is where and when it gets tough. We have to prod little Miss S. Q. onto a foreign stoop, and then whip up a helluva faux cat fight right before her eyes.

I take as great a satisfaction in boffing Miss Louise in the nose as she does in giving me a Swedish massage via her toes. We howl and yeowl to beat the band and a few audience members too.

Squeaker cringes against a potted hibiscus on the porch.

Perfect!

At last, the porch lights come on, and Louise and I split for the front hedge.

A human comes out blinking into the dark. When have they ever done differently?

"What is going on out here?"

Louise and I are silent. All one can hear out here is Squeaker's shoulder blades and teeth clicking together.

"Well." The human, for once, has heard something more subtle than clashing stray cats.

I hear the slap of bare feet on concrete, and then bushes being brushed aside to reveal Squeaker.

"Oh, my. What have we here? No scaredy-cat, no. A pretty little thing. What blue eyes you have, my dear. No. Do not shake. Why, you are quite a fine little pussums."

I hate the expression "pussums," but Louise whacks me in the shoulder and I shut up. Beggars cannot be choosers, and this is Squeaker's last chance.

"What a precious puss." The human has actually lifted her into his arms and she is not doing a thing.

Whoops! Maybe purring.

Yes!

It is a match made in heaven and at Midnight Inc. Investigations.

Danny Dove is now crooning to the little orphan. "Would you like some Bailey's Irish Cream, *hmmm*? You need a name. How about . . . I think you are a little girl, right? How about . . . Alexandra?"

Works for me.

Louise smashes me in the whiskers. "Nice going, Pater the Great," she says.

Well, I guess I would have been a czar in another life, if life were fair.

Chapter 49

Telling Temple

It was three-thirty in the morning when Matt knocked on Temple's door. Loud. He figured he'd better tell her as soon as possible. He was ready to push the doorbell and make a major racket when the door opened.

The Temple of Christmas Future answered, a petite pale redhead in red-and-purple pajamas with goggle-size glasses reflecting himself.

"I want Temple," Matt said, confused, flustered.

"I'm not a madam, don't tell me. Tell her. I'm Kit, aunt. You're Matt, very tasty. I'll get her if you insist. Although the hour is extremely intemperate. I approve, you mad, impetuous boy, you. No relation to the Fontana Brothers, I presume?"

"Are you kidding? Do I look Italian?"

"Northern Italian, maybe. A girl can dream. I am, however, devastated to inform you that I am no girl. *Un momento, favore.*"

Matt was left blinking in the tiny entry hall.

Temple toddled out a few minutes later, wearing a robe that reminded him of nun-wear, no glasses. Apparently, he was not to see her without contact lenses.

The thought was both encouraging and heart-breaking.

"I guess you two . . . neighbors had better confer in the bedroom," Kit said, as delicately as she could probably ever manage. "I'm camping out on the living-room couch so you surely don't want me eavesdropping."

Temple wove on her feet, which were attired in bunny slippers, a little. "There's always the office," she noted with the strange dignity of a drunk or a person drawn out of deep sleep. She nodded to her right, and Matt gratefully followed her in there. He had no desire to view the California king-size bed Electra said Max Kinsella had required.

Temple shut the door behind them.

They stood and stared at each other for a few moments.

"You must have come from the radio station," Temple said, waking up enough to get self-conscious. "And I must look a mess."

"Love the bunny slippers. The robe's a wash but it makes me wonder what's under it."

"Then it's a successful robe," Temple said, running the end of a pink satin tie through her hand.

Conversation stopped. He found himself content, as he often was nowadays, just to stand and look at her. Her sleek new blond hair was uncombed, but even he knew from TV commercials that was a greatly desired look. He took a mental snapshot of her appearing sleepy enough to pick up and take somewhere like a child who's been up way too late. Somewhere not childish at all. It was a shame to spoil that tousled innocence with other people's wrangles.

"Matt? What is it? Why are you here so late?"

"It's all bad," he said. "I've talked to Molina and just now to Max."

"*You* saw Max? Must have needed an appointment with his secretary."

"He found me. Things are . . . a mess. A duel of the Titans is coming and you're going to be squashed between them."

"What do you mean?" Temple yawned as she settled into her computer desk chair, letting the slippers fall off and tucking her bare feet under her on the seat.

Matt paced away, not wanting to say what he had to say. "I can't stop 'em. Molina is going after Max for sexual harassment and stalking. Max . . . you know him. He has too many irons in the fire bigger than his own self-defense."

"Max? Stalking?" She was sitting up, feet on the floor again. "Who? Shangri-La?"

"Molina herself." Matt stopped to take in Temple's reaction, which was incredulous and heated.

"Max stalking her? I thought Molina was wired lately, but is she completely crazy?"

"I can't make him take this charge seriously."

"Maybe because he's seriously innocent."

Matt nodded. "Carmen has a hope chest of evidence for the stalking charge, but only one piece of it damning—"

"Damn *her*, then!"

"I can't. She believes it."

"Do you?"

"I don't think she's crazy," he said.

Temple snorted indignantly.

Matt knelt beside the chair. "No, I don't think Max is her stalker. That makes what I think completely contradictory. It doesn't mean a thing."

Temple leaned back in her chair, away from him. "You're neutral, then?"

"I suppose so . . . if you can believe that two people telling the truth adds up to somebody else's lie? Temple, the only thing I know is that I don't want you to be hurt."

"The only thing *I* know is that you can't ever stop anyone else from being hurt."

"Okay. I'll take a position."

"Which is?"

"For Max. Can you believe it?"

She smiled at him, leaned nearer, put her palm on his cheek.

"Yeah. You always give everyone but yourself the benefit of the doubt. If *you* do think Max is innocent, it means a lot. Are you sure you're not doing this just for me?"

"I'd do almost anything 'just for you.' But . . . I've got that Catholic conscience. No. It's not for you, or me, but for what I believe. God help me, in this case, I believe in Max Kinsella."

"So do I. So did I, well past the point when I looked like a stupid woman."

"Not stupid. Loyal. But now that he's in Molina's sights again—"

"What?"

"It's going to bother you."

"What?"

"Us." He'd said it, put his selfish insecurities out on the table for Temple to see.

Her gray-blue eyes stared into his for a long moment. Then she stroked her forefinger across his lips, a tender gesture recalling their recent intimacies. Was it hello, or good-bye?

"Max will always be in trouble with someone," she said finally. She produced a wry, sad smile. "Maybe me this time, if he's been playing head games with Molina." She frowned. "I may be conceited, but I just can't see him stalking her under any circumstances."

"She wouldn't be convinced he was, though, without some grounds."

"So. You understand what he's up against."

"I understand what he's always been up against." *And that's why you loved him,* Matt thought. *Love* him.

It's hard to compete with a martyr. To win Temple, Matt figured, he couldn't do it over Max's dead body, over his disgrace and fall. Somehow, he'd have to absolve Max and disprove Molina's deepest convictions.

Or this ugly suspicion about Max, so wounding to a loyalist like Temple, would always lie between them.

Chapter 50

Miracle Worker

"Is it all right if Aldo picks me up here?" Kit asked Temple at about six P.M. the next evening.

Her aunt was shifting her weight from foot to foot in her zebrawood-soled brocaded stiletto sandals like an antsy twelve-year-old.

"Why wouldn't it be?"

"Well, you're used to thinking of the Fontanas as a flock. Seeing just one at a time might be . . . overwhelming and confusing."

"*I'm* not the one who has to be very sure about not confusing Fontanas," Temple pointed out. Pointedly. "Where are you going tonight?"

"The Bellagio."

"For dinner? That'll cost Aldo a well-tailored Zegna arm, and probably a leg."

"I'm worth it," said Kit, ducking back into Temple's office and its attached bathroom to finish her makeup.

Temple hoped that she would be that self-confident when she was sixty . . . in thirty years. Right now, the outlook was glum on all fronts.

The idea of Max was bitter in her mind. At best, he was brushing her out of his life. At worst, he was coming on to *her*, their relentless enemy. Maybe there was some ulterior reason for the good of mankind behind it. Even that idea left a sour taste in her mouth. She wished she'd kissed Matt last night. He'd looked so torn and worried and his mouth was always as clean and bracing as springwater to her.

At work, everyone connected with the White Russian exhibition was being regarded as an apparent thief-in-training. Temple's guilty knowledge that innocents were suspected when she knew Max was the culprit was twisting her usually wrought-iron stomach into queasy knots. The media was all over the hotel and her and Randy. In fact, to avoid them snooping into their PR plans to accentuate the positive, Randy had ordered Temple to work from her home computer for a while.

Now, she'd barely settled in to craft totally unworkable press releases—how do you defuse a fatal fall and a stolen artifact in 150 words or less?—and Kit was preparing to exit, way too excited about her fling with Aldo to even notice that Temple was running on emotional empty, six quarts shy of hope.

Temple forced her depleted energy up forty revolutions per minute when the doorbell rang.

"Would you get that, hon?" Kit yelled from the bathroom. "I haven't finished unpacking the bags under my eyes."

"Hi!" Temple greeted Aldo, checking out his smooth, swarthy Italian hide for forty-something wrinkles. He didn't look a day over thirty-two, but Mediterranean types aged well. "Kit'll be right out."

God! She felt like her own mother. She was the young chick here; Kit was, well, not acting her age.

"How is the family?" Temple inquired as she led tall, dark, and Fontana into the living room. The cappuccino color of his suit matched her sofa exactly, although the material was far better.

"Uh, do you mean the family, or the Family, Miss Temple?"

She felt like she'd never been trapped into making small talk with a single Fontana for so long before.

"I mean your terrific brothers. And I haven't even been to the Crystal Phoenix in ages to see Nicky and Van."

"Me, neither," Aldo said, making ready to sit on her sofa.

"Wait!"

"What?" He slapped a hand to his inside breast pocket. "What's wrong?"

"Nothing . . . worth, ah, a sidearm extraction. It's just that you'll get black Midnight Louie hairs all over that pale linen suit."

"Whoa! You mean I am trespassing on the Top Cat's territory here?"

"Sort of."

Temple decided not to mention that Kit had been sleeping there lately . . . when she was home before four in the morning. Temple never thought she'd be the one to uphold the Barr family standards for discreet behavior.

Aldo, perhaps as uneasy as she was, began pacing. Although he wasn't as tall as Max, he was still way too tall to pace in a room this size.

He stopped by the French doors to eye the petite balcony. "Cute place."

"Thanks." Temple felt like a Lilliputian being visited by a rod-packing Gulliver.

"Sorry!" Kit clattered out over the hardwood floors, looking as breathless and perky as a sixteen-year-old. "I'm ready now."

"Bella!" Aldo gathered her into his long-armed escort and steered her to the door.

"We'll be back—" Kit began. "When will we be back?"

"When the night has had enough of us," Aldo said dramatically.

Kit shrugged. "Oh, well . . ."

Temple could have sworn she winked at her before Aldo drew the big coffered door shut on them.

Well, this was a fine how-do-you-do! Kit out on the town, Fontana style. Louie out on the town, prowling style. Matt gunning for Max and not telling her a thing about it until after the fact. Max the usual Invisible Man he'd been for the past few months.

Temple threw herself down on the sofa, unmindful of Louie hairs, put up her feet, and debated calling Matt, calling out for a pizza, calling the Mounties, or the remaining Fontana brothers.

Instead, she did what a future sixty-year-old should do. She fell asleep, feeling rather sorry for herself but too tired to do anything to take her mind off that spineless condition.

When she woke up, the room was dark. Totally dark. Not a lamp lit.

The time on the VCR read 12:00. Midnight! She jolted upright. Wait. She had never reset the VCR time after it went out during one of the few summer electrical storms in Las Vegas. With an annual rainfall of four inches, they were rarer than ace-high flushes. She couldn't have fixed it anyway, because only Max knew how to do it.

Her eyes felt grainy from sleeping with her contact lenses in, even though they were the soft variety.

The peace and quiet was nice, though, after frenetic, long hours on the hotel's marble floors. It was too late to relieve Randy, but she'd be there first thing in the morning and start pulling her weight again. Surely nothing terrible had happened in just these few hours.

Then she saw the red light blinking on her answering machine through the open door to her office. Oh, no. Someone had called.

Temple sat up, fast, and tried to stand, but she ran into a solid piece of darkness that caught hold of her arms and held her back. Before she could scream, she recognized the silky texture of Max's trademark black turtleneck sweater.

"If you won't scream, I'll promise not to fall asleep," he said.

Temple wiggled up high enough in the sofa seat to switch

on the floor lamp next to it. Max had been sitting at the sofa's far end with her feet on his lap, waiting for her to wake up.

"You do look tired enough to fall asleep right now," she told him, as the light searched the deep lines and sharp angles of his features. "What's been going on, Max? I swear I can't take it anymore."

He just nodded. "I've come here on orders."

"Who orders you around?"

"Apparently, your upstairs neighbor."

"Matt? You'd never take orders from Matt. What's going on? He was all rabid to find you, talk to you. Maybe I shouldn't have passed his message on to you."

"He was and I found him. We had a heart-to-heart."

"I heard and I don't like the sound of that. It's much too civilized."

"Just civil. He agreed that I should talk to you."

"Agreed?"

"He insisted. I agreed."

"This is crazy. I don't need Matt as a go-between."

"Maybe you do. He was warning me."

"About what?"

"That fingerprint Molina bullied you out of."

"That was the piece of damning evidence Matt said she had? Then there *was* a fingerprint on that CD?"

"So Molina told Matt."

"Why would she tell Matt about that?"

Max shrugged, a gesture so small she hardly detected it. "It appears she finally has the evidence to draw the net closed on me."

"Oh, God, Max! She just charged in here. I didn't even think until later that I could have stopped her."

"I don't think you could have. She's been pushing the line on what's legal lately, not to mention ethical. I do take a certain pride in driving her to such measures. It will be some consolation when I'm led off in chains."

"She'd have to find and catch you first."

"Yes, well, that may not be necessary. No matter how long I can avoid capture, all she really has to do to ruin me is come here and tell you what she thinks she's got me on."

"Not murder?"

"That too, but nothing she can prove."

"What can she prove, then?"

"Can we take a high-end whiskey break? Still got some?"

"Of course. You don't think I just pass your Millennium bottle out to strangers?"

"Or to neighbors?"

Temple felt her cheeks heat up, probably not visibly, though. "Or aunts," she said, dodging the implication. Had she offered Matt some? Once? Maybe.

Either way, she was glad for an excuse to hustle into the kitchen and slam cupboard doors and fill glasses with a dark potent inch of the pricey Bushmill's Millennium Irish whiskey with which Max had celebrated, and mourned, the passing of his worst enemy, Kathleen O'Connor, who'd taken with her the golden days of his youth and left behind eternally unresolvable guilt. No enemy could do worse.

Temple wondered what Max was mourning now.

She brought him the crystal glass and sipped from hers as she sat down again. "I can't imagine what Molina's done now that you need to fortify yourself against it."

"The whiskey isn't for me. It's for you."

"Me?"

"Molina couldn't find any evidence on the two or three counts of murder she wanted to lay at my door, which she can't find anyway."

"Then what was the whole bit about gleaning a fingerprint off a CD from here about?"

"She apparently now does have evidence on a nasty lesser charge, enough to bring me in, if she can find me, and prosecute. Even if she can't find me, she can just run tattling to you and damage me enough to give her immense satisfaction."

"What is it?"

Max composed his features as if he were on stage. Calm, authoritative, unreadable. "Sexual stalking."

"Of who? Me? She has flipped. We are totally consensual."

Max laughed. "You are a past master of spin. No. Of her."

"Of *her*?"

Tilt! Max was right: Temple needed a belt, even though

she'd heard this first from Matt, especially since she didn't want to admit to Max just how . . . in touch she and Matt had been lately. She assuaged her own guilt by unleashing her spleen on Molina. "That woman! What gall! What . . . conceit. You'd never—"

"Thank you."

"What's given her this idea? Stalking how?" Still playing dumb.

"Sneaking into her house and leaving items. A blue vintage velvet dress in her closet."

"Hey! Wanta moonlight here? I could use a stalker like that!"

"Not so nice, a Gameboy in Mariah's room once, before she evolved into such a game girl, thanks to you. But mostly stuff in Molina's bedroom, including, the latest indignity, according to Devine, a racy teddy. I suspect he didn't know what that was until Molina explained it to him. Imagine, she has two adolescents to rear. I suppose we should pity the woman."

Temple waved away his attempt at humor, as disturbing as it was to picture Matt and Molina discussing racy teddies. "And she found a fingerprint matching the one on my CD to one found in her house?"

"One is the operative number. None of the objects had fingerprints but one, and that had only one print. It matches one of mine from the CD."

Temple swilled Millennium whiskey way too thoughtlessly. "She planted it! Aren't there ways?"

"Nice thought." Max shook his head. "Molina is too proud to cheat. It was there, all right."

"You're too proud to make a mistake like that."

"Thanks for your total trust in my hubris. Won't mean much coming from a character witness on the stand, though."

"How can she think you'd do such a thing?"

"She hates me? No, I suppose she figured I'd upped the cat-and-mouse game we've been playing all over Vegas long before this." His expression grew bitter. "According to your new friendly neighborhood go-between, the last stalker invasion was particularly nasty. In that sense, I don't blame her for going ballistic. A trail of rose petals all through the house, into Mariah's bedroom as well as her own. I think the threat to Mariah sent her over the edge."

"That's proof of your innocence. You'd never include a kid in anything, not even a cat-and-mouse game."

"Again, character witnesses aren't going to save me, as sterling as you are and as sure as you are to be a knockout on the witness stand. The jury would fall for you like babies for saltwater taffy."

His palm stroked her straight blond hair. Temple forgot how different she looked these days, how different she was beginning to feel.

"I've always wanted to be all fifties' overdressed and stalk into a witness box on black spike heels," she said. "And to attend a funeral wearing a big black hat with a veil. But I don't have the height to carry any of it off."

"Not my funeral, I hope."

"She'll never catch you. She can't touch you."

"Probably not. But she can touch you."

"How?"

He sat back, sipped the whiskey. "That's what Devine sent me to tell you. The one . . . minor reason Molina might not be completely unjustified in suspecting me of this slimy crime."

"Matt sent you? Again? Since when do you take directions from him?"

"Since he's right. Molina will tell you. I'd rather be first."

"I can't imagine anything serious enough involving me for you and Matt to collaborate on."

"We have your best interests at heart."

Temple's heart almost stopped to hear that. Max and Matt *conspiring* to . . . what? Spare her? This must be major.

"Remember," Max said, swirling the dark honey liquor in his Baccarat glass so it oiled the sides, "when you were doing that sophomoronic 'Tess the Thong Girl' undercover routine in the strip clubs, trying to prove that I wasn't the Stripper Killer? I could have throttled you myself for taking such a risk when I found out what you'd been doing."

"Molina's always been too ready to accuse you of sleazy

crimes. It's been a slap in the face to me too; that's why I had to do something about it. But, hey, we got the creep."

"We?"

"I never told anybody this, but although the pepper spray you gave me stopped the real Stripper Killer in that parking lot, it was Rafi Nadir coming along and decking him that put him out cold until the police came. Rafi didn't want the credit for some reason, so he vanished, and I got the, ah, capture."

"Nadir!" Max slapped his forehead. "What irony! Molina's hated ex-squeeze saved you from the Stripper Killer and cut out, leaving you sole credit." His chuckle escalated into a laugh as he pulled Temple against him. "I love it."

"You hate Molina almost as much as she hates you, don't you?"

"I'm getting there," he said, grim again. He kept his arm around her, holding on tight. "That wasn't my greatest hour, either, that night. She backed me into this corner I didn't want to be in. She caught up with me in the other strip club parking lot, the wrong one, where the Stripper Killer wasn't planning to strike again. That's when I put it all together, where he'd really be, and that you were there, alone."

"Heck, no, Max. I had Rafi Nadir, remember. And even Midnight Louie showed up with a yowling Greek chorus of feral cats, no less."

"Where is Louie, by the way?"

"Out. Like my aunt Kit. She's dating a Fontana, can you believe it?"

"Knowing your aunt Kit, yes. Knowing the Fontanas, no."

Temple smiled, the tension between them dissipating with their separate visions of a Fontana brother–Aunt Kit tryst.

Max sighed and reached for his glass again, but he didn't let go of her.

"Anyway," he continued, "I knew I *had* to get to you and Baby Doll's. Molina knew she had me in her sights and she wasn't going to let me go anywhere. I'd been in the same spot with her before and got away, but not this time."

"Sights? She'd pulled a gun on you?"

"Right. I convinced her I wasn't carrying and that I'd go anyway and she could justify the shooting however she liked."

"Max! You shouldn't bluff an angry, prejudiced person with a gun."

"Wasn't bluffing."

"Max!"

He shrugged. "She's not a killer, just a damn determined woman. I knew she wouldn't shoot, and she knew I knew that. So . . . that woman has balls, I'll give her that. She slams her semiautomatic on the hood of the nearest Ford 350 and decides to keep me from leaving using hand-to-hand combat."

"She's really crazy. You're strong from all that stage work."

"Used to be. Molina's no lightweight, plus she's trained. And, I didn't want to hurt her."

"You're a gentleman."

"Maybe. Mostly because an assaulting-an-officer charge is hard to defend against if she did manage to haul me in. The point, Temple, is she was costing me time. She was keeping me from getting to where I knew you were exposed to the real Stripper Killer. I tried to overpower her, but she wasn't having any of it. We were too evenly matched, given my overriding concern to get away and get to you. I couldn't clobber her outright. And I couldn't gain enough advantage to get away fast enough and far enough. It was a stalemate. I had her pinned to a van, but the instant I let go, my advantage was gone. I had to get her off-guard, really shock the shield off of her."

By now, Temple was listening like a kid at a campfire ghost-story telling. What would Max do? What clever magician's trick?

"You remember my face after that night?"

"It was scraped." Temple was jolted by the change of topic in the story.

"That's because I let her take me down and cuff me. That finally became the only way I could get out of that damn parking lot and into her car where I could pick the handcuffs and unite her and her steering wheel with them until death did them part, then get out and get to Baby Doll's to, I thought, save you. Except you and Rafi Nadir had already turned the trick."

"And Midnight Louie. He alerted me to someone stalking me."

Max put his head in his hands. "Don't mention stalkers. I never want to hear that word again. Temple, when I had that woman up against that van, all I could think of was how to throw her off-guard. What would distract her the most so I could get away without hurting her or myself. What would shock her. So . . . you had to have been there . . . I sort of came onto her. Loathing me as she does, it was the only trick I had left up my sleeve. And it did freeze her into next week. I almost got away before she recovered and I had to play 'possom. That's really why she ground my face in the asphalt and why she might think I'm her stalker."

"Oh, wow." Temple put her own head in her hands. "Like what did you do, say?"

"It was the heat of the moment. I don't even remember."

"She sure does."

Max cleared his throat. "I might have implied she was . . . frigid. That she was putting all that energy into chasing me because—"

"—she really wanted you."

He shrugged.

"That is so sexist, Max Kinsella! And so is thinking that I always need to be rescued."

"There's the one common denominator in my sins: thinking of you, caring about you, wanting to protect you."

"You have to leave me with no word for a year to protect me? You have to hit on another woman to protect me? I think I'd rather not be protected."

"That's what Devine said. That I had to come clean with you now, before Molina embarrasses you later."

"Embarrass nothing! Humiliate is more like it. And then the fact that you're involved in the Czar Alexander scepter going missing. . . . Creating the worst publicity fallout in my career is not 'protecting' me. I'd be much better off without you doing that."

"Or without me?"

"I don't know! Everything's crazy. I don't know what I think anymore, except that you and I are just not working out. We've tried, God knows, but as long as you have to play peeka-boo with the law, I'm never going to know where you and I really stand, and I can't . . . stand . . . that anymore. I want stability. I want openness. I want—"

"Someone else," he said shrewdly.

"I was going to say 'Molina off my case.' "

"I'll be the first to admit that my secret status quo has changed, and I can't tell you one word about it. But something's changed for you too, and I don't think it has to be secret. You just want it that way."

Temple calmed down and thought. She supposed a parking lot faux-seduction was maybe no worse than some desert dirty dancing.

"Thanks for telling me about Molina. I will be happy to break it to her that you didn't mean anything by whatever you said or did. Unfortunately, I can't report a meaningless . . . crisis in my own life. While we're being so honest, I have something to confess. Matt has proposed."

"To you?"

"Well, not to Molina!"

"Marriage?" Max seemed dazed.

"Yup, the usual."

"He can't."

"He can."

Max finally let her go. There seemed more space between them than one small sofa could produce. He thought it over.

"His stalker is dead, unlike my current bête noir, Molina. He's safe at last, a free soul. He loves you. I've known that for way too long. Makes a decent wage. Has a night job, but you got used to that with me. You could do worse."

"Max! You sound like my mother!"

"I'm just weighing the competition. He's good looking, but too moral to succumb to bold hussies. He's got an edge he tries to hide, so he could protect you the next time you need to masquerade as a murder victim. Outside of Midnight Louie, I can't think of anybody better for you."

"Max, don't you care?"

"I've always cared too much, Temple. My problem, not yours. I thought, swore, when we connected again in New

York that I could elude my past and become what I'd masqueraded as for so long: just your average headlining Las Vegas magician."

He grinned at the immodesty of that description. The grin vanished as fast as a Cheshire cat. "But things have . . . changed. My shadow life is looming larger than ever these days, and a lot more than the Czar Alexander scepter depends on it. I can't guarantee to be there for you. I can't guarantee not to muck up your job site for hidden, but we hope, higher, purposes. I can't guarantee that I won't have to drop out of sight again. I can't guarantee to keep all the flying axes in the air anymore.

"It's time for you to get a life of your own. I can't be a dog in the manger anymore." Max stood. "Molina isn't imagining things, but I never meant anything but a ploy by it, and she almost fell for it. You remember that when she comes calling. Make Matt's day, or night, when the time comes for it. Remember me, now and then."

Temple stood too.

The magician was heading toward her entry hall. He was going to walk out her front door like a mortal man. It was wrong, no argument, no sudden paper flowers, just leaving, it sounded like . . . forever.

"Max—!"

But the door had closed, and when she ran to open it, he was gone.

Temple hung on the door, swung a little with it, so dazed that the insistent sound inside her unit didn't register until it had been so insistent that she feared it would escape her.

She ran back in to pick up the phone a split second before her answering machine kicked in.

"Temple?"

She couldn't speak, but the caller rushed on.

"It's Randy. It's the hugest frigging wonder of the world. The Czar Alexander scepter is *back*! Sitting under its Lexan onion dome as big as life and eight times more glitzy. This will be huge! The publicity will be the best thing the hotel has ever had. 'Now you see it, now you don't! Come view the New Millennium's vanishing scepter while you still can . . .'

Are you there? We are no longer in deep doo-doo. We are saved!"

"Great," Temple managed to say. Randy was too excited to hear the strain in her voice. "I'll be in first thing tomorrow to plan . . . to plan—"

"We'll need a whole new campaign to announce its reappearance. 'The Magic and Mystery of Vegas Strikes Again. Maximum glitz, minimum fuss.' Kiddo, I am so glad to be working with you on this. We can really milk this thing. We'll be the talk of the town, and our careers will be caramel, yours especially, as you're a freelancer and can really capitalize on it. But I'll expect a big raise, let me tell you."

"Great."

"Okay. Get some sleep. You'll need it."

"Will do."

She sat holding the receiver, lulled by the dial tone for a long time. And then the tears came: relief, regret, regret, relief. Regret.

Chapter 51

Maxamillion

"I was worried," Gandolph said when Max came home in the wee hours to find the old man waiting up for him.

"That's kind of nice," Max said. He knew his smile was weary.

"It took longer than it should have."

"I had a detour to make afterward. A personal detour."

Garry Randolph, the man who had been the magician Gandolph the Great, let the graven lines of his sixty-something face lift. "That little redheaded girl you love."

"She's a blond these days, and I can't afford to love anybody while I'm infiltrating the Synth."

"They won't like that you put the scepter back."

"The deal was that I steal it and do with it what I please, giving them a cut of any profits. What I please is to restore it."

"You're trying to win them over."

"Being a wimp won't win them over. They'll be pissed to see all that lovely money gone, but they'll get that I'm my own man."

"You did it for her. It was her show."

"Garry, you have me cold. I did it for her. And it was a hell of a challenge to get it back in place again with all the extra security they have lined up now."

"Yeah? How'd you manage it?"

"I could use a stiff drink and then I'll tell you every little detail."

"Not about your detour, though."

"No. Not about my detour."

Garry frowned at him, as he had years ago when Max—still numbed by the IRA-bomb death of his cousin Sean—had charged into some particularly dangerous situation abroad, He'd been so young—not even nineteen—and wounded, and wild. The perfect counterterrorism agent. He felt that same untamed urgency again, but not the energy. Not any of the energy at all anymore.

But he had to muster it again for one last personal appearance. Tomorrow.

Chapter 52

Leaving Las Vegas

Carmen stopped dead in her tracks.

They hadn't been very purposeful tracks, just the usual domestic homecoming shuffle at the end of a Friday while she totaled all the minor annoying weekend cleaning chores she had been neglecting.

She'd been thinking about something as mundane as washing down her kitchen cupboard doors—Mariah should help—when she realized that Max Kinsella had appeared in her living room not six feet away.

He was all in black—shoes, slacks, trench coat—more like encountering a life-size cutout of Keanu Reeves in *The Matrix* than a real person. No. Larger than life size. Certainly larger than Keanu Reeves. But he looked gaunt, maybe even worn, desperate.

It was enough to stop her heart. Did. For a beat or two.

She'd made a few collars in her day who'd been threatening and creepy. They were always loud and uncontrolled, flailing against their incarceration.

Kinsella was still free, quiet, and way too calm.

He watched her pull the Glock from the paddle holster at her rear right hip and aim it. The muzzle wavered between head and heart.

"I'm not armed, as usual," he said, shrugging, "but don't let that stop you. Maybe your ankle gun is a throwaway. You wipe it clean, paste it in my cold dead hand, and internal affairs goes far, far away."

He was, what was the word? Disarming. Literally. Silver Irish tongue.

She wanted to check to see if her ankle holster showed or he had just guessed. She'd taken a wide, shooting stance the instant she saw him. Her pant leg could have outlined the gun's shape.

That didn't matter. She shrugged in turn, the only gesture she could make without losing the total control she had of the semiautomatic, and of the situation.

"Thanks for laying out the options. This is my home. I'm a police officer. You're a suspect. A stalking suspect. You shouldn't be here. I don't need to salt a gun on your corpse. You're dead either way."

"Don't I know it."

"Me? You blame me for the hole you're in?"

"Blame is too big a word. You're a tool."

It took a split second for her to hear the word as "tool" instead of "fool."

"Oh, everybody's after you."

"Probably." He smiled so faintly she wasn't sure she'd seen it.

"Aren't you special? Aren't you important?"

"Apparently, you think so."

"So. Why walk into the muzzle of a Glock?"

"I'm leaving Las Vegas. One way or the other. On your floor, or on a jet plane."

"You leave? Give up the game? I don't believe you. Why?"

"The only thing keeping me here has been lying in an evidence baggie in your desk drawer."

The ring he'd given Temple Barr, later found at a murder scene. He was right. She regarded it as a personal trophy. And a clue.

He said, "Thought I'd give a word of warning before I go."

"Shoot first?"

"Maybe. Matt told me about what has been happening to you. I just wanted to say . . ." He let the words hang in the air. "I didn't do . . . this." His arms lifted slightly to indicate her violated house.

Her trigger finger tautened at the motion. "Tell it to a jury."

"Sorry. Can't wait around. Unless it's a grand jury, investigating my own shooting."

"Open and shut. Trust me. I hate to play the gender card, but a male suspect stalking a female cop looks especially bad."

"Fine. I didn't do this."

"Who the hell else? Who the hell else knew we'd run into each other in the strip club parking lot and had it out? Who besides you had to get touchy-feely in between the body kicks?"

Again, he denied the charge with a shrug and a faint smile.

"I don't know. I just know that all's fair in love and war, but home invasion isn't my style. You're the detective. Just asking. If it wasn't me—say someone was speculating on the far fringe edge of an open mind—who else could it have been?"

"*No one!* No one was there. No one saw. No one heard."

"And if you investigated every case, every dead body lying there in a parking lot, from that supposition, how far would you and your detectives ever get? Lieutenant?"

There must be someone. That was the investigative motto. Canvas the neighborhood, roust the winos, savage the Dumpsters, check the surveillance cameras within a five-mile circumference. Dumpster dive. *Find someone who had seen, heard.*

"Not at Secrets's," she said. She'd been there. The lot had been deserted. As empty as emotion.

He shrugged, that irritating I-don't-care gesture that jerked her chain.

"Mamacita!" The front door banged open. Mariah. Home straight from school for once.

Max Kinsella shrugged again, genuinely apologetic for the first time.

The bastard had probably seen her car in the driveway, left and watched for Mariah to leave school, made sure the kid was heading for home, then just beat her here.

Molina resisted glancing over her shoulder. She heard herself shouting at her own child, *"Freeze!"*

The schoolgirl scuffles came on. Molina had to risk a direct look, a direct order. "Stop. Drop. Stay back!"

And in that split second, the magician . . . split.

Leaving her hands trembling on the brink of firing. They lowered the gun.

He hadn't needed a weapon.

Molina swarmed her prone daughter, who hadn't even had time to notice that anyone else was on the premises. "Good girl. It's okay. I thought someone was in the house. You did right, *chica*. We're okay."

Unless Kinsella hadn't been her stalker.

Impossible! It was him. She couldn't shoot a man in front of her daughter, but she could sure wish that she had. Maybe a kneecap, then he'd be the one cowering on the floor, not Mariah.

Someone *else* was stalking her? Ridiculous! No one had been in that parking lot but rows of empty cars and pickups and vans. Not a human moving among them. Not even a drifting palm frond blown by the wind.

No one.

So why had Max, aka the "Invisible Man" Kinsella, risked coming here to suggest otherwise?

A huckster unwilling to give up a last con?

A player leaving the stage with everyone hoodwinked?

A deceptive magician taking one last bow?

An innocent man?

Come on!

Chapter 53

Foreplay

"So," Miss Midnight Louise asks in her most scathing tone, "is there a reason we are out clubbing at Neon Nightmare when everything that can go wrong has gone wrong at the New Millennium?"

"Say what?" I growl as loudly as I can over the pounding, thumping sound system. I would not dignify this noxious noise with the term "music."

"You understood me, Pop. You just did not want to answer because you do not really know why we are here."

"Here," is under the end of the long black Plexiglas bar. Above us the cadre of bartenders are slamming piña colada martinis down with lightning speed. Below us, the reflective black floor makes our usual ebony coats blend in with the decor. Those of our kind are generally considered inappropriate customers at such establishments, but most of the people here are too dazed in a pharmaceutical sense to notice our presence. We could come in white rabbit suits and still be ignored. Actually, we might be hit on for illegal substances in that guise.

"Not everything has gone wrong. I checked the New Millennium out earlier. The Czar Alexander scepter is back in place."

"Yeah, and what kind of thief would do that?" she asks.

"I have my suspicions," I say. I do not rat out a born second-story dude like myself, ever. Besides, that is the kind of ambiguous statement that usually shuts up all but the female of the species.

"Your suspicions? Such as—?"

Miss Louise is always a stickler for embarrassing specifics, like how much one weighs or what one thinks one is thinking.

I could tell her "none of your business," but unfortunately these days her business *is* our business, i.e., Midnight Inc. Investigations, so I figure it is time to let her in on my brilliant deduction.

"You know about this Phantom Mage guy?"

"Appears twice nightly, yeah. That is better than your Miss Temple has been getting from Mr. Max Kinsella lately."

"Exactly my point, Louise."

She does not miss a beat now that I have given her a big, fat clue.

"You think this Phantom Mage is Mr. Max in disguise?"

Before I can repeat my "I have my suspicions" mantra she hopscotches right over me. If we were playing a game of checkers, she would be King.

"Oh. And you think he is the one who stole the Czar Alexander scepter. I admit it smacks of a Mr. Max operation. But why? He is ordinarily a law-abiding dude."

"There has been nothing ordinary about this White Russian exhibition. It has had my Miss Temple's brain in a bow tie since she started working on it. Nothing but trouble."

"Rather like Mr. Max himself."

"That is not fair, Louise. Much as I do not want him encroaching on my quilt time, he has only tried to help Miss Temple in her various enterprises and escapades. He has saved her life almost as often as I have."

She snorts. That is not a very ladylike reaction, but I forbear to tell her. Louise does not take direction well. I do not either but that is different.

"That is what you get," she says, "for entering into a mixed relationship. You will always be a third wheel when it comes to nocturnal territory."

She is, alas, right. Humans do not abide by the simplest rules of territory: what smells like me is mine; where I sleep I am king; where I eat I am emperor; who I adopt is my loyal subject forever.

Maybe that should be "whom" I adopt. I am sure glad I did not say that aloud, for Miss Midnight Louise is also a fierce grammarian, as well as a dedicated carnivore and feminist of the first water, which means that she will mark any territory she can ahead of me. I am lucky that she regards Miss Temple's digs as out of bounds or we would be knee-deep in trouble. Even without murderers and thieves around.

Speaking of adopting, Miss Midnight Louise would do well to consider that I have informally done her the honor. Granted it took a little prodding of a needle-sharp shiv on her part.

She has moved on, however, to consider my brilliant deduction, and is staring up hard at the dark apex of the internal pyramid that is the Neon Nightmare nightclub, as if searching for prey.

"I," she points out (literally, by tapping me on the shoulder with a four-flush of extended shivs), "have no territorial disputes with Mr. Max. If he is the scepter thief, he must have more reason then mere material gain."

"You think so? They do not call it 'filthy lucre' for nothing. Our kind has a hard time comprehending the sin of Greed."

"Unless it involves food," she says with a sly sideways glance at me.

"Then it is called Gluttony. And do not deny that you lap up every gourmet tidbit that Chef Song puts in your rice bowl at the Crystal Phoenix."

Miss Louise remains fixated on the ceiling, from which the Phantom Mage is soon scheduled to descend in a sizzling display of pyrotechnics and acrobatic daring. Of course it is Mr. Max! But why?

"He must be undercover," Louise hums softly to herself. "But why?"

"Miss Lieutenant C.R. Molina is making things too hot for him?"

"She has been for ages. There must be another motive."

"Maybe he just misses his regular job."

Louise's gold eyes shine like twin suns. I bask in her approval. "You are so right. One cannot discount that with humans, especially performers. But he has always had two jobs, from what you have told me: as entertainer and as secret agent. He fought international terrorists even before this new breed entered the scene."

"Right," I say. "The IRA. I must admit I do not get it, this endless enmity between the orange and the green. Our kind has no trouble with those colors in both coat and eyes. Though you and I survive only by a miracle, given the human weakness for superstition and ignorance. Witches' familiars indeed. Black is beautiful! That is why we are so prevalent. One wishes people had been born color-blind, as we are."

"I do not know about you but I see some colors, although faintly. Humans have an aura, have you not noticed that?"

"Uh, this is getting very Karma, Louise. I thought you scorned that New Age stuff."

"I scorn nothing that makes sense, and I can tell you that Mr. Max's aura is green. Miss Temple's is red. Mr. Matt's is gold. And Miss Lieutenant Carmen Molina's is blue."

"Speaking of auras," I say, "I have just spotted a gray one."

She follows my glance to Mr. Rafi Nadir, obviously working security for Neon Nightmare. He wears all black, like Mr. Max, but it is harsh where Mr. Max's wardrobe is smooth. He wears black denim jeans and jacket and a T-shirt with a death's head on the front. It is probably for some rock band. They are all very depressed sorts in my observation.

"His aura," Louise corrects me (Louise lives to correct me), "is silver."

I admit I am taken aback. Silver is way too nice an aura for Mr. Rafi Nadir, ex-cop, ex–Carmen Molina live-in, all too *not*-ex father of little Mariah, who is no longer so little.

Nor am I happy to have two such dudes on different sides of the law inhabiting the same space, albeit unknown to each other. Mr. Max is unofficially a good guy, and Mr. Rafi is officially a fallen good guy.

But I am here to observe and learn and test theories, not tail sinister characters around Las Vegas. Although I have gleaned that my Miss Temple is highly upset with Miss Lieutenant C.R. Molina and that it would be fun to sic Rafi Nadir on that woman's tail just to get back at her sins against my nearest and dearest.

However, Midnight Louie is not petty.

I am here to decide whether the Phantom Mage is Mr. Max, and, if so, why. And what that means for my Miss Temple's peace of mind.

And my hereditary claim to one-third of the bed.

Chapter 54

Crystal Shoe Persuasion

"I thought and I thought about where to go," Matt said, looking around the elegant dining room. "I know you've been through a lot lately at the New Millennium. So I decided this place might have the most resonance for you."

Matt had insisted (he was doing a lot of that lately) on taking Temple out to celebrate when he telephoned and heard that the Czar Alexander scepter had been restored to its proper place (unlike her significant other of long standing).

Temple had swallowed that pang and passed on more happy news to Matt.

"Not only is the scepter back, but I scored a *Vanity Fair* piece, maybe even by Dominic Dunne, on the disappearing and reappearing scepter, the sad death of the little Chinese defector girl, and the would-be greedy Russian thieves and thugs. The exhibition deaths have made the Las Vegas papers and are going to dog the exhibition anyway, so I figured a Big Negative can equal a Positive sometimes in the publicity business. Everyone went for it. It lends, they said, 'mystique' to the collection."

"Not to mention the mystique of all those dead Romanovs. Gore sells, I guess."

"Especially if you can add some glitz. A sad reality of the media biz."

"Enough sad reality! This *Vanity Fair* thing is big?"

"This is huge! The New Millennium's paying me a bonus."

"Then we'll really have lots to celebrate."

It was only after Matt hung up that Temple wondered what else they would be celebrating.

Kit was out again with Aldo that night, so much for a related buffer zone, and Temple was both angry and sad about Max's midnight descent into hail and farewell, so she'd agreed.

This was what Max wanted, right? She'd pulled out her purple prom dress/Crossfire hood ornament dress, again dusted off her Midnight Louie shoes—even he had seemed to desert her lately—and decided to celebrate by letting herself wallow in everything about Matt she liked, which was a lot.

Now, Temple gazed around the glittering Crystal Phoenix dining room. When Matt had asked her out to dinner, she'd been too distracted by recent events to wonder why, or even where he'd take her.

"The Phoenix *is* sort of home base for me," she said, "although not lately." Lately, nothing was. "But I've never eaten in this restaurant before."

"Good. I'd like to dedicate this evening to things never done before."

Temple couldn't stop the heat from rising to her face. There was One Big Thing neither had ever done before: Temple with Matt, Matt with anybody else in the whole wide world.

The waiter chose that perfect cue to arrive with a silver-plated champagne stand and a bottle of Perrier-Jouët.

"Perrier-Jouët! I should have worn something better than my old prom dress."

"You look good in purple."

"Even as a bottle blonde?"

"Even as whatever color your hair happens to be."

Temple glanced down at the now-vintage taffeta gown with its halter top and huge, blooming skirt. She did love it. "This is my desert-dancing dress."

She knew she evoked their most romantic moments, even as her heart twisted for other times, other places.

Matt lifted his glass of champagne in a toast. "To desert dancing then."

Temple raised her glass, feeling suddenly bold. "To . . . moonlighting as a hood ornament on a Crossfire."

It was his turn to color, but it was only a faint, passing flush on his fair Polish skin slightly toasted by a Las Vegas tan. Matt was getting way too hard to embarrass, Temple decided. Which was both intriguing and worrisome.

"Did you have designs on a desert ride for dessert?" she asked.

"No. All the dessert I want is right here."

Oh. "You have something to tell me?"

"More like ask you."

Oh.

Thank God. The waiter swooped away their salad plates and assured them their main courses would be "up" very soon.

"Would you like to dance?" he asked.

Oh. That. Sure. She'd taught him the name of that tune, after all.

The dance floor was a tiny peninsula of parquet off the bandstand. The band was mellow, soothing, dedicated to old standards: gonna take a Sentimental Journey into a Canadian Sunset. Corny. Safe.

Temple put her left hand on the shoulder of the brandy velvet dinner jacket she had talked Matt into buying many moons ago.

Thinking of which, the full moon hung like a Christmas tree ornament outside the sweep of windows framing the night. Pale, huge, opaque but gleaming. The full moon always looked like Bing Crosby's crooning face to her. *Ba-ba-ba-ba-boo.* Boo! Was a surprise on the menu tonight?

Her right hand folded into Matt's as they swayed together with a half dozen other couples, some silver haired, some . . . good grief! . . . with gelled hair spikes and visible tattoos.

What happens in Vegas stays in Vegas. Who comes to Vegas, is part of Vegas.

"Frank Bucek told me about your takedown at the New Millennium," Matt said.

"Oh. That. It was the Fontana brothers' takedown."

Matt nodded.

Temple felt the gesture to the bottom of her soles. Solid. They were close, not tentative, and she liked it.

"He gave me some advice," Matt added a minute later.

"Oh."

"Yeah. He said ex-priests were hard on their wives."

"Oh. Really? How?"

Matt shrugged. Temple shivered. "We've been little tin gods in our parishes or wherever. Catered to. By housekeepers. Soccer moms. Looked up to by kids. We can be a tad self-centered, never meaning to be."

"All in the name of serving mankind?"

"Right. The grandiose big picture, not the intimate small picture. I wouldn't want to be that way."

"Of course not. What does Frank's wife do?"

"Keeps him down to earth."

"Sounds like . . . fun."

"And then there's . . . you know, sex."

"Oh. I suppose that would be an issue for anyone who's been celibate for a long time."

"Right. We tend to be overly . . . intense."

"Really?"

He nodded, which brought her cheek in contact with his cheek.

Matt led her back to their table before the heat of his hand had quite branded itself onto her taffeta-clad back.

How many years since her high school prom night? Twelve.

Was it possible? Thirty-one looming? And just yesterday she'd been sweet, dumb sixteen, before high school kids had even thought of "friends with benefits."

"You can dance on wood as well as sand," she said approvingly as he pulled out her chair so she could gather the full skirt under herself and sit. Sometimes vintage was awkward.

A lot of times life was awkward.

Matt sat opposite her. The Crystal Phoenix avoided the usual flickering candle under glass on its table. Instead a Murano blown-glass phoenix spread its tail feathers in a series of fairy-size floating flames.

The flickering uplight made every man and woman look like a soft-spotlit movie star. Matt was a floating, glittering image of himself. Temple hoped she was too. No wrinkles. No worry, just radiant points of light.

The waiter wafted plates before them as if presenting canna lily leaves bearing manna from Fairyland. Divine scents lifted upward.

"How wonderful," Temple said. "Chef Song has outdone himself."

"Even Louie might approve," Matt said, eyeing her.

Even Louie might approve . . . what? The menu? A delicate fish dish for her, medallions of beef for Matt? The two of them together, dining at Louie's old stomping grounds, the Crystal Phoenix? The chef? The place? The atmosphere? The pheromones?

They were silent during dinner, every bite of which was . . . divine.

Temple patted her lips with the heavy linen napkin, thinking about when to refresh her pale lipstick, thinking about the beaded lipstick holder in her teeny-tiny purse on the tabletop. About whether to excuse herself and flee to the ladies' room. Or to reapply her going-out mouth at the table, as etiquette said one could, in front of one's escort.

Matt beat her to it by abstracting a small, gray velvet box from somewhere. It was almost as magical a manifestation as some paper bouquet from Max.

He held it under the flickering crystal gaze of the mythical bird that had died in flame and ashes and risen from them hard, diamond-bright, invincible. Reborn. New. Fresh. Real.

Temple took the box in her hand. Licked her lips.

Opened it.

Glanced away from the laserlike fire.

Lasers healed, lasers struck dead. Lasers dazzled.

"Matt."

She finally focused past the blinding glitter. The bling. A ring of diamonds massed in the mechanically graceful assemblage of curves and angles that screamed Art Deco. Art Deckle. Not even a dead man could push himself between this view and her understanding of it. "Fred Leighton," the inside of the satin lining declared in subtle letters. Estate jewelry. True vintage. Amazing beauty of shape and line, of time and history. Of understanding what called to her.

"This," she said, "is truly Red Carpet bling. It's exquisite. My God, I'm Julia Roberts!

"This is a ring," he said. Corrected. "You're you. It's really two guard rings. It comes apart, see? The band is rubies, for . . . later. I saw it and saw you. That's all."

Temple was agape at the clever way the two halves of the ring separated to admit a band. A band of rubies for a wedding ring. What an exquisite thought, an exquisite execution, the epitome of every reason she loved vintage things, but Fred Leighton, jeweler to movie stars . . . that was way too much.

She said so.

"Listen. I've given triple that to African famine and Gulf Coast flood relief. You can wear it in good conscience."

Of course he would have; that was why she'd always had to spur him into springing for the basic little comforts of American consumer life. But for her, he needed no encouragement. He went big.

Temple bit her lower lip (on which she should have reinstalled lipstick for this truly Kodak moment).

Beauty, the poet had said, is truth. Truth, beauty.

Who was she to deny the perfection of a beautiful gift, a beautiful moment, a beautiful mind, a beautiful heart, a beautiful hope?

"I don't know quite what to say," she said. Anyway.

She held up the corona of light, in her right hand, poised somewhere over her left third finger. Apparently, it was a Kodak moment to someone other than Matt and herself.

A flash exploded around them both, an aurora, a star going nova.

"Photo, folks? Visiting Las Vegas to celebrate an engagement and tie the knot? Your friends and family will treasure this moment as much as you do."

Temple rather doubted that.

"Just twelve dollars."

Matt didn't doubt that at all but reached for his wallet. It was his night to pay, all the way. To pave the way.

The tiny elevator at the Circle Ritz was all theirs at this hour. The Midnight Hour. Monday night. Matt's one night off from his late-night radio shrink show.

The shrink was in.

His finger was poised over the round black buttons with the white floor numbers mostly polished away by other fingers over many more years than they'd been on this planet.

"Floor two or three?" he said lightly. Temple still heard the strain in his voice. It was a momentous decision and it was all hers.

"Three," Temple said. "I've got an aunt cluttering up my living room and a cat claiming my bedroom."

"I've got a brand-new bed and no aunts or cats."

"I know."

"Is there a reason you're huddling in the corner of the elevator?"

"I'm scared?"

"*You're* scared?

"It's a lot of responsibility."

"Don't I know?"

He took her elbow, steered her out of the small elevator car into the deserted hallway and down the short cul-de-sac to his door. Where he got lukewarm feet.

"Maybe some place more . . . unusual. Without a past. A hotel?"

"This is fine," Temple said, trying not to zone out on the way the sidelight fell on his hair, making a blond halo of it.

Angels. They didn't do carnal things like sex.

"Are you—?" he asked.

"Protected? Yes. Is that a sin?"

"That's the way you are. You're perfect. I'm not. Remember? I don't want to hurt you. For what you are or for what you aren't. You're all I want."

"Funny, I feel the exact same way about you."

Inside the apartment, there wasn't a soul around. Not even a cat.

Temple eyed the sculptural red fifties designer sofa she'd found for Matt at Goodwill. Danny was right that it had cost something to give it up to him, to insist he have it. She'd always kinda maybe thought in her wildest dreams they'd make it someday on that sleek suede surface. She'd always kinda maybe thought a lot of inadmissible things, inadmissible evidence, about Matt Devine. Before she'd known he'd been a priest.

And, heck, even after.

She sat on the red sofa knowing her peony of a purple taffeta skirt made her look like a human mushroom. She looked at her left hand with the movie-star-level estate diamond ring on it.

"I don't know if I'm ready for this," she told him.

She didn't tell him that the day after the black dress interlude she'd hied herself off for testing. A small card that declared her free of HIV and other STDs now lay hidden in her seldom-used scarf drawer. She knew Matt came shrinkwrapped, so to speak, and didn't want her virgin would-be bridegroom thinking about ugly realities on such a momentous occasion as first sex. She'd figured she was safe and had sniffled a bit when she read the results, pretty solid proof of her conviction that Max had never been unfaithful.

Matt was still trying to be supremely accommodating. He sat beside her. "If the ring's too much or too much pressure, forget it."

Temple knew that visible symbol of commitment would mean a lot to his conscience.

She stroked his forearm with that hand, watching the diamonds throw out serious sparks. "No, it's beautiful. It just should be our secret for a while."

She touched his lips with a forefinger.

He was watching everything she did with such dreamy pleasure she thought she could die happy right that moment. She'd forgotten what first love was like, but Matt was bringing it all back to her.

"I feel responsible," she said.

"For what? Yourself? Me?"

"I'm the one who knows. I'm the brazen hussy. You're the innocent virgin. I can take. You can only give. It's not fair."

He stood, took her hand, the right one, and drew her up against him as if they were dancing.

"Frank Bucek told me he saw you."

"I ran into him when he was here for crime business at the New Millennium."

"He told me that you'd talked."

"He told you we'd talked? I thought he had to abide by some confessional binding thing or something."

"He only mentioned you in passing."

"What I said . . . oh, no!"

Matt smiled. "Now I'll really wonder. No, he just gave me two words of advice."

"And—?"

"Nobody's perfect." Matt was looking down at her as if he didn't believe that, as if he believed she was really, really perfect.

"I know I'm not. I'm confused. I'm a . . . worldly woman. I'd have an ex, that isn't an easy, cut-and-dried thing, Matt. It'd be messy."

"He wasn't talking about you, Temple. He was talking about me. And I suddenly realized, in all my twisting and turning to do the one right thing, that I didn't have to be perfect or do the perfect thing. That thinking like that was a kind of hubris. Selfish. That I only had to love you, as I have since almost the minute I met you, that I only had to want you, as I have since almost the day I met you."

"What took you so long on the 'want' part?"

"So you were faster?"

"Oh, yeah. It was simultaneous, on my part."

"Really." He pulled her closer. "From my book, I understand that that's the best way. Simultaneous."

"Oh, Matt. There are so many 'best ways.' "

"I want to have them all, with you."

"Even if I'm not ready for marriage right out of the box?"

"I figured something else out, brilliant solver of other people's problems that I am. If I do what's best for you, I can't hurt myself. I've been searching for some overarching spiritual love all my life. And it's there. In other people. Person. Don't be guilty, Temple. I've wasted way too much of my life on that."

He pulled her close enough that she could tug his tie loose.

He was undoing her back zipper, short as it was on her halter-top prom dress.

She was back there again, in Jon Bon Jovi prom night country, two American kids in the Heartland. A virgin again. Feeling true love again.

And having it all.

"I've always," Matt said, his voice husky, "pictured us on this sofa."

He swooped her down like a pirate, stripped her as slowly as a Latin lover, and took her to passionate heights she'd never imagined even in those wildest dreams. She hadn't hardly to do a thing to aid and abet in unleashing years of self-denial, just be there and be willing to be swept away. The resulting emotional and sensual tsunami took their breaths away. He was the most perfect imperfect lover in the world and she wept with the joy of it.

They lay in Matt's new bed in the heart of darkness inside the Circle Ritz.

"This is just us, isn't it?" he asked.

Temple pillowed her head on his shoulder. His bare shoulder.
"Yes."

"No . . . interference from what I was, you were?"

"No."

"What we've figured out we want, what we need?"

"Yes."

"Only us. Only tonight?"

"Yes."

"And tomorrow?"

"Only us, only tomorrow."

"Are you sure?"

Temple took a deep breath. Midnight Louie was the only sure creature she knew on the planet. People were a lot more handicapped. But she and Matt had come damn close to feline certainty.

"Yes."

No wonder Scarlett had swooned before being swept up that fateful staircase, Temple thought. No way was tomorrow going to be just another day after a night like this.

Chapter 55

Maxed Out

Max had literally hung himself out to dry on a line high above the light-stabbed dance floor far below. He balanced unseen in the dark, a wire walker who understood that he was seriously overextended. In all senses of the word.

To the audiences at Neon Nightmare, he was the Phantom Mage, the masked wall-walking, bungee-jumping illusionist who capered nightly above their sound, synthetic substance, and alcohol-dazed heads.

To the Synth, a group of disgruntled traditional magicians who hated those who revealed their tricks, like the Cloaked Conjuror, and who met in a maze of rooms burrowed into the nightclub's pyramidlike structure, he was an ex–Strip magician who'd performed as the Mystifying Max.

To them, he was also a raw recruit, assigned to prove his loyalty by ripping off the art show at the New Millennium and bringing down the Cloaked Conjuror and his illusion-destroying show, a show repped by Max's long-time love, Temple Barr.

And then he was just Max, up to his black turtleneck in a scheme with his mentor and partner in counterterrorism, Garry Randolph, to betray the Synth and uncover the web of international money laundering and mayhem they believed it fostered.

Somewhere in there, he'd hoped he had that relationship with Temple to preserve, for his own self alone, for the dream of having a personal life beyond his brushes with the Irish revolutionary Kathleen O'Connor, who had snagged his teenage heart while engineering his innocent cousin's political death.

Kitty was dead now, but he was convinced her activities in Las Vegas had been part of a larger plot that extended to several unaccounted-for deaths in the past two years. Whatever had been, and was still going on, was big.

"Oh, what a tangled web we weave," said Sir Walter Scott, "when first we practice to deceive."

The Scottish poet had been right enough to remain quoted for the ages. Deception, like magical illusions, took practice. So did stealing rare art objects.

Max smiled to envision the unexpected end he'd engineered for that caper. They would all be flummoxed. It was something the Synth could have never anticipated and, worse, couldn't fault him for, given that it didn't violate the terms of their agreement, although it would sure as heck violate their intentions.

He frowned to consider that nasty tank trap Molina had laid for him. There was no way a fingerprint of his could be found in her house, not even from his recent, lightning personal appearance, suitably Mephistophelean, he hoped. He grinned grimly at that escapade, running the bungee cords through his hands, automatically checking for fraying, breaks, weaknesses in the mechanism, as he did before every performance, every plummet into the widening funnel of neon-lit darkness and noise below him.

When he dove, the dancers parted with *ooohs* of delighted fright. He swooped so low, so close to their frenetic level, that he almost met his own black shadow in the gleaming mirror-black floor.

What a rush. Screaming hordes jousted for the leis of fluorescent flowers he looped over them as the cord pulled him away. They leaped up after him the way people sprang to capture cheap plastic beads at Mardi Gras. Life was a cabaret along the Strip, and Max had to caper for their attention like any Mardi Gras babe seeking plastic beads.

He checked his safety belt, his spandex-gloved fingers pulling on the steel fasteners to test them.

Him. Leave a fingerprint in Molina's house? *Never!* None had existed on any official record until she'd raided Temple's rooms. This was police harassment. The plan was to destroy Temple's unshakable faith in him, and it had worked. A little.

Max knew her faith in his innocence would never waver. Her faithfulness was another thing. Don't guard what you've got, and it's gone. He shut his eyes for an instant. If he hadn't come back from his forced disappearance several months ago, he knew that Temple would be where she probably was now: with Matt Devine. He had only delayed the inevitable. You usually can't save the world, even one little corner of it, and your love life too. And for that he also blamed Molina's relentless opposition.

With all he had going on, juggling his various personae and infiltrating the Synth and the Millennium heist turned booby-trap, the last thing he needed was another of Molina's pathetic games distracting him.

The music paused, then revved into the overblown intro for the Phantom Mage.

No time to dwell on loss or anger, on what he had unwillingly given up and what interfering others had taken from him.

Max leaped off the tiny platform like a diver into darkness. Showers of sparklers sprayed from his figure as the cloak spread out like wings, revealing a lining of leaping flames.

The pale faces gazing up at him drew nearer, grew features ... *O*'s of open mouths and wide eyes. For a moment, he was stronger and more enrapturing than anything they could drink or smoke or sniff or inject, a dark angel falling to earth, spewing gaudy fire.

He knew the instant the bungee cord failed to tauten for the fast flight back up, knew at once it had failed completely. Hadn't he run the entire length through his hands? While his mind had gnawed at the irritation of phantom fingerprints, maybe his hands had missed a weakness in the line.

Was this a mere snag, or a fatal flaw?

Below him the awe-stricken holes in people's faces enlarged into horror. He saw them scattering and did a full body twist to send him away from landing dead-on-down to the floor, away toward the side wall where no one could be hurt. No one but . . .

The bungee cord snapped like a rubber band. He had a split second to—

He hit with astounding force and then had nothing more to worry about at all.

Chapter 56

After Max

"Look!" Miss Louise cries softly, but no less urgently. Sometimes she can mew like a Miss Muffet, although most often she screams like a Wicked Witch of the West.

So I look up. And there is the dark glittering figure, falling. Like a bird. I am almost tempted to leap up, to meet it and bring it down. But I understand this is a giant bird-man, and I am not the size of predator that could contain it, much less kill it.

Besides, I have retired from the predator biz. Now, I track them.

"Oooh," breathe the people above us and all around us.

"Aaaah," they sigh.

And then the flying man plunges to the ground, the invisible leash not tightening and jerking him back into the upper air.

Louise howls. People scream and scatter. Rafi Nadir's motorcycle boots crack hard across black Plexiglas, which shatters as if he wore seven-league boots made of lead.

And the Phantom Mage swings full-frontal-first into a wall of concrete sheathed in mirrors and neon.

Rafi Nadir is defending the perimeter. He sometimes works security here.

He has already dialed 911 with his cell phone. Now he fights to keep hysterical people from rushing the fallen form with a mad conjoined instinct of horror, compassion, and curiosity.

That leaves room for Miss Midnight Louise and me to slink in close.

"Bast!" Louise breathes in my ear. "Is he dead? Let me smell."

"Back, kit. I know his scent better than you." I push my nostrils toward the hidden neck, searching not only for scent, but for the telltale mouse-like flutter of a pulse. I pick up a trace of Brut, sweat, sulphur, and rosin. And my Miss Temple's perfume, called "Delicious." I sense no movement at all.

My heart sinks but I cannot let Louise see that.

Her vibrissae mingle with mine despite my holding her back. "Is it he?" she asks with laudable grammar.

"Maybe."

"Is he . . . dead?

"Maybe."

By now, Mr. Rafi Nadir is turning back to the . . . body.

We retreat into our color-coordinated darkness. No one notices us, then or later.

In three minutes, the emergency techs come, lean over the Phantom Mage, shout orders, load the body on a gurney and roll it out over the sleek black floor.

Suddenly, the canned music starts up but people crowd the bar, not the dance floor. A long black cord hangs down limp, like a string from a bare lightbulb, but there is no light at the top of the pyramid, only darkness. The cord swings a bit in the air-conditioning blowers, its ragged end just missing the floor.

Louise and I hunker down again at the end of the bar. I could use a hit of nip myself.

"What will we do?" she asks with a shiver I can feel.

I look up. "The police will be all over this place all too soon. I intend to claw my way up there and scour the place before they mess it up with their fingerprint powders and such."

"This whole place is as shiny as a chrome scratching post. How will we get up?"

I do not correct her on that "we." I could really use Nose E., but we cannot spare the time to fetch the little bomb-sniffing Maltese, and we can climb better than any canine on the planet, even if the surface is plastic.

"We will just have to use our built-in pitons," I tell her, glad of company on this sad detail. "It will have to be you and me, kit."

"If Mr. Max got up there, we can do it."

"Right. And if Mr. Max got up there and someone messed with his rigging, they could get up there too. We may only have feline noses, but they will have to do. If there has been sabotage afoot, Midnight Inc. Investigations will find out and track the perpetrators to whatever hole they have to hide in."

"And lock them in and call in the dogs."

"You know any dog packs?"

"The Thirteenth Street Bonepickers."

"They will do. Bast grant me the power to console my Miss Temple."

Miss Midnight Louise is already trotting along the sidelines of the dance floor, ignoring any who might spot her. I rush to catch up.

"You console. I am going to kick major butt."

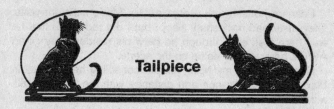

Tailpiece

Midnight Louie Mourns the Status Quo Vadis

The decent thing would have been to warn me that the human misbehavior in this book would erupt to such an extent that it would threaten my happy home.

My Miss Temple and I have had a mutually agreeable working and living arrangement: I was the alpha male on her premises, but would allow her SO, Mr. Max Kinsella, visiting privileges if he did not hog too much of the California king size. I would tolerate off-campus activities with Mr. Matt Devine if my Miss Temple could ever get him off the celibacy shtick.

But I would remain first and foremost in her domestic sphere, i.e., our shared digs at the Circle Ritz.

I cannot honestly say I enjoyed Mr. Max's midnight visits. They disturbed my beauty sleep, but I did recognize that he was here first, even though he blew his residency by going AWOL before I ever came on the scene.

Nor did I mind my Miss Temple consoling herself for Mr. Max's growing absence and distance with the far more reliable and nearby Mr. Matt.

But now I have heard this Awful Word bandied about: marriage. What is *wrong* with unofficial cohabitation? It has served my species well for thousands of years. This official monogamy that humans keep trying has all sorts of evil offshoots.

It causes the couple to contemplate shared quarters. Will it be his? Hers? A new place entirely?

Do you see a comfy niche for Midnight Louie, Esq., in this rush to unification? I thought not. Oh, I am sure I would be accorded some ratty old pillow in a corner of some other bedroom somewhere.

But what if Mr. Matt, being the late-blooming sort, objects to witnesses in the bedroom, even if they are the silent type? I do not cede territory to any male without a fight.

What am I to do at this late date? Move in with dear old dad on Lake Mead? Go begging like a homeless old duffer for quarters back at the Crystal Phoenix from my apparent daughter, Midnight Louise? I would rather be fish bait! Koi, come and get me!

I am not about to throw myself on the mercy of my collaborator either. If she cared a fig or a flying flamingo about me she would not have let these unruly characters mess up my life (not to mention theirs) so much.

What is the use of being an author if you cannot control characters and events? I have long felt the literary game was a sham and a delusion and now that I am in danger of becoming homeless again, I am certain of it.

I just did not expect my very own partner in crime to sell me out to raging hormones.

(Of course, I cannot really say how I feel about all this for publication. I have an image to project . . . I mean protect, and I may also harbor some secret, soul-stirring issues that I cannot share with anyone, not even my Miss Temple, not even my Miss Carole.)

You, Dear Readers, however, are an exception. Yet we can only communicate through the cryptic means of literature. Litterature in my case. The moving finger, or claw, writes. On the wall or in the sand. And moves on. And on.

Surely things cannot be as dire as they look! Not if I have anything to write about it.

Midnight Louie, Esq.

If you'd like information about Midnight Louie's free Scratching Post-Intelligencer newsletter and/or T-shirt and other cool things, contact him at P.O. Box 33155, Fort Worth, TX 76163-1555 or www.carolenelsondouglas.com or at cdouglas@catwriter.com.

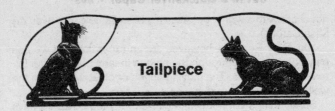

Tailpiece

Carole Nelson Douglas Professes Innocence, or Maybe Just Ignorance

I didn't know they were going to do it, Louie. Honest.

Oh, I knew they were capable of almost anything, including laughing at my attempts to produce some logical behavior on their parts. The problem is, this is fiction. And even in Real Life, people are lamentably unpredictable. Not cats. Never cats. That's why I surround myself with them.

That's why you and I have had a monogamous relationship for thirty-three years, Louie. Thirty-three years. Not bad for my species, and downright metaphysical for yours.

Well, what can we do? We have invested a lot of time, love, and hope in these people. We will just have to have faith.

We will have to have faith that they have learned something

from us (and particularly you) and will come around to surprising us with their good sense, good intentions, and ultimately ideal solutions to all the messy druthers that lives of crime and punishment create.

You want to run them in on a moving violation, Louie?

Be my guest.

You are the driving force here and I don't expect you to take this level of turmoil lying down. You've got your paw on what's going to happen next and will get all these humans herded back into their proper places. Right, Big Boy?

Speak to me!

P.S. Charity auctions at mystery conventions often allow bidders to win the prize of having their or a loved one's name in a particular author's book. Midnight Louie (of course) draws hot and high bidding wars. The pair of Yorkshire terriers in *Cat in a Leopard Spot* resulted from a United Way drawing in Minnesota. The real-life Beth Marble's husband won her a role in *Cat in a Hot Pink Pursuit*. And in this book, Squeaker's owner won her participation. Squeaker is the shy, gorgeous shelter cat, as portrayed, and her shelter "name," was—yes indeed—Fontana. Truth is always stranger than fiction.

Midnight Louie is back on the prowl in the latest mystery from

CAROLE NELSON DOUGLAS!

Cat in a Red Hot Rage

Temple Barr and Midnight Louie are up to their tails in froufrou, chapeaux, and murder when the Red Hat Sisterhood convention hits Las Vegas.

"Don't miss the fun when murder makes a date with Midnight Louie amid five thousand Red Hatters out for a great time. Carole Nelson Douglas's colorful characters are right at home in this sea of purple and red."

—Haywood Smith, *New York Times* bestselling author of *The Red Hat Club*

www.tor.com   0-765-31401-0 • In hardcover May 2007